ONLY
the
BEAUTIFUL

NOVELS BY SUSAN MEISSNER

Only the Beautiful
The Nature of Fragile Things
The Last Year of the War
As Bright as Heaven
A Bridge Across the Ocean
Stars over Sunset Boulevard
Secrets of a Charmed Life
A Fall of Marigolds
The Girl in the Glass
A Sound Among the Trees
Lady in Waiting
White Picket Fences
The Shape of Mercy

ONLY
the
BEAUTIFUL

SUSAN MEISSNER

BERKLEY
New York

BERKLEY
An imprint of Penguin Random House LLC
penguinrandomhouse.com

Copyright © 2023 by Susan Meissner
Penguin Random House supports copyright. Copyright fuels creativity,
encourages diverse voices, promotes free speech, and creates a vibrant culture.
Thank you for buying an authorized edition of this book and for complying
with copyright laws by not reproducing, scanning, or distributing any part of
it in any form without permission. You are supporting writers and allowing
Penguin Random House to continue to publish books for every reader.

BERKLEY and the BERKLEY & B colophon are registered trademarks of
Penguin Random House LLC.

Library of Congress Cataloging-in-Publication Data

Names: Meissner, Susan, 1961– author.
Title: Only the beautiful / Susan Meissner.
Description: New York: Berkley, [2023]
Identifiers: LCCN 2022031862 (print) I LCCN 2022031863 (ebook) I
ISBN 9780593332832 (hardcover) I ISBN 9780593332856 (ebook)
Subjects: LCGFT: Novels.
Classification: LCC PS3613.E435 O55 2023 (print) I
LCC PS3613.E435 (ebook) I DDC 813/.6—dc23/eng/20220707
LC record available at https://lccn.loc.gov/2022031862
LC ebook record available at https://lccn.loc.gov/2022031863

Printed in the United States of America
1st Printing

Title page illustration by Masha Dav/Shutterstock.com

Then God said, "Let us make mankind in our image, in our likeness."

Genesis 1:26

ONLY
the
BEAUTIFUL

PART ONE
ROSANNE

1

SONOMA COUNTY, CALIFORNIA
FEBRUARY 1939

The chardonnay vines outside my open window are silent, but I still imagine the bursts of teal and lavender their summer rustlings always called to my mind. That sound had been my favorite, those colors the prettiest. The leafless stocks with their arms outstretched on cordon after cordon look like lines of dancers waiting for the music to start—for spring to set their performance in motion. Looking at them, I feel a deep sadness. It might be a long time before I see again these vines that had for so long been under my father's care, or hear their leaves whisper, spilling the colors in my mind that belong to them alone.

Perhaps I will never see this vineyard again.

The Calverts won't welcome a future visit from me. Celine Calvert has already made it clear that after today she is done with me. Done.

For a moment the words *if only* flutter in my head, but I lean forward and pull the window shut. What is to be gained by wishing I could turn back the clock? If I had that power, I would have done it before now. I wouldn't even be living with the Calverts if

I had the ability to spin time backward. I'd still be living in the vinedresser's cottage down the hill with my parents and little brother.

The doorbell rings from beyond the bedroom. Shards of heather gray prick at the edges of my mind. I hear Celine cross the entry to open the front door and invite the visitor inside.

Mrs. Grissom is here to take me away.

It's almost a year to the day since I first met Mrs. Grissom on the afternoon my whole world changed, just like it is changing now. On that day my father's truck got stuck on the railroad tracks outside Santa Rosa. In one blinding instant, he and my little brother, Tommy, were snatched away from this life. The next, I was sitting in a ghostly white hospital room for the handful of minutes before my mother slipped away to join them.

"Rosie . . ." Momma's voice was threaded with the faintest colors of heaven as I sat in a cold metal chair next to her bed. She lay in a sea of bandages seeping crimson.

"I'm here." I laid my hand across her bruised fingers.

"I am so . . . sorry . . ." Her voice sounded different from what I'd always known. Low and weak.

Tears, hot and salty, slid down my cheeks and into my mouth.

"Promise me . . . Be happy . . . for me . . . and be . . . careful." She nodded as if to remind me of a past agreement between us. *"Be careful, Rosanne*. Promise . . ."

"Momma, don't."

"Promise . . ."

A sob clawed its way out of my mouth as I spit out the words: "I promise."

"Love . . . you . . ."

I don't know if she heard me say I loved her, too.

The moments after she left me seemed at the time made of the thinnest of tissue paper. I remember being allowed to sit with

Momma after she'd passed. I remember being told my father and brother had been taken to the morgue straight from the crash and that I'd have to say good-bye to them in my heart.

And then I was meeting Mrs. Grissom, a woman from the county who'd arrived at the hospital sometime during that stretch of shapeless minutes. She'd asked Celine—who had brought me to the hospital—if she knew of any next of kin who could take me in. There weren't any. She'd asked if Celine would please consider speaking to Mr. Calvert about the two of them taking on the role of legal guardians for me since I'd lived the entirety of my sixteen years on their property anyway. The county had a terrible shortage of foster families willing to take older children, and the nearest orphanages were full. It wouldn't have to be for forever. Just for the time being. And they had already raised their son, Wilson, so they had experience.

The two women were speaking in the hallway, just outside the room where I sat with my mother's body. I couldn't see Celine's face, but I could sense her hesitation.

"Oh, I suppose," Celine finally said. "I guess that makes sense. Truman and I do have that bedroom off the kitchen available. The poor thing can stay with us. At least for now."

And Eunice Grissom said she'd approve the emergency placement that very day so that I could return home with Celine, and the rest of the paperwork could follow.

I've only seen Mrs. Grissom twice since then. Once two days after my family was laid to rest—Celine and Truman had paid for the arrangements and the simple headstones—and a few weeks later when she came by to let the Calverts know the temporary guardianship had been approved.

And now Mrs. Grissom is here again.

I hear her step farther into the house and closer to where I wait in the little room beyond the kitchen.

"I'm so very sad and disappointed about all this," Mrs. Grissom says. "And here I thought it had been going so well here for all of you."

"Yes. It's very sad." Celine's voice is toneless. "Extremely disappointing."

"I've been asking a lot of questions on my end since your visit with me on Tuesday, and it seems everyone I've talked to agrees," Mrs. Grissom says, "if what you're saying is true."

"I assure you, it's true."

"Well then," Mrs. Grissom says. "We will leave this with those who can help her best."

"Yes," Celine replies. "Wait right here. I'll get her."

A home for unwed mothers, then. That's where I'm headed, since apparently no one else will take me the way I am. Seventeen. Orphaned. Pregnant.

At least it will be a home. At least it will be a place where this tiny life inside me will be protected. It scares me a little how much I am already starting to care for it. This child is the only family I have now. Surely some unwed mothers are allowed to keep their babies. Surely some do.

The sound of a lock turning yanks me from this daydream, and the door to my bedroom opens. Celine stands at the doorframe, her gaze on me like arrows.

"Mrs. Grissom is here for you," she says, and then quickly turns from me.

"Where is she taking me?"

Celine doesn't turn to me when she answers. Her voice looks an icy blue—like rock crystal. "Where you belong."

She walks away, back through the kitchen and dining room to the entryway, where Mrs. Grissom waits.

I don't reach for the bag I packed—Celine has already taken that—but instead for a sweater I placed on the bed next to a maid's uniform that is no longer mine.

Tears brim in my eyes as I move through the kitchen, and I think of Momma as she lay dying, whispering the words "Be happy, be careful." I have failed her on both accounts.

I walk to the tiled entry, where Mrs. Grissom stands with my travel bag by her feet. I see her gaze drop to the slight mound at my waist. She frowns and sighs. *It's true, then,* the sigh seems to say. *The orphan girl kindly taken in by the Calverts let a boy into her bed.*

"Come, then, Rosanne," Mrs. Grissom says, shaking her head. "We've somewhere to be."

I know it's pointless to apologize, but I turn to Celine anyway.

"I'm sorry, Mrs. Calvert."

"Good-bye, Rosie," she says flatly, her words heavy and gray.

"Thank you for doing what you could for her, you and Mr. Calvert." Mrs. Grissom hands Celine a piece of paper from the top of the clipboard she is carrying. No doubt the record of the Calverts' relinquishment of me. "The county is grateful."

"Yes," Celine says.

I walk out to the passenger side of Mrs. Grissom's Buick and place my travel bag on the back seat and then get in the front. Celine pulls her front door shut even before I am fully inside the car. Mrs. Grissom starts the engine, and as she eases slowly past the Calverts' house, I reach with one hand for the necklace at my throat, feeling for my mother's cloisonné pendant and the little key resting behind it. One is a tether to my past and the other to my future.

I look longingly at the vines as we pass them on the gravel drive, rows and rows of them. I love all the colors of this place, and the chuffing of nearby tractors and the neighbor's roosters and my father's whistling. They'd always been such happy sounds, happy colors. Oh, how I will miss them.

As we turn onto the road to Santa Rosa, I reach for my bag and lift it over the seat to make sure all that I put inside it is still there: the few items of clothing that still fit me, my worn copy of *The Secret Garden*, the photograph of me and Tommy and my parents, my cigar box full of my savings, the baking soda tin with the amaryllis bulb and the instructions on how to care for it . . .

It's all there except for the bundle of Helen Calvert's letters inside the cigar box. My money is still inside it, but the letters from Truman's sister are gone.

Before I can even begin to mourn their loss, Mrs. Grissom asks me why of all things I have a dirty old turnip in my travel bag.

I turn to stare at her. "You looked in my bag, too?"

"We had to make sure you weren't taking anything that wasn't . . ." Her voice drifts off.

"Mine?"

"Safe."

"It's not a turnip." I turn back to the window. "It's an amaryllis bulb."

"A what?"

"An amaryllis. A flower bulb."

"But why do you have it?"

I don't want to explain why I have it. And I don't feel like telling her the dirty little turnip is not what it looks like. It is more. It is something beautiful, hidden but there. Helen Calvert, who lives far across the sea, wrote words like those about the amaryllis bulb when she gave it to me. I've held on to them and the bulb because I've needed to believe they are true.

"Because it's mine," I say. "And so were those letters I had in my bag."

"They weren't addressed to you. Mrs. Calvert said they were hers and Mr. Calvert's."

"Not all of them were. Some of them were mine. And they had given the others to me. Those letters were mine."

Mrs. Grissom is quiet for many long moments.

"Care to tell me how you got into this mess?" she finally says, as though it doesn't matter who the rightful owner of those letters is. We aren't going back for them.

"No." I reach again to touch the little key hiding behind the pendant. I don't care to tell her. I won't.

"Things would go easier if you told me the truth about . . ." She glances at the slight bump at my waist. "You know. How this happened."

"Would it change where you're taking me?"

"Well, no."

"It happened the usual way, Mrs. Grissom."

The county worker sighs, shakes her head, and turns her attention fully back to the road.

I remove the tissue-thin paper of instructions on how to care for an amaryllis from within the baking soda tin—which Celine obviously missed when she went through my bag—and place the only letter from Helen left to me inside the cigar box where all the others had been. I return the bag to its place on the back seat.

We drive into Santa Rosa, then through it, and then we pass over to rolling hillsides on its other side, blanketed with vineyards and scattered sycamore and bushy acacia trees.

"Is it a nice place? Where you're taking me?" I ask as we turn onto a road I have never been down before.

Mrs. Grissom purses her lips before answering. "It's a respected place for people who need help, Rosanne. You need help and that's what's important. I suppose in its own way it's nice."

It will be something like a boardinghouse, I imagine, run by tsking older women who will look down on me in disapproval. I'll be rooming with other fallen girls who have gotten themselves in trouble, and we will surely be reminded daily of our failure to make good choices. Why aren't there places like that for fallen men, I wonder, where they are tsked and told every day that their recklessness has led to disaster?

Mrs. Grissom slows and turns onto a sloping driveway. I see a high fence surrounding a multistory brick building with white trim and flanked by lawns just starting to come back to life after the winter. It looks like a school or college. On either side of the gated entry are two oak trees with limbs that reach well over the top of the fence. A sign etched in stone on the outside of the gate reads SONOMA STATE HOME FOR THE INFIRM. Below that in smaller letters are the words: CARING FOR THE MENTALLY EN-CUMBERED, THE EPILEPTIC, THE PHYSICALLY DISABLED, AND THE PSYCHOPATHIC DELINQUENT.

A cold burst of alarm surges in my chest. "Is this where we're going?"

"It is." Mrs. Grissom doesn't look my way as she stops in front of the closed gate. An attendant emerges from a small gatehouse.

"This can't be right, Mrs. Grissom. Didn't you see the sign? This is some kind of hospital for . . . for sick people."

The smiling attendant comes around to the driver's side and Mrs. Grissom rolls down her window.

"Eunice Grissom with County Human Services. This is Rosanne Maras."

"Mrs. Grissom!" I shout. "This isn't the right place. I'm not sick. I'm not . . . infirm."

Mrs. Grissom tightens her grip on the steering wheel and says nothing.

"You can drive on up," the attendant says. "They're expecting her."

Expecting me? *Expecting* me?

"No, wait!" I call out to him. But the attendant is opening the gate wide so that the car can pull through. I turn to Mrs. Grissom. "I am *not* staying at this place!"

She begins to drive slowly forward. "You need to trust the people who have been charged with your care and well-being, Rosanne."

"But I'm not sick. I'm just . . . I just . . ." I place a hand on my tummy. "I made a mistake."

Mrs. Grissom says nothing but keeps her foot on the gas pedal, her hands on the steering wheel.

She pulls up to a cement curb beside the building just as the large wooden front door opens and a woman in a dark blue dress steps out, along with a nurse in a starched uniform and a man dressed in white pants and a matching shirt. The man comes down the steps quickly, opens the back seat passenger door, and reaches for my travel bag.

I swing around from the front and put my hand out to stop him. "I'm at the wrong place. I'm not staying here." He pulls the bag from my reach and takes it anyway.

The woman and the nurse have joined the man at the curb now, and the nurse takes the bag. The man returns to the car and opens the door where I am sitting.

I instinctively move closer to Mrs. Grissom. "Tell them to give me my bag back. I'm not staying here."

"Rosanne, this is for your own good," Mrs. Grissom says.

The woman in blue bends to look into the car. "We have your room all ready for you, Miss Maras. It's a nice room with a bed by the window."

"But I'm not sick! I'm not 'infirm' or 'psycho . . . ' whatever that other word is."

The man starts to reach inside to pull me out. I scoot away from him, as close to Mrs. Grissom as I can be without climbing onto her lap.

"Rosanne! You are making this far more difficult than it needs to be," Mrs. Grissom scolds. Her words are hot with annoyance and peppered with flashes of topaz.

The woman in the blue dress bends further to look me full in the face.

"Miss Maras, we are all here to help you. Here to take care of you. Now, please come on out of the car, mmm?"

My heart is thumping madly in my chest. I can feel my pulse in my ears like a beating drum. "I don't need to be taken care of."

"Well, how about if you and Dr. Townsend have a little chat about that. Just a chat. You aren't afraid to have a little chat, are you? If you aren't one who needs our care, well then, we aren't going to keep you. We couldn't possibly. Our rooms are needed for the people who really do need our help. If you don't belong here, I will see to it that you are on your way."

The pounding in my head begins to ease a bit. "You will?"

"You have my word."

I turn to look at Mrs. Grissom, who nods toward the woman. "If I get a telephone call that you don't belong here, I'll come back for you myself. I promise."

"A telephone call? Why can't you just wait here for me? You should just wait here for me."

Mrs. Grissom sighs. "Fine. I'll wait here."

I stare at her until Mrs. Grissom turns the key and kills the car's engine. Then I turn to stare at the man standing by the open door. "I don't want him touching me."

"Norman won't be obliged to help you inside if you just come out of the car on your own," the woman says.

I hesitate a moment and then scoot the rest of the way across the seat to step out.

"Well then, that wasn't so hard, was it?" the woman in blue says, smiling brightly.

I want to tell the woman it was indeed hard. It was extremely hard to get out of Mrs. Grissom's car and step into an enclosure with high fences and a locked gate.

"And you promise after I talk with the doctor, I can come back out to the car?" I say instead.

"Absolutely. If you aren't in need of our care, I will bring you out myself. We don't have the room here for people who don't need us."

"And my bag?" I look at the nurse, who stands there with the travel bag in hand. Her expression is unreadable. She looks . . . bored. As if she doesn't care that everything of value to me—other than the chain around my neck—is in that bag.

"If you will not be staying with us, your bag will be returned to you," the woman says.

"Why can't I keep it with me now?"

"Those are our rules, I'm afraid. Now then. I'm Mrs. Crockett. I am the matron here. Shall we go inside and have that chat?"

I follow the two women up the steps. The man Mrs. Crockett called Norman is following close behind me. Pale blue dots hover at the back of my eyes at the sound of his footsteps. We step into the building and enter a lobby. A nurse at a reception desk looks up casually when we walk in and then immediately drops her gaze to the papers she is working on.

Mrs. Crockett turns to her left and opens a door, and the rest of us follow her down a hallway with offices on either side. At the end of the hall is a set of double doors, one of which is open. Mrs. Crockett knocks once on it and then proceeds to enter.

"Dr. Townsend, Rosanne Maras is here," she says.

This room is nicer than the reception area. There are shelves lined with books, and certificates and paintings hang on the wall. Behind the large wooden desk sits a man in a white coat. His hair is slicked back, and his hairline, just beginning to recede, is salted with tiny flecks of gray. On his desk are files and papers, a crystal paperweight of a running horse, and a photo of him with people who must be his family. Everyone in the photo is smiling.

"Miss Maras, please." The doctor motions to one of two armchairs in front of his desk. Mrs. Crockett takes the other chair. As I sit down, I look over my shoulder to see that the nurse, with my travel bag on her lap, has taken a straight-backed chair by the door. Norman stands on the other side of the door with his arms crossed loosely in front of his chest.

"I'm Dr. Townsend," the doctor says in a friendly but authoritative voice. "And may I call you Rosanne? Or . . ." He picks up a piece of paper in front of him. "Rosie? Is that the name you prefer to go by?"

"Rosie is fine," I say, wishing with all my might I could see what else is on that paper he is looking at.

"Rosie here believes a mistake has been made." Mrs. Crockett's words are tinged ever so slightly with false sympathy.

"Is that so?"

"I'm not sick," I say. "I'm not infirm. I'm not any of the things on your sign."

"But you are with child, unmarried, without a home or employment, and only seventeen?" the doctor asks.

"Being with child doesn't mean you're sick."

"True, true," Dr. Townsend says, nodding. "But not every illness is characterized by a cough or a fever. There are all kinds of reasons to need the care of doctors and nurses. Let's see if you need our help, shall we? First, can you tell me who the father of your child is?"

He doesn't say it in a threatening way. His pen is poised over the piece of paper to supply the name as if it means nothing, is of no consequence. Just a name on a line on a hospital form.

"It doesn't matter who the father is. It was a mistake. I'd had wine for the first time and I wasn't . . . I didn't . . . it was a mistake."

"But you do know who the father is?"

I see pulsing brown obelisks cast by the doctor's voice. But there is another voice from before echoing in my mind, too. "You're going to need the money, Rosie," this other voice is saying. "You know you will. I can take care of that. But you need to do this one thing . . ." I can feel the key resting against my breastbone.

"Rosie?" Dr. Townsend says.

"Maybe. Yes. No! I don't know. It doesn't matter."

"So it wasn't just one person, then? You've been with several men?"

My face heats with blazing shame. "I'm saying it doesn't matter who it is! He doesn't love me and I don't love him. It was just a mistake."

The doctor stares at me as though he does not believe me. He doesn't believe that I've been with only one man and only once. What lies has Celine told Mrs. Grissom about me? What has Mrs. Grissom told Dr. Townsend? I need to get out of here.

"I would like to go now," I say.

"We've a few more things to discuss." Dr. Townsend looks at the piece of paper again. "I'd like to talk to you about these visions of yours."

My heart seems to thud to a stop in my chest. "What?"

"The woman who has been responsible for you, Mrs. Calvert? She reported to Mrs. Grissom that you believe you see colors and shapes no one else can see. I'd like to hear more about that."

The room seems to close in around me with the crushing weight of disbelief. How can this man know this? How does *Celine* know?

"Rosie? Did you hear me? I said I'd like to hear more," the doctor says.

"I don't know what you're talking about." My voice sounds thin and weak in my ears.

"You didn't tell Mr. Truman Calvert and the Calverts' son about these colors and shapes that you see?"

"I never said anything to Wilson!" Not that I can remember, anyway.

"But you did tell Mr. Calvert you can see invisible colors and shapes when you hear sounds, yes? And you told him that numbers and names and places all have assigned colors that you see in your head? Mrs. Calvert said you told him this."

The breath in my lungs tapers away as if all the oxygen in the room has been sucked out of it. Truman told Celine what I shared with him in confidence. He told her! Why? Why did he do that? I told him no one was supposed to know. Especially not Celine. Unless it was Wilson he told, despite my request, to clear things up. Yes, yes. I could see Wilson sharing with his mother what Truman had to have told him. I hear again my mother's voice as she lay dying telling me to be careful. *Be careful.* But I hadn't been. I'd been stupid. Twice.

I want to remain calm. It seems important that I remain calm in this place. I breathe in deeply and exhale.

"I was just kidding," I say.

"Just kidding?"

I close my eyes. Why is this happening? Why? I want my mother. I want wings to fly away. Far, far away.

"Rosie?" Dr. Townsend says gently.

"It's just a little game I play," I whisper, eyes still closed. "That's all. It's nothing. Just a game."

"Why would you play a game like that?"

"I don't know."

"It's a very odd game to play, and for no reason that seems to be to your benefit," he continues. "I'd like to be able to help you, Rosie. But you will need to be honest with me. No more lies."

I open my eyes to look at him. Ready tears are blurring my vision. "I can't."

"Why can't you?"

"You won't understand." Two tears spill down my face, impossible to stop. "Nobody does."

"I think you'll find that I understand a great deal about what a person can see and hear that no one else can. Don't you think you owe it to the child to get the help you need?"

"The child?"

"Yes."

My child. My baby . . . Oh God! What would they do with a baby in a place like this? I have to get out of here.

"I'd like to go now, please." I flick the tears away.

"That wouldn't be wise, and it wouldn't be humane to let you go in the condition you are in," Dr. Townsend says calmly. "You have no family, correct? No aunts or uncles or grandparents?"

It's true that I have no relatives in California. My parents immigrated to the United States from Eastern Europe as children and my grandparents have long since died. Momma was an only child and Daddy had only one sibling—an estranged brother I've never met. I know there are some distant Marasz relatives—that being the family name before immigration officials removed the *z*—still living in Poland, but I've no idea who they are or how to reach them. "No, but—"

"I couldn't possibly turn you out into a world where there is no one to help you. As an orphan and a minor, you fall under the county's care, and the county has given you to me. You are my responsibility."

"I'd like to go just the same." I stand, and at once Norman is at my side with his hand on my arm, his grip tight. The crushing fear from before slams into me.

"When you are well and ready to be on your own, you will be released, I assure you," the doctor says. "But not a minute before."

"Let me go. Let me go!" I squirm and Norman quickly puts both arms round my torso. The nurse stands, drops my travel bag, and rushes to help him hold me fast.

"Mrs. Crockett, do you have the hypodermic?" Dr. Townsend asks.

"I do, Doctor."

I scream for my mother as the needle pierces my skin.

2

I had seen the little room just off the Calverts' kitchen plenty of times; on all those occasions I'd been called up to the big house to help with dinner parties and holidays. There was a bedstead and bureau of hardwood, curtains trimmed in eyelet, and a chenille bedcover in a pattern of cabbage roses. It had been the Calverts' housekeeper's bedroom, but that woman, Flora, whom Celine had often complained to and about, had been let go the week before, and Celine hadn't yet found her replacement.

As she and I traveled home from the hospital the day of the accident, Celine told me she had decided on a plan to address both her pressing need and mine.

"So I know you're probably not thinking about what you're going to do to get on with life now and all of that," Celine began, "but the truth is, you've been tossed into a situation where you're going to have to start making decisions for yourself. I know all about that. You hadn't been born yet when my parents died, so you probably don't know there was a time when I had to take on the running of the vineyard all by myself. I couldn't stop to feel sorry for myself, because there was so much work to do and I had to do it."

Though my thoughts were still a throbbing tangle of fear and anger and sorrow, I remembered having overheard at a dinner party once that Celine married Truman Calvert when her father, Bernard Rosseau, was still living. Mr. Rosseau had died of a heart attack three years later, when Celine was twenty-five. She hadn't been forced to manage Rosseau Vineyard all by herself; she had a husband. But I looked out at the passing countryside and said nothing.

"I found that work helped me move on from grief," Celine went on. "Trust me. The last thing you're going to want to do is lie on your bed and cry day after day. I know what I'm talking about here. If you want to keep working in the vineyard, I won't stop you, but I think you should work at the big house. You've worked in my kitchen often enough to know how I like things, and I know your mother relied on you to keep house in the cottage when she was out in the vineyard. She often told me what a good cook you are, so if you'd like to give that a try, we can do that. Unless you want to go back to school."

I had convinced my parents to let me quit school four months earlier—on my sixteenth birthday—so that I could work alongside my father instead. Many farmers' children stop schooling at sixteen, I'd told them, and I wasn't suited for school anyway. The colors in my mind were always fighting for my attention, and there were so many sounds at school. Too many. It had been so hard to concentrate. I loved to read, and I was fond of history and geography, but math, because of those numbers and all the colors that went with them, was impossible. And my classmates thought I was strange, even though I'd obeyed my parents' command from years earlier to tell no one what I saw in this big world of sound. "Other people don't see the colors that you do," my parents had said, although Momma had told me once that a dead great-aunt had been able to see them. People wouldn't understand. People would think something was wrong with me. I'd kept the colors to myself the best I could, pretending all the time that I never saw anything out of the ordinary. But my classmates remembered the few times I'd slipped. They whispered about me. So did my teachers.

In the end, it hadn't taken much convincing. Daddy and Momma didn't like the colors, but they liked less that I was unhappy. And I'd already been helping in the vineyard since I was little. I knew everything about the vines. I loved them. They were home to me. And I had promised my parents and kept the promise to continue making bicycle trips to the library in Santa Rosa to borrow books. I'd assured them I wouldn't stop learning. Books would teach me.

"I don't want to go back to school," I told Celine.

"I don't blame you. You're going to need to make a way for yourself in this world. You work for me and I'll see to it that you get good experience as a domestic, and I'll write you a nice letter of recommendation when the time comes for you to move on. You'll get far better experience working for me at the house than toiling away at the vines. And you'll certainly enjoy it more."

I didn't think Celine was right about that. I had grown up chasing a giggling Tommy through the rows, and clipping the bunches of sweet fruit at harvest, and pruning back the branches in the winter to make way for the next year's grapes. The last echoes of my life with my parents and little brother were in those vines.

And yet it wouldn't be the same working for another vinedresser.

"What do you think? Shall we tell Mr. Calvert that's what we've decided to do?" Celine asked.

I said yes.

"Good." Celine seemed happy with herself for having so

quickly come up with a plan that benefited everyone. "There is a retired chef I've been wanting to hire for quite a while, but he doesn't clean houses and he only wants to come a few hours a day. I'll see if I can hire him for the evening meals. You can handle the rest, can't you? I'll call him when we get home."

When we arrived back at the vineyard, Truman seemed genuinely sad for me and suggested to Celine that I be given a couple of days at the cottage to adjust and mourn, and that after my family was laid to rest perhaps then I could join them at the big house. Even though I wasn't sure I wanted to sleep in the cottage by myself, I'd been surprised at his kindness. I didn't know Truman well. Even though I'd been born at Rosseau Vineyard, it was always Celine who would come down to the cottage to speak with my father or who called me up to the big house to help in the kitchen with parties. Truman spent all his time in the tasting and barrel room, a tall, wide stone-and-timbered structure built into a hillside. But Celine said it was a terrible idea for me to be alone in the cottage after having just lost everybody I loved.

"Rosie is our responsibility now, Truman. We can't go around making careless decisions," she said.

So I spent the first night as the Calverts' ward in my new bedroom—the maid's bedroom. I lay awake that night for a long time, numb with grief and disbelief. The sounds in the big house in the midnight hours were new and different. Subtle. Strange. And so were the colors that accompanied them. I kept replaying in my head the policeman coming to the big house, the sound of his car's tires crunching on the sloping gravel drive and creating pinpricks of orange. And me, hanging laundry on the line outside the cottage, watching as he rang Celine and Truman's doorbell. I saw over and over the policeman talking to Celine on the porch and the slow way she swiveled her head to look at me at the bottom of the little hill as I wondered why a policeman was talking to her.

I fell asleep wishing I'd been in the truck with my family.

The following day, Celine and Truman helped me take what I wanted out of the cottage so that it could be prepared for a new head vinedresser. Momma's chipped china and faded tablecloths had still looked so beautiful before, but now everything in the cottage looked old and dull. I asked that the household goods be given away to the migrant farm camp in the next town over, and I took only my clothes, the cloisonné necklace that Daddy had given Momma for their tenth wedding anniversary, my cigar box of loose coins and Helen Calvert's letters, and my bicycle. A book. The following day, at a graveside service attended by the other employees of the vineyard, the caskets containing my family were lowered into the ground at the local cemetery.

On the day after that, I began my new life as the Calverts' maid.

I was now in charge of preparing and laying out the Calverts' breakfast every morning according to a menu Celine would select each week. The Calverts would see to their own midday meal, and the hired chef would prepare the last meal of the day, which I would serve and then clean up afterward. I was in charge of putting away Mrs. Calvert's grocery order every week as well as seeing to the housekeeping of all the other rooms in the house.

"The average pay for a maid is ten dollars a week, but because you're just starting out and all your physical needs are already being met, let's make it five so that you have room to grow," Celine said as she and I sat at the kitchen table the day after the funeral and went over my duties. I would have free use of the telephone for local calls and would have Sundays off and every other Saturday afternoon and evening.

And there were to be no gentlemen callers at the house. Ever.

I blushed crimson at this.

"That was the biggest problem with Flora, you know," Celine added.

"But I'm not . . ."

"You're young and quite pretty, that's what you are. I'm not only giving you a direct order, I am also giving you good advice. Don't make the mistakes Flora made. Staying out all night and sleeping past the breakfast hour and even sneaking men into her room. I won't abide that kind of behavior. And neither would any other employer."

"Of . . . of course not." The idea of sneaking a young man into my bedroom was absurd. I hadn't so much as even been kissed. I'd imagined it. Lots of times. I had even practiced on my bed pillow in the dark after having overheard girls in town giggling about stolen kisses from boys who had wanted more than just kisses. But no boy had ever taken any interest in me. And my heart was shattered from the loss of my family. It was unthinkable.

"So we're clear on that?" Celine said.

"Yes, Mrs. Calvert."

"Good. Now. Do you want to eat with us in the dining room or take your meals on your own? It's up to you. But I'll just tell you that when you work for a family as a domestic, they will not expect you to sit with them. That's not how it's done. And I'm trying to do my best to prepare you for your life ahead, you know. Someone has to."

"I'll . . . take them on my own."

With that, Celine stood up from the table and said she was actually looking forward to having me in the house now that she had given it some thought and everything was settled. It would almost be like having a daughter, something she'd always wanted and never had.

These details finished, I went into my bedroom to change. On the bed was a black dress with a white collar and matching white apron. I closed the door, took off my cotton blouse and twill skirt, and put on the dress.

I didn't know how I felt about the uniform, although it was made well and smelled nice. I turned to face the mirror above the bureau and stared at my reflection. The dress made me look older, but I did not feel older. It made me look as if I belonged there, but I didn't feel like I did.

Celine had said a moment earlier that I was pretty. I cocked my head and studied the girl I saw in the glass. I saw my father's wavy brown hair, my mother's sea blue eyes. Momma's slightly full lips and Daddy's slender nose. A thin waist, arms strong yet slender. My breasts filled out the dress in a way that seemed normal and rather average. Not too big, not too small. Did all that make me pretty? I didn't feel ugly, but was I pretty? I wasn't sure.

Then, from beyond the closed door, I heard the faint sounds of music. Celine had put on a record and the song was floating on the air toward my bedroom. Bing Crosby's "Remember Me?"

The music crept in under the door and filled my mind with tiny orange and yellow spirals.

3

I awaken to the sensation of being underwater.

My first thought as consciousness starts to return is that I have forgotten how to swim and am drowning, yet it doesn't hurt like I've always believed drowning would. It is strangely painless . . .

As I become more awake, the liquid sensation is replaced by that of fabric. A sheet and blanket enclose my body, not water. The material smells of bleach. I am also aware that I have just woken from a terrible nightmare. I can't remember now why the dream was so frightening, and yet I feel a desperate need to awaken completely so that I won't fall back asleep and return to it.

It is so hard to open my eyes. So hard.

As I lie half in and half out of wakefulness, I slowly recall that Mrs. Grissom was in my dream. And a woman in a blue dress and a man in white named Norman. I remember there was a doctor. Dr. Townsend.

Wait. Those other people are real.

I did not dream them. They are real.

I force my eyes open.

I am lying on a bed in a dimly lit room. Above me is one long, narrow window high up on the wall, big enough for perhaps only a cat to get through if the panes could be opened. It does not appear that they could be. A pale light shines through the cloudy glass. There is nothing else in the room but the bed I am lying on. I want to throw back the covers, but I can only push them slowly off of my body. The dress I had on earlier is gone, and I am now wearing a stiff cotton shift I don't recognize. Someone took my clothes off. Someone saw and touched my body to slide me into this nightgown-like thing I now wear. Someone put different underpants on me. Someone saw my naked body. I raise an unsteady hand to my throat. My mother's necklace is gone, too. And the little key.

With effort I swing my legs over the side of the bed and get to my feet. A wave of dizziness nearly sends me back onto the mattress, but I steel myself as I wait for it to fade. When it does, I stagger over to the door, grasping the knob with difficulty. The doorknob will not turn. I am locked in.

Fear floods me as I draw back my hand and then land a weak thud on the door. I bang it again.

"Please, somebody!" I call out, my voice sounding as if my mouth is full of gelatin. "Somebody! Let me out. Please, let me out!"

I keep pounding, and soon a covering over a small window in the door slides open. A nurse stands on the other side. All I can see of the woman are her eyes, nose, and part of her white hat.

"Please let me out," I say.

"Everyone is looking forward to you coming out of that room, Rosie," the nurse replies. "But that depends on you, not me. If you're going to fight me or try to hurt me or anyone else, you're going to need to stay in this room."

Hurt her?

"I just want out."

"Are you ready to go upstairs and settle in?"

"I'm . . . I'm not supposed to be at this place."

"But you are at this place," the nurse says. "And you'll be staying here until you are well again, so unless you are ready to let us help you, you'll need to stay in that room. It's really up to you whether or not I open the door."

"All right," I say in a less-than-convincing tone.

"I want your word, now," the nurse says sternly. "I want to hear you say you are ready to let us help you get well, and I want you to mean it."

I think this through quickly. The needle in the doctor's office put me to sleep and into this room. These people have my things. My bag. My clothes. And they have keys. They have power over me. I will have to do whatever they say until I can find a way to leave. Somehow I must find a way out of this place. But until then I will have to pretend, and lucky for me, I already know how to do that. I pretend every day that I don't see the colors.

I can't fight back like I did in the doctor's office.

"I'm ready to let you help me get well," I say.

"And I have your word?" The nurse sounds like a parent correcting an unruly child.

"Yes."

I hear the sound of a key in the lock, see the handle turn, watch the door open.

This nurse is different from the one who took my travel bag. She is older than that first nurse and larger, almost as tall as a man. She looks strong.

"Now then," the woman says. "I'm Nurse Tipton." She steps aside so that I can exit the room. We stand in a long hallway with doors on either side. The linoleum is cracked in places and there isn't so much as a framed photograph on the walls. From far down the hall I hear a woman scream. A scattering of reddish confetti accompanies it. Nurse Tipton doesn't even look in the direction of the outburst.

"Are you sure you're able to walk?" the nurse says. "You look a little woozy still."

"I'm . . . I can walk."

"Shall we?" The nurse starts down the hall toward a workstation enclosed in reinforced glass. Beyond it is a closed door.

I hold on to the wall with one hand as we walk, feeling balance and control of my movements return with every step.

"Nurse Tipton," I say after we pass a couple of doors with the same cutout windows mine had—all closed. My voice sounds less mushy in my ears. "Where are my clothes? Where's my bag?"

"You don't need to worry about either. We've taken care of everything."

"I'm not worried. I just want to know where they are." I attempt to walk without the aid of the wall and find that I can.

"Your things have been taken to a safe place to be kept until you're well and ready to leave us."

"But I need my clothes."

"The residents all wear clothing we provide. And you won't be wearing your own clothes much longer anyway, will you?" There is a slightly judgmental tone to her words.

I feel my face warm, but I push the shame aside. "Where's my necklace? It means a lot to me." My mother's cloisonné pendant—and the little key that shares its chain—are my only hope of survival now.

"Your necklace is actually safer where it is, right inside your bag," the nurse says matter-of-factly. "Sometimes things get taken from rooms. We don't condone it. But it happens. Other residents have been known to take things that don't belong to them."

If I am to escape this place, I must have my bag. I need that key. I must know where it is.

"So my bag is in a place no one can get to?" I ask.

"There's a locked closet in the administration wing for residents' personal belongings. Residents aren't even allowed in the administration wing."

"The administration wing?"

"That's where you went when you arrived."

I will have to find a way to get inside that closet. Somehow, I must. I have to. "All right," I say. "But the amaryllis bulb needs to be kept in a cool, dark place. Is it cool and dark in there?"

"So that's what that was!" the nurse says as we arrive at the nurses' station. "I'm afraid that's been tossed."

I stop just short of the station. "What do you mean it's been tossed?"

Nurse Tipton taps on the glass to get the attention of another nurse inside, who stands in front of a wheeled tray filling little medicine cups. "I need to sign Miss Maras out," she says.

"What do you mean it's been tossed?" I ask again, struggling to repeat myself calmly.

Nurse Tipton turns to face me. "It looked like something that needed to be thrown out, so . . . it was thrown out." She turns back around and takes a clipboard from the other nurse through an opening in the glass and starts writing on it.

"But it's not trash," I reply with forced composure. "It's an amaryllis bulb and it's mine."

Nurse Tipton glances at me as she slides the clipboard back through the opening. "Well, sorry, but like I said. It's been thrown out."

"But surely we could take it out of the trash. I only just got here."

Nurse Tipton stares at me a moment. "You've been here three days, Rosie."

I feel the dizziness from before start to creep over me, and I will it back, closing my eyes a moment to steady myself. "That's not possible."

"Well, it is possible, because it happened. We had to keep you medicated the last three days because you kept trying to hurt people and escape the room. We had to double your last dose. Your memory's probably foggy now."

I stare at the woman, open-mouthed. I have no recollection of any of that.

"You can ask anyone here," Nurse Tipton continues. "You came here on Thursday morning. It's now Sunday and it's almost lunchtime. So how about we get you set up in your room, get you into some day clothes, and then go down to the cafeteria? I'm sorry about the bulb, but it's gone now."

"But Helen gave it to me," I whisper, and my eyes burn with tears ready to fall. *It was my bit of buried treasure*, I want to say. *My little scrap of hope. The promise of something good that waits for me.*

"Well, maybe this Helen person will give you another one someday. It's not like it was the only one in the world. Shall we go, then?"

I nod numbly. Helen will never give me another bulb. I already know I will never see her again. Nor will I hear from her again, will I? Of course I won't. The bulb she gave me is gone.

Perhaps I deserve for it to be gone.

Nurse Tipton withdraws a key ring from her pocket, opens the door by the nurses' station, and leads me out into a foyer. Across the space and to my left are closed doors just like the one we came through. To my right is a set of double doors with window insets. A staircase is visible beyond the glass, and an elevator is next to it. "Can you handle the stairs?" she asks.

"Yes," I manage.

Nurse Tipton uses a different key to open the door to the stairs, which we then begin to climb.

"We just left Ward 2," Nurse Tipton says as she adjusts her pace to match mine. "I suggest you don't do anything to find yourself back there on that side of the second floor. The other side is the infirmary and surgery. The third and fourth floors are for the residents' rooms. The third floor is for women, fourth for the men. The fifth floor is where the dayroom is, and the library and the therapy rooms. The first floor is off-limits except for the cafeteria and the visiting rooms." The nurse looks back at me as we climb, letting her gaze drop to the round little mound at my waistline. "Female residents have no contact with the male residents outside the fifth-floor dayroom. None."

Again I hear the cool edge of judgment in the nurse's voice.

"You'll find out all the rules tomorrow," she continues as she turns back around. "Mrs. Crockett—she's the matron here—will give you a tour and explain all the expectations."

"Expectations?"

"Yes. There are behaviors that will be expected from you and others that will not be tolerated. We have rules here that every resident must abide by. You can't just do whatever you want. We have five hundred residents here, so our rules are important and necessary."

I cannot let my mind linger on the nurse's critical tone. I feel an urgency—especially after hearing what my earlier defiance resulted in—to play along. Just play along and watch and listen.

But maybe I can ask politely to use a phone. I'm thinking Celine must have known what kind of place Mrs. Grissom was taking me to, but I can't imagine Truman did. If I can just find a way to telephone the vineyard when she's not there to answer the phone. If I can tell Truman what's been done to me, he could do something to get me out.

On the next floor, the nurse uses her key to open the door leading out of the stairwell. We enter a foyer identical to the one below it, with doors on all the opposite walls, marked Hall A, B, and C. Nurse Tipton takes her key, walks to Hall B, unlocks the door, and ushers me through.

In front of us is a nurses' station, similar to the one downstairs but smaller. Behind the glass are a nurse and two orderlies. They are all eating off cafeteria trays. One of the men is Norman. He looks at me for a moment but then returns to his plate, as if I were no one he's met before, certainly not someone whom he had to wrap his arms around to restrain. On the desk is a shiny black telephone.

"I've brought Rosie Maras up from the second floor," Nurse Tipton says to the people behind the glass. The nurse doesn't glance at me but instead looks up at Nurse Tipton in disappointment.

"Do you mind taking her and showing her to her room, Vera?" She nods to her tray. "It's chicken potpie. The only good thing they make here, and only when it's hot. Please? I didn't know she was coming up now."

Nurse Tipton sighs. "All right. Which room?"

The other nurse smiles gratefully. "Room 5. Last bed on the left. Her clothes are on the bed. Norman can take her down for lunch as soon as she's dressed. She shouldn't dawdle or she'll miss it."

"Okay, okay," Nurse Tipton says, and then she turns to me. "Come on."

"Thank you!" the other nurse calls out as we start to walk away.

Nurse Tipton leads me down the long hallway, painted all white with doors on either side, all of which are wide open. I can see that each room holds six beds, and that most of the beds are made and empty. But there are some where a sleeping figure lies curled up under the blankets.

The nurse enters Room 5, halfway down the hallway and empty of other people. She leads me to the last bed on the left-hand side, positioned by a barred window, one of only two in the room. There is a dull blue cotton dress on the mattress and soft-soled slip-on shoes on the floor by a nightstand. On some of the other nightstands are framed photographs or books or small stuffed animals. The one by this bed is empty.

"You're lucky to have a bed by the window." Nurse Tipton nods toward the glass panes and the cross work of bars. From the window I can see below a vegetable garden, a pen full of goats, and a sizable chicken coop, all within the confines of the fence surrounding the property. Inside those enclosures are women in the same kind of somber dress that lies folded on my bed, some hoeing in the garden, some tending the goats, and some raking up chicken feces in the coop.

Nurse Tipton notices me looking down at them.

"The residents all have little jobs to keep them busy," she says. "Most choose the area they want to work in. It's better if you choose. If you don't, one will be chosen for you. We have another vegetable garden as well as a dairy barn and a small orchard on the men's side. The male residents take care of those. Not everyone has to find a duty outdoors, though. Some residents work in the kitchen or the laundry room or hair salon or managing the library. If you want a little free advice, you should quickly choose what you want to do and then do your best at it. It's one of the ways we gauge whether or not you are ready to be discharged. If you have learned a skill and can make a living for yourself outside and not be a burden on society, we know you're ready. And if you can't, it is one of the reasons a person remains a resident here."

Nurse Tipton waits a moment to let that sink in. "All right, then. You heard what Nurse Andrews said. If you want lunch, you should get changed. The women and men have separate eating times, and you don't want to miss yours."

I turn from the window. "The women that we passed still lying in their beds, why didn't they go down for lunch?"

"That is not behavior any of them should continue if they want to be released. Any able-bodied resident who persists in remaining in their bed more than a day or two will be removed to Ward 2, where they will be sure to receive nourishment. But returning to Ward 2 is like starting over. You are in one of the halls in Ward 3 that has the most opportunities for you to make independent choices. Again, I would suggest you do everything you can to remain here on the third floor and in this ward. Time to get dressed."

I pick the dress up off the bed and let it unfold. It's several sizes too large for me. A brassiere, not the one I was wearing the day I arrived, falls onto the bed from within the folds of the dress, as well as a pair of plain white socks.

"I suppose Nurse Andrews was thinking this would be the best fit for now," Nurse Tipton says, looking askance at the overly large dress. "We do have maternity smocks for women who are farther along. I'm sure you will transition into one of those soon enough."

Nurse Tipton makes no move to leave so that I can change in privacy. I slip off the cotton shift and put on the bra, also a bit too big, and then the dress, which surely looks like a tent on me. When I am done I slip on the soft-soled shoes, which thankfully fit.

"Can you take me down to the cafeteria instead of that orderly?" I ask when I'm finished.

Nurse Tipton cocks her head in curiosity. "Are you afraid of men?"

I can already sense it is important that I not appear to be overly fearful of anything here.

"No," I answer quickly. "When I arrived I was . . . you know, not expecting to stay. That orderly had to . . . restrain me. I'm embarrassed."

Nurse Tipton shoos away my concern as if it were a housefly. "I assure you Norman has dealt with far worse. And I wouldn't be able to anyway. I need to get back to my own ward."

"Before you go, may I please use a telephone?"

Nurse Tipton blinks at me. "You want to use a telephone?"

"Yes, there is someone I would like to call."

"Residents don't have telephone privileges. But you can tell Mrs. Crockett and she can call that person for you if it's important. It would have to be pretty important."

"I won't be able to use the telephone ever while I'm here?"

"You can write letters if you want. As many as you want, although they will be viewed before they are sent. But the telephone is off-limits."

I swallow my disappointment the best I can, but I can feel tears of frustration begging for release. Writing a letter won't help me. A letter to the big house would be opened by Celine. In all likelihood, Truman would never see it. A well-timed phone call to the barrel room would have been different, though. Celine isn't in there as much as Truman is . . .

But I can't think of that now. If I happen upon an unattended phone, I will find a way to use it. Until then, I'll have to bury this frustration along with all the others.

The two of us walk back out into the hallway and to the nurses' station.

"She's ready," Nurse Tipton announces.

Norman slips another forkful of his lunch into his mouth, wipes his face with a napkin, and then comes out. He says nothing as he withdraws a key and walks to the door. Nurse Tipton and I follow him into the foyer and then into the stairwell. At the second-floor landing Nurse Tipton pulls out her own key ring to leave us.

"Thank you." It seems like the right thing to say in that moment, though I'm not sure what I'm thanking Nurse Tipton for.

"Take care," the woman says with a casual tip of her chin.

I follow Norman down the rest of the stairs to the first floor and to the large cafeteria at the back of the building. It is a large space filled with long tables where dozens upon dozens of women of all ages are seated and eating. There must be close to three hundred diners. Some look like they are only twelve or thirteen, and others have gray hair and faces lined with age.

Only a handful raise their heads to look at me, new and pregnant and arriving late to lunch. The rest continue to eat and talk.

The sound of their voices in a room empty of anything soft to absorb the noise casts an arc of drab green as I walk into the room.

4

I didn't feel—not for a moment—that I worked for both the Calverts, even though it was the couple's house I cleaned and both of their clothes and towels and linens I laundered. I knew it was Celine Calvert who made all the decisions and instructed me on every detail of what I was to do. Truman had few comments on my duties as their maid and fewer still in his role as a co-guardian of my welfare, which seemed to suit Celine just fine.

Daddy had started working at Rosseau Vineyard before I was even born, and while he never spoke badly about his employer, I caught on early that Celine was someone he never wanted to disappoint. Despite her petite stature and being a woman, Celine had always been fully capable of running the vineyard's business without much help from anyone, near as I could tell. She expected every employee's absolute best effort, just as she gave the vineyard her own. I had always thought of her as not only being in charge but loving that she was in charge.

Celine Calvert was the only vineyard owner in Sonoma County

I knew of who wasn't a man. It was known around the county that years earlier, before the new Prohibition laws took effect, Celine had contracted with Catholic dioceses up and down the West Coast to make sacramental wine, the only kind that would be allowed to be made. Rosseau Vineyard hadn't only survived during Prohibition; it had thrived. Daddy told me once that when Prohibition began, there had been more than seven hundred California wineries. At its end, only fifty were still active. Celine's was one of them.

To me, Truman Calvert had always seemed the exact opposite of his wife. He was tall—a good ten inches taller than Celine—and he walked with a slight limp from a battle injury in the Great War, making his gait slower than hers. When they walked the property together it seemed like she was in a hurry and he was always trying to catch up with her. Truman spent most of his time bringing in restaurant owners and hotel managers to sample the Rosseau vintages. He was a quiet man who didn't come down to the vinedresser's cottage much, and he seemed to let Celine make all the major decisions related to the vineyard. I had long supposed it was because the vineyard had been Celine's inheritance, not his, but it was almost laughable how tiny Celine ran the show while her tall husband just watched.

The Calverts' only child, Wilson, was away at college at Berkeley. It had been a long time since I had seen him up close. There had been one year, when I was six and Wilson was ten, when he liked to come down to the vinedresser's cottage to play with me, and we would build forts in the vines or kick a ball to each other. Tommy was just a baby then. But it was just for that one year. By the time Wilson was fourteen, he was attending a fancy boarding school in San Francisco and was home only on holidays and term breaks. Those early days of our friendship were never repeated, not even during the summer months when Wilson was home.

On my days off, I would walk the vineyards. When I climbed the hill back to the big house, I often paused on the flagstone patio that overlooked the acres and imagined my parents and Tommy hovering just above me in paradise, perhaps just beyond the clouds. Not so very far, just far enough not to be able to reach them with a touch. Celine had been right about the work being a way of distracting me from the heaviness of not being able to bridge that gap. The work was its own kind of consolation.

A month into my new life at the big house, Celine reminded me—just after the evening meal and after she'd downed several glasses of Rosseau wine—that she'd always wanted a daughter and had been disappointed to have been given only a son and no other children.

"I was going to name any baby girl I had Francine, after my mother," she said as I started to clear away the supper dishes. It was nearly eight thirty. Celine was lingering at the table and Truman had long since left it. "I suppose we would've called her Francie. That sounds nice alongside Rosie."

Celine giggled and reached out for my hand to hold it. She was clearly tipsy. Drunk, perhaps.

"Um, yes," I said. "It does."

"You're very pretty, you know that, don't you?"

I felt the cool weight of Celine's hand in mine and said nothing.

"My Francie and you might have been friends when you were little," Celine went on dreamily. "Just think of it. Francie and Rosie. My Francie would have been fair-haired like me, though. That's how I would have been able to tell you two apart." She swung her other hand out, nearly knocking over her wineglass. "I'd look out over the vineyard, and I'd see you two playing together. Pretending to be princesses with daisy-chain crowns in your hair. I'd see your two heads, and I would know which one was mine."

I searched for appropriate words for a reply. None came to mind. I was still considering the awkwardness of the situation when Celine suddenly closed her eyes and the hand in mine grew limp.

"Mrs. Calvert?" I said.

No response.

I said her name again and touched her shoulder. Celine slouched in her chair and tucked her chin to her chest, letting out a snuffled snore. I stepped back, unsure what to do. I started taking plates to the kitchen and kept hoping each time I came back to the table that Celine would have roused. But when the table was clear of all the supper dishes and Celine still sat slumped in her chair, I left her to search for Truman.

I found him in the study. The room was filled with comfortable furniture and bookshelves, a stone fireplace, a cocktail bar, and a mahogany desk that had been Bernard Rosseau's and was now Celine's. Truman's framed war medals and photographs from when he was a young man in the army hung on a paneled wall by a window. He was sitting in one of the chairs facing the cold hearth and smoking a cigarette. A glass of brandy sat on a table next to him.

"Mr. Calvert?" I said.

He slowly turned his head and looked at me with slight surprise. "Please just call me Truman, Rosie. What is it?"

"I'm afraid Mrs. Calvert is . . . well, I think she is . . ." My voice fell away.

"She's what?"

"She has fallen asleep at the table. I can't wake her up."

Truman turned back around. He waited a moment and then

ground out his cigarette in an ashtray. He picked up the tumbler of brandy, polished it off, and then stood.

I stepped aside as he walked past me, and we headed for the dining room. When we got there I was going to leave him to it and return to the kitchen.

"I might need your help," he said.

Celine was in the same place where I had left her. After a couple of attempts to awaken his wife, Truman bent down and scooped her up.

"If you could just follow along and open the bedroom door and pull back the bedspread, please? That would be helpful," he said.

Truman walked through the silent house with the slight hitch in his step and his sleeping wife in his arms, and I followed behind, seeing scarlet diamonds when Celine let out a snore. When we arrived at the master suite at the far end of the hallway, he stepped aside and I opened the door quietly and stepped in. I went to the four-poster bed across the room, plucked off the decorative pillows and set them on a window seat, and then pulled back the bedspread.

"So, um, will that be all?"

"Yes, thank you."

I turned and quickly left the room.

I was washing up the dishes when Truman came into the kitchen a few minutes later with his empty brandy glass.

"She probably won't remember what just happened now," Truman said as he placed the tumbler next to the sink. "And it would be wise not to mention it. I don't think it would go well for you if you did." He leaned up against the countertop and folded his arms across his chest as if he planned to stay for a while and chat.

"Oh. All right," I said hesitantly.

"No, I mean it. Don't ever bring it up. Celine won't like it that you saw her that way. She doesn't like to look weak in front of people."

I felt for the next dish in the suds. I wanted to be done. I wanted to forget about this night, too. Truman's being that close to me was making me feel strangely uncomfortable.

"It's one of the things her father bequeathed to her, unfortunately. The ability to worry too much about people seeing her as vulnerable."

"Oh."

"Fathers tend to do that, don't they? Foist on us their own fears."

I stared up at Truman and then quickly looked away. I wasn't sure what it meant to foist something on someone, but I could tell from his tone it was something fathers shouldn't do.

"I doubt, though, that your father was as hard on you as mine and Celine's were on us," Truman said. "Unless I'm wrong about that."

I felt a ripple of both pride and unease zip through me. Daddy hadn't been hard on me. But he didn't like my colors. He hadn't been able to trust that I could keep them secret. It was hard to pretend sometimes. I'd told him this. He'd actually seemed relieved when I asked to quit school, though he tried to hide it. "I . . . He was a good father," I said.

"So he never had impossible expectations of you, eh?"

I set a rinsed dish in the wooden drainer but didn't look at Truman. He had hardly ever spoken more than a few words to me at a time. Not in all those years before the accident and not now, and never about anything personal. "No."

"Never? Really?"

I glanced upward to look at him again. He was gazing at me in earnest.

"Never," I said.

He nodded, smiling lightly. "Celine does that, too. She'll defend her father to her dying day. Just like you're doing now. It's okay. I know why. You miss your father. His memory is sacred to you. But I watched your father with you from the day you were born. Just because I live up here on the hill doesn't mean I don't see what happens down below. I think both your parents expected a lot from you. Let me just say that you don't have to try to live up to something that never fit you in the first place. If your parents had lived longer, you might've figured that out for yourself. But sadly they're gone now, and you'll end up holding on to what they wanted for you because you think to honor them you must. You don't, though."

An odd mix of anger and shame flared. Both felt like a rush of wind. "My parents were good to me."

"I'm not saying they weren't. I could tell they loved you. You were very lucky in that way. I'm not talking about that. I'm just saying it's okay to plan your own path, Rosie. And I'm saying it because you're still able to. It's a nice place to be in, and it doesn't last."

I plunged my hands back into the sink. "Okay," I said.

"Do you have everything you need?" he asked a moment later. "Is there anything Celine and I can do for you?"

"I . . . I don't need anything."

Truman stepped back from the counter. "All right. Good night, Rosie. You'll remember what I said, right? I mean about what happened tonight with Celine?"

"Um, yes. Good night, Mr. Calvert."

"Truman."

"Truman."

In the morning, and to my relief, Celine didn't remember having fallen into a drunken stupor. She came to the breakfast table a little after nine, holding a cool cloth to her head and asking for coffee and a glass of peppered tomato juice and for me to please save any need to bang pots and pans for later. Truman followed minutes later, giving no indication that anything out of the ordinary had taken place the night before.

Days and weeks passed after that. Winter gave way to spring, and spring to summer. Celine began giving me additional tasks to ready the house for company.

Wilson was coming home.

5

The first several days, I work hard to appear as though I'm adapting well to life at the institution. My five roommates neither aid nor hinder me. None seem overly eager to get to know me. The two whose beds are directly across from me, Lenore and Ruth, spend every minute together, whispering to each other after lights-out. Both act as if they are still ten years old rather than eighteen and nineteen. They giggle and laugh and hold hands like schoolgirls. Their sweet round faces even look childlike. I cannot guess what medical condition brought them here other than their oddly childish behavior.

The young woman at the head of the opposite row of beds does not speak at all, while the one at the top of my own row spends a great deal of time mumbling to herself or shouting at invisible threats. In the bed next to me is a girl named Charlotte, who is only fifteen and who routinely cries herself to sleep.

On my third night in the room, the mumbler yells at Charlotte to shut up. I get up to try to comfort her, but I'm scolded back to my bed by the night nurse. When it is lights-out, I am told, no one is allowed out of their beds.

I am left to myself to get used to everyday life at the institution and its routines: the scheduled time of getting up in the morning, the days for showering, appointed times for meals and outdoor recreation and exercise, the classes in the morning required of everyone still of school age or without a high school diploma, the hours in the dayroom to read or play checkers or write letters.

At night in my bed I sometimes recall snatches of those blurry first three days after I arrived. I can taste the fear on my tongue and feel its weight on my chest. I sense my utter desperation, and I vaguely remember swinging my fists. I am embarrassed by these images.

On the fourth day, I am asked to choose a job. At first I thought I'd ask to be assigned to one of the vegetable gardens, as those women work so close to the outside world they can touch the blades of grass that poke through the metal fencing from the other side. But as there is only one gate, which is always locked, I change my mind and offer to work in the kitchen helping to prepare the meals. I figure grocery trucks must make periodic deliveries to the kitchen's back door. There has to be a time when a member of the kitchen staff takes in the grocery delivery. The door to the outside has to be open for that, as well as the outside perimeter gate. Only those who work in the kitchen know when that time is. If I can find a way to sneak down to the first floor to retrieve my necklace and the money out of my travel bag—both of which I can shove into my brassiere as I sneak back to my own floor—maybe I can also find a way to hide inside the grocery truck before it leaves. The head cook is happy to take me on when she hears I have experience in the kitchen. I am put on the lunch shift.

The food that is prepared at the institution is nothing like the exquisite dinners the hired chef created for the Calverts. Grandfatherly Alphonse found great delight in showing me how to make delicious French entrees like coq au vin and ratatouille and quiche, dishes that Celine's French mother had made and that she missed. I learned a lot from him in the year I spent living at the big house, but I am given no opportunity to enhance the dishes the institution's head cook decides on each day. I and the other residents with kitchen duty simply do what we are told.

There is a telephone in the kitchen, but it is in the head cook's little office under lock and key. Still, I know I will be ever on the lookout for a chance to use it.

My new job is rather humdrum, but it does make the days go by faster. I spend my free time alternating between imagining breaking free and attempting to ease Charlotte's distress. Charlotte is the only roommate who likes to sit with me during day-room time and the other mealtimes. And after a few days, Charlotte not only seems to want me near her but expects it, and she seeks me out if I'm not. But she says no more than a few sentences to anyone, including me.

When I ask her one afternoon why she is at the institution, she looks away as if she hasn't heard the question. The next day, Charlotte is not in her bed when I awaken. She doesn't return to our room until that evening just before lights-out, arriving in a wheelchair pushed by Norman. Charlotte is grimacing as if in pain. Nurse Andrews walks behind them.

The nurse pulls back the covers on Charlotte's bed, and I watch as Norman carefully eases her onto the mattress.

"Is she sick?" I ask with concern, partly for Charlotte and partly for me and my unborn child. I don't want to catch whatever Charlotte has and endanger my baby.

"She'll be fine," Nurse Andrews says easily, pulling up the bedcovers over Charlotte. "She had a procedure. She just needs to rest for a few days."

Charlotte does not cry herself to sleep that night.

———

When the room stirs to the seven o'clock morning alarm, Charlotte does not awaken like the rest of us in the room. Her blanket is half on and half off, and a thin line of scarlet low on her abdomen peeks through her nightgown. It looks like a slender trail of blood.

"It's the gas," Lenore says when I get up to make sure Charlotte is okay.

"Beg your pardon?"

"That's why she's so sleepy. It's the gas."

"What gas?"

"The gas for when they cut you."

"When they . . . what?"

"When they cut you," Lenore says, and she grabs Ruth's hand and the two of them start to leave the room for the toilet.

"What do you mean, 'when they cut you'?" I call after them, and the mumbler, still abed, yells at me to shut up.

I want to stay until Charlotte opens her eyes, but I'm sent to breakfast with the rest of the room. It isn't until I get back to the ward after the lunch shift that I see Charlotte is awake, but she is still in bed and still in pain, so I don't ask her what happened.

But a few minutes after I sit down in my own bed, she suddenly says, "My mother said they were going to take out my appendix," and the sound of her voice is a yellowed beige.

"Oh."

I have heard of people needing to have their appendix taken out, but only after having been sick with terrible stomach pains just before. That's how doctors know the appendix has to be removed. But Charlotte hadn't been in pain. Had she? And when had she talked with her mother? "You want me to get a book for you to read while you get better?" I ask her. "I can get one from the library in the dayroom."

She shakes her head. "I don't like to read."

Three days later, Charlotte is gone. I return to the ward after outdoor time and the bed next to mine is stripped and the nightstand empty. I hope it is because her mother came for her. But none of my roommates know if that's what happened, and when I ask Nurse Andrews, she tells me I don't need to concern myself with other people's situations, only my own.

Mrs. Crockett comes to see me the next day, before I start my lunch shift.

"I think you're ready to begin your therapy sessions with Dr. Townsend," she says. "It was important that you become acclimated to your new surroundings first, but now that you have done that, we can begin in earnest the process to help you get well."

I don't know what she means. Therapy sounds like it could be painful. Most things involving a doctor are. "Will it hurt? Are there needles?"

Mrs. Crockett smiles. "Not usually. Many of your therapy sessions will be just so that Dr. Townsend and you can talk."

"Talk."

"Yes. Your sessions with the doctor will play a significant role in you getting well, more than anything else you will do here. Are you ready to take the next step?"

It's as she's asking this that I realize Dr. Townsend will want to talk about the colors. It's why I'm here and not at a home for unwed mothers, isn't it? He thinks something is wrong with me. My parents told me this could happen, warned me that if I was not careful it would, and so had told me to tell no one. And what did I do? I told Truman, thinking I could trust him. Apparently I also told Wilson, though I don't remember it. Somehow Celine learned of what I said and then told Mrs. Grissom. How else can Dr. Townsend know about them?

I don't see how talking about the colors will help me get out of this place. Dr. Townsend told me that first day that he understood a great deal about what some people can see that others don't, but unless he sees the colors, too, he can't possibly understand them. And I could tell by the way he asked me about them that day that he doesn't. I decide I will tell him it was a childhood prank gone too far, a selfish, foolish way to get attention from my parents. From Wilson. From Truman. I will need to be convincing.

"Yes, Mrs. Crockett," I reply. "I am ready."

"I'm glad to hear that," the matron says. "The doctor would like to see you Tuesdays and Thursdays in the afternoons for an hour right after your shift in the kitchen. One of the orderlies or the nurse on duty will see to it that you are escorted to the fifth floor at that time."

I spend the rest of the day, and into the night as I lie in my bed waiting to fall asleep, practicing how I will tell Dr. Townsend the colors had all been a game.

Just a silly game.

6

Before . . .
JUNE 1938

Wilson's visit home was to be just for a week, not the entire summer term break.

Celine, when she heard the news, was not happy about this change in plans. It was lunchtime when she'd taken Wilson's telephone call. I'd been asked to heat up and serve the leftover boeuf bourguignon that Alphonse had made for dinner the night before. Truman was already seated at the table with the day's mail. I was filling their drinking glasses with lemonade while she talked with her son, and both Truman and I heard her end of the conversation. When the call ended, Celine slammed the telephone handset onto its base and then walked back into the dining room from the telephone table in the entryway.

"A friend asked him to spend the summer at his family's house on Cape Cod," Celine said, falsely sweet, as she took her chair. "The friend's family has a mansion overlooking the water. The friend's family has tennis courts and a putting green and a billiards room! The friend's family has horses."

"He's not a child anymore, Celine," Truman said. "He's not always going to spend his summers with us."

"But we made plans!" Celine grabbed the lemonade glass at her place setting. "We're going to miss celebrating his birthday with him. He should've thought about that."

"Let's not begrudge him spending the summer at a house that sounds amazing. If we make him feel terrible about it, he won't want to come home for Christmas."

Celine glowered at Truman as though he'd crossed a line. Then she swung around to face me. "Is there something you wanted, Rosie?"

I realized I'd been standing as if glued to the spot because I had been looking forward to having Wilson home for the whole summer, too. I hadn't understood how much until Celine announced he was only coming for a week. There had been a time, long ago when we were little, when Wilson had been my friend. I didn't have any close friends anymore. I hadn't for a while. I'd also realized I'd wanted Wilson to see that I had grown up and was no longer a child.

"No, Mrs. Calvert." I spun around and headed back into the kitchen, letting the hinged door between the two rooms fall closed.

"I did *not* make him feel terrible about it," Celine said, her voice gruff but controlled and clearly audible from the other side of the wooden door.

Truman didn't say anything for a moment. "I can only tell you what it sounded like," he finally replied. "It sounded like you were mad at him."

"Well, I wasn't. I was surprised. And disappointed. But I didn't make him feel *terrible*, Truman."

"Good. Glad to hear it."

"You don't have to use that tone."

I grabbed my own lunch and headed for the back door and the

patio so as not to have to listen to them discuss this the way they were.

I wondered as I ate if Truman usually said as little as he did because it was nearly always easier. Celine was . . . opinionated. And she liked being in command. Of everything. When I took my dish back into the kitchen some minutes later, Truman was at the sink rinsing off his lunch plate.

"I can do that." I moved to take the plate from him. Truman stayed where he was.

"Sorry you had to hear Celine and me . . . discussing things," he said. "Is that why you decided to eat your lunch outside?"

"It's all right."

Truman reached for my dish. I hesitated and then handed it to him.

"I'm sorry Wilson won't be home for the whole summer," I said.

"I'm actually not. That probably sounds awful, but I'm not sorry he found something fun to do the last summer before he graduates. He'll probably get a job next year in San Francisco or Seattle and we'll be lucky if we get to see him even at the holidays. He has no interest in running a vineyard, and he knows Celine won't let him anyway. I'm glad he's going. It sounds like a once-in-a-lifetime opportunity."

"It . . . it does sound like a nice place." I watched with surprise as Truman tossed soap flakes into the sink and began to fill it with hot water.

"Disappointments like this would be easier for Celine if we had been able to have other kids, but with Wilson being our only one, she tends to hold on a little too tight." Truman lowered the lunch dishes into the soapy water.

"My mother wondered why you and Mrs. Calvert didn't have more children." As soon as the words were out of my mouth, I wanted to snatch them back. Momma *had* wondered why Wilson was the Calverts' only child, but she would've been mortified to know I'd said so aloud. "I'm sorry. I shouldn't have said that."

Truman shrugged the apology away. "We wanted others. There was a time, many years ago, when Wilson was to have had a little brother, but Celine . . . we lost that baby. There were no others after that."

"Oh. I'm so sorry." I contemplated telling Truman my mother had miscarried two babies in between me and Tommy. I was about to when he went on.

"I think Wilson would have been a good big brother. Having a sibling would have taken the focus off himself, and that probably would have been a good thing, too." He turned to look at me with his hands in the suds. "It must be hard for you now with the loss of your own brother. I would often see you at the cottage with him. Even from up here on the hill, I could see he was very fond of you."

A lump bloomed quickly in my throat. "I do miss him. Very much. Tommy liked trailing around after me, even with six years between us. But . . . I could tell things were starting to change for him. He was starting to want to spend more time with his friends at school than with me."

Truman turned his attention back to the dishes. "I know what you mean. Helen is eight years older than me and we were close when we were young, but we didn't like the same things after a while. The older we got, the more the gap widened. And of course, with Helen living so far away in Europe, I hardly ever see her. She is my sister, though, and the only one I have. But you already know that."

I had met Helen Calvert twice. The first time I didn't even remember, as I'd only been two. She'd apparently taken a fancy to me. Or maybe it was more like I had taken a fancy to her. Helen had come at harvesttime, and everyone at the vineyard, even

Celine and Truman and Wilson, participated in harvest. Helen had played with me in the vines while my parents clipped fruit, and the way Momma remembered it, I had charmed her. After that, whenever Helen wrote to Truman and Celine, she'd tell them to say hello to me.

Once when I'd been called up to the house to help polish forks and spoons, I'd marveled at the pretty foreign stamps on the envelopes of Helen's letters. With Helen's blessing, Celine and Truman had begun routinely giving me the letters when they were done reading them.

The second time Helen came to California for a visit was when I was nine.

By then, I had a little pile of her letters all collected over the years. I was excited to meet her because of those letters and all the greetings she had sent me through Celine and Truman. Even though I didn't know her, she felt like a friend. I knew that she worked as a nanny in Europe and I thought she must be a very good one. I could tell by the way she treated Wilson and little Tommy and me that she loved children.

When we talked, I confessed to her that it wasn't the stamps I loved most about her letters; it was what she'd written about her life in faraway places. I knew she'd traveled across Europe and had even visited Egypt and India. The names for the places Helen had been to and the children she cared for and the names of the food she ate had such happy sounds when I said them out loud. And the colors of those words were just as magical. I'd been forbidden by my parents to tell anyone about what I could see that no one else did, but I couldn't help whispering to Helen that her letters made me see all the colors of the world. It was the closest I'd come to telling anyone what I saw in my mind when I heard words like Paris and Cairo and Bombay.

Helen had loved that. Loved the way I'd said "all the colors of the world." She didn't know what I'd truly meant by it, but I didn't care. It was enough that she'd been delighted to hear me say what I did. I felt the glow of her attention and friendship then.

After she returned to Europe, she occasionally wrote a letter addressed only to me. When Helen moved to Vienna the year I turned ten, she wrote to me about the opera house and the taste of good Viennese coffee and how big the horse fountain was in Salzburg and how beautiful the meadow flowers were in summer, high up in the Alps. I wrote her back, as I always did, careful to mind the secret I'd promised I'd keep, even though it weighed on me to do so because Helen's words brought so many colors to mind.

In time it became easier to stop replying to Helen's letters than continue to withhold the truth from her. It seemed deceptive to say nothing of the colors when she'd ask how I was, how my family was, and especially how the vineyard was. The two letters she wrote to me when I was twelve I left unanswered. She did not write to me again, though in her subsequent letters to Celine and Truman she always ended them with "and give my love and the stamps to Rosie."

Helen had surely supposed I'd outgrown my interest in her letters. That was not the case. I still read the contents of every envelope Celine gave me.

Truman now set a wet dish on the drainboard. "I forgot to tell you we've just had a new letter from her. She spoke of you in it."

"She did?" I grabbed a towel and lifted the clean dish to dry it.

"She was very sad to hear of the accident. But glad to hear we'd taken you in."

He kept his eyes on the bubbles in the sink.

"How is she?" I said.

"She says she's fine, though I don't expect Vienna is a pleasant place to be at the moment with Germany having marched in there like it owns the place. She loves it there, though, and is devoted to that family she works for. She won't leave. Not even now, when it seems like there might be a war."

I had been hearing the radio broadcasts from the Calverts' living room when I cleaned up the supper dishes. I knew there was unrest in Europe and that an angry man named Adolf Hitler had risen to power in Germany. I knew this man had marched his troops into Austria a few months earlier to absorb the whole of it. The sound of those broadcasts had summoned willowy streaks of gloomy gray.

"She's not afraid?" I asked.

"Europe is home to her now, she says. And that family she's with in Vienna has six or seven children. I can never remember. She'll be an old woman by the time the last one's out of that house."

"My goodness," I said, imagining for a moment the colors I might see if I lived a life as thrilling as that. "I think she's very brave."

"*Brave* is an interesting word to describe it. Her deciding to become what our father said is an overpaid babysitter drove him nuts. God, how he blew his top over that. And then he blew it again when she announced she was leaving for England to be a nanny over there. All these years later, he's still not happy about her choices. But then Pops has never been an easy man to please."

"What does your mother think?"

"She died when I was four. It wouldn't have mattered if she thought it was a great idea. He wasn't a fan of things that happened without his say-so. Helen going off to Europe because she wanted to travel and then staying there happened without his say-so."

"Oh."

"He liked it when I married Celine, though. He sure liked that. Until he realized it wasn't going to benefit him in the least."

I didn't know what to say to this. I wiped a drinking glass dry and said nothing.

"I don't know why I told you all of that." Truman felt for the stopper and pulled the drain open. The dishwater swirled and gurgled as the sink emptied. In my mind's eye, pops of aquamarine went with it.

"You see your father very often?" I hadn't known Truman's father was still living.

"No. He lives in Oregon now. In a cabin in the woods. A decade ago, he decided to become a hermit, basically."

"Oh."

Truman dried his hands on a second dish towel. We were finished.

"Thanks for helping with the dishes," I said.

"Used to do them all the time growing up. Wouldn't want to forget how. I'll find out where Helen's latest letter is. I know you like the stamps." He turned and left.

The kitchen seemed to diminish in size the tiniest bit after he was gone. It had been nice talking with Truman. I realized with a start that I missed that more than anything now, talking with someone while doing an ordinary task, like I used to do with Momma and Daddy and even Tommy.

When Alphonse arrived to start supper, I went into the kitchen to assist, and the promised newly arrived letter from Helen Calvert was sitting on the countertop. I slipped it into my apron pocket to read later.

When the supper dishes were cleaned and put away and I was alone in my room, I opened the envelope:

May 4, 1938

My dear Truman, Celine, and Wilson:
  I hope this letter finds you all well. Thanks for your package, Truman, and the boxes of Boston

Baked Beans! They are the only American candy I miss. That was sweet of you. And many thanks for the letter with all the news of home.

I was so touched to hear that you have taken in Rosie, and so sad to hear of the terrible accident that took her family from her. Please pass along my heartfelt condolences. I am sure the loss has been tremendous. My thoughts and prayers are with her.

I appreciate your plea for me to come home before tensions rise further here, but I feel that I must stay. I belong here. I can't recall if I've told you that the youngest of the Maier children, Brigitta, was born with only three fingers on each hand and a few other health problems. She is learning to master skills with six fingers that the rest of us can do with ten, but she still struggles with almost every developmental step a child takes as she grows. My guess is she will likely always remain at home. My employer, Captain Maier, had a demanding position before, in what had been the Austrian Army, and it is even more so now that he is part of the German Wehrmacht. His duties often mean travel. And Frau Maier is heavily involved in the related activities expected of an officer's wife. They need me here to help care for Brigitta during this especially tumultuous time in Vienna.

It is actually quite important that Brigitta is seen to be well cared for and not a burden to society. The government here doesn't like people who are different in any way, and there are more and more rumors about what they are doing to people seen as inferior. The new leadership here feels toward the weak and disabled the way they feel about the Jewish residents.

They do not like them. It is appalling. So you see, it is important that I remain here and make sure the child is cared for. Surely you can understand.

I have to say that in spite of all this, Brigitta Maier is a sweet child, nearly made of sunshine. Always happy, always laughing, always in good spirits. Life did not give me a family of my own, but with Brigitta, it is almost as if I do have a daughter. And with the rest of the Maiers, I almost have a family like yours.

Please turn your concern for me into prayers for the Maiers and this country and the world. These are dark days. I fear they may grow darker.

I hope to write again in the summer.

All my love,
Helen

I folded the letter and put it back inside its envelope and then added it to the collection of letters from Helen Calvert that I kept—even though this letter wasn't full of the usual descriptions of gardens or concerts or the ski chalet that she and this family she worked for sometimes went to. I found myself worried for this little girl named Brigitta whom I did not know. That night when I went to bed, I said a little prayer for her, like Helen had asked of us.

But then my thoughts turned to Wilson's expected visit, a much happier thought, and one that I wanted to fall asleep thinking about, rather than a little disabled girl in Vienna who apparently needed to be shielded from her own government. I nodded off imagining Wilson liking the idea that I was now living in his house. And that I was a young woman now.

Over the next few days, I allowed myself to daydream about what it was going to be like to see Wilson again. I wondered if he'd notice how much I had changed since the last time we were in the same room together.

On the day I changed Wilson's bed linens with fresh sheets, I wondered crazily what it might be like to be kissed by him. The thought made me giggle, and the giggle felt good. It had been a long time since I'd laughed.

As I fluffed Wilson's bed pillows, I fantasized that maybe after seeing me again he'd end up wishing he hadn't planned to stay on Cape Cod for the whole summer.

It was a silly thought. So silly. But still . . .

Maybe he would tell me that he hoped the next time he came home for a visit, I would still be there.

7

I've been to the fifth-floor dayroom and seen the therapy rooms situated directly across, and I've heard nurses talking about treatments received in those rooms. None of them sound like they entail a great deal of time talking to Dr. Townsend, not as Mrs. Crockett described it.

From what I have seen, residents who have trouble speaking or walking properly or who struggle with manners or simple sums are given exercises to practice their skills. Those who suffer terrible fits or from severe melancholy are placed in warm, bubbling baths or icy-cold ones. I have seen others that the nurses describe as "exhibiting deviant conduct" listening to a recording of a gentle-voiced woman reciting standards of good behavior. Some do appear to spend time talking with Dr. Townsend about why they are here, and some probably have to endure a combination of all these things. There are a handful of other doctors who use the rooms, some on staff and some who come in on weekdays from the outside world. Some of the residents never go into a therapy room at all but sit in chairs and drool, or they pace in the corners of the room while endlessly muttering to themselves.

I have seen Dr. Townsend only from a distance since my arrival. He sometimes pops into the dayroom to say hello to some of the residents and to perhaps see who is there and who is not. He often has a teenage boy with him, who I now know is his son, Stuart. I've also learned that Dr. Townsend and his family live in a nice house outside the gate but on the property, and that the doctor spends a great deal of time at the institution, even on weekends. Stuart is often with him. It's obvious by the way Dr. Townsend behaves with his son that he is grooming him for a career like his own. I overheard Norman tell another orderly that Dr. Townsend has even put the boy on night sentry duty and given him a whistle and an hourly wage.

"Next thing you know the kid will be signing our paychecks," Norman said to this other orderly in a disgruntled voice.

Dr. Townsend, with Stuart at his side, waved to me from the entrance to the dayroom the day after Mrs. Crockett said my therapy sessions would begin. It was a polite acknowledgment that he remembered me and maybe even that he was looking forward to our first session. I hope he is as fatherly to his patients as he is to his son.

On the first Tuesday that I am shown into a therapy room, Dr. Townsend is already seated at the plain wooden table, waiting for me. Several large boxes are stacked around him. There is nothing else in the room but the table, two chairs, the doctor, and those boxes. The sight of them startles me, and I lay a hand instinctively over my tummy to protect my baby.

He smiles slightly. "Not to worry, Rosie. Nothing in the boxes will hurt you."

"I'm glad to hear that." I sit down across from him, hoping I sound at ease.

The doctor's smile intensifies. "We're all pleased to see you have settled in well here."

"Yes. I am sorry about what happened when . . . on my first

day. I wasn't . . . I hadn't been properly prepared. I thought I was going to a home for unwed mothers. That's not what this place is, so I was . . . unprepared."

Dr. Townsend studies me for several seconds. "Do you still feel that you don't belong here?"

I'd said too much. I should've said nothing but "thank you" when he praised me for adapting well.

"I . . . I didn't at first."

"And now you do?"

I lick my lips, which are suddenly very dry. "Um. Yes."

"I'd like to hear more about that. But first there are a few things we need to go over again for our records." He opens a folio of papers in front of him and takes up his pen. The piece of paper on top is filled with lines upon lines of typed words that I can't read. They are too small, too far away, and upside down. "The state requires we go over this, as you are now in our care," he continues. "Now then. One more time. Are you able to tell me who the father of your child is?" His pen is poised above the piece of paper, ready to record my answer.

I hesitate a moment. "No," I say simply.

"Because you can't or you choose not to?"

I decide on the answer that seems the least defiant. "I can't."

"Because you don't know who the father is?" he presses.

"Because I can't."

"Have you been threatened in some way? Do you feel you are in danger if you answer this question?" I sense concern in his voice, and for a moment I waver. But only a moment.

"No."

"Then why won't you tell me?"

"If I tell you, will you let me go?" I ask, fairly certain he won't.

"I'm afraid not."

"Then it doesn't matter if I know or don't know."

"All right," Dr. Townsend says in a resigned tone, almost as if he doesn't have an opinion on the matter, but he had to ask and he had to record that he'd asked. Twice. "We also need to talk about what will happen when your baby is born." He glances down at the piece of paper. "Our Dr. Melson here projects a mid-July due date for you."

"But I haven't seen a doctor here."

Dr. Townsend looks up from the folio. "He saw you when you were on Ward 2. He examined you there. You don't remember that?"

I very much don't. "Those first few days are a little foggy," I reply, licking my lips again.

"You had to be sedated much of the time. The narcotics often impact short-term memory."

I feel my face flush at the reminder and the slight recollection that I had been so uncontrollable. "I'm so sorry about that."

Dr. Townsend smiles at me, but he returns to the conversation at hand. "A mid-July due date, then. Dr. Melson says your baby appears to be healthy and developing normally. A good sign."

I don't know what to say to this. How had this Dr. Melson been able to discover all this? What had he done to me? I say nothing as I ponder this.

"Since you will not be an adult when the baby is delivered, nor married, and since you do not have any responsible adult family members or next of kin, and as the state is custodian of your care, and hence your baby's care, it is the state's decision that the infant be transported to a state-approved facility after delivery so that a proper home with two parents can be found through adoption. I need to know if you understand this."

I know it is to my benefit to say yes, I do. But the words are slow in coming and my eyes burn with ready tears. This place would likely take my very soul if I let it. But I will not let it. I have a plan. I just need to get out. I blink the tears away as he waits for my answer. I don't care what he thinks or what he writes down on that piece of paper. I will not be here when my child is born. I won't. It is only coming on March now. I have four months to find a way.

"I understand," I say.

"Good. I'm glad we've taken care of that." The doctor makes a notation on the paper in front of him and then looks up. "Now we can concentrate on you. Mrs. Crockett says you've adapted well to our routines here. You have duties in the kitchen, a job you chose, yes?"

"Yes. I like to cook."

"Good." He again consults the papers in front of him. "And you're in our modified classroom in the mornings, I see. Behind in your studies, though. You have some catching up to do."

"I stopped going to school so that I could work."

He looks up. "Why is that?"

"I didn't enjoy school that much."

"Any particular reason?"

I am about to say math had been hard and the colors relentless and the looks from my classmates upsetting. But I lasso those words before they fall from my lips.

"I liked working better."

He studies me for a moment. "I hear from Nurse Tipton that you were unhappy about a flower bulb that was in your bag when you arrived here and which had been disposed of."

He continues to study me, waiting for me to acknowledge that this is true. The loss of the amaryllis still haunts me, but I don't want him to know it and somehow use my sadness over it against me.

"Yes," I say hesitantly.

"Nurse Tipton said you were quite upset about it."

"Well, it was mine," I say, as though the offense wasn't that my amaryllis was tossed into the garbage but that something that belonged to me was taken.

"But it was more than just a flower bulb to you, yes?" he asks. "It had additional meaning? It might assist me in helping you if I understand why."

In my mind I see an amaryllis brilliantly in bloom on Celine and Truman's kitchen counter, a gift from Helen Calvert to help me bear my first Christmas without my family. I see the note in her fine handwriting explaining to me that a blooming amaryllis at Christmastime has been lovingly coaxed into life by a gardener who has convinced it that it is spring, and that it will continue to bloom every year if I care for its bulb the same way. I was enchanted by the way the word *amaryllis* fell on my ear, and the color that filled my mind when I said it out loud. It was such a beautiful word.

And I loved even more the notion that its bulb was a promise of beauty to come, despite the harshness of winter.

But I will not share this with the doctor. The bulb is gone now. What does it matter that I feel this way about it? "The person who gave it to me said it would bloom every year if I took care of it," I say with a casual lift of my shoulders. "I was upset because now I can't. The bulb wasn't trash, but it was treated like it was. I should've been asked."

I wait to see what Dr. Townsend will say, and after a moment he seems satisfied with my answer.

"Fair enough," he replied. "Now. You mentioned a few moments ago that you understand now why you are here. I'd like to hear more."

I'm glad to move on from talking about the amaryllis. I wasn't prepared to talk about it. This conversation, though, this I have practiced for. As I open my mouth to speak, I feel as though I am stepping onto a stage. Donning a mask. I have indeed been rehearsing my next words for several days.

"It's because of the colors I told people I can see. I shouldn't have been doing that. It is wrong. I realize that now. Lying to people, especially to my parents, was a wicked thing to do. I'm ready to learn how to be the kind of person who doesn't lie."

Dr. Townsend sits back in his chair. "So you are telling me you don't see colors and shapes in your mind when you hear sounds? That names and places and titles don't all have assigned colors?"

"That's right," I say. "I lied to my parents about it and I lied to Mr. Calvert when I told him."

"And why would you do that?" the doctor asks. "Why would you make up such a falsehood?"

"I guess because I got attention from my parents when I first started pretending, and then I didn't know how to stop pretending. Some people seemed to be more interested in me when I told them I could see the colors."

"People like Mr. Calvert and his son?"

I will myself to shrug indifferently. "It didn't matter who I chose to tell it to. Everyone I told the lie to gave me attention."

"But you didn't tell everyone you could see these colors, right? No one at school?"

"I did when I was younger. My teacher in second grade didn't appreciate it and the other kids made fun of me, so I stopped telling people at school. I stopped telling nearly everyone. My parents insisted on it."

"So you kept up the lie in front of your parents, even though it alarmed them, and Mr. Calvert and Wilson Calvert, all for their attention, but never around any other people?"

I can see how what I am saying doesn't make much sense, but I shrug as if I had just been a stupid girl who hadn't thought things through.

"If we're going to be able to help you, Rosie, we need to be truthful with each other."

"I am being truthful." The fib tastes sour on my tongue.

"I don't think you are."

"I am."

The doctor turns to one of the boxes next to him and lifts off the lid, revealing a portable gramophone with a shiny silver crank that he obviously turned in preparation for my session. Dr. Townsend sets the turntable spinning and lowers the arm with its needle onto the record already placed there. Music from Tommy Dorsey begins to fill the room. It is a bright, happy tune. I instinctively put my hands over my ears as ribbons of sky blue begin to fall all around the insides of my mind.

"Put your hands down, Rosie," the doctor says, plenty loud enough for me to hear.

I slowly obey, lowering my arms as the music continues to play and the colors swirl like flags in a breeze.

"I'd like to know what you are seeing," Dr. Townsend said.

I swallow hard. "I don't see anything." I tighten my grip on the armrests of my chair and hold his gaze—and my breath—willing the colors to fade.

The doctor stops the turntable and switches recordings. The next beautiful array of sounds I recognize from Celine's set of Christmas albums. "The Waltz of the Flowers" from Tchaikovsky's *The Nutcracker Suite* fills the space around me, and instantly magnificent puffs of yellow and pink and scarlet began to burst like fireworks in the folds of my mind.

"Tell me what you see, Rosie," Dr. Townsend says.

"Nothing!" I shout. "I don't see anything."

He leans toward me as the recording continues, the music becoming more enchanting with every measure. "I could attach electrodes to your head and monitor your brain waves and I could prove that I know you're lying," he says, gently and yet forcefully. "You're seeing the colors right now. I want to know what you see."

"Stop, please stop," I beg.

"Tell me what you see."

I stare at the doctor as the music plays. Perhaps as a doctor he is curious. Curiosity is different from fear or shock or disbelief. Perhaps because he is a doctor, especially the kind of doctor that he is, he is intrigued by my ability to see the colors. Perhaps if I tell him what he wants to know, he will decide that I have a talent—a strange one, yes, but still a talent, and not a handicap. Perhaps he is the only kind of person who will. And yet there is risk in telling him. I need some kind of assurance that my cooperation will benefit me, too, not just him.

"If I tell you, will you let me leave?" I ask. "I'd like you to let me go if I tell you."

"Discharge you?" he says. "You are a homeless, pregnant, unmarried seventeen-year-old without a means of supporting yourself. You will not leave this place until after you're able to demonstrate that you can maintain a responsible life, with a proper job and a suitable place to live, and that you aren't a liability to society. But I can assure you that will not happen until you successfully complete these therapy sessions. If you want to be discharged from here, that process starts today with you telling me what you see."

I can't imagine staying in this place for endless months or years. It is an impossible notion. I know now for certain that my only hope of escape with my child is if I appear to willingly submit to every requirement of me—every single one. I simply must gain Dr. Townsend's trust. So even though the puffs of yellow, pink, and crimson are beginning to diminish, I tell the doctor I see them. I describe their shape, their hue, their radiance. Their beauty.

And Dr. Townsend writes down my every word.

8

Wilson arrived home late in the afternoon. Alphonse had taken the night off but had prepared dishes the day before and had left instructions for me on how to reheat and assemble them. I'd been busy seeing to all this and hadn't heard Wilson come in the front door. I emerged from the kitchen a little after five o'clock to prepare the dining table and there he was, standing with his parents across the entry in the open living room, sipping an aperitif.

He'd turned toward me and smiled when I stepped into the dining room.

Wilson had grown tall and good-looking like his father, with the same sandy-brown hair and strong build. But he had Celine's nose and cheekbones, and even from yards away he radiated the same confidence as his mother. He seemed a perfect blend of his parents' best physical qualities.

"Rosie, come here a moment," Celine said.

I crossed the entry to the living room, wishing with all my might I'd had a moment to redo my hair and check a mirror for smudges on my face.

"You remember Wilson, don't you?" Celine asked.

"I . . . Yes."

"Well, hey." Wilson's self-assured smile deepened. His voice was draped in forest green. "So you're living and working for my parents here in the house now, eh?"

"Y-yes."

He was even more handsome at only a few feet away.

"Are you liking the new job okay?"

I couldn't tell if he was joking, his smile was so deceptively charming. Did he really expect me to say if I didn't like my new situation with his parents standing right there?

"I . . . I do. I mean, I am."

"She's doing great," Celine interjected, almost proudly. "And she makes the most wonderful omelets. You'll see, Wilson."

"They are quite good," Truman added.

I felt my face blush a little at the praise. "My mother was a good teacher."

Wilson tipped his head up slightly as if suddenly remembering. "Oh yes. I heard about what happened to your parents and brother. That's so awful."

His tone was mysterious. Was he sincerely sad for me? Or was he just saying what one would be expected to say? I couldn't tell. The color of his voice was the same, yet different somehow.

"It was," I said. "It was awful."

An uncomfortable hush filled the room. It was obvious no one knew what to say next.

"Well, go on with what you were doing, Rosie," Celine instructed, breaking the silence. "We don't want to keep you."

Half an hour later, the family came to the table just as I was setting down the last dish. As they took their places, Wilson asked why there were only three place settings.

"Rosie doesn't eat with us," Celine said amiably. "She prefers to take her meals on her own."

Wilson turned his attention to me. "You do?"

"I doubt that's how she would describe it," Truman said under his breath as he reached for the wine bottle.

Celine leveled her gaze at her husband. "I told you before, we are trying to help this girl prepare for her life on her own. She is going to make an excellent domestic with the training she is getting here. It would be ridiculous of her to think she could sit with the family she works for at their dinner table."

"Yes, but she doesn't just work for us," Truman said as he poured wine into his glass. "We're guardians of her care."

"Like foster parents?" Wilson asked.

"Something like that," Truman said, setting the bottle down.

"No, it is *not* like that," Celine said. "We are not her foster parents. We are just her custodians until she can make her own way."

"It's all right," I interjected. "I don't mind." I wanted nothing more than to go back to the kitchen and not be the cause of a family squabble.

"Well, I think you should join us," Wilson said, and then he turned to Celine. "One meal can't hurt, Mother. I am sure Rosie won't start asking for the keys to the Packard after one meal."

Wilson's invitation startled me. Delighted me, too. But still. "I don't know if I should," I said. "I'm in my uniform. And it's family time."

"No one cares what you're wearing," Wilson said. "Sit and eat."

"Why don't you?" Truman added easily.

"Oh, all right, then," Celine said. "Get another place setting, Rosie."

"I can do that," Truman said, rising from his chair. "You can go change if you really want to."

"Oh . . . okay."

I hurried to my room, stepped out of my maid's uniform, and put on a soft cap-sleeved dress printed with daisies that fell to my knees in a flared hem. I usually wore it only for special occasions. It was my favorite. I yanked my long brown hair out of its ponytail and ran my fingers through the strands. I pinched my cheeks for color and was back at the table in less than five minutes.

We filled our plates and began to eat. It was such a pleasant sensation to be there at the table with all of them. I could almost see myself as a part of this family—and in this way, not as a maid. The food was wonderful and the music Celine had put on the phonograph so lovely, I felt happier than I'd been for a long time. I wasn't contributing to the conversation—I was more than content to just listen and imagine—so I was only half-aware when they began to talk about the time Truman and Celine had taken a very young Wilson to see a staging of *A Christmas Carol* and he'd been so afraid of the Ghost of Christmas Past that they had to leave the theater. I was smiling, imagining a young Wilson wailing at the specter of the Ghost of Christmas Past while audience members laughed or shook their heads in annoyance. I didn't hear Wilson say my name. It wasn't until he said it a second time that I realized he was asking me a question about ghosts.

"Beg your pardon?" I said.

"I said, didn't you tell me once a long time ago that you can see ghosts? Or something like that?"

The air in the room seemed to turn cold. "What?"

Wilson furrowed his brow in thought. "I'm trying to remember now what you said. Let me think a minute. We were hiding in the vines from . . . I can't even remember from what . . . and you told me you could see ghosts or hear ghosts?"

"Oh, for heaven's sake, Wilson, what are you talking about?" Celine picked up her wineglass and took a sip.

"It *was* ghosts, wasn't it?" Wilson said the words as if it was nothing to ask this question, the simplest thing in the world. Darts of bright purple spun around his question.

"I don't . . . I . . ." But I couldn't form a reply. What had I told him about what I could see? And when?

Wilson laughed. "It's nothing to be embarrassed about, Rosie. I've never met anyone who saw ghosts. That's pretty keen, if you can."

All three of them were looking at me, waiting for me to answer a question I wasn't prepared in the least to answer.

"It's not ghosts!" I blurted, words finally flying out of my mouth. But they weren't quite the right ones. The Calverts' stares widened.

"*It's* not ghosts?" Celine said, echoing me.

I blinked back my rising alarm. "I mean, I can't see ghosts. Of course I can't see ghosts."

Celine turned to her son. "How long ago was this?"

Wilson kept his eyes trained on me. "I don't know. I was probably ten or eleven."

Celine waved her hand. "Oh, for heaven's sake, Wilson. She would've been only six or seven. Of course she was pretending. You always were too trusting."

Wilson didn't break his gaze. "Were you pretending?" He looked at me as though I was holding back on him now and this saddened him. Hurt his feelings, maybe.

"Of course she was!" Celine laughed. "Or she was teasing you. Girls like to tease boys as much as boys like to tease girls. Don't they, Truman?"

Truman was looking at me with concern. "Yes," he said, but he didn't sound like he meant it.

I attempted a smile and a light laugh. "I guess we do like to tease."

"Well, there you go," Celine said. "No more talk of ghosts, now. It's creepy."

Wilson shrugged like he didn't mind overly much that the conversation was going to be moving in a different direction. But he reached for his wineglass and looked at me over the rim.

Perhaps you don't see ghosts, his look was saying to me. *But you see something. And when you were six and I was ten and we were friends, you told me what it was.*

9

For the next six weeks, every time I attend my therapy sessions, Dr. Townsend extracts some type of noisemaker from within the boxes in the room, produces a sound, then asks questions about what I see. He has brought out a metronome, a cuckoo clock, a train whistle, a duck call, a bell. He has dropped a porcelain dish, clapped his hands, bounced a ball, dragged his chair across the floor. He has played recordings of farm animals and chugging locomotives and opera singers and gunshots and falling rain and a crying child. He writes down what sounds produce vibrant colors and which ones nearly hueless shapes. He has placed colored numbers in front of me to find out which are the right colors according to me and which ones are wrong. He has had me list the colors for January, February, March, and so on; the color for his name, my name, the names of my family—my dead family in heaven. And even though he said the electrodes would be used only if I refused to tell him what he wanted, he nonetheless straps them to my head and has me listen to the sounds all over again while he watches a skinny stretch of paper become splattered with ink from a moving needle.

Sometimes Stuart Townsend comes into the room during our sessions. Dr. Townsend asked me if I minded the first time he came, and since I thought it would be to my benefit to say that I did not, I told him I was fine with it. Stuart is polite but curious, and I often catch him looking at the mound that is my tummy. But I have made a point to be nice to Stuart on the off chance that doing so will help me gain favor with his father. And I do in fact like Stuart. I have been able to tell as the days have progressed that Dr. Townsend expects much from him and is insistent that Stuart pay attention to everything he shows him regarding the running of the institution. I now have the impression that Stuart's future has been decided for him, and I am wondering if he would have set his sights on being a doctor like his father if the choice had been left to him.

Also during these six weeks, another woman from my room, the childlike woman across from me named Ruth, is taken to the surgery on the second floor and comes back to the room the next day with the same little incisions on her abdomen that Charlotte had. Lenore cried for her friend when she left and cries when she comes back. Again when I ask Nurse Andrews if my roommate is all right, I'm told Ruth will be fine; she had a procedure and just needs rest. This time, though, when I ask, I am at the nurses' station. This time I can see Ruth's medical chart. It is facing the glass and I can see what the procedure is called. A salpingectomy. There is no mention of the appendix at all. Ruth—and presumably Charlotte—had a salpingectomy. I have no idea what that is.

Finally something nearly good happens, though. Charlotte's bed is given to a new resident. Her name is Belle and she is nineteen, auburn-haired, green-eyed, and beautiful. Unlike the others in my sleeping room, Belle accepts my friendship from the get-go. She has relied on me to tell her what she needs to know, sits with me at mealtimes, plays checkers with me in the dayroom, tells me jokes that make me laugh. Belle seems so normal. She isn't given to fits, doesn't walk with a limp, isn't slow of speech, doesn't fade into a fog of melancholy or slide into bouts of anger.

After she has been at the institution a week, I decide to ask her why she is here.

"My mother dumped me here because I am an embarrassment to her," Belle says. We are lying in our beds after lights-out, talking in low tones. "I spent a little too much time with the gardener and the next-door neighbor and her best friend's husband, if you know what I mean."

"Too much time with them?"

"Having sex with them. With them and with others. I'm good at seducing men. I can get them to do whatever I want. Anything. My mother thinks there's something wrong with me because all I want is sex. She's wrong, though. I don't want the sex, really, I just want the power."

Power? I have no idea what she is talking about.

"Is that why you're here?" she asks. "Because you like sex?"

A little laugh escapes me. It is almost like the start of a sob. "No."

"My mother, when she found out what I was doing, called me a whore. She kept yelling, 'What is wrong with you?' So I told her. I told her it all began when her cousin—the rich family relative—raped me. She stormed off with her hands over her ears when I said it. Didn't want to hear it. Told me I was a liar."

"A liar? She . . . she didn't believe you?"

"Nope. She called this place up and told them I was a sex-crazed, lying lunatic and a danger to society and myself."

It is dark in the room, and I can't see Belle's face, only the outline of her body curled up into her blanket. "But your cousin *raped* you," I say, appalled.

"Her cousin. And yes. He held me down, put his hand over my mouth, had his way, and then told me if I told anyone, he'd deny it. Didn't matter, because when I finally did tell my mother, she didn't believe me anyway. The cousin has loads of money. He's wealthy. So of course he wouldn't do such a thing."

"That's . . . terrible." I wish for a better word for what Belle has just told me.

"I hated that he was able to use his body against me that way. And I hated that I could control nothing," Belle goes on. "I vowed I would be the one in charge of my body from then on, and I have been. Every man since has begged for it. Begged."

I can scarcely imagine what Belle endured. I can't imagine at all how she's chosen to recover from it, nor can I understand how openly she talks about it. She sounds almost proud.

"How old were you when he did this to you?" I ask her.

"Thirteen."

"Oh, Belle! How awful! What does your father say about all this?"

"Nothing. I haven't seen him since he left my mother for another woman ages ago. It's why Mother won't rock the boat with the cousin. She needs what that side of the family gives her."

In the darkness of our room, I can't see how or if Belle is affected by talking about this. She doesn't say anything for a few seconds.

"So why are you here?" Belle finally asks, seemingly unmoved.

I decide in that moment to tell Belle how I wound up at the institution. I like having a friend, my first in years. True friends are honest with one another, aren't they? Belle has been honest with me; I will be honest in return. She doesn't seem like she'd be put off by me having an odd ability, so I tell her about the colors. And I tell her about the accident that took my family from me, and how the Calverts took me in and made me their maid. I don't tell her exactly how I came to be with child—just that I made a mistake with someone—but she doesn't seem to care about specifics.

"Damn," Belle says when I am finished. "But . . . but that doesn't explain why you're here."

"The colors are why I'm here. It's not normal to see them, and that makes me not normal."

A moment of silence passes between us. This is when I think she will ask who the father of my baby is. But she doesn't. I am beginning to understand sex means nothing to her other than a means to an end.

"So is it nice? Being able to see colors that no one else can see?" she says.

The question makes me smile. It is the kind of response I was hoping for from Belle. But the very next second, I am saddened by it. Truman had a reaction not so very different from this when Wilson's prodding got the better of me and I finally confided in Truman that day we were walking in the vines. I can't help but think he must have told Celine even though I'd told him not to.

"Most of the time it's nice. Beautiful, even," I tell her. "Not in here, though. Here they think something is terribly wrong with me. Dr. Townsend won't leave me alone about it. Every session I have with him, he is playing sounds and asking me what I see. Sometimes he puts wires on my head. I wish he'd just stop. The colors don't hurt anyone."

We are quiet again, and I am thinking perhaps Belle has fallen asleep, but then she sighs and murmurs, "God, I would give anything for a cigarette. I'd scale the wall if I had better shoes."

"Would you really?" I ask.

"Right this minute."

"I'm going to escape." The whispered words pop out of my mouth before I can consider if Belle is completely trustworthy to hear them.

She doesn't say anything right away. "How are you going to do it?" she replies a few seconds later.

"I don't know yet, but I got that job in the kitchen so that I could pay attention to when deliveries come. I'm thinking maybe I can sneak into a delivery truck."

"Hmm. That could work. Maybe. But are you ever near that truck?"

"Well, no. I haven't figured out how to do it yet."

"I suppose the staff takes in the deliveries? And the truck only comes during the day?"

"Yes." I can see what Belle is thinking, that my plan won't work. "I have to try, Belle. I have to." My voice is growing louder. "They're going to take my baby from me. I have to try."

"Shh, shh. Of course you do. You just need a better way, I think. Where do you plan to go when you get out?"

I choose my next words carefully. "I have money. In a safety-deposit box in San Jose. I have the key for it in my bag that is locked up downstairs. It's on a necklace that was my mother's. No one here knows about it."

"How much?"

I hesitate. "A lot."

"Really?" Belle's quiet tone brightens. "Where'd you get it?"

I pause a moment. "It was given to me."

"Why were you in San Jose?"

"I wasn't. But it's there."

"You've seen it?"

"No. But it's there." It *has* to be there.

Another moment of quiet passes.

"I bet I can get us out," Belle says.

I don't know what to say to this. Maybe my plan isn't the best, but it is a plan. Belle's confident tone makes me think she doesn't appreciate how difficult pulling off an escape is going to be. I am fairly certain I will only have one shot at it. If I am caught, Dr. Townsend and the rest will never trust me again. They might put me back in Ward 2. They might never let me out of this place.

"How?" I finally say.

"I'll use what I've always used to get what I want."

"What do you mean?" But I think I know what Belle means. "Are all the orderlies male in this place? And the doctors?"

"I think so."

"And they all have keys, right?"

"Probably."

"Then just leave it to me," Belle says. "Now tell me what Dr. Townsend is like. I'm going to be seeing him the day after tomorrow."

"I . . . I don't think you'll be able to get the keys from him," I say hesitantly. "And I don't think you should try with him. He is quite devoted to his family, and I think he's pretty smart."

"Well, we'll see about that. Who is that young fellow always hanging around him?"

"That's his son, Stuart."

"Have you seen the way that kid ogles me?" Belle says with a whispered laugh. "I could have that boy in my back pocket in no time."

"He doesn't have keys," I say quickly, feeling an immediate concern for the boy. "And Stuart and his father are close. The Townsends live right here on the premises. In that big brick house in back on the other side of the fence."

"Oh, then never mind. I'll find someone else, some employee who lives in town. I'll take care of everything." Belle yawns and turns over. "It'll be fun," she says. "Don't worry about it."

Belle, for all her beauty and cleverness, also seems reckless.

I fall asleep doing the exact opposite of what she told me to do.

10

As I lay in bed the night of the dinner with all three Calverts, I tried to remember what I'd actually said to Wilson all those years ago. I cast my mind to the past, back to when he and I were just children playing in the vineyard. I could see those days in the folds of my memory, but they were fragmented, postcard-like images of uncomplicated times, when I wished everyone could see the colors and was surprised when confronted anew with the truth that everyone could not.

I couldn't remember the day I told Wilson about the colors because for me it surely hadn't been a remarkable day. The opposite would've been true for him. He'd apparently been fascinated. But as we aged, he'd forgotten exactly what I'd said. The memory of that day had come back to him because the family was laughing about the time he'd been afraid of the Ghost of Christmas Past. Wilson had suddenly remembered me at a very young age telling him something extraordinary. Bizarre.

I didn't know if I should pretend for the next six days that Wilson was remembering that day wrong or confide fully in him.

I wanted us to be friends again, like we had been when we were little. I wanted *more* than to be just friends. But even so, I wasn't sure I could trust him with my secret. I barely knew Wilson anymore. I tossed and turned much of the night.

In the morning, when I served Truman breakfast, he apologized for Wilson having embarrassed me at the table the previous evening. I said it was nothing. When Wilson came into the dining room half an hour later, I served him the requested omelet and pretended not to notice how he studied me. Celine decided to have breakfast in bed, and when I brought her a tray, she asked what in the world Wilson had been talking about the night before. I shrugged and said it was so long ago I couldn't remember, but that Wilson and I had pretended many things while playing in the vines, including that the leafy bower was actually a pirate ship and that we were pirates.

I hoped that was the end of it so that if I did decide to tell Wilson, it would be on my terms and my timing. But in the afternoon, Wilson came into the living room, where I was dusting, and declared that he suddenly remembered the whole story. He said it wasn't ghosts I had told him I could see.

"You told me you saw colors and shapes that danced in your mind, invisible to everybody but you. Like ghosts." His tone was curious and coy and playful. I wanted so badly to sense from his voice and manner that I could trust him, but I couldn't.

Truman was in the room and heard Wilson say this, too.

I forced myself to stay calm. "That sounds as silly as saying I see ghosts." I was relieved to find that it was easier for the lie to roll off my tongue when I wasn't facing him across a dinner table.

"But . . . why say it?" Wilson said.

"Give it a rest, Wils," Truman said from the sofa, where he sat reading a newspaper full of headlines about the turmoil in Europe.

The telephone rang then, and I was happy to answer it and tell Wilson that the call was for him.

Wilson took the receiver from me and let his gaze linger on me as he did so. He could obviously tell I wasn't being truthful, but I could also tell he didn't seem to mind. It was almost as if he liked that I was being vague, because it was like we were playing some kind of game.

I turned from him, wanting the relative privacy of the kitchen. Seconds later I was at the sink pondering the situation. I wanted very much for Wilson to be interested in me, but his fascination about what I'd apparently told him when we were little didn't feel like attraction as much as a desire to satisfy his curiosity—even at the expense of embarrassing me. There likely weren't going to be stolen kisses from him anytime soon. My half-spun dream of Wilson and me falling in love, and me one day sitting at Celine's table as her daughter-in-law and not her maid, felt as though it was floating away from me like a cloud on the wind.

And I couldn't help but feel silly for having allowed myself to imagine it.

Later, just before Alphonse arrived to begin supper preparations, I took a walk in the vineyard to calm myself. The vines were heavy with young fruit and the air was electric with the buzzing of summer insects. A dappling of peaceful blue spheres soothed me as I walked. I came upon Truman, talking to Sam, the new vinedresser, as they studied a cluster of unripened grapes. I smiled and nodded as I walked past them. Truman called out to me to hold up a minute.

I waited until he joined me.

"Is it all right if I walk with you for a bit?" He asked as if he understood I cherished my private moments alone in the vines.

I said yes, but inside I was reluctant. I suspected that Truman had been able to tell there was some truth to what Wilson had said the night before, and again in the living room.

"Look," Truman said after we'd taken a few steps away from Sam. "If you don't want to talk about this, we don't have to, but

I could see you were upset by what Wilson was talking about. You don't have your parents to go to, and you've not had any friends come up to the house, and you haven't gone anywhere to visit with old school chums, so I just wanted you to know that if you want to talk to someone about this, I'm here."

The kind way he said this made me immediately want to tell him everything, but the pledge that I'd made to my mother on her deathbed came pulsing back to me at the same moment. I'd promised to be careful, and I knew what Momma had meant when she'd extracted that promise. But had she meant I must live the rest of my life without telling anyone about the colors? Ever?

When I said nothing, Truman went on. "What Wilson said today in the living room, is it true? Do you see colors and shapes no one else can see?"

It was a question that ordinarily I would've been afraid to have asked of me, but his words were wrapped in a tone I hadn't heard before. It was almost as if he wanted me to say yes. Almost as if he needed to believe magic still happened in the world, because he had stopped seeing evidence of it. Before I could think about what I was doing, I turned to him and nodded.

"When do you see them?" he asked.

"All the time. Whenever I hear a sound, I see them. Even silence has a sound, so I always see them."

"Like, hovering in the air?"

It had been a long time since I had described what the colors were like. So long that I couldn't remember how best to do it. I was quiet for a moment.

"No, not like that," I finally said. "It's more like, I see them in my mind. Like if I told you to picture a running horse, you would see it inside your head. It would have color and shape and it would be moving. But no one has to tell me to picture the colors. The sounds make them come, all on their own."

"Every sound does that?" Truman said, intrigued.

"Yes, but it's not just sounds that have colors. Names and places and numbers have colors, too."

"What do you mean, they have colors?"

"They have a color that doesn't change. It's like it's been given to them. Your name is mint green. Celine is pale peach. Wilson is red. The number seven is red, too. June is gold. Tuesday is white."

"That's amazing," Truman said. "What happens when you close your eyes?"

"I still see them. Sometimes different colors appear, but they still come."

"And they never stop?"

"Sometimes if there are many sounds at once, they will dissolve and fold into one another. Sometimes one set of colors lasts longer than another. Sometimes if I concentrate, I can make them brighter."

"You talk about these colors as if . . . as if you're fond of them," Truman said.

"I guess I am. They can be so beautiful. But . . . but they caused a lot of trouble for me in school. I had a difficult time concentrating, and arithmetic with all those numbers was just . . . it was too frustrating. When I was younger, the other students teased me, and teachers didn't like it when I told them they wrote the names of the days of the week in the wrong colors. My parents told me to stop telling anyone about them. I didn't like school, for lots of reasons."

"That's why your parents let you quit."

"I wanted to quit. They wanted me to be happy. And they were afraid for me. They were afraid if it got out that I was still claiming to see the colors, people might think I was crazy."

"Did your parents ever take you to a doctor or anything?"

I stopped walking. "Why would they do that? I wasn't sick. And I'm not crazy."

"No, I know, but—"

"And what kind of doctor would they have taken me to? What kind of doctor would believe me?"

"All right. I can see how that would've been a problem. My apologies. Please?" Truman nodded so that we could resume our walk.

We strolled in silence for a few moments.

"Do you see them right now?" Truman asked.

"Of course."

"Can you tell me?"

In the distance a tractor snorted. Starlings were chirping in a nearby pepper tree. One of Sam's workers, Felipe, was singing a tune in Spanish several rows away.

"The sound of that tractor is lines of brown and gold," I said, "and the birds' singing is swaths of orange, like strokes of a paintbrush. Felipe's voice is blue bursts lifting up like a fountain."

"That's incredible. And it's always been this way for you?"

"For as long as I can remember. My mother had a great-aunt who saw the colors. But I never met her. She died before I was born."

"Wow." Truman's voice was laced in salmon-colored fringe and utter amazement. "But you don't remember telling Wilson any of this?"

I shook my head. "I don't. But I must have. I stopped telling people when I was in second grade. My parents insisted on it. And you can't tell anyone, Truman. Okay? No one is supposed to know. I don't even think I want Wilson to know."

"But he does know."

"He just thinks he does."

We walked on for a few moments in silence.

"I think I understand now why it always seemed to me that your father had expectations of you," Truman finally said. "He was probably afraid for you."

"Which is why you can't tell anyone. Please? You can't."

He nodded as we started back for the house.

That nod, I would confidently assume, had been a guarantee—a vow to keep my secret.

A promise not to mention it to anyone.

Including Celine.

II

MAY TO JUNE 1939

As April eases into May, I marvel at how my body is adapting and changing, cocooning the little one that moves inside me now with what seems like great delight. I saw Dr. Melson for a routine checkup in mid-April, and even upon seeing him—he is a dour-faced older man who seems bored with his job—I had no recollection of having met him before.

I am not the only pregnant woman at the institution; there are at least six others that I have seen. Since the maternity appointments all take place on a particular Tuesday, I sat with three of them in the waiting room on the day of my checkup. It was the closest contact I'd had with any of the other expectant mothers. With more than two hundred and fifty women at the institution, I have only seen the others from afar, either in the cafeteria or the dayroom or during our required outdoor time, when we wander around on the back lawn with nothing to do, separated from the men by a metal fence. As I waited for my name to be called, the woman next to me started singing lullabies to her unborn baby as if she were holding it in her arms. She leaned over to me and whispered that her child was the Baby Jesus.

When it was finally my turn to go in, the indifferent Dr. Melson measured my abdomen, weighed me, and listened to the baby's heartbeat with something he called a fetoscope. He then pronounced me and the baby healthy and told me that unless I had complications, he wouldn't be seeing me again until the first of July, just a week or so before my due date.

I was glad to leave the second-floor infirmary when he was finished. Having to pass the door to Ward 2 on my way to the stairs brought back the memory of waking up in it as if from a bad dream, only to realize the nightmare was real.

Not only was it real, but it is now worse. Dr. Townsend is no longer interested in just recording what I see when I hear sounds or what colors my mind has assigned to numbers and names and places. Now he wishes to remove the colors from me in every form that they appear. During my sessions, when the doctor produces sounds and I describe the colors I see, he gives me a tiny electrical shock—enough to startle me, enough to hurt. It does no good to pretend I am sick to avoid my therapy sessions, because I am brought down anyway. It likewise does no good to tell Dr. Townsend I don't like the shocks, that they hurt me and frighten me.

"But this is how we will cease the colors from appearing, Rosie," he says in reply to my protests.

"Why must I stop seeing them?" I answer. "They're not hurting anyone."

"On the contrary," Dr. Townsend says solemnly. "They're hurting you. Why do you think you're here?"

The plan to escape is consuming my thoughts. The bigger the baby grows, and me with it, the less I am able to imagine hiding myself in that grocery delivery truck. Plus, the paid kitchen staff never lets the residents who work in the kitchen unload the truck. Nor do they let us anywhere near the door when the truck is being unloaded. Belle was right that my plan has major flaws.

Belle's insistence that she is coming along well on her own scheme is my only hope. At night when the other women in our room are asleep, Belle updates me on her progress. She has switched jobs three times to scout out the best options. After flirting with nearly every orderly and male staff member, including Stuart—and despite me asking her to please leave the boy alone—Belle has decided to work solely on the custodian's unassuming assistant, a lanky, pimply faced young man named Rudy.

The plan is to have Rudy come to believe that Belle has fallen in love with him. That will be different from seducing him, Belle tells me. If all Rudy thinks Belle wants is a quick whoopee in the broom closet, he might easily oblige. But that won't get us out. He has to believe instead that Belle is mad for him and that he and Belle should run away together. But first she has to make him think spiriting her out of the institution is his idea.

"It will happen," Belle quietly assures me as we lie in the darkness one night. "I'm already halfway there with him."

"But how will I escape with you?"

"I'm going to tell him that it's very important that no one suspects him of helping me," Belle explains. "So on the night of the escape, he won't even be here. He will have given me his keys before leaving for home, and he'll be the last of the day workers to clock out so that he can leave the gate latch unlocked. He doesn't have the key to that. I'll escape that night, with you, of course, although he won't know that part. He'll think I'm going to meet him at the bus station in Santa Rosa in three days' time. I'll have told him that if he waits three days to join me, they won't consider him an accomplice because he'll still be right here when they start looking for us. And even if they should suspect him and they search his house, they won't find me. He will up and quit that third day, and he'll come to the bus station, where he will expect to find me, but I won't be there. We will be long gone."

I have to admit it is a good plan and seems nearly foolproof, but I feel bad for the janitor's assistant.

"Isn't it a bit cruel to Rudy, though?" I ask.

"And what about what has happened to us?" Belle says. "Isn't that heaps more cruel? Rudy will get over me. I guarantee it."

For the rest of May, I watch Belle carefully to make sure she isn't being too obvious in her pursuit of Rudy. Belle's plan is our only plan, and the nearer the time draws for the baby to come, the more important it is that nothing happens to thwart it. We simply have to escape before I deliver. Belle continues to be coquettish around other men besides Rudy—including Stuart—so that if anyone notices her flirtatious behavior, it will not appear that she has singled him out.

I can see that Stuart is now infatuated with Belle and is practically addicted to her attentions. Her constant whispers to him that he is such a handsome fellow who will soon be breaking hearts have worked on him like a love potion. Belle sees it, too, but thinks nothing of it. She is used to boys and men being smitten with her. One more doesn't matter. Stuart will often look for ways to be in the dayroom and on the lawns without his father present so that, I'm supposing, he can hang about wherever Belle is and not have his father notice. I'm glad he is being sneaky about it.

Stuart has also noticed that I am Belle's closest friend at the institution. He comes to me in the dayroom one day to ask if I know when Belle's birthday is, as he'd heard Belle mention she has one coming up, and he wants to get her something, something in secret. I answer truthfully that I don't know, and then I gently tell Stuart that Belle is a girl who is not likely to settle down with just one person, that she likes many people all at once and that he deserves the affection of someone who cares for only him. He seems to understand what I mean, but it makes him sad and he walks away from me sullen.

I am afraid he will go to his father about his feelings for Belle. Extra attention thrown Belle's way could foil our plan. But as it turns out, Belle is already on Dr. Townsend's mind, and not because of anything having to do with his son. In my next session, the doctor begins not with stimuli and shocks but by telling me that he is concerned that I spend too much of my free time with Belle.

"Belle is no one you want to be influenced by, Rosie," Dr. Townsend says. "She could easily derail your progress."

"I don't know what you mean."

"She's here for a reason, just like you. You need to be careful."

"Careful of what?"

"Of listening to and being manipulated by what she says. Belle is, among other things, a pathological liar."

I remember Belle telling me that she hadn't been believed when she said she'd been raped by her mother's cousin. Her mother had called her a lunatic. Sex-crazed. A liar. Apparently Dr. Townsend doesn't believe her, either. But this other word he used—*pathological*—is strange to me.

"I . . . I don't know what that is."

"A pathological liar is someone who lies compulsively and for no reason that benefits them," he says simply. "Most people who lie, like you did to me when you first came here, do so because they think telling the lie will benefit them. They think it will keep them out of trouble or help them avoid an embarrassing situation. They don't particularly like lying; they don't make a practice of lying. They do so only at times, because they think they must. Pathological liars lie habitually, and they absolutely do make a practice of it. And for no apparent gain."

I feel my mouth drop open slightly. Is it true, what Dr. Townsend is saying? Has everything Belle told me to this point been a lie? The rape when she was thirteen? All those men she said she'd been with? Her plan to get us out? Is none of it true?

"Is everything she says a lie?" I hope he cannot hear the ribbon of dread in my voice.

"Not everything. But you can't assume she's always telling you the truth, because she's likely not. You are probably a good influence on her, so I'd rather not relocate her to a different ward. But it concerns me that you spend so much time with her. If I have to move her, I will. But I am hoping you will adjust how you spend your free time. Will you do that?"

I will myself to calmly answer him. "Yes, of course. Thank you for telling me."

Dr. Townsend doesn't mention anything about Stuart's having come under Belle's spell, or even Belle's excess flirtations of late, and I hope it is because it has been obvious only to me, and only because I've been watching Belle so closely. In fact, the conversation about Belle quickly ends as the doctor proceeds next to unbox his noisemakers and electric shock apparatus.

For the rest of the day, I am one minute anxious about what Dr. Townsend told me, and the next perturbed. I don't want to believe what he said is true. And why should I assume it is? He doesn't know everything. I know he just had an article published in some big medical journal, because the staff are tripping over themselves to congratulate him, but even that doesn't prove Dr. Townsend knows everything. I asked him if he knows why I see colors when I hear sounds, and he answered it is tangling in my brain. It's like crossed wires, he said, and it is abnormal. But he didn't tell me why, only how. Crossed wires. Why are they crossed? I don't think he knows.

That night after lights-out and after the rest of the room is asleep, I share with Belle that Dr. Townsend is now monitoring how often I am with her, and that he's expecting me to use my free time in other ways.

"I need to spend less time with you or he'll move you to a different room," I tell her.

"I was actually going to suggest you not spend so much time with me, so that the staff doesn't suspect we're up to something," Belle replies, and I immediately wonder if she really had been going to suggest that.

"You are planning our escape, aren't you?" I cannot help but ask. "You swear to me you are?"

"Of course!" Belle says in a big-sister kind of voice. "My plan is working. I cornered Rudy just today in a linen closet and gave him a kiss to knock his socks off. I pretended that I was embarrassed at being so taken with him and unable to control myself. He was like clay in my hands."

"Which linen closet?" I need to know if she really did yank Rudy into a closet and kiss him. I need to know beyond a doubt that Belle is telling me the truth. About everything.

"Don't worry!" Belle laughs. "I was careful. Nobody saw us."

She thinks only that I fear she was observed. I must choose to believe her. I just have to. What other option do I have?

"It's almost June," I say a second later. "I only have six weeks left before the baby comes. We can't wait much longer, Belle."

"I know, I know. I've got it. You fret too much." She turns over in her bed, the conversation finished.

May turns to June, and I begin to fear that when Belle and I escape, I will be so close to delivering the baby that we won't be able to get away fast enough. I feel immense. I am starting to waddle when I walk. And where will we go after getting the money in San Jose? How will we even get to San Jose? Do I have enough savings in my cigar box for bus tickets and food for both of us until we get there? If the authorities are dispatched to look for us, will they search the bus depots?

During my hours in the dayroom, which I am careful to spend separately from Belle, I now look at maps of California in an atlas in the library, studying and memorizing towns far from Sonoma County that we could flee to quietly with the money and where I could safely deliver. I tell Belle about these places—Redding, Eureka, Klamath, and other towns across the border in Oregon—but Belle seems uninterested in where we go when we get out. The thrill of planning our escape is all she cares about.

I start to miss my mother in fresh new ways the first days of June, especially since I no longer have Belle's constant attention to distract me from my fears of the coming delivery. I hadn't often imagined what it might be like to bear a child, but those few times that I had, I'd always pictured Momma there with me, holding my hand or putting a cold cloth on my head, encouraging me with kind words, eager to meet her first grandchild. I'd pictured a pacing husband on the other side of where she and I were. I never supposed there wouldn't be a husband. This thought and my mother's absence keep me awake at night, along with the anxiety of awaiting Belle's pronouncement that the moment of our escape is at hand.

But the worst of my worries soon starts to haunt me. I already observed that two women in the room across the hall had been sent to the surgery for a "procedure" and had come back the next day with incisions low on their abdomens. I would look up the word *salpingectomy* in a dictionary in the dayroom library if there was one. As there isn't, and as Nurse Andrews is of no help, and since Belle hasn't any idea what one is, I decide to ask Dr. Townsend at one of my sessions why this keeps happening.

Dr. Townsend has just unboxed his portable gramophone for the day's therapy, and he regards me for a moment before answering. "I don't discuss someone's medical condition with other people, Rosie," he says. "You should be glad I don't. I haven't discussed your medical history with another resident, and the only time I disclosed someone else's with you was when I gave you much-needed advice regarding Belle. I was doing you a favor. It's not something we usually do here."

"But none of these women had tummy troubles before, and—"

But Dr. Townsend cuts me off. "Your only concern should be your own health," he says as he reaches to his right to take the cover off the electroshock apparatus. His tone is curt, his expression one of irritation as he prepares his devices. He isn't making progress in his efforts to halt the colors, and I can tell this morning that this annoys him. He sets the dial on the electroshock machine to the highest setting yet.

I leave the session half an hour later with tearstained cheeks and welts on my hands from where the electric bands burned me.

That night in our beds, I tell Belle that Dr. Townsend refused to explain what the procedure is that women on our floor keep having.

"I'll find out from Norman what it is," Belle says. "He'll know."

"Norman?" I say in a startled whisper.

"I can get him to tell me. I know what he likes."

"What . . . what are you . . ." But I can't find the words to ask Belle what she is up to with the orderly.

"Norman's just my backup plan in case Rudy falls through."

"Belle!"

"But he won't! He won't. It's close now. I'm sure of it. We'll be out of here in no time."

"The baby will be here in less than a month," I remind her.

"We're almost there. Don't worry."

Belle is soon snoring lightly, but it is a long time before sleep finds me.

The next day at dinner, Belle seeks me out to sit with me. "We've got to get out of here," Belle says under her breath, her tone awash with alarm.

"Why? What is it?" I whisper back to her.

"I found out what they're doing here. It's not just women they're cutting into. They're doing it to some of the men, too. I bet you and I are on the list to have it done. They'll wait for you because of the baby, but they could have me in there tomorrow if they want. We have to get out."

"Why? What are they doing?"

Other female residents take seats next to and across from us, talking loudly. Belle turns from me and begins to butter her roll.

"What are they doing?" I ask again.

The other women stop talking with one another to look at me, thinking perhaps I am talking about them.

Belle ignores my question for several seconds until the women begin talking among themselves again.

"They don't want people like us having children," she finally whispers.

"What do you mean, people like us?" Fear makes my voice tremble.

"Like us, Rosie. Like us. They think you're a freak and I'm a demented sex addict. They don't want us having children and passing on our bad blood. They're sterilizing people here."

"What do you mean, sterilizing?" The word sounds like merely something dirty being made clean. Its color is a sharp yellow.

"I mean they are cutting into people and changing them so that they can never have children. Ever. We have to get out."

I stare at Belle in horror and I cover my abdomen with my hand as if to protect my baby from an unseen enemy. "When?"

"Eat your food. Stop looking at me like that. You need to be ready to go at any moment. Not tonight, but maybe tomorrow night. Or maybe the next."

"And my bag? We have to get it. Will Rudy's keys open that closet on the first floor?"

"They'd better. We need to stop talking about this and eat."

Belle begins to shovel food into her mouth, but my appetite has left me. I am picturing my body being sliced open and Dr. Melson shoveling out everything that makes me able to have a baby.

How can they do that here to people? How can they decide who should bring children into this world and who shouldn't? How?

I leave the table with my dinner untouched.

Two days later, Belle tells me that Rudy has at last pledged his undying love to her and that he'll find a way to get her out so that they can run away together. She kissed him, cried like a moon-struck schoolgirl, and told him our idea as if it had just occurred to her. The escape is now in play. We will leave Sunday night.

But the very next morning, I stand from my bed upon waking and a great splash of water gushes out of me, down my legs and onto the floor. As I stare incredulous at the puddle, a queer pain grips me. I turn in shock to look at the bed next to me. Belle is sitting up and staring at me wide-eyed.

"What's happening?" I whisper.

Belle yells for the nurse.

12

Autumn spilled golden and glorious onto the vineyard, and with it came my seventeenth birthday.

I awoke early that October morning achingly aware that my parents and Tommy should have been there to celebrate it with me. It was all wrong that they weren't. I dressed for the day slowly and was late getting the coffee started. Celine came into the kitchen looking for it with an empty cup in one hand and a beribboned box of chocolates in the other.

"There you are!" Celine said in a mockingly disgruntled voice. "I was going to give you this in the dining room when you came in with the coffee, but I can give it to you in here just as well. Happy birthday, Rosie."

She extended the box of chocolates.

"These are my absolute favorite confection in the world," Celine went on. "You can only get these from a certain chocolatier in San Francisco. I made a special trip!"

I looked down at the pretty box and its pink satin ribbon. I needed to thank Celine, but the kind gesture only made me miss my family even more, and the words stuck in my throat.

"Don't tell me you don't like chocolate." Celine was smiling but with her eyebrows pinched.

"No, I do, very much," I finally replied. "I'm . . . I'm surprised you remembered. Thank you, Mrs. Calvert."

"Of course I remembered, and you're very welcome. You'll have to hide them from me, though, because they really are quite wonderful."

"I'm sure they are, thank you."

"I was thinking you might want the afternoon off for your birthday," Celine went on. "Maybe you'd like to ride your bike into town and see a motion picture with a friend or something?"

It was on the tip of my tongue to respond with, *When have I ever wanted to do something like that, Mrs. Calvert?* but I did not say this. It would have been rude. Celine surely meant well. The box of chocolates was well intended, too, but even as I thought this, I realized that what I wanted more than anything was out of this house. Not just for an afternoon but for good. I did not want to spend another birthday like this one, even though in all likelihood I probably would have to, maybe a couple more, actually. A person wasn't considered an actual adult until twenty-one.

Celine had already decided that I was destined to be a maid, would always be a maid, but I wondered now, as Celine waited for me to answer, what I might be able to do with my life if I decided for myself. What if I took professional cooking classes and then got a job at a fancy restaurant in San Francisco, or even Seattle? I might like that very much. And I was already a good cook. But I would need money to make that happen, probably more than I was already making and saving as a maid. I would need cash for a room to rent, and for classes and supplies and bus fare and food until I found a job. At this same moment, I remembered Celine and Truman recently discussing the need to hire someone to help on weekends and selected evenings in the tasting room. I wasn't sure what I was truly capable of, but I knew this. I didn't want to spend the rest of my days cleaning toilets, washing someone else's dirty dishes, and hanging up their laundry.

"Actually, Mrs. Calvert," I finally said, "what I'd really like to do is ask you about that position assisting in the tasting room. I couldn't help overhearing you and Mr. Calvert talking about it at breakfast yesterday. I could help with that. I don't work evenings or Sundays, and that's when you said you needed someone."

Celine's eyes widened in surprise. "Why on earth would you want to work every minute of every day, Rosie? You'd be giving up all your time off."

"I know, but I don't have much to do on my hours off. I get bored." That was true enough. "I'd like to work."

"Well," Celine replied, thinking aloud. "You do have a professional-looking uniform. And you already know the wines, and you're polite to people. You already know what I expect in an employee. And we really only need someone when there are multiple clients at once. Hmm. All right, then. I'll talk to Mr. Calvert about it."

And then Celine went off to announce her decision to Truman as if she'd thought of the idea herself.

The next few weeks passed with new purpose for me. It was Truman whom I worked for during tastings, not Celine, and this was a refreshing change. Truman treated me more like an equal than a servant, and he'd ask about my well-being from time to time, mindful that my sorrow lingered. He didn't specifically ask about the colors, either, which I appreciated, but I would see him glance my way when a sound reverberated in the cavernous space.

The tasting room was a part of the much larger barrel room—a two-story building that abutted a steep ridge—where the Rosseau vintages aged in large oak casks, turned on their sides, in three caves that had been hewn out of a rocky hillside of the Mayacamas mountain range. My father had told me long ago that fifty Chinese laborers had dug those caves when Celine was just a baby, and that those men lived for several years at the vineyard in makeshift dormitories that Bernard Rosseau dismantled as soon as they were finished.

The barrel and tasting room was built of honey-colored stone on the outside and timbered on the inside with a cross work of redwood rafters that made its interior look like a church. The tasting room, set off by itself near one of the caves, was the one place Truman Calvert seemed content, almost happy. I supposed it was because the tasting room was the one and only aspect of the family business that Celine let him manage with few intrusions from her.

He showed me how to care for the bottles, uncork and pour, swish and sniff, and even how to describe the vintages with clever words that never failed to bring exotic colors to my mind, and which he would occasionally ask me to describe. Working alongside Truman in the tasting room was almost like working in an expensive restaurant kitchen. It was good experience. Not only that, but I was meeting chefs and sommeliers from San Francisco whose names I was filing away for a future day.

October also meant the harvest was underway. It was a time of year that I had always loved because everyone took part. Even Celine and Truman donned work clothes and grabbed shears to cut the clusters from their vines. It was always a race against time to get the fruit picked at its peak of readiness, before a sudden rainstorm ruined the grapes or high winds damaged them or a wildfire—all too typical in early fall—scorched them. The harvesting would begin at daybreak each morning of the season and last until the sun set.

Working alongside the hired hands that autumn reminded me of all the harvests in my past, when my father had chosen the picking teams and my mother and I made the harvesting crews lunch every day. I'd loved how we all gathered for a celebration at the end of the season and there would be a grape stomp and a whole roasted pig on an outdoor spit and a piñata for the migrant workers' children. Someone always had a guitar, so there'd be singing and a bonfire and hot cocoa when the evening chill fell across the vineyard.

Nearly nine months had passed since the accident, nine months since my life had entirely changed. But I had kept busy and had saved a nice bit of money. I was finally starting to feel hopeful that the future might yet hold some happiness for me.

In the first weekend of November, even though the harvest wasn't finished and Wilson was expected home for a couple of days, Celine accepted an overnight invitation to visit an old high school friend who now lived in Berkeley and whose daughter was getting married. She left for her overnight trip on a Saturday morning after giving me instructions on all the details that needed to be handled in the house while she was away.

Enough time had passed that I was again looking forward to seeing Wilson. I was hopeful that, now that we'd put that old memory behind us, he might see that the child I'd been when I said those strange things was no more. I was seventeen, a young woman who his own mother had said was quite pretty. He hadn't meant to make me feel uncomfortable before, I told myself. He just hadn't known my mother had sworn me to secrecy. And it wasn't as if he'd ridiculed me about the colors or even the false notion that I could see ghosts. He'd been curious. Interested. Interest was almost like attraction, wasn't it?

As soon as Celine was gone and all the sandwiches for the harvest workers were made, I changed into field clothes to spend the day alongside a crew of pickers from Los Angeles, all while watching the gravel drive for Wilson's car. It felt good to do the arduous work of bending and clipping and to listen and watch for the colors that were always so stunning at harvest.

In the late afternoon, I finally saw the silver Ford De Luxe that Truman and Celine had bought for Wilson the previous year. I watched as it took the slope up to the big house in a cloud of dust. The row I was working obscured the rest of my view as the car parked up near the front of the house. Wilson honked a cheery hello and I saw ribbons of happy orange. I heard Truman calling out from another part of the vineyard that he'd be right up.

It was too early for me to return to the house, so I kept at it until a few minutes before four o'clock, so that I could clean up before beginning on the supper that Alphonse had half prepared the evening before.

I returned to the big house through the kitchen's back door so that Wilson would not by chance see me in field clothes and with my hair dusty and plastered to my neck and forehead. My muscles were tired from the day's work, and the warm bath would be comforting. I took my time in the tub, making sure to wash every inch of my body with scented soap. After I dried off, I reached for my maid's uniform, but then I turned from it and put on a cotton dress of pale pink instead. It was Saturday night, my evening off, I reasoned. I had told Celine I would make sure Wilson and Truman had a hot meal, but I hadn't told her I'd be in uniform when I did it. As I checked my reflection in the mirror, I heard voices in the kitchen. Truman's, Wilson's, and that of a third person.

A woman.

I opened my bedroom door, and there, standing near the sink in between Wilson and Truman, was a stunningly beautiful woman, petite and pretty with curls the color of corn silk. Her white teeth were framed by perfectly applied red lipstick. She wore a periwinkle-hued linen suit and glossy black pumps.

Wilson had brought a girl home for the weekend.

He'd been turning toward a kitchen drawer at that same moment, and when he saw me, he smiled. "Hey, Rosie. Perfect timing. We're looking for the old corkscrew. The new one in the breakfront broke. Is it in this drawer somewhere?"

I couldn't find my voice. I could only stare at the woman, unable to wrest my eyes from her.

Wilson had brought home a girl.

"Uh . . . I . . . Maybe." I forced my feet to move toward the three of them, toward the drawer that Wilson had just opened. Toward the woman with the perfect body and smile.

Wilson had brought a girl home. For the weekend.

I started to rummage through the utensil drawer, but I couldn't remember what I was supposed to be looking for.

"I've got plenty down in the tasting room," Truman said after a few seconds. "I'll be back in a flash. Wilson, you should introduce Alice to Rosie."

"Oh. Right," Wilson said as Truman walked away. I pushed the drawer closed and turned to face him and his guest.

"Rosie, this is Alice Barrow. Alice, this is Rosie. Rosie's kind of like our . . ." Wilson stopped and looked at me. "What are you? I'm not sure."

Again, for several seconds, my voice was lost to me.

"Pleased to meet you, Miss Barrow," I finally said mechanically. Like a thing made of clockwork. "I am . . . uh, I live here and I take care of the house and kitchen. I'll be serving the evening meal."

"A pleasure," the woman said genially but somehow also distantly. Then she turned to Wilson. "I thought we were going into the city tonight."

"We are." He turned to me. "We're just going to have a quick glass of the family vintage before heading down to the Sausalito Ferry. I want to show Alice San Francisco this weekend."

"Ah. How nice." I barely recognized my voice.

"I know! Let's go down to the barrel and tasting room and have our wine there," Wilson said to Alice. "I can show you the caves."

"All right," his guest said in a tone that told me it made no difference to her where they had their glass of wine before heading out for San Francisco. Wilson was trying to impress this woman. I could tell he hadn't been successful yet.

"Nice to have met you," Alice said languidly as they turned to leave the kitchen.

"Yes. Enjoy your evening," I returned.

Wilson had his hand on the small of her back as they started to walk away. He looked back at me with a smile as they crossed from the kitchen to the dining room. "Bye, Rosie."

I waved, and then they were gone.

For several seconds, I just stood there wondering what to do with my immense disappointment and feeling like a fool for having imagined—again—that Wilson would have any interest in me. Perhaps it wasn't actually Wilson that I longed for as much as I just longed to be wanted. It had been exhilarating to think he could have feelings for me. I'd loved imagining it was possible.

I changed into a blouse and trousers and then began to pull out the things to make dinner, moving about the kitchen as if in a disjointed dream. The long day in the fields was catching up with me now that there was nothing exciting to look forward to for the weekend. I just wanted to finish the dinner preparations, serve Truman, clean up, and be done with this day.

Wilson and Alice were already gone when supper was ready. The harvest crews had left, too, and the house and the property were quiet.

I served Truman in the study, where he decided to take his meal, and I ate in the kitchen while I absently flipped through a magazine. By eight o'clock, I was bone-tired in body and soul, and I went to retrieve Truman's dinner plate so that I could clean up for the night and crawl into bed.

He had a cheery fire going and music playing on the phonograph that I'd never heard before. As I stepped into the room, I was nearly swept off my feet at the sound of it. Swirls of lavender and bright yellow hovered on the tripping piano notes and an accompanying horn. A saxophone, I thought.

Truman was sitting in one of the two chairs in front of the fireplace, a bottle of whisky in front of him, and a glass. A lit cigarette resting on an ashtray on the table next to him was sending curls of smoke into the air.

"What is that music?" I asked him.

He turned to face me. "Ah. That, my dear, is Duke Ellington. Do you like it?"

"I've never heard anything like it." The colors were swirling in my head as if they were living things. How beautiful they were.

Truman sat forward on his chair. "You're seeing good ones, I can tell. I mean those colors of yours. You're seeing something wonderful, aren't you?"

"I am," I said tentatively.

"Tell me." Longing graced his voice. I liked hearing it.

"Purple and yellow," I said. "Like flowers."

He sat back, lifted his glass to me in a salute. "You don't know how lucky you are."

I felt my eyes widen. I didn't know what to say to this. I certainly didn't feel lucky. I hadn't for what seemed like a long time. And especially not today.

"Celine doesn't like the Duke." Truman raised the tumbler to his mouth, tipped it back, and swallowed. "She doesn't like jazz.

Can you believe it? She won't let me play it in the house when she's home."

"Is that what this is? Jazz?"

He poured another swallow from the bottle into his glass. "It is indeed. The best there is."

I started to reach for his dinner plate sitting next to the ashtray, but Truman waved me away from the dish as he rose from the chair. "Just leave it." He walked over to the bar, grabbed a bottle and two wineglasses, and came back to the chair. "Join me in a drink? You need to try this. It's our newest vintage. A sherry. The most exquisite we've ever made."

He began to pour from the bottle. The liquid was a robust red, almost brown.

"Oh, I don't think—"

But he thrust the little glass toward me. "I just found out you had a birthday."

"Yes, I did, but—"

"And nothing was done for it, right? No cake? Nothing?"

"Mrs. Calvert gave me some chocolates. Nice ones."

"I can't believe it came and went and Celine just now told me. Come. Let's toast your seventeenth year properly. You haven't tasted sherry this fine in your life."

I took the glass with hesitation. "I've never tasted sherry at all."

"Then I insist. Did you know Columbus traveled to the New World with barrels of it? It's Spanish. Sherry is Spanish. We don't have the right grapes here in California, but the Rosseau muscats have helped us create something quite nice. Try it."

I raised the glass to my lips and sipped. The wine was honey-sweet and warmed me like sunshine.

"Impressive, right? Especially for our first try."

"It's . . . delicious." I took another sip, and another. The drink was easing my disappointment of being startled at seeing beautiful Alice Barrow in Celine's kitchen and Wilson's hand on the small of her back when she walked out of it.

Truman poured more for me and then set down his wineglass. He picked up the tumbler from before and splashed more whisky into it.

The phonograph began to play a new tune, this one as captivating as the one before it. I was feeling toasty all over, and the aches from the hours in the field were falling away as though my sore muscles were knotted threads being untied.

"Have a seat." Truman motioned to the second chair. "We'll pretend that today is your birthday, since we sadly didn't do anything proper to celebrate it. We can play a game of cards and sip our drinks and listen to the Duke."

I knew I should take his plate to the kitchen and get to bed, but my birthday had in fact gone by pretty much unnoticed. And today had ended up being a terrible day. I sat down in the other chair, telling myself it was just for one game of cards, one more glass of the delectable wine, and then bed.

Truman poured himself another tumbler and dealt the cards for gin, and soon it really did start to feel like it was not an ordinary day. We played three hands while he drank whisky and I consumed a third glass of sherry. And while we played, he told me stories of the Great War, how he'd loved being a soldier.

"I never regretted enlisting, even though it nearly killed me," he said. "I've never been as close to death as I was in the trenches of Montreuil, but I swear, I've never felt as alive as I did then. I was part of something grand, something that mattered."

I wasn't entirely sure what he meant, but the room was starting to tilt a little, and I knew I needed to get to my room before I fell asleep right there in the chair.

"It's late. I need to turn in." I rose from where I sat, but my head was spinning. I took a step and immediately began to fall. Truman shot to his feet to catch me.

"Hold on, there," he said, steadying me in his arms.

The phonograph started to play an enchanting melody, the kind that begged for dancers. Truman grinned and began to dance with me in his arms, but I wasn't a good dancer, and the amount of sherry I'd consumed was making me even less of one. He started laughing when I stepped on his feet, and then I laughed, too, when he stepped on mine. We'd both drunk too much to manage even the simplest steps. The more we attempted to dance anyway, the more we stumbled. This was hilarious, too. I couldn't remember the last time I'd laughed like that. The sound of my own laughter spun white orbs around my thoughts. We circled to a stop when the song ended. When the next one began, Truman cupped my face with his hand.

"I wish I could go back to when I was seventeen," he said. "You are so lucky, so lucky."

His hand on my cheek felt so wonderful. Like the petal of a rose. "I don't feel lucky," I said.

"But you are. Think of it! You're young and pretty and smart. And you have this amazing gift. You have everything."

"I don't think . . ."

He was staring at me in unmistakable awe and envy, one arm still around my waist. And then he bent forward and touched his lips to mine in a gentle and merely seconds-long kiss. It was my first. Truman's lips were soft and warm, and his kiss instantly made my insides ache with an odd mix of desire and alarm. I tasted the whisky on his breath, tart and tantalizing. A ripple of unfamiliar longing sped through me as Truman pressed his lips to mine again, and this time he kept them there.

It was wrong, I knew this. A kiss from Truman was wrong, wrong, wrong. But it felt so perfect to be held like that and to be kissed like that and to be told I was smart and pretty and lucky. Everything I'd wanted Wilson to do, Truman was doing.

Before I knew it, I was kissing him back.

Truman's arms circled my waist fully as he brought me closer and his kiss intensified. I knew I needed to break away. Truman was married to Celine. What we were doing was absolutely not a good idea, but I didn't know how to stop him. I wanted to be kissed, and I didn't know how to stop wanting it.

"You're so beautiful," he whispered into my hair, slurring the words a bit, but I didn't care. He sounded like he meant it. I wanted to believe it.

My arms went around his neck as he kissed me again. The room was now swirling with color and sound and the novelty of being desired. It was like being on the roller coaster at Ocean Beach. The Big Dipper. I'd been on it just the one time, when I was twelve. It had been thrilling and terrifying at the same time.

Then Truman was lowering me slowly onto the thick rug in front of the fireplace, and a thousand sirens went off in my head.

"Wait," I said, gulping for air and control. I seemed unable to grab hold of either one.

He was over me, kissing my neck as he slid his hands up under my blouse.

"I . . . I don't . . . Wait, Truman," I sputtered, and I felt like I was being devoured alive by both unrelenting desire and dread. "Stop."

But he didn't stop. The buttons of my blouse were suddenly undone, and his hands and lips were all over my body. He was covering me with kisses and his touch. I hadn't known being touched by a man could feel like this. No one had told me; no one had yet touched me. Momma had only ever spoken in vague terms about the ways of men with women. I knew what sexual intercourse was, Momma had told me that much, but I hadn't known the act began with *this*. This unstoppable, racing need to be wanted. Nor that it would make you feel as if you were flying.

But it was wrong. Truman had to stop.

Truman should not be doing what he was doing.

"Don't, Truman," I whispered, nearly choking out his name as he tugged at my underwear and then at his own trousers. But the room continued to spin with the effects of alcohol and his touch and the chilling horror that he was not listening.

Then Truman was above me and somehow inside me and I felt like I was being sawn in two as he moved. The room went golden with pain and heat and brilliance and desire that didn't seem to belong to this world. The next moment Truman fell against me, and the scorching brightness faded, the fire in my body subsided. He rolled off and lay down next to me, breathing like I was, as if we had run a great distance. It seemed like we lay that way for a long time, but it was only seconds.

"I don't know why we did that," Truman said, breathless. He sounded perplexed.

We, I wanted to say. *We?* But my voice was frozen in my throat.

"Oh God. This . . . this can't happen again. You know that, don't you?"

I couldn't think straight to answer him.

"Rosie?" Truman turned his head to look at me.

Still no words would come.

"We're drunk. We made a mistake, okay? I let myself get carried away. We both did. This can't happen again." He swiveled his head to stare at the ceiling and run a hand through his hair.

I sat up and pulled my clothes about me, my thoughts a blur. I wanted my bed. I wanted sleep. I wanted to be anywhere but in this room with Truman Calvert lying there with his trousers undone.

As I rose unsteadily to my feet, Truman reached out to me. "You okay?"

I didn't think I was, but I nodded.

"Did you hear what I said?"

Again, I nodded, and then turned to walk away.

"Hey. I'm sorry," Truman called after me, but the phonograph was playing a happy tune, and I wasn't sure what he was sorry for.

13

All is a blur of light and sound as Belle yells for Nurse Andrews to come. I bend forward as the sense of fullness I've been experiencing in the last few days turns to a peculiar churning.

Something is happening. Something not good for our plans.

"Belle!" The imagined escape begins to flit away in my mind like a panicked butterfly, and the room seems to tilt. We were so close. So close.

"Hush," Belle whispers, mindful of our other roommates, all awake now. "You'll be fine. We'll go on Sunday just like we planned. You, me, and the baby. All three of us."

"But it's too early. It's too early for the baby to come. Something has to be wrong!"

"Stop talking like that," Belle murmurs urgently. "We'll get out of here, just like I said we would. No more talking about it."

Nurse Andrews sweeps into the room to see what all the fuss is about.

"All right, then." She looks calmly at the puddle, as though I had merely spilled a glass of water. "Nothing to get all worked up about."

"But I have three more weeks!" I say in a terrified voice.

"Babies come when they want to come," Nurse Andrews replies. "You're likely going to be fine and the baby probably will be, too. We just need to get you downstairs into the maternity ward. I'll have Norman get a wheelchair. Just hold on to the footboard there. Don't sit on anything and make a bigger mess." She leaves to go find Norman.

Belle turns to me. "To hell with her. If you want to sit on your bed, sit."

"I'm okay." I grip the rail at the bottom of my bed. "I'm so sorry, Belle."

But Belle gives me a quick shake of her head. The escape is not going to be discussed—all eyes in the room are on us.

Moments later Norman comes into the room with the wheelchair. As I'm wheeled away, I look back at Belle. I don't know if it is the last time I will see my friend. What if they keep me in the maternity ward for more than three days? Will Belle leave without me? I want to tell her to go and I want to tell her to stay, but I can only stare at her as I am pushed out of the room.

I was told by the nursing staff that my labor pains would feel like monthly cramps, only much worse. The fiery twisting and turning inside me would be opening a door into my uterus through which the baby will pass, and I should not fight it. I am given an enema and shaved, and as the rest of the day wears on and the pains intensify, I try to remember the pain is a door. A door for my child to come through to me.

Dr. Melson comes late in the afternoon and pronounces that it is now time for the gas that will put me to sleep for the hardest part of the delivery.

"I don't want gas!" I say through gritted teeth as a labor pain envelops me.

"Of course you do," says one of the nurses.

"I don't care if she doesn't want it," Dr. Melson says tonelessly. "It's easier for me if she pushes the child out. And she's narrow. The forceps might be a problem. Let her push if she wants to."

For the next twenty minutes, all I am aware of are the door and the pain and the work. At the moment my baby slips from my body, I feel as if a long frigid winter has ended and at last spring is here. The infant girl the doctor holds up is tiny and beautiful. She is like a perfect bloom that has pushed its way up out of the dark ground, just like the amaryllis Helen gave me. Beauty out of nothingness, hope out of the darkness. The baby cries out, and the very room seems electrified with orbs of December red.

The name comes to me that same instant. The only name for my baby girl.

"Amaryllis," I say as I gaze in awe at the flower that emerged from the dark confines of my body.

"What, dear?" says one of the nurses.

"Her name is Amaryllis."

"Oh. Well, I suppose we can call her that for now if you want. That's a pretty name, Rosie."

"Let me hold her."

The two nurses in the room look at each other and say nothing. Dr. Melson, who is kneading my abdomen in a not very gentle way to encourage the afterbirth to come out, does not look up when he says, "We don't recommend that."

"She's my daughter!" I say, grimacing as he works on me.

The doctor looks up. "Holding the baby will only make it harder for you. I should know. I've seen it a dozen times." He drops his gaze back to his task.

What has he seen a dozen times? His words make no sense. "Harder for what? What are you talking about?"

Dr. Melson looks up again. He is frowning. "Do I need to call in Dr. Townsend?"

I suddenly remember then that it is their plan to send my baby girl to a receiving home so that a suitable family will adopt her. My parental rights are already scheduled to be terminated.

Because I am not a suitable person to be a mother.

My instincts war inside me. I want with all my might to snatch that baby from the nurse who is now washing away my presence from the little bloom's flesh. But I have to keep pretending that I am ready to do whatever it is they expect of me. Belle promised me that delivering the baby today will change nothing. She assured me we will still escape. I don't know how we will do it now; I only know I refuse to believe that we won't.

My baby is still crying out to be held by her mother. "I still want to hold her," I say.

Dr. Melson thinks for a moment and then shrugs. He swivels around to address the nurse holding Amaryllis. "Only for a few minutes," he says.

The nurse wraps my wailing baby in a blanket and places her in my arms. She quiets as soon as I begin to speak her name, over and over. "Amaryllis. Amaryllis, Amaryllis."

The minutes I am allowed seem to condense to mere seconds as the two of us—mother and daughter—stare at each other, eye to eye. Every time I say her name, I am making a promise. *I will come for you. I will come for you. I will come for you.*

Dr. Melson signals for the nurse to take my child, and I feel my heart will burst. *It's only until Sunday*, I tell myself as the baby is pulled out of my arms. Only until Sunday.

The nurse who handed Amaryllis to me rewraps her in the blanket and starts to walk away.

"Where are you taking her?" I call out as I try to maneuver myself to see where the nurse is going. A cramp grips me.

The doctor is seated back between my legs again, and he is tugging gently on the curly cord that tied Amaryllis to me. "You'd be wise to stop asking questions about the baby."

"We have a nice little nursery," the nurse interjects when Dr. Melson says nothing else.

"And when does she . . . ? When is she supposed to . . . ?" I can't finish the sentence. I will burst into sobs if I actually ask when they are planning to send her from this place, away from me.

"The child—," the doctor begins.

"Amaryllis," I correct him.

"*Amaryllis* will stay in our care for two weeks so that we can make sure she is ready for travel and so that the institution taking her in can prepare for her arrival. She came early, you know."

An immediate sense of relief floods me. They aren't planning to send Amaryllis away until well after Sunday. The three of us will be gone by then.

"When can I go back to my room?" I ask. "I want to go back to my room."

"You need to push right now," Dr. Melson says, ignoring my question. "The afterbirth needs to be delivered."

I obey and I feel something soft and wet fall away from inside me. Dr. Melson slides the afterbirth into a basin and gives it a cursory glance. Then he turns back to me. "You're going to need a few stitches. Hold still."

He pricks my tender flesh with a needle and I wince at the sting. And then he is sewing me back together. I wait until he is finished and he stands to pull off the surgical gown he's been wearing over his clothes.

"Can I go back to my room now?" I ask.

"You'll stay here overnight. Maybe longer."

"But if I am fine by tomorrow, may I go back to my room?"

The other nurse in the room laughs. "You should take advantage of having a little peace and quiet in the maternity ward. You're the only one here right now. It will be like having your own room. The kitchen brings you your meals. And you really should rest."

"I just want to go back to my room."

Dr. Melson frowns at me. "That's my decision to make, not yours. But if you're recovering nicely by tomorrow, I might allow it." He turns to the nurse. "Take her to the ward."

It is past suppertime when I am escorted on shaking legs to a ward down the hall, a room with four beds in it, all empty. The nurse gives me a package of sanitary pads and tells me I'll bleed for several days and not to worry—heavy bleeding is normal.

"And don't express any milk from your breasts," she says. "You'll be tempted to, but don't. You'll just make it worse. When the milk starts to come in, I'll give you some warm compresses for the pain."

The nurse leaves me, and I study my breasts under my hospital gown after she is gone, anxious for my milk to appear. Amaryllis will need it.

Dinner is brought to me on a cart, and I devour the meat loaf and whipped potatoes on my plate.

I am beyond exhausted, but sleep eludes me. The nursery is somewhere close, I am sure of it. Amaryllis isn't far. I finally fall asleep gazing at yellow feathery wisps that float on my mind at the sound of an infant's tender cry. Somewhere here on the second floor, Amaryllis is crying for me. My breasts ache to nourish her.

In the morning, I awake from fitful sleep that has been interrupted by after-birth pains, soreness in my breasts, the lingering echoes of Amaryllis's cries, and dreams of escaping. One of the delivery room nurses from the day before brings me breakfast and asks how I slept.

"Fine," I say. "Can I go back to my room now?"

The nurse gives me a mildly quizzical look. "Dr. Melson won't be by until the afternoon."

"But I'm fine! I just want to go back to my room."

The nurse gazes at me for a moment and then says she'll check. But an hour later, it isn't Dr. Melson who comes to my room, but

Dr. Townsend. He does not congratulate me on having given birth to a beautiful baby. "I hear you'd like to go back up to the third floor," he says.

I tamp down alarm that I've tipped him off that I'm up to something. "It's hard for me to be on this floor. I can hear the baby crying and I'd rather not."

He studies me carefully before answering. "I suppose I can understand that. I hear you forgot yesterday what the plans are for the baby." His gaze is penetrating.

"I didn't forget," I said, holding that gaze. "Dr. Melson wasn't being clear."

Several seconds tick by before he continues.

"If you are allowed back to your own room, you'll still be on a minimal schedule," Dr. Townsend says. "You will not be returning to your job at the kitchen for a week or two, and you should stay off the stairs between floors."

"I understand."

"All right," he says. "I'll have Dr. Melson come in to make sure the postpartum bleeding is under control, and if he sees no problems, you can go back to your room this afternoon."

"Thank you, Dr. Townsend," I say.

"You're welcome." He turns to leave the room.

He has only been gone a few seconds when I rise to go to the lavatory in the hall to change my pad and use the toilet. I stop just short of the entrance to the hallway when I hear the nurse and Dr. Townsend talking, obviously about me.

"I'm sure you know best, Doctor, but I don't see the point in her returning to her own room when she's only going to have to come back here in two days," the nurse is saying.

"The procedure will go better if she's had a few days to recover from the birth in a room where she feels comfortable. It's not as if it's difficult to bring her back down." The doctor starts to walk away.

I clamp a hand over my mouth and back away from the doorway, my stitches pulling and stinging. I turn to the wall so that Dr. Townsend won't see me if he comes in my direction, but the doctor's footsteps lead him to the door out of the hospital ward. It is only after the outer door clicks shut and he is gone that I let out the stifled gasp.

There is only one reason to bring me back to the hospital ward. They are going to cut into me, change what is inside so that I can never have any more children.

Dr. Townsend hasn't been able to fix me. He hasn't been able to rinse the colors from my head. He knows the colors also appeared to a great-aunt on my mother's side of the family. Or maybe he already knew this flaw of mine can be passed on to babies just like it was passed on to me.

Tomorrow's escape has to happen. Has to.

14

When I awakened in my bed, head pounding, I believed for a handful of hazy seconds that what happened the previous night with Truman had all been a ridiculous dream—the wine, the dancing, the confiding, the kissing, the touching, the unspeakable act on the rug—all of it a dream. It had seemed like one in those first moments of sleepy consciousness. I would never have sex with a married man, my employer's husband no less, and someone old enough to be my father—drunk or not. I would never do that. The memory of having done so was a creation of my imagination.

But as I became more alert and the throbbing in my head did not clear, I knew I had imagined none of it.

Waves of regret and shame rushed through me. God Almighty, how could I have done such a thing?

Yet it hadn't entirely been my fault. Truman had given me too much to drink. He'd kissed me and I'd wanted him to stop.

But then I kissed him back.

I had liked his kisses. I'd wanted them. And then I hadn't found a way to stop him from doing the rest. I should have tried harder to push him away. I should have insisted. I shouldn't have let him tug at my underwear or push my legs apart or . . .

I felt the contents of my stomach roil and I dashed out of my bed to heave over and over into the toilet. I sat back on my knees when my stomach was empty, trembling with the realization that even with the retching, I would not be able to rid myself of what I had done and what I had failed to do. Minutes passed before I rose to my feet. I dressed in my uniform and made my way gingerly into the kitchen. Everything ached—my head, my stomach, the private place inside that had been invaded, my inner being.

I laid out Truman's breakfast before I heard him moving about the house and retreated into the kitchen when I heard him coming down the hall. I listened as he sat down at the table, opened the newspaper that I'd placed at his chair, lowered his coffee cup onto its saucer. I heard the faint scraping of fork tines against his plate.

It was usual for me to refill the Calverts' coffee cups as they ate breakfast without them having to ask, and though I wished I could just stay in the kitchen until he was finished eating, Truman called for me. He wanted more coffee, please.

Seconds passed before I reached for the coffeepot and pushed open the kitchen door, which was usually latched open unless there were guests. I had unhooked it that morning so that it would swing shut.

Truman was wearing a starched white shirt and twill pants, and his hair was plastered neatly into place with pomade. Even so, he looked disheveled. Tired. Out of sorts. I walked over to where he sat and began to pour. My hand shook, and coffee spilled off the rim of his cup and onto the saucer.

"Rosie."

I stopped pouring and slowly raised my head to look at him.

"Why is the kitchen door closed?" His voice was both gentle and earnest.

"I . . . I was . . . ," I stammered. "I don't know."

"We need to go back to the way our lives were before. Exactly the way they were before. It's important." His tone was quietly insistent, his gaze intense. "What happened last night needs to be forgotten. Like it didn't happen. We had too much to drink. Things got out of hand. I shouldn't have kissed you. We shouldn't have . . ." His voice dropped away.

I nodded, unable to speak a word.

"The kitchen door should be open this morning, right?"

He waited until I answered.

"Yes," I whispered.

He reached out to touch my arm, but it was not like last night. It did not make my insides ache to be held. It was the touch of someone in quiet distress. "Can you do what we both must do? I need to know."

In his voice I heard the unhappy man who told me he wished he could go back to when he had been my age. When he'd had options.

"Yes," I said, even though I wasn't sure I could.

He removed his hand and exhaled. "How about you try again with the coffee?"

This time when I poured, my hand stayed steady. He thanked me. I went back to the kitchen and relatched the door open on its hook.

This, then, was how we were to go back to the way things had been before. We were to pretend, as if it had only been a dream, just like my waking thoughts had suggested. I could pretend having sex with Truman Calvert had been merely a dream, but I knew I'd never be able to pretend I didn't remember it. That was impossible. No one could do that.

By the time Celine arrived home a bit before noon, I was scrubbing toilets and Truman was in the tasting room with a restaurateur from Sebastopol.

Over the next few days, I saw little of Truman. He either skipped breakfast or took it down in the tasting room. He made himself lunch when I was busy doing other chores, and he came to the dinner table after I had laid out Alphonse's dishes. I was glad one minute and irritated the next that he kept his distance. I found myself reluctantly reliving the feeling of having been in his arms, of being kissed, of being touched. Nothing had taken the sharp, deep edge off my losses like being with Truman—in that way—had. Nothing had come close. Not walking among the vines, not the colors. I was not in love with him, and I knew he was not in love with me, but what I'd felt when I'd been with him was the closest thing to love I had felt in months.

But even so, Truman should have stopped when I asked him to. I should've stopped him. I should've been stronger, should've drunk less wine.

If only he had stopped. If only I had made him stop.

The next weekend arrived, and I was expected in the tasting room to assist Truman with a group of East Coast tourists. I reported for duty half an hour before the group was to arrive to polish the stemware and prepare little plates of aged cheddar and dark chocolate. It was only the second time Truman and I had been alone since the night in his study. As we readied the room, Truman uncorked a zinfandel to let it breathe.

"Everything all right?" he said, but he did not look at me.

"Everything is fine," I said, not looking at him, either.

We said nothing else to each other. The awkward silence between us lifted as soon as the guests arrived. The group was relaxed, cheerful, and easy to please. They enjoyed the wines and one another's company, even when their conversation drifted to the news of the day—the chaos in Europe. I had seen the latest headlines in the Calverts' morning newspaper. Over a period of two days, raiding parties of National Socialists, angered by the murder of a German diplomat in Paris by a Jew, had vandalized thousands of Jewish homes, schools, and businesses—in Munich, Berlin, Leipzig, everywhere. The Nazis—as they were being called—had littered thousands of streets with broken glass from smashed windows and had burned hundreds of synagogues. Dozens of people were dead and thousands of Jewish men had been arrested.

When one of the guests mentioned trouble in Vienna as well, Truman looked up from the bottle he was uncorking. "What's this about Vienna?"

The man, who'd been speaking to his friends, turned, surprised that Truman had put himself into their conversation. The group of guests had moved from the oak bar where Truman had introduced the wines to a little table of their own.

"Sorry. I don't mean to intrude, but my sister lives in Vienna," Truman said.

"Ah, well. Not the safest place at the moment. The violence and vandalism happened there, too. And it seems the archbishop of Vienna is now under house arrest. His residence was also smashed up during all that hullabaloo."

"But," Truman said, "the archbishop is Catholic."

"He apparently spoke out against how the Jews are being treated," the man said. "He continues to speak out. He's in hot water now, you could say."

"It's just terrible what is happening over there to the Jewish people," said the woman next to him.

"If I were Jewish, I wouldn't stay another minute in Germany. Or Austria," said another man in the party.

"Nor would I," said the woman. "But where would you go? Who would take you? You couldn't come to America, you know. Not unless you had family here already, and even then you could only come under the quota."

"All those poor mothers and their children," said another woman, shaking her head. "How will they keep their little ones safe from such brutality? And look what happens to you if you speak out against it."

The people around the table nodded and sipped. No one had any answers. I glanced at Truman; his brow was furrowed in thought. He turned and handed me the next vintage for the tasters to try. I could not read his face.

I walked over to the little table and began to pour.

Wilson didn't come home at Thanksgiving—he'd met a new girl and was visiting with her family over the four-day break—so the Calverts accepted an invitation from friends to have the Thanksgiving meal with them. Celine told me I could join them if I wanted to, but I had no desire to tag along and Celine seemed relieved that I didn't.

As the month eased into December and the many boxes of Christmas decorations came out, Celine asked me to help make every room look festive, but I hung the garlands and trim with a growing sense of emptiness. Pretending around Celine was exhausting, and the approach of Christmas made me miss my family with an intensity that surprised me. It was as if they had all died just yesterday. Worse, I felt as though I deserved to have lost them all. My mother and father would be horrified by what I'd done.

And yet I also battled thoughts that my parents had abandoned me to this fate, and now I was stuck in a house that felt like a prison, reminded every day when I made Truman's breakfast or washed his clothes or cleaned his bathroom sink or made his bed that he'd not stopped when I asked him to.

The hope I had begun to nurture on my birthday in October was starting to fade, and I wasn't the only one in a restless state. The merry decorations couldn't relieve the uneasiness that seemed to seep from the very walls of the Calverts' house. I saw it in the way Celine would watch Truman when he didn't seem to know he was being watched. She surely suspected he was troubled about something, but I could also tell, to my relief, that she had no idea what it was. Truman's unexplained moodiness irritated Celine; that was also obvious.

A week before Christmas, a deliveryman came to the door with a flowering plant, beautiful and exotic, with trumpetlike blooms of crimson flounced by a loose wrapping of translucent gold paper. I could see that the sender's address on the accompanying note was in Vienna. This was surely a Christmas gift to the family from Helen Calvert, a world away in Austria.

I brought it in to the Calverts as they finished a late breakfast.

"What in the world is that?" Celine said.

"I think it might be from Mr. Calvert's sister." I extended the plant to her.

"Is that so?" Truman said, looking up from his newspaper.

"Is it for the house, then?" Celine looked at the plant suspiciously, as if it might contain a family of aphids under its green, waxy leaves.

"I'm sure it's meant to be enjoyed inside the house, Celine. It's very pretty. And it was very thoughtful of her to have it sent."

"Yes, I suppose. I'm just not a fan of plants in the house, Truman. You know it, and I thought she knew it."

Truman folded the newspaper and set it down by his empty plate. "I imagine the last time Helen was here, you and she did not talk at length about having plants in the house."

Celine retrieved the note attached to the plant, opened it, and then clucked her tongue. "This plant isn't for us at all," she said to Truman. Then she turned to face me. "Helen sent this for you, Rosie."

"What?" I said, though I'd heard her perfectly.

"She did?" Truman said.

Celine handed the little teletyped note to me. I felt her and Truman's gazes on me as I read it.

Dearest Rosie: It's been a few years since I've written you, but that doesn't mean I've forgotten you. I am especially mindful now of the loss of your sweet family and that this will be your first holiday season without them. I hope this bit of Christmas cheer will bring you comfort. See my letter to Truman and the family for how to care for the amaryllis.

With love, Helen Calvert

I read the note twice, stunned at her kindness. I didn't know how to pronounce the name of the plant, and yet I loved how the letters looked on paper.

Truman rose from the table. "That was very thoughtful," he said, but his voice sounded a bit wooden.

"Yes, very nice," Celine said. "Well then, Rosie. Why don't you take it into the kitchen so that you can enjoy it there."

"Yes, Mrs. Calvert."

I could scarcely believe the captivating thing was mine or that Helen Calvert had sent it to me. To me. It was so beautiful. And I didn't deserve such thoughtfulness. I set it on the countertop by the sink, and I spent the rest of the day admiring its blooms and unable to feel worthy of them. Helen, too, would no doubt be appalled at what her brother and I had done.

When Alphonse arrived at four o'clock to begin dinner preparations, he swept into the kitchen, set down his kit of knives, and noticed the plant.

He turned to me. "Whose is the amaryllis?"

At the sound of the word, shades of pink and red flitted across my mind like confetti. What an enchanting word. *Amaryllis.*

"Is that how you say it?" I said.

"*Oui.*"

"Truman's sister in Austria sent it to me."

"Ah. My brother grows those sometimes. You need a greenhouse to have them in wintertime, though. They are from Africa, where it's hot all the time. They are not a winter flower."

"Is that why they are called amaryllis?" I asked, gazing at the flower, which now had a name that I knew would forever be a kaleidoscope of delight to me. "Because they are able to bloom in winter?"

"That I do not know." Alphonse slipped his apron over his white shirt. "But I do know what to do when it stops blooming." He nodded toward the crimson petals. "The amaryllis is like a tulip or daffodil. There's a bulb down in the dirt. You dig it up when it's done. When you want it to bloom again, you plant. *Voilà.*"

"*Voilà?*"

"This means 'there you go.' The flower comes back."

Alphonse set me to trimming asparagus, but I found my gaze traveling to the amaryllis as I worked. So beautiful in the present moment and containing the promise of beauty always. I was mesmerized by it.

———

Wilson came home for the Christmas break, but I could easily tell I was no longer of any interest at all to him. He took several phone calls and made several of his own. All to the new love interest, Barbara. He was polite to me, but that was all. I was just the maid and nothing else.

Two days before Christmas, Celine declared the family would spend the holidays in San Francisco at a posh hotel. She said I could join them if I wanted, but it was clear in her tone that the invitation was merely a polite gesture, as I was only temporarily a member of the household. I was more than content to decline. Celine gave me three days off and pearl earrings wrapped in silver paper.

Before the Calverts left for San Francisco, Celine came into the kitchen and handed me one of her Christmas cards that had come in the mail earlier that week.

"You're probably going to want this."

I could see from the postmark that it was from Vienna.

"Helen has instructions inside for you on what to do with that plant," Celine said.

I tucked the letter in my apron pocket. When the Calverts were gone and the lunch dishes put away, I went into my room, took out the envelope, and withdrew a Christmas card picturing a snowy chalet, evergreens, and foreign words—German ones that meant nothing to me—embellished with silver glitter. Inside the card was a tissue-thin letter.

Merry Christmas, Truman and all!
I hope you all have a very happy Christmas. I know you are worried for me, but I promise I am all right. Things are different here in Vienna than they used to be; what you are probably hearing about life

under the rule of the Reich is sadly true. But I'm not afraid, and I know that I'm supposed to be here with this family. The Maiers did not ask me to stay; I offered.

I'm right where I want to be.

Much love to you all, Helen

P.S. to Rosie: I hope you are enjoying the little bit of paradise I had sent to you. I've always loved an amaryllis at Christmastime. It blooms in winter because it believes it is spring. After the first of the year, pull the bulb from the dirt. Keep it cool and dry, like in the barn or barrel room. Next year, if you repot it in November, it will bloom for you again at the holidays. Just like it is blooming now. An amaryllis is always waiting to delight and surprise you, even when your world seems cold and dark.

I ran my fingers over the words above her postscript to me. *I'm right where I want to be.* As I whispered those words aloud, bursts of peach and lime green bloomed in my thoughts, and it was as if I could see that future day, hidden from me now like an amaryllis bulb in a dark place: that day when this life would be behind me and my new one would be starting, and I would say those words for myself and mean them.

When the holiday season was over and the scarlet petals had withered and fallen, I unearthed the amaryllis bulb, brushed off the dirt, and wrapped it in cheesecloth I'd taken from the kitchen. I put the little package and Helen's instructions in an empty baking soda tin and shoved it into the darkest part of my closet. And then I penned a thank-you note that felt more like a confession as I wrote it.

> *Dear Miss Calvert,*
>
> *Thank you very much for the amaryllis. It was so kind of you. I have never seen a more beautiful flower or heard a more beautiful name. I am keeping your note on how to take care of it. I hope to do my best by it. I promise I will try.*
>
> *Yours sincerely,*
> *Rosanne Maras*

I posted the letter on a bike ride to the library.

Every day thereafter when I dressed, I'd see the little tin in the back of the closet, and I would be reminded that things wouldn't always be the way they were now.

It wasn't until the third week of January that it occurred to me that I hadn't had my monthly bleeding in November or December. My heart immediately began to pound as I counted back the days to be sure. No cycle at Christmastime. No cycle before Thanksgiving. And now none in January. As the full understanding of what this meant flooded my thoughts, I sank to my knees in my room. My mother had told me what happened to a woman's body when a child was coming. The cycles stopped. They stopped like they had for me now. I spent the next quarter hour on the floor next to my bed, rocking back and forth on my knees, begging God for my bleeding to come. *Let it come, let it come, let it come.*

Days passed and the prayer went unanswered—my cycle did not return—and I began to plead to heaven with a new request. I wanted God to take the child from me. I wanted him to take it away. Celine had had a miscarriage. Momma had had two in between me and Tommy. It happened. Women miscarried all the time. I prayed for mercy and forgiveness for wanting the child gone. It was a terrible thing to wish for. I hated myself for wanting it gone.

But my cycle of blood did not come. And still I begged every day to be delivered of it.

By the first week in February, I could no longer zip up my uniform. I let out the side seams and sewed them up by hand. A week later when I was bathing, there was no mistaking the rounded swelling, like a little melon, across my abdomen. I touched it and felt not a sloshing bag of waters as I'd expected but a protective wall, like layers of leather, meant to keep something safe and secure. How could I have ever hoped I would miscarry? There was a life growing inside me.

I stroked the slight mound, astonished to realize the little thing nestled inside my body that I had wanted gone was actually precious and amazing. And mine. I was suddenly glad that my cruel prayer to be rid of the baby had not been granted. But I also knew in that same instant I could not hide what was happening to my body.

It seemed I had three options. I could tell Truman and ask for his help, but the truth was, I didn't want to tell him. I didn't want him knowing his child was growing inside me. It was my child, only mine. And what would he be able to do? What would he *want* to do? Send me away to some secret place of his choosing, not mine?

Or I could tell Mrs. Grissom, but I sensed only heartache awaited me if I did that. She'd likely confront the Calverts to question them on how I got into this predicament. I didn't want Celine to ever find out what had happened that autumn night she was away. Plus, the county surely wouldn't let me keep the baby.

Or I could sneak away before anyone noticed I was with child and start a new life for myself and my baby far away from here—and without having to tell anyone.

It was only this last choice that I liked. The other options would put me right back where someone else was deciding my future instead of me.

As the next few days slipped past, I couldn't decide if I should flee to San Francisco or San Jose or somewhere else, much farther away. It seemed such a weighty, impossible decision. And there was no one to turn to for advice.

Had I saved enough money, and would I be able to convince the outside world that I was already an adult, just widowed young? Would I be believed if that was the story I told? Perhaps a church would help me. Wasn't that what churches did? Helped people in need? As I lay in my bed wondering what to do and when to do it, I felt a fluttering, like tiny moths, inside me. The child was moving, stretching its small arms and legs, telling me, *I am here*.

I curled up into a ball, and the movement stopped. But only for a moment. Sleep eluded me for hours.

The following morning, I could not zip up the uniform whose side seams I'd already let out. I looked down at my middle, at the little bulge that refused now to be hidden. There was no more time to ponder where I would go. I would have to leave. Today.

I would have to feign sickness that morning, but not such that Celine would insist on my seeing a doctor. I knew Truman was leaving after breakfast for an overnight trip to San Leandro to negotiate a contract with a hotel there. If I waited until Celine had an errand to run, I could sneak away and ride my bicycle to the Santa Rosa bus station without either one of the Calverts seeing me. Heading to San Francisco, where surely it would be easy to get lost in the crowd, frightened me, but it now seemed the best plan. It was a huge city; there had to be plenty of churches there. And there was no more time now to come upon a better idea. I would leave a note for the Calverts saying I was grateful for the home and job for the last year but that I was sad living at the vineyard without my family and was setting out for a new start in Los Angeles, a place to which I had no intention of going.

I put my nightgown back on, and my bathrobe, cinching it loosely over the bump. I grabbed my travel bag from the closet shelf and put in the cigar box with Helen's letters and the money I'd saved, my toiletry things, my mother's necklace, a photograph of my family, a book I loved, and a few items of clothing. The last thing I tucked in was the baking soda tin with the amaryllis bulb inside it. I zipped the bag closed, shoved it under my bed, and waited to hear the sounds of Truman or Celine coming into the kitchen to see about breakfast.

I heard Celine first and was glad it was her and not Truman. Celine was just on the other side of the door, getting the coffee out of the pantry, huffing surely because I should have made it by now. I opened my bedroom door just a little and coughed.

"I'm so sorry," I said in a forced, scratchy voice, and then I coughed again. "I have a bit of a cold, Mrs. Calvert. I'm sure if I just rest today, I'll feel better."

"Oh," Celine said. "Are you running a fever?"

Before I could say I was sure I wasn't, Celine had her hand on my forehead. "You don't feel warm."

I willed Celine not to look down at the little round thing puffing out the fabric of my bathrobe.

"All right. Go back to bed," Celine said. "I'll make you some tea in a little bit. Let me just get Truman on his way."

"I'll be all right. I don't need anything."

"I'll be the one to decide that." Celine turned for the pantry. "Go on. Go back to bed."

I obeyed, closing the door and returning to my bed, to listen and wait.

I waited as the Calverts got their own breakfast. Waited as I heard Truman open the front door to leave for his trip and Celine call after him to make sure he got the good year when he loaded up the Riesling. I waited as he finally drove away, and as Celine brought the promised cup of tea and some toast. Waited for Celine to have a reason to go to town in their other car or to the barrel room. Anywhere.

Finally, a bit before noon, I heard Celine open the back door. I got out of bed and peeked through the curtain. Celine was watering her potted geraniums. When she was done, she crossed the patio to head down the path to the barrel room. Finally.

I shed my nightgown and robe, grabbed the travel bag from under the bed, and shoved them inside. I pulled on a pair of pants but could not button them closed, and I kicked them off, tossing them into the closet and pulling out a skirt. I couldn't zip it closed, either. Tears of frustration burned my eyes. I stepped out of the skirt and tried a cotton dress better suited for summer, but I could button every button. It was a tight fit, and the buttonholes puckered in an unflattering way, but it was going to have to do.

I grabbed a piece of writing paper and scribbled the hasty note that I'd waited to write until I was sure Celine wouldn't hear me moving about in my room. I apologized for not telling them in person and signed my name. Leaving the note on the dresser, I checked the window that looked out on the patio for any sign that Celine was returning to the back door, and then picked up my bag.

I opened my bedroom door, saw that the kitchen was empty, and turned to close the door behind me. The button above my navel popped off, and as I bent to retrieve it, a second button popped off and skittered across the floor.

"No!" I whispered as I chased after it. "No, no, no!"

My fingers had just curled around the second button when Celine walked into the kitchen from the main part of the house. She had returned through the front door.

"What's this? What are you doing?" Celine gaped at me crouched on the floor with a travel bag only a few feet away.

An arrow of dread zipped through me. I couldn't think of any words to answer her.

"Rosie?" Celine said, annoyed now. "What is going on?"

I knew there was nothing to do but stand and hope Celine wouldn't notice the two missing buttons and the widening opening in my dress. Or that if she did, she wouldn't surmise why it was there. Maybe she would think it was just two missing buttons on a dress I had outgrown.

"I need to go." I rose to stand.

"Go? Where do you think—" Celine stopped midsentence, her gaze fixed on the opening in my dress. "Are you . . . ? Have you . . . ?" Her words fell away as she stared.

I reached for the bag on the floor. "I'm sorry, Mrs. Calvert. But I need to go."

I tried to walk past Celine, but she shot out an arm and stopped me. "Good Lord, child. Are you *pregnant*?"

I tried to wrench myself free, but Celine held me fast.

"Please," I begged. "I won't be any trouble to you. I'll go. You won't have to see me again."

"Who did this to you?" Celine's angry tone was also achingly maternal.

"I need to go." My eyes brimmed with scorching tears.

"Was it Sam down at the cottage? Or that new man he hired? Tell me! Did one of the workers force himself on you?"

"No, no, it's nothing like that."

Please, please just let me go, I cried within.

But Celine's grip tightened. "Are you saying you *let* this happen?" Her eyebrows arched in disgust and disbelief. "Are you saying you brought someone into this house, into your room, when I specifically told you not to? Are you running off with this man?"

"I need to go!" I cried out. "Please!"

Celine suddenly let go of me. Clarity, like a veil being lifted, seemed to spread across her face. She was fitting the pieces together: the night she'd stayed in Berkeley with a friend, Truman's unexplainable restlessness of late, my own anxiousness.

"No," she whispered, even as she was done putting all of this together and realizing it fit. "No, no, no . . ."

Then the look of clarity morphed into one of rage. Celine swept an open hand hard and fast across my cheek, nearly knocking me to the floor.

"After all I have done for you!" Celine yelled. "How could you do this?" She hit me again and I fell the rest of the way to the tiles, tasting blood in my mouth.

Celine paced away from me, raising a hand to her forehead as if to rub away fire-hot thoughts too painful to consider.

"I'll go." I half rose to a sitting position, my face stinging. "I can just go. No one needs to know."

Celine wheeled on me, eyes blazing. "No one needs to know what? That you're a slut? A lying whore?"

"I won't tell anyone. I won't tell."

"What? You won't tell anyone *what*?" Celine screamed, daring me to say the words.

"Please just let me go," I pleaded.

Celine knelt down, just inches from my face. "Let you go? So you can spread lies about my family to whoever will listen to you?" She spat the words, and saliva speckled my cheeks.

"I won't tell anyone! I swear!"

"You think I'd be stupid enough to trust you twice?"

"Mrs. Calvert, I—"

"Go to your room."

"Please just let me leave. I promise I'll say nothing."

"*Go!*" Celine screamed.

I got to my feet unsteadily, took a step, and then reached for my bag.

"Leave it," Celine commanded.

"But—"

"I said leave it!"

I turned and walked slowly toward my bedroom. I could feel my lip beginning to swell. As soon as I was inside, Celine grabbed the door handle.

"You open this door and I swear to God I'll break your arm." She slammed the door shut.

I folded myself onto my bed, dazed and aching. Many minutes later I heard Celine talking on the telephone three rooms away. I couldn't make out the muffled words. Celine was speaking relatively calmly, though, definitely not to Truman.

Then I heard a key turn in the lock of my bedroom door. I hadn't even known there was a key for that lock. Some minutes later, Celine was on the patio outside my window. I rose from my bed to peer out. Celine was standing there with my travel bag in one hand, her purse and car keys in the other. One of the vineyard employees, an older man named Horace, stood next to her.

"If she so much as opens that window an inch, you slam it shut," Celine was telling the man. "I don't care if you bring it down on her fingers. She has stolen from me."

I watched as Celine handed the man money. It looked like a lot, surely enough to buy his participation. The man pulled up one of the patio chairs and set it within yards of my window and took a seat. Celine stared at me through the lacy curtain and then walked off, taking my travel bag with her, knowing that I wouldn't go far without it.

From the window, I couldn't see Celine getting into her vehicle, but I heard the engine turn over, heard the tires on the gravel, saw pricks of pale brown.

I returned to my bed, curled up on it, and tried to think where Celine was driving off to. What was she doing? Who was she telling? And how was I going to get away now? How in the world was I going to get away now? After a long while lying there in terror, my troubling thoughts exhausted me into sleep.

When I woke up, it was nearly three o'clock in the afternoon. The house was still quiet. Horace was still seated outside my window, nodding off but not in deep sleep. I was thirsty. I went into my bathroom, turned on the cold-water tap, and drank from my cupped hand. The cool water soothed my swollen lip.

At four o'clock, Celine returned and Horace left.

Half an hour later, Celine opened the door, and I sat up on my bed.

Celine's gaze was like steel, but her voice was calm. "Arrangements have been made for you."

"Please, Mrs. Calvert. You don't have to arrange anything. If you will just give me my bag, I—"

"You'll go where I say."

"Where . . . where am I going?"

Celine regarded me coolly. "Where you belong."

"Please, Mrs. Calvert." I felt new tears spill from my eyes, making the cut on my lip sting.

"Give me your shoes."

"What?"

"Your shoes. Give me your shoes."

"What? Why?" I sputtered.

"Why do you think? Mrs. Grissom will be coming for you the day after tomorrow. I intend to make sure you go with her and nowhere else. You'll get your shoes back then. Now, give them to me."

I sat back down on my bed, removed my shoes, and handed them to Celine.

"I don't care what you do between now and then, but you will not leave this house or touch the telephone or answer the door. And I don't want to see you. Do you understand? If I were you, I'd stay in here except to get something to eat. Because I don't want to see you."

Celine turned and left, closing the door behind her.

Minutes later, Alphonse arrived to make dinner. I heard him ask about me.

"She's not feeling well," Celine said.

15

When I am finally allowed to return to the third floor, the room I share with Belle is empty. I want to go looking for her, but I am told to stay in my bed. I wait until shortly before suppertime, when Belle at last returns to our room, congratulating me heartily on the birth of my baby girl. Only then can I tell her what Dr. Townsend has planned for me in just two days' time.

"We're getting out of here tomorrow, just like I said we would," she says softly, confidently. "You've got nothing to worry about."

"Rudy's keys have to open the door to the nursery, Belle," I continue, my tone as quiet as hers, but not nearly as confident. "I can't leave without Amaryllis."

"Amaryllis? That's her name?" Belle looks at me quizzically, but this is no time to explain anything.

"His keys have to open the door to the nursery!" I whisper insistently.

"They will, they will. His keys open all the doors. He told me."

"And there's sure to be a night nurse in the nursery. You must get my baby without her seeing you."

Belle waves my concern away. "Not to worry, Rosie. I can be as stealthy as a cat. You'll see. I've taken care of everything. Rudy's going to be leaving some clothes in a suitcase for me on the outside, behind a gas station he knows of about a mile from here. We can't be seen in these clothes, you know. And you probably won't fit in anything in that bag of yours."

"Which we have to get."

"I know, I know. And, hey, I won't be able to vouch for the style of the clothes Rudy gets. I have a feeling he's going to be stealing them from the back of his mother's closet. They're going to be dresses even she doesn't wear anymore." Belle laughs lightly.

Far from putting me at ease, Belle's confidence is unnerving. The last time I tried to escape from somewhere, I was sent to this godforsaken place. I want to believe, as she so easily does, that I can have a happy life again. I had one once. It was a simple life. There wasn't much money, and I felt a bit alone, but I had been happy. I hadn't realized this was true until this moment. When I had my family, the vineyard, and my colors, I had been happy. It had been a good life. My family is gone now, and so is the vineyard, but I still have my colors. Surely a new kind of happiness is still within reach.

That night, my sleep is again interrupted by my breasts, which ache, and by dreams of escaping, of holding Amaryllis. Several times I wake with a start when I realize my arms are empty.

On Sunday morning, I lie in my bed as the rising sun slowly replaces the darkness with mellow light. This is the last time I will open my eyes in this room.

I am allowed to go with Belle down to the cafeteria for meals, for which I am grateful. I don't want to while away the entire day in our room waiting for the sun to set, waiting for the midnight hour, waiting for freedom.

Belle is in high spirits, seemingly intoxicated by what will happen tonight. Her cheeks, flushed with excitement, make her more beautiful than ever. I spend the day quietly wishing she would just act like herself. But all throughout the day, whenever I see her, Belle is full of laughs. She has learned Stuart Townsend has been charged with outside security tonight, and she finds this exceedingly convenient.

"Even if he does see us, he'll let us go," Belle murmurs to me just as the dinner chimes ring. "He's in love with me."

"But you can't let him see us!" I reply in an urgent whisper. "He won't!"

Minutes later, Belle and I see Stuart on the first floor as we emerge from the elevator on our way to dinner. It is the beginning of his evening shift. Belle immediately makes a comment about how handsome he looks in his uniform and with that shiny whistle around his neck. The observation makes Stuart blush with obvious infatuation. He walks with us to the cafeteria, and Belle prattles on about how safe she feels with him in charge and I wish she would just shut up. When we get to the cafeteria doors and the queue to go inside, Stuart has no choice but to round the corner and continue on his way, though he seems reluctant to do it.

"Belle, can't you please just leave him alone?" I say softly when he is gone. "Must you lead him on like that? You don't need to."

"For heaven's sake. I'm just having a bit of fun with him," Belle answers, loud enough for anyone to hear—if anyone in the queue with us cares to listen. A couple of residents turn their heads.

"But he thinks you really like him. It's not kind, what you're doing."

"Honestly, Rosie," Belle continues at normal volume, and sounding a bit peeved with me. "He's just a child. Probably doesn't even know what his pecker is for." This Belle says plenty loud enough for others around us to hear. There are gasps and laughs, and I turn to see who else heard Belle. Belle turns, too, and we both see that Stuart has returned from around the corner, and he heard it as well. His face is a mask of humiliation and hurt.

"Oops!" Belle says, and a laugh escapes her. Several other residents laugh, too, but before she can think of a quick explanation for what she said, Stuart turns and hurries out of sight.

"I was only kidding, Stuart!" Belle calls after him.

I feel bad for the boy, but I must dismiss it. I need to concentrate on supper and eating a full plate. Neither I nor Belle knows when or where we will get our next meal. Soon we will be gone, and hopefully Stuart will forget Belle and that he had his heart flattened by her.

The rest of the evening seems to pass at a snail's pace. When it is finally lights-out, I get under the covers to lie awake until Belle says it is time to set our plan in motion. We talked it over during outdoors time that afternoon. When the rest of the room is soundly asleep, we will put our day clothes back on and then wait for the nurse on our ward to go downstairs for her nightly snack of tea and toast, which usually happens around midnight. While I'm not supposed to use the stairs yet, I know I must, as not only will the elevator be noisy, but the night nurse from our ward will be taking it. We will quietly sneak down the stairs to the second floor, where Belle will use Rudy's keys to open the door into the infirmary to get inside the nursery. I will hold the door slightly ajar so that she will not need to use the keys again to open it from within. We do not know how long this part will take because Belle will have to find the nursery, take the hoped-for sleeping baby out of the room, and all without being seen. And then we will head to the first-floor administrative closet, and then the front door and freedom.

When we are finally able to start executing the plan, the first part goes off seamlessly. In mere minutes after leaving our room—after molding our bed pillows and nightgowns into body-shaped mounds under our blankets—I am standing at the door to the infirmary, holding it only slightly open. I pray Hail Marys repeatedly, dreading every second I stand there that I'll soon hear shouts or an alarm sounding. I don't know how long I wait, but finally Belle is at the door with a bundle in her arms—sweet Amaryllis, asleep and wrapped in a blanket. She hands my daughter to me and quietly closes the door behind us so that it clicks nearly silently.

"The old bat is asleep in her chair," Belle whispers with a laugh, speaking of the nursery's night nurse, and the only staff member she saw in the infirmary.

Back to the stairs; we go to the first floor. My stitches are starting to burn, but I ignore the pain. Belle opens the stairwell door slowly and quietly, but there is no one in the hallway or in the dimly lit reception area. Belle has to try several keys to open the door to the administration wing, but once we are in the hallway, the same key opens a closet next to a file room.

"That's it." I point to my travel bag on a middle shelf on the right side of the enclosed space.

Belle grabs the bag and then pulls the closet door shut. We hurry back into the hall and to the front door. Belle chooses a different key to open the lock, and we quietly step out into the night.

Belle runs down the steps and onto the gravel drive, and I struggle to keep up, the burning sensation between my legs now feeling like fire.

"We've got to be quick about this part," Belle whispers over her shoulder urgently.

"I know," I say.

"Let me take Amaryllis." Belle slings the travel bag over her shoulder and reaches for the baby as we continue to run.

"No, I've got her."

A sallow moon is throwing pale light onto the gravel. Ahead are the darkened gatehouse and the two massive oak trees that frame it. No one comes through the gates after lights-out, and Rudy does not have a key to the gate, but he promised to leave it unlatched when he left for the night. As we near it, I hope against hope that he has done so.

We are nearly at the gate when a figure steps out of the shadows cast by one of the oak trees. Belle and I startle to a stop.

Stuart comes into the light spilled by the moon. He looks angry, defiant, and in charge. He also looks a little out of breath, like he ran to the shadow of the tree ahead of us before Belle even opened the front door. He must have seen us creeping down the stairs or entering the infirmary. He had to have seen us in the darkened halls to be here now, standing in front of the only way out of this place. He could've sounded the alarm when he first saw us, but he's waited until Belle and I are just seconds away from our escape.

My heart begins to hammer inside my chest. In my arms, Amaryllis stirs.

"What are you doing here?" Belle says impatiently, clearly not concerned about how Stuart has come to be standing in front of us, blocking our way. But then she quickly softens her tone. "Come now. I know you care for me, Stuart. Let us be on our way. No one needs to know you saw us. You'll be our hero."

Stuart is staring at her as if he wants to be the hero of our story. As if maybe he is considering it, imagining what it might be like to be that man in Belle's life, the man who saved her. But then his look goes stony.

"Why should I do anything nice for you?" He reaches for the whistle hanging around his neck. "After what you did to me?"

Belle takes a step forward. "Don't—"

But Stuart puts the whistle to his lips and blows.

"Damn you!" Belle screams. She grabs me with one hand, throws open the gate with the other, and we dash out past the gatehouse and into the road. Amaryllis is wailing in earnest now.

Behind us, Stuart is blowing into his whistle again and again as he runs back to the building. Over my shoulder, I see lights flooding the first-floor windows.

"Run!" Belle yells.

And I do. I try, but Amaryllis is screaming and Belle is running too fast and the night is dark and the road uneven and I can feel blood trickling down my legs. I stumble, and as I begin to go down, I cocoon my daughter against my chest so that my own head and cheek and shoulder take the brunt of the fall. For a second as I lie at the edge of the roadside ditch, I see only brilliant starlight. I raise myself up as my vision begins to clear, with blood and dirt in my eyes and my screaming baby still in my arms. I see Belle, with my travel bag over her shoulder, a speck in the distance.

Then there is the sound of a vehicle, and then headlights and loud voices.

The blood from inside me is warm on my legs, and the night is cold. And then my world goes black.

16

Before . . .
FEBRUARY 1939

Truman arrived home from his overnight trip to San Leandro in the late afternoon.

I had been instructed that when I heard his car, I was to stay in my bedroom. I was not to be seen or heard if I knew what was good for me.

It was a warm day for late February, and Celine had opened some windows in the house, including the one in the master suite. Perhaps Celine wanted me to hear what she was going to say to her husband, because she didn't close it when, after having seen no one in the front of the house upon his arrival, Truman proceeded to their bedroom. My window was open as well.

Celine wasted no time.

"I have very distressing news about Rosie." Her words were clipped but clear, floating on the air from her window to mine like they were pinned to a connecting ribbon.

"Oh?" Truman said.

"Yes, very distressing," Celine continued icily. "She got herself pregnant."

A slight pause. "What was that?" he said.

"She got herself pregnant, Truman."

"Are . . . are you sure?" He sounded uneasy.

"Oh yes. I'm very sure. It happened sometime in November, I'd say. She's far enough along you can see it." The pitch of Celine's voice had risen several degrees.

"No, that's not . . . not . . ." Truman's voice sounded weak. Airless.

"What? Not possible? Oh, it's possible. It's not only possible, it's true. Rosie is pregnant. Easy enough for it to happen, you know. All a girl has to do is open her legs to a man."

I felt the contents of my stomach churn, and I swallowed back the bile. There was no doubt in my mind that Celine knew. If there had been any question before, it was now crystal clear. Celine knew Truman was the father.

"God, that's . . . disappointing," Truman said.

"Yes. It is disappointing, isn't it?" Celine's voice was mocking, her words wrapped in venomous yellow.

Seconds of silence followed.

"Did she tell you . . . um . . ."

"Did she tell me who the father is? No. She did not. I imagine it's some boy she met in town. Or maybe one of the field hands. Or any number of young men she has probably met up with in town on those so-called bicycle rides to the library. Maybe she herself doesn't know who the father is because there have been so many."

"Celine."

"What? Isn't that what had to have happened, Truman? Isn't it? It had to have been someone she met in town or across the road. Because *you* would never risk all that you have here for a few moments of carnal pleasure, would you? You wouldn't risk this beautiful house and all the money and your nice car and a relationship with your son for a romp with the maid, who, let's just remember for a moment, also happens to be your ward? Can you imagine the consequences for this family if you had in fact risked it all? The charges that could be brought against you? The damage to the family business and my late father's legacy? Why, it's unthinkable. You would never, ever put Wilson and me through something like that. So of course that's what happened. She's been out sleeping around. You've probably seen her coming in late a time or two from a bike ride in town, haven't you? I'm sure I have."

That's not true! I want to scream. *It's not true!* But fear that it could be worse for me if I screamed that there had been only one man—Truman—kept me silent. Several seconds passed. I heard nothing from the room at the end of the hall for a span of seconds. Not a sigh, not an intake of breath, not a creak of a floorboard. Nothing.

Maybe it is the time to tell the truth after all, I thought in that moment. *Not here to Celine. But to Mrs. Grissom.* Mrs. Grissom, who had placed me at the Calverts', thinking I'd be safe.

"What happens now?" Truman finally said.

"Thankfully there are places for girls like her, who've done what she has done. Mrs. Grissom is coming to retrieve her tomorrow."

"And . . . what about the baby?"

"What about the baby, Truman?" Celine said evenly.

"What will happen to it?"

"I don't really give a damn. Do you?"

"Maybe we should find out."

"Maybe you should be careful what you ask about. In fact, I suggest you think very carefully about the steps you decide to take next."

Again, several long seconds of silence hung in the air. Hot

tears slid down my face. The child moved within me, a fluttering of tiny winglike limbs.

Then I heard Truman's footsteps as he walked away from his wife. Something made of glass shattered after being hurled against a master bedroom wall. Bright orange filled my head.

I closed my eyes, but the hue only intensified.

An hour later, when Alphonse should've been driving up, I opened my bedroom door cautiously. I hovered at the doorway waiting for the chef to arrive, but he did not come. Celine had probably canceled him for that evening. Of course she had. Celine and Truman wouldn't be sitting down to dinner together like they would on a normal day. It had not been a normal day. Tomorrow, after I was gone, I supposed they would. They apparently had a charade to keep up.

I decided to make myself a sandwich before either one of them came into the kitchen to see about their own evening meal. I was so hungry I was feeling light-headed. I had just taken out of the refrigerator a paper-wrapped package of sliced ham and a block of Swiss when Truman stepped into the kitchen, startling me.

"We need to talk," he said.

"But . . . Mrs. Calvert." I looked past him to the open kitchen doorway and the rest of the house.

"She's in the barrel room."

"But what if she doesn't stay there? What if she comes back?"

"That's not our biggest problem at the moment." His voice was agitated, strident. Dark red.

"I think she knows," I said softly, embarrassed to say those words.

"Of course she knows!" Truman snapped.

I flinched. Truman had never used that tone of voice with me before, or with anyone else, that I could remember. Even when he and Celine argued, he'd always kept his composure.

"I'm sorry," he added quickly. "God, you can't imagine how sorry I am." He exhaled heavily. "Look, if we're going to get through this, we're going to have to play by her rules. And that means I need for you to do something. I'll make sure you're compensated for it. I'll make sure you have what you need to make a fresh start for yourself. I promise you. But I need something from you."

"What do you mean, compensated?"

"I mean I will give you money. You're going to need it. You know you will. But I can only give it to you if I'm free and able to give it. You understand? I need for you to do something in return. If Celine kicks me out or the county finds out about this, who knows what will happen to me or my family. You can be sure there will be no money for you then. I very much want to make sure you're taken care of, Rosie, and this is the only way I know how to do it. I feel bad about all of this."

All of this? *This?*

"What do you want me to do?" I asked, but I already knew.

"You can't tell anyone it was me. I'm not exactly asking you to lie. I'm just asking you not to tell anyone it was me. It's nobody's business anyway. This is the only way I'll be able to help you make a fresh start somewhere other than here. After the . . . after you're on your own again, you're going to need money."

"Where am I going? Where is Mrs. Grissom taking me?" I said, unable to answer his request.

"I don't know. You're not the first seventeen-year-old to fall pregnant and be unmarried. Celine said the county has access to places that can accommodate you and . . ." He glanced down at my stomach. "And the baby." He winced slightly as the last two words left his mouth.

It had been on the tip of my tongue to tell him then that I was keeping the child, but I bit the words back. I didn't want to share this child with anyone, especially him. And if Celine were to find out I was keeping Truman's child, what would she do? Nothing good.

There was no reason to tell Truman what I was planning to do.

"Please," Truman said hoarsely. "Please let me help us both. Please say you'll do it."

"How will you get the money to me?"

"I have a safety-deposit box at First National Bank in San Jose. I'll give you the key. I've been putting away money for years, money that I thought Celine wouldn't notice was gone so that I could have some resources of my own. I think she knows I have it after all. I think she wants me to offer that money to you in return for not telling anyone it was me. She wants from you what I absolutely need from you. Your silence. You'll be paid well for it."

"How do you know this? How do you know she wants you to do this?" I said, incredulous.

"Because the key for that money was on my dresser just now! I keep it hidden in my cuff-link box in my closet. It was lying right there where I would see it. Who else would have done that? No one."

Truman reached into his pocket and held out a slender silver key. I looked down at it. Such a little thing, and what a promise it was making. I would in fact need the money, and he should be the one to provide it. But I wanted nothing else from Truman Calvert. Ever. He was a sad, pathetic man. If I hadn't been disappointed about Wilson and hadn't drunk the wine, and if the music hadn't cast a spell on me, I might've run from the room when he'd tried to kiss me. Told Celine the next day I wanted Mrs. Grissom to come for me.

"Is it enough?" I asked.

"It's four thousand dollars."

I felt my mouth drop open at such an enormous sum.

"It's all I have," he continued. "I don't know if I can give you more at a later time. I doubt Celine will trust me after this. Please, Rosie. I made a terrible mistake and I'm very sorry. You're going to need the money. I can give you what you need if you give me what I need. When you go to the bank, tell them I've left a note with my signature in the box instructing you be given its contents. It will match the signature they have for me on file. I'll get down there and take care of that as soon as I can. It might take me a month or two. Once you have the money, you will never have to come this way again. You can be done here. Please?" He looked past me, to the kitchen window overlooking the driveway, and then swung his gaze back. "Celine's coming." He picked up my hand and put the key in it. "Please?"

I closed my hand around the key and slipped it into my pocket.

"It's what's best for everyone," he said, relief thick in his voice. "Now, go on back to your room. I'll take care of this."

When the front door clicked open, I was silently shutting my bedroom door behind me and Truman was at the kitchen counter, making himself a ham and cheese sandwich.

I stretched out on my bed in the maid's room, waiting for the next chance to get something to eat without being seen, musing on what I could make of myself with four thousand dollars to assist me. Feather-soft movements beneath the skin and muscle of my abdomen reminded me I would not be alone.

17

I feel as if I'm made of thistledown, drifting high above the weary world. I can hear Momma in heaven calling my name, which means I am dead. My next thought isn't that my life is over so quickly but that my arms are empty and they ought not to be.

Gradually the feeling of lightness begins to fade, and I realize I'm not dead after all. I am waking from a bottomless slumber. The more awake I become, the more I'm aware of pain—everywhere—from deep within but also on the outside of my body. Everything hurts.

I open my eyes slowly. There is a woman standing over me, saying my name. Not my mother, but a nurse in a white dress and starched hat. I am in a bed, not on a cloud. My head hurts, as do my cheek, my hands, my shoulder, the space in between my legs, my stomach. The nurse peers down at me.

"You need to wake up now, Rosie," the nurse is saying. "Time to wake up."

I want to close my eyes and go back to the sky, but I know something is wrong about where I am, something is missing.

Amaryllis. Where is Amaryllis?

"Where's my baby?" I whisper as the nurse's face comes into better focus.

"How about a drink of water?" the nurse says.

"Where is Amaryllis?" My voice sounds as if I have grit in my throat.

"Can you sit up a tiny bit?" the nurse asks, and I see that she is holding a glass of water.

"Where's Amaryllis?" My gaze darts about the room. Amaryllis is nowhere in sight.

"How about if I prop up your pillows and then you can take a drink? You'll feel better after you've had some sips of water." The nurse sets the glass down on a bedside table.

As I allow the nurse to bend me into a semi-sitting position, a burst of heat spreads across my abdomen. I reach down instinctively to put out the flame and the nurse gently bats my hand away.

"Now, you don't want to be pulling at the bandages," the nurse says. "Nor do you want to sit up too fast and tear the stitches on your tummy."

Alarm shoots through my sore body. "What stitches?" I push back the covers.

"Careful, there. It's just three little incisions," the nurse says calmly. "Nothing to fret about."

With shaking hands I pull up the hospital gown someone has put on me and I look down at my stomach, at the three bandages: one over my navel, one on the lower left side of my tummy, and one on the right.

"What have you done?" I groan, wanting to yell the question, but it feels like there is no air in the room to draw across my vocal cords. None.

"It was a simple procedure, dear. You'll be feeling like yourself in no time."

"What have you done to me?" I look up at the nurse, but I know what they have done. They cut into me. Changed me. Sterilized me. Just like they had done to Charlotte. To the childlike young woman in the bed across from me. To who knows how many others here.

"Why in the world don't they tell you people ahead of time what's going to happen?" the nurse mutters in an exasperated tone. "How about that sip of water?" She reaches for the glass.

"Where is my baby? Where is Amaryllis?" I swing my legs over the side of the bed and attempt to stand. I have to get out of here. Pain sends me back to the mattress.

"You need to calm down," the nurse scolds, pulling the covers back over me.

I sweep them off again. "Where's my baby?"

The nurse takes out a hypodermic from her pocket. "If you don't stop thrashing about, I'm going to have to give you something to make you stop, and it will just slow down your recovery time. Do you understand?"

But I keep screaming for my child. Another nurse comes into the room.

"Hold her down," says the first nurse. Arms are across my body, pushing me back to the mattress, and then there is the burn of a needle, and then nothing.

When I wake the second time, it is not to the imagined voice of my mother but to the voice of Dr. Townsend, standing at the foot of my bed, saying my name. I do not feel weightless this time; I feel like I am made of iron—a statue. It's as if I have been turned to stone. I realize my arms and legs are tied to the bed.

"I would like to have a conversation with you," Dr. Townsend says, "about what you did and what's been done to you, but we can't have that conversation unless you are in control of yourself. Do you understand what I'm saying?"

"Where is Amaryllis?" My voice sounds mushy in my ears.

"She's back in the nursery where she belongs. You could've done that child great harm doing what you did. You're lucky she's all right."

Tears burn my eyes, and I can't rub them away. "I would never do anything to hurt her."

"But that's exactly what you did. Are you ready to talk, Rosie? We have matters to discuss."

"Where is Belle?"

"Belle is not your concern. Are we going to be able to have that conversation or not?"

I nod.

"Your foolish attempt to escape could have cost you your life. The stairs, the running, all of it caused you to start bleeding. You also could have easily dislocated your shoulder, and you have a sizable contusion on your head and a fractured cheekbone. But that's not the worst of it. You could've killed the baby with the fall you took."

"I protected her," I whisper through my tears.

"You endangered her life."

A sob escapes me, and he goes on.

"I told you Belle was a bad influence and you did not listen to me. We shall be careful hereafter who you room with."

I swallow back another sob. "Where is Belle? Did she get away?"

"Belle shall be found. Your concern should be on what's going to happen next with you."

"You cut into me."

"You had a simple procedure from which you will quickly recover."

"You cut me open! You cut something out of me! I know you did. And now I'll never have another baby! How could you do that to me?" Fresh tears course down my cheeks, and Dr. Townsend seems to soften.

"Listen to me, Rosie," he says. "I've been a doctor for a long time. I have seen what happens to people like you who are burdened and who burden others with an inherited abnormality. It is inhumane for you to likewise force that abnormality onto another person."

"My . . . abnormality?"

"What happens to you with auditory stimulation is an aberration. It's abnormal. It is nothing you should wish to inflict on another person."

"But they're just colors! Seeing them isn't some terrible thing!"

"Look at where you are and all that has befallen you and tell me again it's not a terrible thing. The wires in your brain are crossed, Rosie. They are mixed up. If you were any kind of suitable mother, you would realize that you should not pass on this disability to a child. A good person would not do that."

Sobs wrack my body as I ponder that maybe he is right.

"Does Amaryllis have it?" I ask through my tears. "Did I give it to her?"

"No one will know for several years if you have saddled her with it. I hope she has been spared. I really do."

I am quiet for a moment as my sobs subside. "Is that why you do this here? Why you cut people open like this?"

"I'm assuming you think it is unfair," he says, "but it is the fairest thing we can do for you and for the rest of the human race. It is selfish and cruel for people like you to bring into the world children who will suffer what you have suffered. It's a simple thing to keep it from happening. You'll come to thank me in the end."

Only people like you make me suffer because of it, I want to say. But I don't. He has my child.

"Then just let me take Amaryllis and go. I can't have any more children. You've seen to that. Just let me and my child go. Please?"

The doctor sighs. "We've already talked about this. You know I won't do that."

"Please!" I beg. "Please just let me and Amaryllis go."

"And where exactly would you go, Rosie?" he says matter-of-factly, the gentleness in his voice from a moment ago gone. "Your parents are dead and you have no other family. You are a minor who does not have a home or a job or a high school diploma. You have nothing. You have been placed under the state's care, as has your child. She will be taken to a facility licensed by the state to be adopted by a good family who can give her what you cannot. You would be thinking of her right now if you were a good mother."

His words slice into me like a knife. Cold and sharp and deep. His words are true. I can give nothing to Amaryllis. Nothing but love, and in this world, love isn't enough.

"Please let me say good-bye to her," I say, barely able to form the words.

"No. It would only make it harder for you, which would make it harder for the staff. No."

"Please!" I plead. "Please!"

But he turns and starts to walk away.

I am screaming Amaryllis's name—over and over—as he leaves the room, and I am still screaming it when the nurse comes in moments later with the needle.

When I awake the third time, it is morning again—another day has begun, just like it always does. Dawn is relentless. Even on my worst days, the sun never fails to rise. My family is gone, the Calverts are gone, the vineyards are gone, Belle is gone, and Amaryllis is gone. The little silver key is gone. I have no one and nothing except the colors and each new day.

As I lie in the bed hearing the sounds of the institution coming to life, I know that my parents were right to fear the colors. They are dangerous. A dim memory of my father praying at my bedside when I was little comes to me. He pleaded with heaven for a miraculous favor. For the colors to leave his daughter. He was afraid for me. People will always distrust what they don't understand. And what they distrust, they cannot love.

My father didn't get what he asked for, but nor had he promised anything in return. I would do better than he had. I would offer something I loved more than life itself in return for my request.

I close my eyes. "I have failed everyone," I whisper. "I know I have, but, God in heaven, in your great mercy, I ask for this one thing. I will give up my child to be someone else's daughter if you will promise not to give the colors to her. Please don't give them to her. Let this sacrifice of mine pay for what I've done and what I've failed to do. Please. I give my Amaryllis to you if you will do this one thing for me. This one thing."

I pray this request again as a nurse comes into the room and releases me from the straps.

I pray it as I eat the soup and bread they bring to me.

I pray it for the five days I am in the infirmary recovering from my injuries and my surgery.

Dr. Townsend comes to see me on the sixth day, and he seems surprised and pleased to see me sitting up in bed, without the restraints, and eating my lunch.

"I'm so very glad to see how much you have improved since I last saw you," he says.

"Yes," I reply with little inflection. "I'm feeling better."

He is watching me carefully. I can see the doubt in his eyes.

"I have made my peace with what you did to me." My voice sounds older, like I have aged twenty years in the days between the attempt to escape and now.

"I think that's wise. Very wise," Dr. Townsend says. "Dr. Melson says you can return to the third floor if you like. To a different room, though."

"All right." I shrug. I don't care about getting off the second floor; I don't care that I'll be in a different room on the third floor. I only care about my one prayer being answered.

"Perhaps you'd like to be wheeled out onto the lawn for some sunshine and fresh air."

"All right."

He gazes at me for several long moments before telling me he'll arrange for an orderly to take me down. I don't care that he stares in doubt at me. I only care about the prayer and the bargain I have struck.

After lunch, an orderly is dispatched to bring me down in the elevator in a wheelchair to the back lawn. Women loll about in the generous summer sun, some in little groups talking to one another, but most are sitting alone or standing alone. I do not see Belle.

"Is here okay?" the orderly asks as he wheels me under the shade of a sycamore.

"It's fine," I say. "Thank you."

He leaves, and I look out over the grass, past the people, to the horizon beyond the fence. As I do, I whisper the memorized prayer. I am still saying it when someone crosses in front of me and stops.

It is Stuart.

"I'm sorry about what happened." The boy looks and sounds tense with remorse. "About what I did."

I stare at him a moment. "I suppose you were only doing your job."

"Still," he says. "I'm sorry. I should've held Belle back and let you go. I was just . . . mad at her. I was so mad at her I wasn't thinking. I should've let you go."

"I don't know," I say dully. "Maybe it's for the best. Your father doesn't think I'd be a very good mother. He's probably right."

We are quiet for a moment.

"They're taking her today," Stuart says a moment later. "Your baby. They're taking her to some orphanage. I can find out which one if you want."

I close my eyes a second to steel myself from reneging on my pact with the Almighty. We have an agreement as far as I'm concerned. I mean to keep my end.

"Thank you, but no, Stuart," I say, eyes open again. "My daughter needs a home with a mother and a father who will care for her and provide for her. She deserves that."

Stuart is quiet again. He seems disappointed, as though his finding out the name of the orphanage and passing on the information to me would have relieved him of some of his regret.

"Would you do something instead for me?" I ask him.

Stuart says nothing and waits.

"Would you make sure everyone knows my daughter's name is Amaryllis? Will you make sure it's written on the papers that they send with her? Her name is Amaryllis."

"Ama . . . ?" The word is foreign to him.

"Amaryllis." I spell it for him. "It's the name of a flower. A very beautiful one."

"I'll make sure." He turns and leaves me.

That night, when I go to bed in a different room in a different hall, I can feel that Amaryllis is gone from the nursery, gone from my life.

Tears slide down my face and into my mouth as I lie in bed— next to a new girl—and whisper the prayer.

When two weeks have passed and I have recovered sufficiently from my injuries and surgery, I begin working in the kitchen again and I return to morning classes. I spend my days doing what is asked of me and reading whatever I can get my hands on in the library, and my nights in my bed reminding God in heaven of our agreement. I wonder about Belle, where she is, and if she ever gives me a thought. I wonder if she has used the little silver key for herself and taken the money in Truman Calvert's safety-deposit box. I didn't tell her the name of the bank in San Jose, but has Belle been able to find out which one it is? Was it always her plan to take the travel bag and leave me stranded without it? I don't want to believe that could be true. In my darker moments, when I miss Amaryllis the most, my thoughts tell me that Belle has betrayed me. But in the morning, I tell myself that surely she has not.

Dr. Townsend is no longer interested in "curing" me. Since he has been unable to eliminate the colors, the therapy sessions no longer consist of sound makers and electrodes but detailed questions and experiments about my other senses—what I taste on my tongue when I pat a dog or what I smell when I see a photograph of a clock. He seems disappointed that the colors are the only tangling of the connections in my brain, but he keeps at it, writing down every one of my answers even if the response to a given stimulus is no response at all. We also begin to have conversations about my readiness to reenter the world as a responsible adult who keeps her bizarre colors from being a burden on society—his words. It is a condition of my future release that I be able to hold down a job, live independently, and stay out of trouble.

"You're not going to just be shown the door when you are deemed ready to live outside these walls," he says to me one morning just before my eighteenth birthday. "You will be discharged under the state's care into a situation where your progress will be monitored both at the licensed home where you will reside until your twenty-first birthday and at a place of employment that shall be arranged for you. I will decide when you are ready to make that transition to life outside, whether it's this year or the year to come or the year after that. Once you have proven yourself fully capable of living your adult life without making foolish and harmful decisions, you will be released from custodial care, ideally on your twenty-first birthday. But that depends on you. Everything you do the next three years matters, Rosie. Be smart with your choices. Don't do anything to spoil it."

Three more years. Three.

His words are too much to contemplate. The heaviness of them has a color all its own, a shade of purple so dark it is nearly black. I leave the therapy room for my shift in the kitchen weighed down by those words and their dense hue.

The thought of possibly three more years in this place has sapped all strength from me, and it's with immense effort that I put in my work hours in the kitchen for lunch. I decide I'll head up to my room after the meal and lie down. I don't care who frowns on me for it. When the serving line is finished and I start to dish up my own plate, the nurse who brings the residents' mail during the lunch hour comes to the serving window.

"You've got a package, Rosie," she says, handing me a small cardboard box with my name on it and no return address. It is the first time I have received anything in the mail, and the nurse who gives me the package studies me as she hands it over. The package, postmarked from Santa Barbara, has already been opened.

I look up at the nurse as I take it.

"We have to check incoming mail and packages," she says. "It's the rules."

I lift the top of the small box. Inside is a tissue-wrapped bundle no bigger than a few saltine crackers stacked atop each other. Underneath it, there is a note on a folded piece of paper. I open it and read, *Happy Birthday, Rosie! Hope you don't mind I smoked the cigars. See you around . . .*

I unfold the tissue paper and see that it isn't ordinary tissue paper that the bundle has been wrapped in but a letter on onionskin paper. It's Helen Calvert's Christmas letter with the instructions on how to care for the amaryllis. I see her words to me and the words she penned to her brother, Truman.

I am right where I want to be.

Snuggled in the folds of Helen's letter is my mother's cloisonné pendant and the little silver key resting on the same chain. I clutch the necklace to my chest as tears prick at my eyes. Belle hasn't forgotten me, nor has she taken what Truman left for me. Belle wouldn't have sent the key if she had. I don't care that the savings I had in the cigar box aren't in the package, too. Belle needed that cash to stay free, to get to Santa Barbara. It is enough just to have my mother's necklace and Truman's key.

"We've a pretty good idea who that's from, you know," the nurse says.

I have nothing to say in response. It's been three months since Belle escaped and there has been no word from her or about her. I am glad she can easily pass for someone over the age of twenty-one.

"Belle's mother is concerned about her," the nurse continues. "She shouldn't be out on her own like this with no one to help her. She was getting good care here."

"Was she really?" I say with only the slightest challenge in my voice.

"Yes. She was."

"I don't know where she is."

The nurse exhales with a frown and shakes her head. "You should let me keep that necklace locked up for you in the administration wing. It looks expensive."

I fit the clasp at the back of my neck and let the pendant and key slide on the chain down my throat to rest beneath the top button of my dress. "No, thank you. I'll not be taking it off."

"Suit yourself, Rosie. If it gets stolen, you can't fault the hospital."

"I'll not be taking it off," I say as I put Helen's letter into my pocket.

The nurse shrugs and walks away with her little cart and her emptied mail basket.

I am not interested in eating anymore, and I do not want to head to my room, not now that I have the key and my mother's necklace and Helen's letter. I can see my future again, for the first time in too many weeks. A promise of a new life still awaits.

I go to the door that leads to the back lawn, even though an early autumn chill has settled over the yard.

As I step outside, I breathe in the cool air, drawing it into my lungs and relishing the tang of its wild taste. Air can't be fenced or kept back or held in. It goes wherever it wants.

Air is free.

Someday I will be, too, though not soon enough. There doesn't seem to be any way of getting to San Jose before my twenty-first birthday unless my next placement is with someone who will allow me some freedom. But that is not likely. I was caught trying to escape the state's care. Freedom of movement is likely not something I'll be trusted with again. Still, Truman Calvert has to know where I was taken. Has to know I still have his key and his secret. Celine and Truman both have to know I will not be stuck like this forever. Have to know the smartest thing Truman can do is leave that four thousand dollars in the safety-deposit box untouched. That money is mine. He paid for my silence with it. It is mine.

I now have five things that belong to me. The sun every morning, the cloisonné pendant, the silver key, Helen Calvert's letter on how to care for an amaryllis, and the bargain I made.

Six things, actually.

I still have the colors.

18

I measure the long, bleak months between my eighteenth and nineteenth birthdays with little victories that most likely go unnoticed by everyone around me.

In February, I mark without despair the second anniversary of the accident that robbed me of my family, and in June, I survive the day of Amaryllis's first birthday with only two short episodes of weeping, both of which I am able to hide from the staff. In August, I pass a proficiency exam that allows me to receive a modified diploma from the local school district.

There has never been another letter from Belle. No one mentions her name anymore. It's almost as if she was never here. I'm thinking if she was caught, even if she was sent somewhere else, Dr. Townsend would tell me, if only to assure me that what he predicted—that she'd be found—did indeed happen. I miss her, but I'm glad she is still free, still in possession of everything inside her body that belongs to her and no one else. I want to believe she has found someone who truly loves her for who she is and not just her stunningly beautiful body. I want it so much I start to think it's true.

As summer begins to wind down, there is finally talk of releasing me to a group home in the coming weeks, provided I continue with my progress. Continuing to progress is Dr. Townsend's way of saying I must remain resolutely compliant—as in, no more escape attempts—and exhibit no highly charged emotional outbursts or bouts of melancholy, as well as zero resistance in my therapy sessions.

I manage these expectations, all while overhearing from time to time the nursing and kitchen staff speak in quiet tones about the ongoing war in Europe and whether or not the United States will get involved. I have learned from these hushed conversations that Germany has already invaded Poland, France, Holland, and five other countries. I've heard that Jewish men, women, and children in those countries are being persecuted in the most inhumane of ways. I've even heard the cook and the grocery deliveryman talking one day about the thousands of children who have been transported out of countries where the persecution is the worst, sent away on ships—without their parents—to England.

"Those little ones are veritable orphans," the cook said. "They don't know when or if they will see their parents again. Nobody knows."

The deliveryman replied that these *Kindertransports*, as the newspaper called them, would stop because England is now at war with Germany. The last group of children left by ship from a Dutch port in May, one day before Holland surrendered to the Germans. There will be no more transports of children across the North Sea to England.

"Any child still in Europe will have to live through the hell of war, just like their parents will," the deliveryman said.

"If they can," the cook replied.

I saw ribbons of pastel yellow and gray when the cook and the deliveryman were talking about those children, pulled from their parents' arms and taken to a foreign land where they knew no one or even the language spoken there. I ached for those children. I ached for Amaryllis. I ached to feel my own mother's arms around me.

On the day of my nineteenth birthday, a Saturday, Mrs. Crockett comes to my room just after breakfast and tells me Dr. Townsend has a surprise for me and wants to see me in his office. She also has a button-down dress on a hanger over her arm. Red polka dots on a field of yellow cotton.

"The dress is a birthday gift from Mrs. Grissom. Isn't it pretty?"

"Mrs. Grissom?" I haven't heard the woman's name mentioned since the day I arrived at the institution. Not a single time.

Mrs. Crockett cocks her head. "You remember her, don't you?"

"Of course I remember her. She brought me here. I haven't seen her since."

"Oh. We've seen her, dear. Every four or five months, she stops by to talk to Dr. Townsend and get an update."

"Why doesn't she ever talk to me?"

Mrs. Crockett smiles. "She doesn't need to, Rosie. We fill her in on your progress. We're all pleased with how you've come along. Very pleased. Go ahead and put on the new dress. I think you'll be glad you did. And then I'll take you down. As I said, Dr. Townsend has a nice surprise for you."

I step out of the plain blue day dress that all the female patients wear and slip on the new one. It smells like it has just come from the store. The fragrance is one I haven't experienced in such a long time. The buttons feel slick in my fingers.

"Shall we go, then?" Mrs. Crockett says brightly when I am finished.

I follow the matron out of my room, out of the C wing, and down the stairs to the first floor. Mrs. Crockett uses her key to open the door to the administration wing, and we step inside.

The last time I was in that hallway, it was the middle of the night, Amaryllis was in my arms, and Belle was opening a closet door to fetch my travel bag.

We walk down the hall toward Dr. Townsend's office. As we pass the records room, I catch a glimpse of Stuart inside it. I only see Dr. Townsend's son on occasion now that he is involved in sports at school and practicing every day after class. We have not spoken much to each other in the year that Amaryllis has been gone. In truth, I think Stuart has avoided me the last fifteen months, perhaps because regret over what happened on the night of the attempted escape still haunts him. He must still wish he'd allowed me and my baby to flee. I'm not sure I still wish that anymore. I have protected Amaryllis the only way I could with the bargain I made. Wishing to have her back isn't part of the deal. Stuart glances at me as I pass him, and he raises a hand in greeting.

We arrive at Dr. Townsend's office. He is seated behind his desk. Little about his office has changed.

"Please." Dr. Townsend motions to the same chair I sat in so many months ago. Mrs. Crockett takes the same chair she sat in that first day, too.

"It seems you are to be leaving us today," the doctor continues. "The state has decided you are fit to be released back into the county's care. Mrs. Grissom is coming to take you to your new home." His words are bronze-colored, vibrant and pulsing.

Several seconds slip by as I struggle to grasp what he is saying, even though I've been hoping for this day for weeks upon weeks.

"I'm being discharged?" I finally say.

"Back into the county's care," Dr. Townsend says in a corrective tone. "You're still a minor, still an orphan, still without a home or means of income. Mrs. Grissom will be taking you to a group home, where you will want to continue your progress in all the ways we have been working on here."

"What is a group home?"

The way Dr. Townsend says the word *home* doesn't sound like a home at all.

"It's a special place licensed by the county where girls like yourself who are not yet able to be on their own can reach their majority while learning the life skills they will need to live as responsible adults. A job has been found for you where you can continue to gain work experience."

"What kind of job?"

"Working in a hotel. I don't have the details. You will have to ask Mrs. Grissom about it. My task in this moment is to remind you of how far you've come and how important it is for you not to revert to the troublesome behaviors that brought you here. You do remember what those behaviors were, don't you?"

"I remember everything about what brought me here."

Dr. Townsend regards me for a moment. "Good. Well then." He stands and extends his hand for me to shake.

I realize as I stand and clasp it that this is the first time he has touched me in any kind of way that might be considered kind or thoughtful.

"I wish you the very best, Rosie," he says. "But I also wish I could have done more for you."

"You've done plenty."

I wonder as those words fly off my lips if he knows what I mean by them. I guess by the quick arching of his brows that he does.

Mrs. Crockett stands and smiles nervously. "Right. Normally at this point I'd be returning to you the belongings you arrived here with, but we no longer have your bag, as you well know. Your discharge papers have already been given to Mrs. Grissom. So. I can take you back upstairs to get your toothbrush, hair comb, and anything else in your nightstand, and to say good-bye to your roommates if you would like?"

I drop Dr. Townsend's hand but keep his gaze. "No. I don't need to do that."

"All right," she says. "Let's go out to the reception area, then, and wait for Mrs. Grissom."

"Good-bye, Rosie," Dr. Townsend says calmly, as though there wasn't a moment of tension between us just seconds before.

"Good-bye." I turn and walk away from the doctor. I don't look into the rooms we pass. I can hear my soft-soled shoes slapping on the linoleum like flippers on a fish, and I realize I despise these shoes. I hate that sound. Hate the blueish-gray rods they conjure. Mrs. Crockett and I exit the administration wing and the door behind us clicks shut. She leads me to one of the couches in the reception area and we sit. An uneasy silence falls between us.

"It isn't right what you're doing here," I say softly, feeling safe enough to say it now.

"What did you say?" Mrs. Crockett says in a tone that suggests she heard me perfectly.

"You shouldn't have cut into me. You shouldn't have cut into that girl Charlotte or my other roommates as if we are less human than you. You shouldn't have done that."

Mrs. Crockett sits up straighter; the skin on her forehead instantly puckers in consternation. She opens her mouth, but I speak again before she can say anything.

"I know you're probably going to say what do I know about what is best for people, but I had to say this before I left. I had to say it, and you had to hear it."

For a moment, Mrs. Crockett appears too stunned to speak. Before she finds her voice, the phone at the reception desk rings, and both of us turn to the sound.

"All right," the nurse says into the handset. "I'll let her know." She hangs up and lifts her gaze from the telephone to Mrs. Crockett. "Mrs. Grissom is driving up."

I stand.

Mrs. Crockett rises to her feet, too. "Indeed you don't know what is best for people, Rosie," she says.

"And you think you do? You think Dr. Townsend does? Or Dr. Melson, who sliced into me and took out what God put there?"

"As a matter of fact, yes. We do."

"But why do you get to decide what is best, Mrs. Crockett? Why do you get to decide what the best looks like? Why do you get to decide *that*?"

The woman doesn't have a ready answer. I walk to the door and wait for Mrs. Crockett to approach with her key ring. When the matron has slipped her key into the lock, I open the door myself. I turn to Mrs. Crockett as I step across the threshold.

"I will have to live with what was done to me here," I say to her. "But so will you, Mrs. Crockett. All of you will."

I don't wait for a response but take the steps quickly to where a familiar car is now pulling up.

As soon as Mrs. Grissom's vehicle comes to a stop, I open the passenger-side door.

"My goodness!" Mrs. Grissom, who looks exactly the same as last I saw her, laughs lightly as I get into the car. "Hello to you, too. I take it you're in a hurry to be done with this place."

I will never be done with this place, I think, but say instead as I pull the car door shut, "You would be, too."

Mrs. Grissom waves to Mrs. Crockett, standing just outside the door on the first step. I don't turn to do the same.

"Come on, now," Mrs. Grissom says as she eases away from the institution and heads down the gravel. "Was it really so terrible?"

I turn to her. "You do know what they did to me, don't you? What they do to other people in there?"

Mrs. Grissom nods to the gatehouse attendant as we pass through. "Look. The decisions regarding your care at the institution weren't up to me."

"How can you say they weren't up to you?" I shoot back as we turn onto the main road. "You brought me to that place. And you abandoned me there."

"I didn't abandon you there. That place was where I had been instructed to bring you. It was believed by everyone who looked at your case file that it was the place where you needed to be assessed so that you could get the help you required. The fact that you were an orphaned minor and pregnant and unable to name the father—"

"I never said I was unable to name the father."

"All right. Unwilling to name the father, plus those hallucinations of yours—"

"They're not hallucinations. I just see colors in my head when I hear sounds. It's that simple. They're not hallucinations."

Mrs. Grissom shakes her head as if in annoyance. "That's certainly not what anyone else sees when they hear sounds, I can tell you that. And, Rosie, you had better be just letting off a little steam right now, because we're all taking a risk by letting you out of that place. I was told you were ready for this. Ready to be out. You want to go back to the institution, then by all means keep this up. I doubt they have filled your bed already."

I shut my mouth and turn to face the road ahead. My heart is pounding not only in irritation but also in panic that Mrs. Grissom might turn the car around. "I do not want to go back."

"I'm relieved to hear that. Please tell me you're ready for this next step. That you're ready to be out."

I swallow the knot of fear bobbing at the back of my throat. "I am."

"Then you need to stop it with this talk of visions of colors. You understand? You need to stop it. I don't want you talking about them at the group home and I don't want you talking about them at the new job, you understand? You talk like that and it sounds like you're delusional. I don't care how harmless this all seems to you. It's actually pretty weird to everybody else, so just stop it."

We are quiet for a moment. I feel two hot tears escape my bottom eyelids and start to slip down my cheeks. I swipe them away.

Mrs. Grissom casts a glance at me and then exhales heavily. A gentleness returns to her voice when she speaks again. "I am sorry about what they did to you there. I am. They felt it was necessary, and I am not a doctor. It was their decision to make and they made it. I can see that you're upset and angry about it, but Rosie, your life is not over because of this. You can still have a happy life."

"I can't have children now. And the only one I did have was taken from me."

"Let's not pretend you were ready to be a mother when that baby was born. And I understand you are sad that you can't have more children. But you can still have a full life. Some people can't have children or don't marry, so they never have the chance. My husband and I wanted kids; we never had any. But that doesn't mean we haven't been happy."

"But your husband married you thinking you could have children. No one's going to want me. Not now."

"You don't know that. Sometimes you have to go relentlessly looking for your happiness, Rosie. You might have to be more intentional than most. I know a lot of terrible things have happened to you, but one day when you are fully on your own, you will be able to start making more of your own decisions. Today is the first step toward that. Do you understand what I'm trying to tell you?"

I hesitate only a moment before saying yes.

"Now, if you're done being angry about the past, I would like to spend the next few minutes here in the car talking about the future. Your future. And I don't mean the future way off in the distance. I mean tomorrow and the next day and the next day. Can we talk about that?"

"Yes."

"Good. We're headed to Petaluma. It's down the road another half hour or so. There's a group home there licensed by Sonoma County that will be your home until your twenty-first birthday unless you do something to mess that up. The woman who runs the place is Mrs. Clark. She's a bit like a mother and a bit like a parole officer and a bit like a landlord. You will be expected to comply with her expectations. I mean it, Rosie. You need to do what she says. The world is full of rules, honestly it is. For all of us. So you're going to have to learn to live by them. You cannot attempt an escape of any kind, do you understand?"

Mrs. Grissom waits until I say yes, I do.

"Your every movement will be monitored, and if all goes well with Mrs. Clark and the group home and at your new job—it's in the kitchen of a very nice hotel—then on your twenty-first birthday you will be fully released from the county's and state's supervision. You can start making all your own decisions then. If at that point you want to tell people you see strange colors that no one else sees, I won't be able to stop you, but I am telling you that no good will come to you if you keep going on about them. All right?"

I know how to keep the colors a secret. Mrs. Grissom is acting as if I haven't any idea how or why I need to. I know exactly why I need to.

"Yes," I say.

"Great. I'll be checking in with you and Mrs. Clark from time to time, and I am expecting to hear only glowing reports. Glowing. Now, first I'm taking you to lunch and then we'll do a little shopping, since you have practically nothing and it is, after all, your birthday. Plus, those shoes you're wearing are hideous."

A limp grin tugs at the corners of my mouth. I want to say, *You should see what they sound like*, but I don't think Mrs. Grissom will find it funny.

Instead, I thank her for the new dress.

19

Mrs. Clark is a former high school social studies teacher, mother to two grown sons, and the widow of a retired mailman who died too soon. When she found herself single and without purpose at fifty-two, she moved from Oakland back to her family home in Petaluma, which she had inherited the year before her husband's passing. She applied to have her six-bedroom house made into a licensed group home so that she could have meaning again to her days, and easily met the requirements.

"I ran a tight ship with my boys, and I run a tight ship here at this group home," she tells me as we meet in her living room. "But it's a ship where everyone aboard can feel safe. I don't care about any mistakes you might have made or that were made against you, and I don't count those mistakes as defining who you are. I know life can be unfair. I know things can happen to you that you don't deserve. I also know there might be decisions you made in the past that you'd like to undo and can't. But here in this house, we look to tomorrow, not yesterday. Does that sound like something you can agree to?"

I nod. I think I'm going to like Mrs. Clark. I like her wide smile, and her queenly bearing despite the simple clothes she's wearing. I like how she doesn't want to peel back any layers from my earlier life as the orphaned daughter of a vinedresser or the Calverts' irresponsible ward or the young woman who got locked up in an institution where they sterilize flawed people.

"That's all I want, Mrs. Clark," I say. "I want to move forward. I'm never going back to where I was or who I was."

The woman smiles. "Then I think we will get along just fine, you and me."

Mrs. Grissom, seated next to me on the sofa, stands up. "I'll be off and let you settle in, Rosie. I'll stop by in a couple weeks to see how you're coming along." She turns to Mrs. Clark. "And you're all set with getting her to the job on Monday?"

"As soon as the other girls are off for school, we'll be off, too. It's only a short walk. I'll make sure she gets there on time."

The two women go to the front door. As Mrs. Grissom steps over the threshold, she turns and looks past Mrs. Clark to me. She gives me a nod that probably means, *You be good, now.*

Mrs. Clark closes the door and retraces her steps to where I sit surrounded by several shopping bags. Mrs. Grissom bought me new underwear and socks, pajamas, a sweater, two pairs of slacks, three button-down shirts, two more dresses, and a few toiletry items. The new shoes she bought are already on my feet.

Mrs. Clark retakes her chair opposite me. "Is there anything you'd like me to know now that it's just you and me?"

Surely Mrs. Grissom has told this woman how I wound up in the custody of the state: the death of my parents, the indiscretions that left me pregnant at seventeen, and maybe even the hallucinations I claim to have and which the state hospital addressed through more than a year of therapy sessions. I like Mrs. Clark, but I do not yet trust her. I shake my head.

"Do you have any questions about the rules of the house, then?" Mrs. Clark has already told me about her expectations for her residents. Everyone pitches in with the chores and kitchen duty. Each girl does her own laundry. There is to be no fighting, no male callers, no vandalism to the property, no sneaking out at night, no alcohol in the house, and no travel—not even on foot— to anywhere except to work and home again. Shopping trips and excursions to the library or the park or the river will be group events scheduled by Mrs. Clark.

"Are there ever any day trips?" I ask. "Like to San Francisco. Or . . . or other cities?"

"You have reasons to go to the city?" Mrs. Clark's tone is tinged with suspicion.

"No. Just wondering."

Mrs. Clark regards me for a moment. "We don't take day trips like that. If we go anywhere together, it's close by."

I can't recall how far away San Jose is from Petaluma. Seventy miles? Eighty? A hundred? It doesn't really matter. It's surely an impossible distance. I will have to wait—quite possibly two years—to see if Truman's money is still waiting for me.

"Okay," I say, as if Mrs. Clark's answer is of no consequence at all.

"Well, let's head upstairs with your things and get you settled in," she says. "And then I'll take you into the common room to meet the other girls. They're waiting for us."

Mrs. Clark picks up two of the shopping bags and I grab the third. I follow her to the ample staircase to the right of the living room. The bags make crinkling noises—blue and white—as they rub against each other. I am embarrassed by the sound.

"I suppose this is the first time a girl has arrived here with her things in paper bags," I say.

"On the contrary," Mrs. Clark replies easily. "Some girls arrive here with nothing at all."

We continue on to the third floor, and Mrs. Clark leads me to the room farthest from the stairs but which appears to be the largest room on this level.

"You're my oldest right now, and I typically reserve this room for girls who are finished with school. It's a nice room. It was actually mine when I was your age."

The room runs the width of the third floor but has slanted ceilings on either side, so it is both a large room and cozy and close, too. There is a bed with a quilted coverlet, a dresser, a writing desk and chair, and a gloriously full bookcase with some titles that I can see at a glance. *Heidi. Little Women. Captains Courageous.* A braided rug lies on the floor, and paisley curtains hang on the dormer windows.

"There isn't a full bath on the third floor, just a commode and small sink at the end of the hall, but there is a large bathroom on the second floor and it's right by the stairs. There's another full bath on the first floor. I had it put in. It's off the kitchen. I leave it to you girls to work out how you'll take turns with the two tubs. So far, there's only been one tussle over it."

I look at her. A fight over the tub? "Really?"

Mrs. Clark smiles. "Those two aren't here anymore. They just liked to spar. They fought about everything. I think that was the only way those two girls knew how to express how afraid they were of all the things in life they could not control."

I nod toward the bookcase. "Is it okay if I take those books out and read them?"

Her smile widens. "Absolutely. You like to read?"

"I do."

"So do I. I have others downstairs when you're finished with the ones in here. Come. Let's hang up your new clothes."

It does not take long to put away my few things.

"Let me show you the rest of the house, and then we'll go into the common room and you can meet everyone," Mrs. Clark says.

"I'm surprised the girls have been so quiet. It's been a while since we've had someone new join us."

As we pass the other two bedrooms on the third floor, I see now that one is clearly being used—a pair of loafers is askew at the closet door, a sweater hangs on a bedpost—and one looks as if no one is occupying it.

We return to the first floor, go through the living room and dining room, with its large table for ten, and Mrs. Clark points out her bedroom, a former breakfast room, and then we head down a short flight of stairs to an addition to the back of the house where there is a sitting room with sofas and bookcases and a game table. A console radio is softly playing a Billie Holiday tune. Spirals of goldenrod flit about my peripheral vision as I take in the sight of the four girls in the room who are my new house-mates.

One sits on a couch, legs tucked under, reading a magazine. Another is at the game table playing checkers with a third. A fourth, the youngest it seems, pigtailed and freckled, is standing just inside the room with a poorly decorated, lopsided cake on a plate.

"Happy birthday!" the youngest girl says. "I made you a cake."

"This is Vera," Mrs. Clark says to me. "She's thirteen and likes to bake."

Vera bursts into a smile that crinkles her eyes to slits. "It's chocolate."

"Um. Thanks," I say.

"And over on the couch is Lillian; she's sixteen. She's in the room next to yours. Cora and Maxine at the table there are fifteen. They share the second floor with Vera. Girls, this is Rosie Maras."

The other girls seem cautious at my entrance into the room—and their lives—but they settle around the game table as Mrs. Clark cuts the cake and then eat slices of it willingly enough. As we eat, I learn Vera was abandoned by her unmarried mother at the age of ten—she'd simply awakened one morning to an empty bungalow. She happily sits by me as we eat. I get the impression the girl is hungry for affection. Starved for it.

The others—Lillian, Cora, Maxine—seem hardened, though, like the outside of an orange that has sat too long in the heat of a harsh sun. Lillian tried to stab her stepfather—in self-defense, she says—and her mother doesn't want her in the house anymore. Cora, who was orphaned at twelve, ran away from her aunt and uncle for the last time, and they were done with her. And Maxine helped her brother rob a jewelry store. He is twenty-three and in prison. She is here.

None of them have been with Mrs. Clark longer than a year. All of them lived in some other county home before this one.

They ask about me. And I tell them only that my parents are dead and that I took something from my last county placement that didn't belong to me. Maxine especially wants to know more, but I say nothing else.

I have nothing in common with these girls except our shared predicament; we are under the county's thumb and have been sent to live with a woman who is not family. Nothing good brought these girls to Mrs. Clark's doorstep.

That is probably something we have in common, too.

I resolve to mind my own business, hide the colors from everyone, obey Mrs. Clark's rules, and quietly count off the twenty-four months. I don't know yet what I want to do with myself and Truman's four thousand dollars, but I know I want to create a life that will allow me to say, as Helen Calvert said, that I am right where I want to be.

A life that will allow me to buy amaryllis bulbs to my heart's content—the only "children" I will ever have. And I will have them. Windowsills full of them.

A life where the colors are my well-kept secret.

A life that is good.

My job at the Hotel Pacifica, an elegant multistory building with ballrooms and fancy paintings on the walls and thick carpets on the floors, is located six blocks away from the group home. Mrs. Clark walks with me that first Monday morning and reminds me that I am expected back home immediately after my shift ends at four. I can tell by the way Mrs. Clark smiles at me as she drops me off that this is my first test, and that if I'm smart, I'll pass it easily.

I'm greeted at the back door to the kitchen by an older woman in a gray dress and white apron. Mrs. Delaney is the supervisor of the kitchen and laundry staff.

The Pacifica's gleaming kitchen is outfitted with long metal prep tables and rows of hanging pots and pans, three large ovens, and a walk-in refrigerator. If the other workers in the kitchen know from where I've come, they do not let on. Perhaps it is only Mrs. Delaney and the manager of the Pacifica, a Mr. Brohm, who know that my employment here was arranged and is subsidized by the state.

The head chef, Tony, is from New York and insists everyone do everything exactly as he instructs, down to the smallest detail. He reminds me of Alphonse and I quickly sweep away that memory when it surfaces. I don't want to think about Celine's chef or her kitchen or anything pertaining to her at all.

I settle in quickly to my new role as a kitchen assistant and someone who does little more than wash dishes and pans all day long and put them away. In time, though, I am given more responsibility, especially as my willingness to be useful is appreciated more and more. I find I can lose myself to the sights and sounds and colors of the kitchen in much the same way I did when I was a child among the vines. The kitchen is a place where ideas are hatched and beautiful things come together. I like being able—finally—to finish Tony's beautiful dishes with bits of fresh flowers or greenery. I am reminded that there was a time when I thought I might take cooking classes and then find a nice job in a fancy restaurant. That dream again appeals to me.

When I have been at Mrs. Clark's for a little over a month and am fairly certain she likes and trusts me, I ask her if I might be allowed to make a phone call to the family with whom I first lived after my parents and brother were killed.

"You mean the Calverts," Mrs. Clark says.

"Yes," I continue. "I want to let them know where I am now. I grew up on their vineyard." I hope I sound a little nostalgic. What I really want is to talk to Truman and assure him that I am coming for my money someday soon and that it needs to be there when I do come for it.

"I suppose that would be fine," Mrs. Clark says.

When I ask her if I can make the call in private, she studies me. "All right," she says a few seconds later.

It's a Saturday afternoon, and I'm counting on Truman being in the tasting room, hopefully alone. Mrs. Clark nods toward the telephone in the living room and tells me to mind the time, as it is long distance to Santa Rosa. I assure her I won't be long.

But when the tasting room telephone is answered, it's not Truman who answers; it is Celine.

I hang up.

"They weren't at home," I say when I come back into the kitchen, where Mrs. Clark is.

"You can try again tomorrow if you want," she says, and I do. But the next time, the phone rings and rings and no one answers. I try again on the following Friday, and again Celine answers, and again I hang up without saying anything. I'm finally successful the next day. Truman answers, and I hear in the background the chatter of other voices. He's not alone.

"Truman," I say. "It's Rosie."

I hear the intake of breath. The whisper of God's name on his lips. He is surprised to hear from me.

"I can't talk right now," he says, both softly and forcefully.

"I don't want you to talk, Truman. I want you to listen. I'm out of that terrible place Celine sent me to, and yes, it was unbelievably terrible. I'm coming for the money you promised me. It might be a while before I can come for it, but when I do, it needs to be there. If it takes a year or two years, it needs to be there. I need to hear you say you promise it will be. That's all you need to say."

"I haven't touched it. It's all there," he whispers. "And it wasn't me who sent you to wherever it was you went. I didn't know. I didn't—"

"Wherever it *was*?" I interject, scarcely able to believe he has no idea what I went through after I last saw him. "Did you not even ask where I'd been taken? Did you not even wonder?"

Truman hesitates. In the background, I hear laughter and then a woman's voice. Celine's, perhaps.

"It wasn't up to me to—," he whispers, but again I cut him off. I don't want to hear him excuse away the last two years of my life.

"I'm counting on you to keep your promise," I say.

"The money is there," he says.

"Good-bye, Truman."

I lower the receiver to the telephone base. I place it carefully in its cradle, hoping that while Truman Calvert is a coward, he is also a man of his word.

As my twentieth birthday approaches in the fall of 1941, I am still the oldest in the house. I feel like a much older sister to young siblings who don't think I have anything worthwhile to say. I don't care that the other girls don't seem interested in my companionship. I have made it through the first year at the group home. I am doing well; Mrs. Grissom and Mrs. Clark have said so on several occasions. Only one more year to go. Sometimes I think of Belle, and I hope that she is all right, that she is still free. Sometimes I think of Amaryllis and I try to picture what she looks like. I still say the prayer from time to time. I have kept my part of the agreement.

I am decorating miniature cakes with tiny poinsettias made of icing when the news flies through the hotel in December that a naval harbor in faraway Hawaii has been bombed by the Japanese. The hotel staff are all saying that the United States will now likely enter the war that has already been raging across much of the world.

The mood in the kitchen is somber and fearful: So many sailors died in Hawaii; so many more American servicemen are likely to die in the days and months ahead. I don't know what it means to be at war. As days and weeks pass, it seems like all the young male waitstaff have enlisted, and by the first of the year they are gone.

The early months of 1942 are filled with restrictions that seem opposed to my slowly approaching freedom. In the spring, Mrs. Clark is issued ration stamps to buy everything from meat, sugar, and butter to clothing and fuel oil. The hotel is suddenly under the same constraints. Everyone is.

"You'll likely be entering a world fraught with problems," Mrs. Clark tells me in September. Mrs. Grissom had been by earlier that day and said everything is in place for me to be released from the county's custody on my twenty-first birthday.

"But I'm used to problems," I say with a slight smile. The two of us are in the kitchen washing up cups and plates from a before-bed snack of saltines and milk. The other girls have all gone to their rooms.

Mrs. Clark smiles, too. "That you are."

We are quiet for a moment.

"Any thoughts of what you'll do?" she asks.

Tony the chef and the hotel manager both want me to stay on as a regular employee. Mrs. Grissom found a room available to rent not too far from the hotel if I am interested. The older couple who have the room already expressed interest in welcoming me as their tenant. If I want to stay in Petaluma, I can.

I have to admit, I do like working at the hotel. I am learning so much from Tony. He has noticed my interest and has started teaching me recipes and techniques he learned in culinary school.

But there is something I need to do before I decide.

Go to San Jose and get my money.

Perhaps when I have it I'll come back to Petaluma and get my own place. Or maybe I'll finally feel like I have the means to strike out for somewhere totally new. Mr. Brohm has already said he will write a good letter of recommendation if I decide to move on.

Both options seem good. One is safe; one is a bit risky.

I don't know yet which one I will choose.

"I'm not sure yet," I answer honestly.

"I'll miss you, Rosanne. I will," Mrs. Clark says as she places a plate on the drainboard. "I hope you do stay in Petaluma so that you can come visit from time to time. You've been the easiest girl ever to care for. You certainly must know by now that I'm fond of you."

I do know. And I am grateful to have had Mrs. Clark as a stand-in parent for the last two years. Mrs. Clark isn't like Celine or Mrs. Grissom or Mrs. Crockett. She is in charge like they were and as unflinching in her expectations of me, but she is sympathetic and kind in a way those other women weren't. Of all these women, she has been the most like my own mother and, in a way, most like my father, too. I have felt safe with her. Cared for by her. I matter to her. Mrs. Clark has been interested from the get-go in how I am feeling, not just how I am progressing. There was even a moment during those long months when I was tempted to fully confide in Mrs. Clark about the debilitating loss of my parents, what happened at the Calverts', what happened at the institution, and the overarching dilemma of the colors. But then I asked myself: When had honesty about the colors ever helped me? Never. So I said nothing. Even now as I smile at Mrs. Clark, I say only that I am very fond of her, too.

On the day of my birthday, Mrs. Grissom arrives during breakfast with my release papers in hand. She, too, wants to know if I've decided what I'll do next.

"I think I'm just going to take a little break from everything," I answer. We are all gathered in the common room for doughnuts as my send-off. "And then I'll decide."

I have already asked Mr. Brohm if I might have a week off to sort things out, and he has agreed.

"Well," Mrs. Grissom says. "That sweet couple is going to keep the room open for you through the month because I've told them what a responsible person you are, but they're going to need an answer soon, Rosie."

"And I will have one for them, I promise."

For my birthday, Mrs. Grissom gives me a new suitcase with a shiny brass handle, and Mrs. Clark gives me a pretty blue tweed suit, as fashionable as can be found in the middle of wartime shortages. The girls of the house have chipped in and bought me a used wristwatch. They sing to me and wish me well. I am almost sad as I gather my things.

I leave well before noon on a Greyhound bound for San Jose.

20

The bus south to San Jose makes so many stops, it takes three hours to complete the ninety-mile trip, but I use the time to prepare myself to enter the bank and ask for what is mine. When we at last arrive, I use money I saved from working at the hotel to take a taxi to the First National Bank. I am glad for the new tweed suit, glad I decided to put it on before leaving Petaluma. I feel like I look responsible and mature as I walk into the bank and head to the area where the safety-deposit boxes are located. I took off the little silver key from the necklace while still on the bus and placed it in my pocketbook.

But Truman did not discuss with me how to open the box, other than to mention the note with his signature inside it, and now I realize as I am approaching the clerk who sits at a desk in front of the open vault that I don't know how one initiates that. Truman must have thought I would know. I clear my throat and the man looks up and smiles at me.

"May I help you?"

"Yes," I say, feigning confidence. "I'd like to open a safety-deposit box, please. I have the key."

"Certainly." He holds out his hand, palm up. "And the name?"

I look at his outstretched palm, unsure. Am I supposed to hand over the key to him? Just like that? I don't want it out of my sight for a second. Having it is the only proof I've got that the money is mine.

"Your key?"

I swallow the little knob of anxiousness at the back of my throat. "I would like to open the box myself."

The man blinks several times as if needing a moment to find the right words. "Of course, but I must see the number on your key so that I can get its companion."

I hold the key out so that he can look at it. I have studied it often enough to know that engraved on the key is the number 104. The man looks at the number and then gazes up at me, studying my face for a second. I fight not to look away.

"And the name on the account?" he says again, still studying me.

"The name on the account is Truman Calvert. There is a note inside the box with his signature, instructing that I take out what's inside it."

The man gapes at me as if I said the account belongs to Mickey Mouse.

"Mr. Calvert knows I have this key." My voice sounds somehow both assured and nervous at the same time. "He gave me this key. When I open it, I can show you his signature."

"I am guessing you have not been in contact with Mr. Calvert in a while?" the man says, his polite demeanor from seconds earlier starting to weaken a bit.

"What difference does that make?"

The man motions to the chair in front of his desk. "Perhaps you'd like to have a seat."

"No, thank you," I say as calmly as I can. "I just want to open the box as Mr. Calvert instructed me to. I have the key."

"And when were you instructed to open this box, Miss . . . ?"

"Maras. My name is Rosanne Maras." I don't care if he now knows my name or shares my name with anyone. I am done protecting Truman Calvert. "And I don't see what difference it makes, as Mr. Calvert specifically asked me to open the box."

"It matters," the man says, all pretense of politeness gone, "because Mr. Calvert is dead."

Seconds tick by as I struggle to grasp these words. "What do you mean he is dead? How? When?" My mind is a thunderstorm of color.

"Mr. Calvert was killed in an army training accident. His account at this bank was closed. The box has been emptied."

"What do you mean he was killed in a training accident? That doesn't make any sense." The sound of his words makes the whole room seem as if it is spinning with trembling shapes of sallow yellow and brown.

"Are you an employee of the Calverts or a distant family member?" the clerk asks, his brows puckered in consternation.

"No."

"Then what relation are you, Miss Maras?"

"I . . . I find that question . . . rude," I stammer, unable to think of a more refined word. I can feel the hopes I had earlier that morning evaporating as if made of morning mist.

"This is a bank, Miss Maras. Our customers expect us to be careful with the assets they entrust to us."

"I'm . . . I'm just a friend."

"Well, I regret to tell you then that Mr. Calvert reenlisted in the army and was killed in an unfortunate training accident in March."

"But he . . . Who . . . who came for the contents of the box?"

The clerk exhales a breath and levels his gaze at me. "His *wife*. Mrs. Calvert came for the contents of the box." There is no mistaking the accusing tone. This man surely can't conceive of a single good reason why I have this key. Only bad ones. "If that will be all, Miss Maras?" he says.

He again holds out his hand for the key.

Burning tears of embarrassment and frustration are rimming my eyes, but I rein them in as I give it to him.

"Yes. Good day." I turn and walk briskly out, head high, but as soon as I am on the sidewalk I allow the building tears to slip out. For a few seconds as I walk away from the bank, I imagine getting back on a bus and heading north to Rosseau Vineyard to demand from Celine my payment. But just as quickly I realize there is no longer a secret to be kept, is there? There is no pregnant maid. There is no baby. There is no Truman. He's dead. Truman is dead.

Celine would laugh—probably chase me off the property without a penny—if I went there. And if I threatened to tell anyone, who would believe someone who spent twenty-one months in a mental institution and who is now claiming to have borne a child fathered by a respected man who had just given his life for his country? No one.

As I walk aimlessly down streets I don't know, I realize with a jolt that I don't want anything from Celine anyway. Nor from Truman. Three and a half years ago, that money was the only way I could see to make a fresh start. But now I am seeing things differently. I have forged my way in pain and suffering and without any favors from the Calverts. I have my new life in my grasp. It is beginning today, and I will leave San Jose with no remnants at all of the life I knew before. I will make my own way now, the Calverts be damned.

I return two days later to Petaluma, and I tell Mr. Brohm I would like to keep my job. Then I contact the couple, the Newtons, who offered me a room to rent. We arrange to meet the next day.

This couple's only daughter lives on the East Coast with their son-in-law and two grandchildren. The Newtons want very much to have a young person living in the house with them, as they see their own family too infrequently. They see me as a perfect fit for them.

My new room on the Newtons' second floor includes its own bathroom and is decorated in a calming shade of cornflower blue.

I find that I very much like living with the Newtons. They are cheerful with each other and with me, and they never fail to ask me about my day. Within days of my moving in, they begin inviting me in the evenings to play board games with them or listen to their favorite radio programs or the news of the war. I can tell the Newtons enjoy my company, too.

My newfound freedom is nearly intoxicating. To be able to go to the library whenever I want or the cinema or a department store or to stroll through the park unsupervised is almost too wonderful. Experiencing such a profound sense of liberation seems so odd when the whole world is at war. But I find that I like coming home to a place where I will be missed if I were to suddenly not show up. I have the independence I have been hungering for, but I am not alone in it. The Newtons care about me.

The only echo of my old, shackled life that I allow myself to hold on to is the lingering ache of losing Amaryllis. It is a pain that I both hate and love because it reminds me that I *am* someone's mother, despite not knowing where my child is, and despite what was done to me. Remembering her hurts like no other pain I have ever experienced, but the thought of forcing myself to forget her is impossible. I won't. I can't.

Just before the holidays, I am promoted to managing the dining room service, a position that gives me more responsibility and better pay. I'm sad to be leaving the kitchen, but the money will be helpful for when I do decide to move on. My new uniform is not unlike the black dress Celine made me wear. But this one is tailored to my figure and trimmed in expensive white lace. When

I wear it, I do not feel like the girl who was seduced by an unhappy married man.

As the months progress, I start to ponder how much longer I want to stay in Petaluma. I have made a few friends at the hotel, though I keep to myself so much that most of my coworkers no doubt assume I'm shy around other people. I enjoy my responsibilities in the dining room and the money I'm making, but I can't see past each unfolding day. I have a new life, but I still don't know what to do with it. What does a person like me do with a life? The colors are an ever-present reminder that I am different from everybody else. My altered body—the fact that I can never give anyone children—reminds me of that, too. I always thought I'd be married by now, and I still want that kind of companionship for my life. I want what my parents had. But will I ever meet a man who will want someone who can't give him a baby?

One evening a few weeks before my twenty-second birthday, and while I am preparing the dining room for a small assembly of scientists who have gathered for a conference, I pass by one of the ballrooms where they are meeting. I hear a man speaking at the microphone about a sensory anomaly. He is explaining to his colleagues that it is a neurological condition in which a stimulus to one of the senses—hearing, for example—triggers an automatic and instantaneous response in another sense, such as vision. He calls it *synesthesia*.

I am at once glued to where I stand.

"Synesthetes might hear a bell and see a color or experience a taste on their tongue," the man says. "Their minds might assign colors to names and places and numbers. The senses for someone with synesthesia overlap, sometimes in more ways than one."

I am frozen as I listen, forgetting I am supposed to be readying the dining room for when this group breaks for dinner. I hurry away, my thoughts tumbling. My ability to see the colors has a name? It has a *name*? An explanation?

And other people see the colors, too?

I hover in the dining room when the meeting adjourns and the conferees begin drifting in to be seated. I linger as if obsessively interested in making sure everyone has what they need at their table. I watch for the man who was speaking to enter the room. When he does and is seated, I don't take my eyes off his table. I must speak to him. I simply must. I sprint to refill his water glass after he has taken only two sips. He looks to be a few years older than me, maybe early thirties. Dark brown hair, even darker brown eyes.

The man thanks me, and when I see that the other people at his table are engaged in conversation, I say quietly, "I was listening to you speak just now, from the doorway, and I heard you talk about that condition called sin . . . sin . . ."

"Synesthesia," he finishes for me, smiling.

"Yes. How do you . . . I mean, how . . . ?" I don't know which words to use to form my questions. I have so many. "How do you know about it?" I finally ask.

His smile broadens. "I've been studying it for a while."

"And so . . . so there are many other people that have it?"

"Other people?"

When I say nothing in return, he adds, "You experience this, miss?"

I nod slowly, achingly aware that I am doing what I have vowed never to do again. Confide in someone about the colors. "I didn't know it had a name. I didn't know other people saw the colors, too."

He leans forward in interest. "What is it that you experience, if you don't mind my asking?"

I can feel my pulse quickening its pace, in both apprehension and expectation. "When I hear sounds, I see colors and shapes,"

I say quietly. "In my mind. It's like they are there but not there. I have always seen them. I've tried to stop them, but I can't. No one has been able to understand it. And I . . . I have suffered."

He regards me for moment, his interest shifting to compassion.

"I am so very sorry to hear that." The man's words are so gently spoken that I nearly fall to my knees in gratitude that at last, at last, I seem to be understood.

"No one has ever been able to tell me why," I say.

"It's a condition we are only just now starting to understand."

Unbidden tears begin to rim my eyes, and my gaze flits about the room to see if any of the other hotel staff are observing me speaking to one of the guests while holding back tears.

He notices and pauses a moment before continuing. "I would really like to talk with you about your experiences, Miss . . ."

I sense in this moment, this very stretch of seconds, that now is when my new life is truly beginning. In this room, with this man telling me what no one has been able to tell me before. My new existence didn't begin when Mrs. Grissom handed me the release papers or when I left the bank in San Jose with nothing. It is beginning now. Right now.

I am Rosie no longer. That girl is gone. In her place is the woman who has been shaped from that pitiful child. The woman whose second life is beginning today.

I am not Rosanne, either. A new start calls for a new name, pulled from the crucible of my old one.

"Maras," I say. "Anne Maras."

"Miss Maras. I'm Dr. Robert Drummond. Would it be all right if we spoke further? I think I may be able to help you."

"I . . . I would like that."

"What time do you get off this evening?" he asks.

"Nine thirty."

"Would you care to meet then at that diner across the street? I'm leaving early tomorrow morning, but I think I can help you understand what is happening to you if we can talk for a short while tonight."

I look at this young scientist and see not curiosity or judgment or fear or ridicule. It is something else in his facial expression, something that I have never seen with anyone to whom I mentioned the colors. Not even with Truman. It looks like respect.

"I'll be there," I say.

When my shift ends, I can barely contain my eagerness to make my way to the diner. I take a table near the door and wait. When ten minutes have passed and the doctor hasn't appeared, I begin to worry that he has forgotten. Finally, at ten to ten, he sweeps into the diner, apologizing as he takes a seat across from me.

"I'm so very sorry," he says. "I needed to talk to my sons in Los Angeles and the call went longer than I expected. They needed to talk, and I let them, I'm afraid. Please forgive me."

"Of course," I say.

A server brings him a cup of coffee, and as he takes a sip, I notice he is not wearing a wedding ring.

"How old are your sons?" I ask.

"Seven and five. And yes, I know it's a bit late for them to be up, but they're missing their mother. Especially with me being out of town tonight. It's harder for them when I'm away. My wife . . . passed last year," he says, as if needing to explain how he could've kept me waiting so long.

"I'm so sorry for your loss," I say, genuinely sad for him. I know too well the weight of grief.

"Thank you. It's been a rough road, but we're getting through bit by bit. Some days are harder than others. In the end, though, Molly wanted us to be happy again, and we're slowly figuring that out."

He is quiet for a moment, and then he shakes his head. "I apologize. I did not mean to come here and talk about myself. I really just wanted to let you know that what you experience with sounds and color is explainable. I can explain it. It's nothing terrible."

He says those words so easily that for a second I can't respond. "What I experience with sounds and color has made my life a hell on earth, Dr. Drummond," I finally say.

The doctor pauses before responding, just like I had. "I can't tell you how sad I am to hear that, Miss Maras. Please let me be the first to tell you it doesn't have to be that way anymore. I promise you, it does not."

His voice is so calm and sure and warm. I see petals of holiday red as he speaks, as stunning as that flowering bit of heaven Helen Calvert gave me all those years ago. I was pregnant with Amaryllis that Christmas and didn't know it. I wasn't aware that deep within my body, buried and hidden, life was being created.

My darling girl. My only child. Gone from my arms but still residing within me somehow. I think I understand now that a person doesn't stop being a mother just because her child is taken from her. Amaryllis will always be my daughter. I will always be her mother.

"Miss Maras?" Dr. Drummond says. "Are you all right?"

The bright crimson blossom of the doctor's voice fills my mind's eye as if his words are illuminating a path out of a great chasm. I am crawling out of the shadows that held me, out of the earthen darkness that is a bulb's world until it breaks through.

I am right where I want to be.

And my Amaryllis is right here with me.

"I am," I say, nearly tasting dirt on my tongue. "And please. Call me Anne."

PART TWO
HELEN

21

I watch from the window as people hug one another good-bye on the platform, and I wonder for the hundredth time if I am making a mistake. When I arrived in Europe forty years ago, I thought I'd stay until my dying breath, yet here I am about to begin the journey back to California, for good. By choice.

I remind myself—also for the hundredth time—that the last few years haven't been at all like I thought they'd be. They broke my heart more cruelly than any man ever had. All the places I treasured—London, Paris, even Vienna—they've been shattered. The Europe I fell in love with as a young woman is a different place now.

I am different.

For many months, I wanted to believe I'm just like the devastated world, which has begun with great courage to rebuild itself, but I know now that I'm not. I still feel the ashes of war falling on my head.

"There is no shame in recognizing you are exhausted and in

need of rest," Sister Gertrude said when I confessed to my closest friend in Lucerne that my tattered soul was so weary. So very weary.

"I don't want to leave, and yet what else can I do?" I was sitting with her a month earlier, after finally revisiting Vienna and returning with a heavier heart than before I'd gone.

"If you're being tugged home," the nun said, "I doubt you'll find the peace you're aching for until you go."

"I'll be leaving in defeat," I replied softly.

She leaned forward, sought my gaze. "I don't think that's entirely true. But even if you are, there is also no shame in going home to rest after having lost a hard battle. I should think that would be the first thing a person would do."

When the war finally ended, I assumed the sting of my losses—and my failures—would lessen, just as the bombings had ceased and the Nazis had been stopped and the killing had ended.

How shortsighted I was, looking at newspaper stories of demolished buildings being cleared away, the debris being swept up and buried, and thinking the same was surely happening inside me. I should've known better. The human heart isn't made of stone and wood and brick like the ruins of Europe are.

The human heart is nothing at all like that.

My late brother, Truman, told me once that war changes a person, whether you put on a uniform or not, but especially if you do. If you are standing on the battlefield, he said, the reason you are there, ready to kill or be killed, permeates your being. It seeps into your very bones and it stays. It becomes part of you.

But watching the violence as a horrified spectator becomes part of you, too.

The train whistle blows now, and we begin to chuff past the station and away from what was my city of refuge. I turn from the window, not wanting to watch Lucerne pass from my sight. The first leg of my journey—the commute to Zurich—will take an hour. Then there will be a taxi to the airport, then a flight across the Atlantic—my first—to New York, and finally a transcontinental train to California.

"Why aren't you flying to California, too?" one of my students asked at my farewell party. I didn't want to confess to the eleven-year-old boy, a lover of all things aeronautical even though he's never been on an airplane, that I was already dreading the flight to New York. I wasn't going to subject myself to that fear twice.

"I like the train," I told him. "I haven't seen America in a long time. It will be nice to see it again. That way."

"But . . . ," he said in a polite tone that nevertheless suggested I hadn't thought this through. "You could see it from the sky. You've never seen it that way. And you'd be home in hours instead of days."

And then he guessed without my saying it that it was already proving too much for me to believe that a winged cylinder full of people could soar birdlike across the ocean, let alone the whole of the United States.

"The DC-4 is a good airplane, Fraulein Calvert," he said. "I can show you a picture of one in my aviation book."

The model number of the plane meant nothing to me. And I really hadn't wanted to see a photo of it; all I cared about was wrangling the courage to board one. Just the one. But I glanced at his book with half-closed eyes and then tried to forget what I saw. As the days for my departure neared, I wondered if I was simply too old to do something so innovative as air travel.

I don't feel old at sixty-two. I'm trim and I've always treated my body with care and respect. For the nearly forty years I've been a nanny and then lately a teacher, I've felt full of energy, eager to guide and protect my young charges, ready to help them seize the most from every day and prepare for a meaningful life beyond their childhood years. But my dear Truman had been right about what war can do. It changes everything. It changes you. It changes how you look at the world, how you look at yourself.

Sister Gertrude was also right, I tell myself, as in my peripheral vision the city disappears and countryside begins to fly past.

I am tired and ready to go home.

What a strange concept home is, though. I'm headed to the vineyard, a place that has never been my address. When I wrote Celine and asked if I might come home for the holidays while I figure out my next steps, she said yes, without so much as a hint of correction that her home had never been mine. And yet the vineyard—strangely so—feels like the only home I have now. Celine and Wilson are my only family.

Even after five years, I still have trouble accepting the fact that Truman is gone. I still think of things I want to tell him, or I'll sip a cocktail and think to myself, *Truman would like this*. When the news of his death reached me, I wasn't prepared to be the last of my immediate family. Our father had already passed, dying of a heart attack the same day the Japanese bombed Pearl Harbor. Then, four months later, Truman was killed in that horrible accident. I have no one now, really, having never married or had children of my own. Celine and my nephew, Wilson, are all I have left.

I know I don't want to stay with Celine indefinitely, though I am yearning to walk her peaceful acreage and to bask in its beauty. There is so much I want to forget, so much I want to forgive myself for, if that is possible. I'm trusting that the vineyard—blessedly untouched by the hell of war—will provide the solace I need to come to terms at last with what happened in Vienna. For I know I must.

My old college friend Lila Petrakis and her husband, George, have invited me to stay with them in San Francisco after the holidays while I figure out what is next for me. The idea appeals to me. Lila and I have kept in touch by letter all throughout the years. I didn't complete my teacher's certificate like Lila did, but she and I have stayed good friends. George and Lila even visited me years ago in Paris, when they sailed to France for their twentieth wedding anniversary. In my darkest hours during the war—and after it—I missed having a friend like Lila to lean on more than any other deprivation.

In what seems like only a handful of minutes, the train is pulling to a stop at the Zurich station. I trimmed my belongings such that everything I own now fits into two suitcases and an overnight bag for taking onto the plane. A porter helps me take my luggage to the taxi rank.

I look out the window as the driver maneuvers the streets of Zurich, and gazing at the busy people and the zipping cyclists and the mothers pushing young ones in prams momentarily eases my nervousness about the impending flight.

I need help checking my luggage through and finding my gate, but there are seasoned travelers at every turn who lend a hand or offer a word of advice. When it is time to board, I follow the other passengers outside to the brilliantly shining airplane; it looks just like the picture my student showed me.

I take steadying breaths as I step aboard, find my seat, buckle myself in. I close my eyes and count to two hundred as the rest of the passengers board and the engines began to roar and the propellers to spin. I grip the armrests tight as the plane gathers speed on the runway like a locomotive and then leaves the ground and begins to climb into the sky. I slowly open my eyes to peer out the oval window next to me. The sight of the city below takes my breath away. How small Zurich looks. How tiny the automobiles and buildings are. How big the generous sky stretches! Like a never-ending and translucent sea where no evil and dark things swim.

So this is what it is like, I muse to myself, *to soar far, far beyond where you used to be.*

22

I arrive at the Santa Rosa train station more than a week after leaving Switzerland and to weather that is balmy compared to what I left behind. A happy sun is shining in the bold California sky, and the temperature hovers at sixty-five pleasant degrees.

I wrote to Celine earlier not to worry about coming to get me, that I would just get a taxi for the six-mile jaunt to the vineyard.

As the taxi pulls away from the station, I can't keep my gaze from the window. It has been seventeen years since I set foot on the land of my childhood. So much has happened since then.

Truman and I were raised in Sebastopol, a sleepy little farming town seven miles west of Santa Rosa where our father once owned a hardware store. My wanderlust grew out of wanting to escape country life but also out of nighttime cuddles with my mother before she died. It was my mother who told me about faraway places that she longed to visit someday. She was the one who wanted to see London and Paris and Cairo and Rome. When she was taken from us by a blood disease no one understood, I grieved for her by assuming all of her dreams. I didn't know at the time that she never actually thought she would go to those places, that she knew my father was far too practical a man to indulge in fantasies like that when there would never be the money to indulge in them. When I turned eighteen and all my friends went off to either secretarial or nursing school or teachers' college—or to chapels to get married—my father insisted I make my choice. The world will always need teachers and nurses and secretaries, he said, and since I didn't have any marriage proposals, those were my only choices. I didn't want to be a nurse and I hated the idea of sitting at a typewriter all day long, so to college I went to become a teacher. I enjoyed being around children, had always enjoyed it, but the truth was, I didn't want to be a classroom teacher, either. It took three years of college and nearly finishing my teaching certificate before I figured out I didn't have to become what someone else had chosen for me.

I got my first nanny job in San Francisco working for a British family with twin boys. When they returned home to London eighteen months later, they took me with them, as they'd promised they would when they'd interviewed me. My father was still barely speaking to me then, he was so angry about my leaving college to "wipe the noses of other people's children," and when I came home to say good-bye to Truman, Pops left the room.

"I can't watch you make this mistake," he grumbled on his way past me.

I couldn't wait to get away. And then I loved Europe so much, it was easy to stay.

But even though I longed for city life and all the places my mother had dreamed of, and even though I wanted to get as far away from Pops's disappointment as I could, I still loved Sonoma County—the acres and acres of plum and apple trees and vineyards and rolling hills and the tall pepper trees and scrub oak and sycamores. As the taxi drives me out to Celine's, I am so happy to see the landscape is the same. When I arrive at the Rosseau

Vineyard, it's as if nothing has changed here, either. The trees are taller and there is a different car in the driveway, but the grapevines are the same, and so is the stuccoed house with its red-tile roof and terra-cotta pots of hardy geraniums. The driver helps me retrieve my luggage, and as I am paying him, Celine opens the front door. She also looks virtually the same; the years have been kind to her. The only discernible difference I can see is faint lines of weariness under her eyes. Truman has been dead for five years, but I can see that Celine still has sleepless nights.

I wasn't in the States when Truman married Celine, and when I finally did meet her, I was surprised this assertive and confident woman was the one Truman had fallen for. He seemed so deferential around his petite wife. In quiet awe of her more than in love with her.

"How did you know Celine was the one for you?" I asked him when we were alone. I was curious, but also worried that my little brother was in a marriage that might one day disappoint him.

Truman thought for a long moment. "It was Celine saying that I was the one for her, I guess. Here was this beautiful woman raised in wealth and privilege, declaring she wanted *me*—a lowly clerk at the firm that did the vineyard's taxes. She wanted me. I fell for that like a stone in water."

I remember wondering—as I still wonder five years after his death—if it was Celine my brother had fallen in love with or just the idea that she'd chosen him.

"Hello, Helen," Celine says, coming down the steps and giving me a featherlight kiss on the cheek.

"It's so wonderful to see you," I say in return.

"Is this everything?"

I look down at the two suitcases on the gravel. Check to see that I have my purse and overnight bag on my arm. "Yes. I think I'm all set."

We step inside the house after the taxi leaves, and I'm happy to see that Celine decorated the house for Christmas. There is a tall Douglas fir in the living room draped with lights, sparkling ornaments, and garlands. The tables and shelves and mantel are lined from end to end with festive evergreen boughs and candles.

"The house looks so pretty," I say.

Celine casts a glance around her. "I suppose it seems silly to decorate it just for me."

"Not at all. And it's not just for you."

"I don't even know if Wilson and Louise are coming up during the holidays."

"Louise?"

"His fiancée. He proposed last week. They're going to her parents' for Christmas. In Pasadena. I don't know when I'll see them."

"Oh. I'm sorry to hear that. I'll miss seeing him, too. But I am happy to hear he's engaged. What wonderful news."

Celine shrugs. "I suppose I knew this would happen at some point. Children grow up. They leave home." But then she seems to catch the irony of her words. She is fifty-two years old and still living in the house she grew up in. Celine starts down the hallway with my suitcases. "So I have you in Wilson's old room. It's a guest room now," she says over her shoulder.

I follow her.

A moment later, Celine is setting the luggage down in the spacious bedroom.

"Do you want to unpack or do you want to lie down or do you want something to eat?" Celine asks in a rush. I am getting the impression that it's been a while since she has had company.

"I don't need to unpack right now, and I had breakfast on the train. Maybe we can just sit on the patio and have some coffee?"

Celine nods casually, as though it does not matter to her what we do next.

I follow her back through the house and to the kitchen, where she begins to get a percolator going. I notice the door to the room that was the maid's is open, and that there is no longer a bed inside it, but a desk and shelves and filing cabinets. Celine is moving about the kitchen as if she knows exactly where everything is and is quite at home in it.

"You don't have a maid anymore?" I nod toward the little room.

Celine glances over her shoulder at the room and then brings her attention back to getting cups and saucers out of the cupboard. "No. That room is my office now. I decided I didn't like having people who weren't family in the house, living in it as if they were. The last maid was an utter disappointment. I should have guessed she would be."

"Oh. I'm sorry to hear that."

"And there I was trying to help her out by giving her a home here and a job, and because her parents had just died. I should've known better."

I feel my mouth drop open a little. I know whom Celine is talking about.

"You mean Rosie?"

Celine tips her head to look at me curiously. She is frowning. "You remember her?"

"Of course I remember her. You and Truman took her in after her family died. She was a pretty little thing."

Celine is staring at me like I don't know what I'm talking about.

"You and Truman started giving her my letters after they'd been read so that she could have the stamps. I wrote to her a few times so that she could have her own envelopes."

And still she is staring at me as though I'm recalling it all wrong.

"Celine, I sent Rosie the amaryllis that first Christmas after she lost her family. Remember?"

"I remember the amaryllis you sent," she says evenly, but her gaze on me is hard and strange.

"You told me the county found a different place for her not long after that. I had written her a couple more times in the New Year, and you told me to stop."

"That's right," she says, but not as if we are finally talking about the same girl.

"I didn't know Rosie was your maid, too," I say. "Wasn't that kind of . . ." I search for the right word. *Cruel* is too harsh. *Odd* is too vague.

"Kind of what?" A slight note of irritation creeps into Celine's voice.

"I don't know. Unkind? Shouldn't she have been in school?"

"How was it unkind to give her the work experience she'd need as an adult? Her parents left her nothing."

"Of course, but—"

"And they were the ones who took her out of school, not me," Celine continues. "Rosie did poorly in school, if you must know. I was doing her an immense favor by giving her a job and a paycheck. I was the only one thinking about her future. The only one."

I have annoyed Celine with this conversation, and I'm not sure why. "I see," I tell her.

Celine opens up a drawer and gets out two spoons, and then shoves it closed. "No, I don't think you do. You weren't here. It was a mistake bringing that girl into this house. I never should've let the county talk me into it."

"I really am sorry to hear that. It was very kind of you and Truman to try to make a go of it with her. I didn't mean to suggest it wasn't."

Celine exhales heavily and closes her eyes a second. "I really don't want to talk about her."

I'm curious as to what became of Rosie Maras—I actually

have been for a long while—but I sense the need to change the subject. "All right. We don't have to."

Celine turns to me. "Are you sure you don't want a cookie or something? I have some pastries."

"A pastry would be nice."

Minutes later, we are out on the patio, and I'm glad I suggested it. The late morning is golden, and the little that remains of the spent vines is toasty brown in the sun.

"It really is so beautiful here," I say, letting the vista freshen my spirit. "No wonder you love this place so much."

Celine takes a sip of her coffee and gazes out over her inheritance. "Sometimes I think it's only the vineyard that hasn't failed me. Everything else in my life . . ." She lets her words die away.

I can see so clearly that Celine is still grieving. It must be so difficult to lose a husband the way she lost Truman.

I wonder if she was as surprised as I was at my brother's decision to reenlist. He wrote to me shortly after Pearl Harbor that the army didn't care that he was forty-nine years old and that he'd learned to hide the slight limp in his step from the last war he'd fought in.

Letters from Celine after Truman died were few. The war made correspondence between us a problem, to be sure, but her short and sparse notes led me to believe she was adapting to the loss of my brother the way she did everything—or so it always had seemed to me, even from thousands of miles away: with resolve and control.

But now I wonder.

"Are you managing all right, Celine?" I ask as gently as I can. She hesitates only a second. "I'm fine."

"Truman's passing must've been very hard for you."

Celine sets her cup down on its saucer on the table between us. "Many things about having Truman as my husband were hard. So, yes, it was all very hard."

Her tone tells me in no uncertain terms that she does not want to talk about Truman or how his death is affecting her. She doesn't want to invite me into her grief or her life as a widow or even her life in general.

In fact, over the next several days, I get the distinct impression that Celine has allowed me to come only because I have no place of my own yet. She is not expecting or wanting me to stay for any great length of time. I can see this in the way she keeps me at arm's length. She is polite and attentive but only in the most distant of ways. She asks no questions about my experiences during the war or what it was like in Europe after it or what I plan to do now. It's almost as if I am a traveling stranger at her home and not her sister-in-law of thirty years.

I begin to look at advertisements in the *San Francisco Chronicle*, which Celine has delivered every morning, for an apartment and a job. By the first of the year, I hope to be on my own so that Celine can have the solitary life she seems to want. And if I haven't found my own place by then, I'll take up George and Lila's offer to come stay with them for a time.

Christmas Eve arrives, and I try to make the day as pleasant as possible for Celine. I offer to make *faschierter Braten*—a savory meat loaf—for our dinner, served alongside a creamy potato mash and pickled red cabbage. As I dish up our plates, Celine opens a bottle of wine. The food is delicious and the wine, too. Celine ordered a cherry torte from a bakery in Santa Rosa, and as she cuts into it, I remember the muscat dessert wine that Rosseau Vineyards bottles and that I loved the last time I was here. I ask if Celine wouldn't mind opening one of those, too.

We've already had two glasses of wine each at dinner, and now, with our dessert, the third glass of wine is starting to go to my head. I know I need to stop. But Celine continues to pour from both bottles into her glass, alternating from one to the other.

Perhaps her many pours are how she deals with her lingering sorrow, especially at the holidays. I'm glad she is acknowledging her loss and loneliness, but I'm thinking that alcohol is probably not the best way to do it. I reach across the table and lay a hand on Celine's arm.

"Do you want to head on to bed, Celine? I can take care of these dishes."

Celine withdraws her arm and picks up her glass. "I'm not done with my wine," she says, her words a bit slurred.

"You don't have to finish it."

"Oh yes, I do." Celine tips back the glass and takes a large gulp.

"Maybe you can just give me the glass," I say gently.

"Maybe you can just mind your own business." Celine sets the glass down and pours more, her hand wavering a bit. A few drops of wine splash over the side of the glass and onto the linen tablecloth.

"I'm just trying to help," I say.

"Well, you're not helping. You're actually making it worse."

"I don't understand."

"What don't you understand?" Celine's tone is quick and terse.

I sit back in my chair, dumbfounded. "How am I making this worse?"

Celine regards me for a moment, narrowing her eyes. "You really want to know?"

"Yes."

"All right," she says, her words dripping with cynicism. "Having you here in my house right now is not helping me. At all."

"Because you'd rather be alone?" I reply, genuinely perplexed.

"Because I'd rather you weren't here."

"So you're saying it's me? I am personally making it hard for you? I honestly don't understand, Celine. If I have offended you in any way, please tell me, because I assure you it was unintentional, and I am so very sorry."

Celine shakes her head as if I am dense. "I don't want you here, because you remind me of Truman. You're his sister and you look like him. And you sound like him. Every minute of every day that you're here, I see him when I see you, and I hear him when I hear you." Celine says this with a tone of revulsion, not sorrow. It's not grief in her words but contempt. I am momentarily at a loss for words.

"Oh, Celine," I finally reply. "What happened between you?"

My sister-in-law picks up her glass, takes a sip, and swallows. "Of course, you wouldn't think it was his fault, would you?" She sets the glass down hard. "Because you think Truman was wonderful and I was terrible to him and he deserved better than me. So of course you think he couldn't possibly do anything to hurt me."

"Celine, that is not what I'm thinking."

She locks eyes with me, as if daring me to look away. I don't. She leans over the table.

"Your brother betrayed me." She sits back in her chair as though triumphant, her head bobbing slightly to and fro.

"Betrayed you? You mean . . . he was unfaithful to you?"

"Want to know who it was with?" Celine asks, a false and crooked smile on her face. "You'll never guess."

"I don't need to know that. That's personal." I'm sure it is the alcohol talking and that Celine would not want to have this conversation if she were sober.

"It was Rosie," Celine continues, her voice oozing venom. "That girl I let into this house out of the goodness of my heart. Truman got her pregnant."

I feel the room go cold. It can't be true. Truman would not sink to that level, no matter how unhappy he might have been in his marriage. He wouldn't have done that, couldn't have.

"You don't believe me, do you?" Celine grabs her wineglass. "But it's true. Your brother humiliated me and I hated him for it. I hated him because I could do nothing to get back at him. I had to pretend he hadn't done what he'd done, and I had to pretend that girl wasn't carrying his child. I had to pretend all was well in front of everyone, including Wilson. And I hated it. When I got the telegram that Truman was dead, I was glad."

Tears are slipping down my cheeks. I have no ready words of response. None. Celine barrels on.

"I was glad because I could finally stop pretending I had a happy marriage. He got what he deserved after what he did to me."

"What he did to you?" Tears continue to stream down my face. "What about Rosie? What about what he did to her?"

"Oh, you would be thinking about her and not me!" Celine's voice is just on the edge of rage. "She wanted it!"

I wince at the unwanted image of my brother, in his forties, taking a teenage girl—his ward!—to his bed. Impossible. I try to shake the image away. "Are you sure? How do you know?"

"Because I asked her!"

"And she said those words to you? She said it was consensual?"

"I could see it in her face. And after all I had done for her, too! I took that whore into my home to be kind to her. I treated her as my own child!"

"But . . . you brought her into this house as a maid," I say, my own voice rising in volume.

"I treated her like a daughter!"

"By making her wash your clothes and clean your toilets?"

"You weren't here!" Celine spits back. "You were never here. You don't know what I did and didn't do."

I raise my napkin off my lap to wipe away my tears, but they continue to fall. It is all so incredibly depressing—the ruin of a marriage, my brother's stunning lack of judgment, a young girl getting pregnant, the enraged woman who was wronged.

"Oh, Celine, let's not fight," I say in a softer tone. "This is all so terribly sad. I am heartbroken—for all of you."

"I don't believe you. You're not sad for me. You're just sorry your brother got that girl pregnant; you're not sorry for what he did to me."

"But I am. I am sorry for all of you. What happened? Did Truman get arrested?"

Celine downs the rest of her wine and then sets the glass down. "Nothing happened to Truman because no one knew it was him who got Rosie pregnant. Truman bought her off."

"What?"

"You heard me. He promised to pay Rosie for her silence. And she agreed. So you see? She *was* a whore. Just like I said."

"What about the child? Please tell me. What became of the child?"

That baby is Truman's baby. My brother's son or daughter. A child of my blood. My heart is suddenly aching to know where the child is.

Celine leans over the table again. "I made sure Rosie was sent to a place that takes girls like her, white trash girls who are as crazy as she was."

"What do you mean, as crazy as she was?"

"She said she saw things—colors and shapes floating around that no one else could see! Completely delusional. You couldn't trust a word she said. About anything."

"Celine, please tell me where she was sent. What happened to the baby?" I don't even try to hide the begging tone of my voice. If what Celine is saying is true, there is a child out there who is my niece or nephew. My family.

"I bet you'd like to know." Celine rises unsteadily to her feet.

"Please tell me. What became of the child? What happened to Rosie?"

Celine plasters a sick smile on her face. "I don't care what happened to her. They didn't let her keep the baby, if that's what you're wondering. It went to some orphanage, 'father unknown' on its birth certificate. And I hear they sterilize people like her at that place."

"What . . . what do you mean?" I feel the blood rush from my face. Horrific images from my last years in Vienna threaten to crowd in. I push them back with effort.

"You heard what I said. They *sterilize* people like her." Celine turns from the table, needing to hold on to her chair as she does to keep her footing. "You better hope there are taxis running on Christmas morning, because I want you gone in the morning." Then, without another word or glance backward, Celine sways out of the room.

I hear my sister-in-law head down the hallway, leaning against the wall as she goes, and then slamming the door shut after staggering into her bedroom.

For many long minutes, I can only sit at the table in shock and disbelief.

I will call the taxi tonight. I will not spend another night in this house.

But first I need to know where Celine sent Rosie Maras. The baby that young woman bore was Truman's child. My only family now besides Wilson. I rise from the table, wiping my tears. I head for the office off the kitchen, which, years before, was the maid's bedroom, to search every inch of it.

Celine had to have a record of what happened with the teenage girl she and Truman took in. There had to be a file, a document, a note. Something.

I'm afraid something awful happened to Rosie when she left here, and my brother and his angry wife are the reason why.

I fear a terrible injustice has occurred to someone I care about.

Again.

If that's the case, I won't be able to rest until I can make it right somehow.

And this time, I will succeed.

I must.

23

In all the years I'd been employed by families with multiple little ones, I'd always had equal affection for all of them. But with seven-year-old Brigitta Maier, it was different.

I wasn't certain if the other Maier children sensed I had a special affection for their youngest sister. I'd long supposed the children's parents, Johannes and Martine Maier, could tell. If they knew, no one ever mentioned it, not even Hanna, the second-to-last born and only eighteen months older than Brigitta.

Perhaps the other children didn't mind because Brigitta had been dealt a heavy blow compared to them, and the extra love I gave Brigitta helped to offset that. Werner and Karl, the two oldest at fourteen and twelve, could run, ski, and shoot a bow and arrow; Brigitta could not. Hanna and the ten-year-old twins, Liliana and Amelia, could play hopscotch and take ballet classes and would one day gain the notice of the boys in the neighborhood; Brigitta could not and likely would not.

She'd been born prematurely and with misshapen limbs, including arms that ended in three fingers on each hand. She'd had problems from the start with breathing on her own and had struggled with almost every developmental step a child takes as she grows. She walked with an unsteady gait, and her other motor skills were likewise unrefined. She struggled at times to find the words she wanted to say. She would likely always remain at home, unsuited to living an independent life.

But Brigitta Maier was never without a smile on her face, and the thought that this sweet child would never outgrow the need for my care, tragic as that was, also filled me with a sense of lasting purpose, an immense comfort since I'd been unlucky in love and had no children of my own. I felt fortunate that in this family I had what my own life hadn't given me.

It wasn't for lack of trying. I'd given my heart fully to three different men over the decades. All three had swept me off my feet, courted me with affection, professed love, and then left me.

The first had been when I was twenty-six and still in London. I dated Byron for two years and had been ready to give up a posting and family I loved to be his wife and move with him to Calcutta for his job. But he abruptly ended things just when I thought he would propose, telling me that he had met someone else.

Devastated, I'd waited six years before allowing myself to fall that deeply in love again. This time I was nannying in Paris and the world was at war. I met a Frenchman who wooed and charmed me for a year and a half, and to whom I wrote perfume-scented letters that he read in muddy trenches. It was when I spoke of marriage upon his safe return that he confessed he already had a wife, and that I was actually his mistress, that he had no plans to divorce, and that he liked things just the way they were. This time it was I who ended it, but I was just as broken.

The third time, after having spent a decade casually dating and being supremely cautious, I had fallen for Marcel, a divorced Parisian with two grown children. I had just celebrated my forty-third birthday. Marcel was kind and gentle, and for the four years we dated, he spoiled me with jewelry and weekly bouquets and summer vacations to Provence. I'd just begun to believe Marcel was the one I'd been waiting for all those years when he was killed in a traffic accident involving his motorcycle. It was at his funeral that I learned he and his ex-wife had started seeing each other again.

The blow had been hard and swift, and I'd been ready for a change. A big one. The Parisian family I'd been working for at the time, whose last child was going off to boarding school, had heard through friends that there was a couple in Vienna who were looking for a new nanny. The Maiers had five children already and were expecting their sixth. They'd been greatly interested in me not only because I now had more than twenty years' experience but I spoke French, knew a lot of German already, and was of course fluent in English.

I had eagerly accepted the position, and I immediately fell in love with Vienna, just as I had with London and Paris.

But the years since I'd first arrived in Europe were filled with political and civil unrest. When Adolf Hitler and his army marched into Austria to annex it, Truman wrote and begged me to come home. He even offered to wire me the money for my passage on the next ship out of Marseilles.

Johannes Maier had also told me if I wanted to return home, he'd understand.

But leaving Brigitta wasn't something I could consider. Johannes, now an officer in a German panzer division, had been deployed to Berlin for training.

Martine needed me more than ever.

The Austria that I loved was hiding now under the flapping of thousands of red flags bearing the Nazi swastika. With the German troops' arrival came their anti-Jewish laws and hatred for Jewish people. SS officers routinely forced Jewish men and women to get on their knees and scrub off graffiti critical of the annexation. The Schutzstaffel expected Viennese civilian spectators to witness these humiliations and toss in our own insults.

Most of the synagogues in Vienna lay in ruins. Businesses owned by Jews had been ransacked. Thousands of Jewish people had been arrested and deported to penal camps.

"I don't understand Herr Hitler's hatred for Jewish people, Johannes," Martine had said one evening when he was at the town house and all the children were in bed. It was his first night home in weeks, and we were all sitting in the parlor having a nightcap. "Why does he want them gone?"

"Because he sees what most cannot," Johannes replied. "He can see a strong Germany where her people can thrive in every way. A strong Germany for Germany's people, and that includes us. The Jews aren't German, *Liebling*. They aren't even European. They immigrated from elsewhere, you see? Palestine is their ancestral home. That's where they belong. It is fine to live in a place for a time, like Helen here is living in Vienna with us. But she is American. Her true home will always be America. Am I not right, Helen?"

I didn't know what to say. I'd not heard Johannes talk this way before. It had never been a practice of his to discuss politics at home.

"Well," I said after a moment's thought, "what is an American, though, Captain Maier? America is a nation of immigrants."

"Yes, I'll grant that America is a young country settled by foreigners, as you say. But Germany is not. Austria is not. Hitler sees all the economic troubles facing us and he sees a solution. Germany is for Germans."

"What about this campaign the Germans have brought into Austria to prevent people from having children who might pass on genetic flaws? What does that even mean, Johannes?" Martine said. "How is that making Germany for Germans or Austria for Austrians? And what does that mean for people like you and me? What does that mean for someone like Brigitta?"

Johannes crinkled his eyebrows in consternation. "The führer doesn't see the merit of perpetuating weakness, that is all, Martine. Not in politics, not in economics, and not in people. A strong, healthy Germany needs strong, healthy citizens. Weak people make for a weak country. We want a strong country, don't we? It's that simple."

"I don't see anything simple about it," Martine said. "There was talk at the sewing circle today that people who aren't perfect are being sterilized. I didn't believe it could be true, but now to hear you talk, I wonder if it is."

"This is nothing that concerns us," Johannes said, still frowning. His tone was unconvincing, though, even to me.

"Would the Germans sterilize people like you and me because we had a child who isn't . . . perfect?" Tears had suddenly sprung to Martine's eyes.

He paused before answering. I sensed that this had been weighing on him, too, and that he was still formulating an answer to satisfy himself but that he hadn't arrived at one. "I don't know. Probably not. But I suppose they might sterilize someone like Brigitta even though she is likely never to marry."

"Johannes!"

"Why are we talking about this?" he said, raising his voice, his tone suddenly dismissive. "It's people of childbearing age who might burden the society with defective offspring—like epileptics and alcoholics and those with intellectual disabilities—the feeble-minded. These are the ones that have been targeted. Brigitta is just a child. We don't have to worry about it."

"I don't like this, Johannes. It frightens me," Martine said. "It's as if they are saying only perfect babies should be born."

"But . . . but perhaps we are looking at it selfishly," he said slowly, as if thinking aloud. "We love Brigitta, but what kind of life will she ultimately have?"

"A *happy* one!" Martine exclaimed.

"Yes, of course, I know that. I know we can give her a happy life. We are able to. But what about people like her who have no one? What about the ones in institutions where day after day their lives are meaningless and no one loves them or truly cares for them? Maybe it would have been better for those people if they had never been born."

Martine gasped and rose to her feet. "Who are we to say their lives are meaningless! Who are we to say a person has no value?"

Johannes stared at his wife and didn't reply. He appeared to be struggling to construct an answer.

Tears spilling down her cheeks, Martine left the room.

I waited a moment to see if Johannes would try out his answer to Martine's question on me, but he just gazed at his drink and said nothing. I excused myself and followed Martine upstairs to my bedroom, next to Brigitta's.

I went to bed that night, my resolve to stay in Austria as strong as ever, but I lay awake, not knowing what to make of the conversation I'd just been a part of. I wasn't able to stop thinking about what Johannes had said about weakness. *Who defines what is weakness?* I'd wondered. *Isn't it only the strong who get to decide that? Isn't it only the strong who have the power to act on what they decide? How can that be right or fair or good?*

Sleep had been long in coming.

24

The taxi drops me off at the one hotel in Santa Rosa that is still giving out rooms at nine thirty at night on Christmas Eve. There is a lively party going on in the hotel dining hall, open to all the guests, but I head upstairs to the room I've been given and collapse onto the bed fully clothed.

I found what I'd been hunting for in Celine's office after an hour of searching. Buried in the back of a file cabinet in the closet were documents that detailed the signing over to Sonoma County of the Calverts' responsibility for one Rosanne Maras. There was also a letter dated February 26, 1939, from a county social worker, Eunice Grissom, thanking the Calverts for their efforts and informing them that Rosanne Maras had been transferred from their home to the Sonoma State Home for the Infirm if they wished to visit. Visiting hours were Saturday afternoons from two to five.

Those documents are now in my handbag.

I will call Lila and George Petrakis in the morning to first wish them a Merry Christmas and to then ask if I can take them up on the offer to stay with them for a bit. And to see if they'd be willing to perhaps loan me a vehicle in the coming days so that I can drive up to the institution where Rosanne Maras was taken. I don't want to wait until I have my own place and my own car to start looking for what has become of my niece or nephew. I know after nearly nine years that whatever befell Rosanne Maras has long since happened—finding out exactly what that was, even if I can, will change nothing. But still. I need to know. And I won't be at peace until I've made every attempt to find Truman's child.

My heart and mind are weary from the day's revelations. I kick off my shoes, burrow under the comforter, and am asleep in minutes.

I awaken Christmas morning to the sound of bells from a nearby church. I dress in fresh clothes and make my way to the place that pealed such a happy greeting to the day, to sit in a pew and pray for favor as I try to discover the whereabouts of this baby and its mother.

I wait until after lunch to call my friends, apologizing for disturbing them on Christmas. But Lila is just as I've always known her to be, cheerful, kind, and welcoming. She and George are insistent that I have Christmas dinner with their family and begin my stay with them this very day. She offers for one of their sons to travel the one-hundred-mile round trip to fetch me. It seems to me too great an imposition.

"I'm sure I can get on a train tomorrow to you," I say.

"Nonsense. It's Christmas. And Garland loves that drive. You'll get to see the new bridge, Helen. It's beautiful. Majestic even."

By four o'clock that afternoon, and after crossing the new Golden Gate Bridge—a glistening marvel that looks like a castle just begun—I am sipping eggnog with my friends in a lovely Victorian house in San Francisco's Laurel Heights. George and Lila's three sons were young boys the last time I saw them, and now they are all married and have given George and Lila seven grand-children. The Petrakis house on Christmas Day is full of merri-ment and happy voices and laughter, the exact opposite of the home I was in the day before.

I offer to help in the kitchen with the last preparations for din-ner, and Lila agrees so that we can talk and so that her daughters-in-law can enjoy visiting with one another.

"I can't thank you enough for inviting me to come today," I say as I grate a carrot. "And for allowing me to stay with you for a little while so I can figure things out."

Lila looks up from draining a can of pineapple bits. "It's our pleasure, Helen. Truly. You can stay with us as long as you want. We never use the third floor anymore now that the kids are grown and gone. There are two rooms up there, and a toilet. You'll be quite comfortable. It will be a treat for us to have you."

"That is awfully kind."

We are quiet for a moment.

"I take it things didn't go well with your sister-in-law?" Lila finally asks.

"You could say that." I pick up another carrot. "Celine prefers to be alone, I think."

"I'm sorry." Lila sounds genuinely sad for me. "And I'm sorry again about Truman's passing. Coming home must have brought it all back. He was so brave to do what he did, reenlisting like that at nearly fifty."

"Yes," I say, but there is hesitation in my voice. Lila notices.

"You don't think it was brave?"

"No, I do. It's not that. It's . . . I've learned some things about Truman that I was unaware of before. Things that have made me very sad, and I . . . Oh my. We don't need to talk about this today. It's Christmas."

Lila reaches out and stills my hand. "The carrots can wait. Tell me what happened." My old friend has sensed somehow that I need to talk with someone about what I now know. And so I do. I tell Lila all that Celine told me and what I now feel compelled to do. When I'm finished, tears are slipping down my face. Lila wraps me in her arms as if I were a child.

"I had forgotten what a good listener you are." I laugh nervously, and Lila breaks from the embrace.

"I'm so glad you told me." Lila hands me a handkerchief from inside her apron pocket. "You shouldn't have to shoulder it alone, Helen. That's a lot to take in when all you were expecting was a quiet Christmas with your brother's widow."

I dab at my eyes. "I suppose you're right."

"Of course I am. And if for some reason you end up needing a lawyer to sort all this out, you only have to say the word and George will do whatever he can for you, I know he will."

"I don't know what I'm going to need or what obstacles I am going to face. I just know I need to find out what happened to Rosie. And I simply must know what became of her baby. That child is my niece or nephew, and aside from Wilson, whom I barely know, the only other blood relative I have left."

"George and I will find a way to help you. We will. George knows the law. And he knows how to use the law to get information. Don't you worry," Lila says. "Now, let's finish up here and open the prosecco! Today we have Christmas. Tomorrow we figure out how to help you."

Lila and George's children and grandchildren begin packing up for their homes in Berkeley, San Jose, and Napa at eight thirty. By nine o'clock, the last of them have left and the house is quiet. Lila turns on the radio for some Christmas music and pours glasses of port while George builds a fresh fire in the fireplace. When we are settled in comfortable chairs in front of the hearth, Lila and I fill George in on my dilemma.

"I know of that state institution where the girl was sent," George says when I am done. "It's true what Celine said about it.

It's my understanding they've been sterilizing patients there for years."

"For *years*?" I can scarcely believe what he's telling me. "How long?"

"Well, let me think. California has been at it since 1910 or so. Maybe a little earlier. Other states were doing it before California, though. I think Indiana was the first."

For a second, I can only stare at George. "You're saying this was happening to people here, in America, long before the Nazis started doing it in Germany?"

"I'm afraid so."

I am aghast. "I don't understand this," I say. "You know that's how Hitler began, right? He began by sterilizing people he didn't want having children. I know how he got away with it. But how in the name of heaven can it be happening here?"

"The law makes provision for it. I'm pretty sure many states still have eugenics laws on the books."

"Eugenics laws?" Lila asks.

"I mean legislation that allows states to decide who among the institutionalized with so-called genetic flaws should be made unable to have children."

"For what purpose?" Lila says, frowning.

"So that they can't perpetuate a burden on society," I say. "That's the rationale behind it, isn't it?"

George nods.

"And I'm assuming these people with so-called genetic flaws don't have any say in the matter?" I ask.

"I'd wager a certain percentage do, but most are likely deemed unable to make decisions about their health, especially if they are already in the state's care."

"But what about those who are able to make decisions and don't want that procedure?" Lila asks. "I don't see how forcibly sterilizing them can be lawful."

"They can do it because there's a precedent for it," George says. "I remember the Supreme Court case that ruled on this. It was a while ago, in the late 1920s, I believe. There was a young woman considered an imbecile by heredity. Her home state of Virginia wanted to sterilize her, but they also wanted to make sure they had the constitutional right, even with the laws in place, to do that. Her case went all the way to the Supreme Court. All the other states with eugenics laws were watching. That majority decision made it possible for other states to rest easy with the same kinds of laws."

"Was this young woman actually an imbecile?" I ask.

"I never saw the documentation proving it," George replies. "And, granted, I wasn't in the courtroom. But I remember someone being quoted in a newspaper after the fact saying she actually had average marks in school, which a true imbecile would not have. But that fact apparently was never brought up in the proceedings. She'd gotten pregnant at seventeen while living at a foster home, and unfortunately that was seen as a sign of her low intelligence."

"Plenty of smart girls fall pregnant," Lila says.

"Indeed. I remember thinking there were holes in the argument, but it wasn't my case. And I didn't practice that kind of law. I just know that case is why a lot of states have eugenics laws."

"This is exactly how the madness in Germany started. Exactly. They . . ." I let my words drift away. I will not open *that* door. Not on Christmas.

"I know it sounds a bit shocking now, but the movement was quite popular years back," George says. "There was even an extensive exhibit at the 1915 World's Fair right here in San Francisco. It was all about education back then, teaching people that the best way to strengthen society was to bring into it strong, healthy, and intelligent children. But the focus morphed rather quickly to the practice of sterilizing those with genetically undesirable traits. It went on for years, all in the name of bettering society. It's still going on, though less now, I think. After what happened in those concentration camps in Europe, the idea of building a race of only perfect people sounds far too much like what the Nazis were trying to do."

I stiffen involuntarily. A bit of port sloshes out of my glass and onto my hand.

"George," Lila says softly.

George looks quickly to me. "I'm so sorry, Helen. That was careless of me. I can only imagine the things you must have witnessed."

"There are no words to describe it," I say, fingering away the tiny spill, my voice catching in my throat.

The three of us are quiet for a moment. The fire snaps and pops, and the radio station begins to play a choral selection from Handel's *Messiah*.

"Do you really think that place could have sterilized this young woman?" Lila finally asks. "Why would they, if all she was to them was an unmarried pregnant teen?"

"I don't know." George turns to me. "How well did you know her?"

"I was with her twice. Once when she was a toddler and again when she was nine or ten. She's not an imbecile, I can tell you that."

"But your sister-in-law said she was delusional?" George asks.

"She said Rosie claimed to see colors and shapes no one else could see. But she also said Rosie was a liar who couldn't be trusted. So maybe this claim was a lie? I don't know. Celine saying this about Rosie seems very odd to me, because that girl had lived her whole life at the vineyard. She was the vinedresser's daughter, and Celine and Truman knew her well. The way Celine tells it, Rosie was pretty much in charge of the entire upkeep of the house when all of this happened. That's a lot for one so young, and she was managing it. I don't see how Celine could have given Rosie all of those responsibilities if she was delusional. Celine is smart. I would've asked her to explain, but by this point in the conversation she was furious with me and she stomped off to her room."

"Well, hopefully you'll get the answers you're looking for when you visit that institution," Lila says. "George and I can drive you there, if you'd like. It might be helpful to have him with you in case you need help getting the information you want."

"I think having a lawyer there with me might put them on the defensive so they tell me nothing," I say.

"Helen's probably right about that. Legally, she won't have any rights to information about Rosie," George says to Lila. "I agree she'll need to strike a non-adversarial tone."

"We can still drive her up to Sonoma County and just wait in the car when she goes in," Lila says.

"Certainly. Would you like for us to do that, Helen?"

"That's kind of you, truly it is," I reply. "But I can manage if you don't mind me borrowing a car for a day. I'm a good driver, honestly. I've been driving for decades in Europe, and my international driver's license is still valid. I do plan to get my own vehicle at some point. I just don't have one yet."

"She can take the boys' old Studebaker, can't she, George?" Lila says. "I hardly ever drive it anymore. It's just sitting in a shed in the backyard."

"That's true," George says. "I'll need to see if the engine will turn over and make sure there's air in the tires and all that."

"That would be wonderful," I reply. "I really would be so grateful."

"You want to look for this young woman right away, don't you?" Lila asks. "As in tomorrow, if the car is running?"

"I do, yes."

George sets down his empty port glass on the coffee table. "I'll see about firing it up tomorrow morning."

We wish one another a good night and a merry Christmas and then we are off to our beds.

In the morning, after George tinkers with the Studebaker, freshens the gas in its tank, and refills its tires with air, I get inside and make my way to the beckoning Golden Gate Bridge and the answers I hope to find on its other side.

25

Before . . .
MAY 1940

The morning the government official rang the bell at the Maiers'
townhome on Rainergasse was unseasonably chilly for spring and
seemed a commentary on the uncertain times all of Vienna was
living in.

The Reich had by now marched into Czechoslovakia and Poland. France and Britain had declared war on Germany, but nothing had changed. The Reich, which had taken Denmark only a
month earlier, was still moving ever-steadily forward in its quest
for dominance and racial purity. In the newly occupied territories, Jews were now required to wear identifying armbands. Hundreds of thousands of Polish citizens had been driven from their
homes and forced into ghettos, and ethnic Germans were settled
in their place. Dissenters and itinerants were likewise treated as
castoffs to be disposed of. Viennese Jews who could leave had
left, but those who had nowhere to go continued to suffer daily
persecutions. I saw it happening every day, and I felt powerless to
do anything about it.

But on this particular May morning, the streets were largely quiet. Werner and Karl, wearing the new school uniforms that all Hitler Youth wore, had left for school. The twins and Hanna had been dropped off at their school by Martine, who was then headed to the army post to help plan a charity event with other officers' wives. Brigitta and I had not yet left the house for Sonnenschein Grundschule, a special academy that offered adaptive classes for children with educational and physical challenges. Brigitta attended every weekday from ten until two, and I regularly took her there and picked her up again.

In the months to come, I would wonder if the government official had specifically come at a time in the morning when I would be alone with Brigitta. I would spend many endless nights wondering.

The Maiers lived in an attached townhome on a tree-lined street in the Wieden district, not far from the former imperial palace. It was narrow and four stories tall, as were all the homes on the block. A parlor, dining room, and kitchen comprised the first floor. The second floor was where Johannes and Martine and Hanna and the twins had their bedrooms. Brigitta and I had separate bedrooms on the third floor, and the two tiny fourth-floor bedrooms belonged to the boys. A small garage located in the alley behind the house was where the family's Opel Olympia was kept. On rainy or snowy days, I used the car to take Brigitta to school.

Brigitta and I had been working on a puzzle in the parlor when the doorbell rang on that cool morning, a few minutes after nine.

A woman stood on the front stoop wrapped in a lightweight coat, with a clipboard in her hands and an official-looking badge on her lapel.

"Good morning," the woman said in German. "I am Fraulein Platz with the children's health department. This is the Maier residence, yes?"

"Good morning. Yes, it is."

Fraulein Platz looked to be in her early thirties. Pretty, flaxen-haired, and with a statuesque bearing.

"Can I help you?" I asked.

"I'm here to evaluate Brigitta Maier. She is on our list of children residing in this district requiring special care. I am here by law to make sure all of her needs are being met and to record statistical data."

I instantly felt the need to be on my guard. "I'm afraid Captain and Frau Maier are not at home at the moment."

"And who are you, please?" the woman asked.

"My name is Helen Calvert. I am an American citizen on a work visa, and the Maiers' nanny."

"So you look after the children when Captain and Frau Maier are not at home?"

"I do. And also when they are."

"Then we should be able to take care of this right now. If the child is at home and you are able to speak to her care, then we can attend to this and I can be on my way. By law I must make this assessment."

"Or you could come back this afternoon when Frau Maier is home?" I suggested, still wary.

"But I am here now," Fraulein Platz said. "And you are here, and I assume the child is here, and since you take care of her . . . That is what you are for, isn't it? To take care of this child?"

The unnerving conversation with Johannes and Martine from months ago regarding the disabled person's quality of life pricked my memory. Perhaps the wisest thing I could do was let this woman in and let her see how well Brigitta Maier was being taken care of. That was something I could easily do for the Maiers and for Brigitta. And in doing so I would also be showing this woman my role in ensuring that all of Brigitta's needs were being met and would continue to be met. Brigitta was not a burden to society. She was not a burden at all.

Plus, Johannes had told me right after the annexation that he expected compliance from Martine, the children, and me when it came to anything having to do with the new regime. He did not want to be embarrassed or, worse, penalized at his army post over reports that his family or the American he'd hired had refused to comply with a government request.

"If it won't take long." I struck a more conversational tone. "Brigitta has class in a little while and we don't want to be late."

"It should only take a few minutes," the woman said. "I have only a few questions and observations to make."

I invited Fraulein Platz inside, hung up her coat, and ushered her into the parlor. Brigitta was seated cross-legged on the floor, still working on the puzzle. She looked up at the woman, squinting a bit to see her clearly. I was glad Brigitta did not try to rise to her feet, as getting up from a sitting position was always a little difficult for her.

"Brigitta, this is Fraulein Platz. She's come to say hello and talk with you," I said cheerfully.

"Hello there, Brigitta," the woman said.

The child stared at the woman and said nothing.

Fraulein Platz turned to me. "Can she hear me?"

"Of course," I said with a nervous smile. "But you are a stranger and she's been taught to be careful with strangers." Then I quickly added, "All the Maier children have been taught to be careful. The world isn't always safe, you know."

The woman looked at Brigitta again, seeming to size her up even as the little girl sat there with puzzle pieces around her folded legs.

"And how old are you, child?" the woman said.

"You can answer her, Brigitta," I said when she did not answer. "She is not a stranger anymore because we've invited her in and shared our names. So now you know each other."

"I'm nearly eight," Brigitta said, a shy smile curling her lips.

"Can you stand up for me, please?"

Brigitta rose unsteadily to her feet using the coffee table as leverage. Fraulein Platz cocked her head and watched. I prayed that Brigitta would not stumble or collapse after having sat on the floor with crossed legs for so long. When she was finally standing, the woman set down her clipboard on a chair and drew closer to her. She tipped Brigitta's face up to look into her eyes and turned her head to study the shape of her forehead and ears. Then she held up one of Brigitta's misshapen arms, studying with a slight frown the three fingers at the end of it.

Brigitta giggled as the woman turned her arms this way and that and scrutinized Brigitta's strangely shaped palms and missing digits.

"She can write her name and paint and tie her own shoelaces," I said anxiously as the woman picked up Brigitta's other arm and studied it, too.

Fraulein Platz let Brigitta's arms drop, picked up her clipboard, and wrote for a few seconds. "And how old are your brothers, Brigitta?" she said a few moments later, not raising her gaze from her task.

"Werner and Karl," Brigitta said, smiling wide.

Fraulein Platz looked up. "I did not ask you their names. I asked you how old they are." The tone of her voice was neither kind nor unkind, but I felt a cold ripple of unease rush through me.

"Oh. Werner is fourteen. Karl just turned thirteen. And I'm nearly eight!"

"Yes, you told me already you are nearly eight. And can you tell me what street you live on?"

Brigitta looked puzzled for a moment. Then she cracked a little smile. "This one."

The woman pursed her lips and started to write something.

"Perhaps if you asked her—," I began, but the woman cut me off.

ONLY THE BEAUTIFUL 249

"I know you think you would be helping, but it is important that you do not interfere with the assessment, Fraulein Calvert. Thank you." The woman turned back to Brigitta. "Can you walk across the room for me, Brigitta?"

Brigitta's smile intensified as if this was a funny game. The little girl obliged, lurching forward to the far window in an uneven gait that I had grown used to but which now looked quite alarming. Brigitta turned and walked back.

"Thank you, Brigitta," Fraulein Platz said. "Just one more question and we are finished. Can you tell me what my name is?"

Brigitta stared, smiling but open-mouthed. She could not remember.

But why should she be expected to? What seven-year-old remembers a stranger's name after just meeting them? "If you were another child on the playground, she would've remembered your name, Fraulein," I interjected. "It's just the wrong question, that's all."

I expected another warning from the woman not to interfere, but she smiled at me instead. "You are very fond of this little girl, aren't you?"

"Very!" A surge of relief replaced the alarm from before. "She is such a sweet child. She has limitations that you and I don't have, but she makes up for whatever she lacks physically with having such a sunny disposition. She makes every day brighter, she truly does."

The woman continued to smile. "And you have been her primary caregiver from the beginning?"

"I have. She is my main responsibility, although I am nanny to the other Maier children as well. And I assure you I have no plans to return to the States. Ever."

I could see that the woman was paying close attention and listening to my reasoning. This was the moment to let Fraulein Platz know that Brigitta would always be cared for.

"I could have returned to the States before the war began," I went on, "but I chose to stay here because I am committed to this family and to Brigitta."

The woman seemed to take in my words with great interest. She was quiet for a few seconds, as if meditating on the wonderful relationship the Maiers had with their disabled child and how lucky Brigitta was to have such a doting caregiver. Me.

"Thank you very much for your time, Fraulein Calvert."

"We're finished?"

"We're finished."

We walked to the front entry. I retrieved Fraulein Platz's coat and handed it to her.

"Good-bye, Brigitta," the woman said, turning to the parlor, where the child stood in the entry, leaning on the doorframe. Brigitta smiled and waved.

Fraulein Platz turned to the door, and I leaned forward to open it. "Will there be anything else?" I asked, needing last-minute reassurance that I'd done the right thing in inviting the woman in.

"No," the woman said with an easy smile. "That was all."

Fraulein Platz said it with such a note of finality that I sensed a great weight lifting. I'd been smart to let the woman in so that she could see the wonderful home that Brigitta lived in and the environment in which she was thriving.

"Good-bye, Fraulein Platz," I said genially, and the woman responded in kind.

When Martine returned to the house that afternoon, I pondered the wisdom of mentioning the visit from Fraulein Platz. Perhaps it would ease Martine's mind to know that there would be no further inquiries into Brigitta's health issues, because there had been some sort of test that morning and she had passed it. It was finished. On the other hand, there had been rumors of late that disabled Austrian children were being moved from smaller institutions to larger ones to centralize their care, and that some were even being moved from homes where their families struggled to keep pace with the level of care needed. Martine had asked Johannes if these parents were given a choice in the matter, and he had assured her they had been. It was for the children's own good that they were being moved to better-equipped institutions.

But I had seen how troubled Martine had been by this. She lost several nights' sleep until Johannes convinced her that no disabled child was being pulled from the family home without parental permission. Martine had relaxed and had begun to be herself again. Bringing up the visit from Fraulein Platz would bring all that back again—the worry, the dread, the anxiety—though now it would be misplaced. And I felt confident that I had proven that day that Brigitta was not someone who would ever bleed resources from the government. It pained me to think about what might be happening to disabled children not living the fortunate life that Brigitta had, being taken from home and sent to live in faraway institutions. It was too much to consider. I could only think about Brigitta and her safety. Which I had secured that day.

Still, I waited to see if Brigitta would mention to Martine when she returned that there had been a visitor. She did not. Johannes was away with his platoon for several weeks, and so he did not come home asking how everyone's day was or if there had been callers to the house, which he sometimes did. So it was easy for the day to spend itself without my bringing up the visit.

The world was an uncertain place at the moment. Martine worried every day about Johannes, as there were resistance fighters in the former Czechoslovakia and in Poland and even in Austria. She had confided in me that every time someone came to the door, she was terrified it was with news that Johannes was dead or critically wounded.

So even when it was just me and Martine in the parlor that night, enjoying a cup of tea before bed, when I could have told her there had been a visitor that day, I believed I was doing the right thing in saying nothing at all.

26

The hour-long drive to the Sonoma State Home for the Infirm is easy and peaceful and takes me through undulating hills of vineyards and fruit trees and hamlet towns where it seems nothing terrible ever happens. The pastoral scene outside the car soothes me as I mentally prepare for what I might learn this morning. As much as I want to find Rosie Maras, and quickly, I hope that she isn't still at this institution after nearly nine years. But if she's not, I will need to win the hospital administrator's trust if I am to find out where Rosie was discharged and what became of the child she bore.

I follow the map George drew for me, skirting Santa Rosa proper, and soon I see the institution from the road: towering redbrick walls, paned windows, gleaming white trim, and a tall perimeter fence. Two majestic oak trees flank the gate. I approach the entrance and see the sign for the facility etched in granite. I read in smaller lettering beneath it, CARING FOR THE MENTALLY ENCUMBERED, THE EPILEPTIC, THE PHYSICALLY DISABLED, AND THE PSYCHOPATHIC DELINQUENT. I involuntarily shudder, and a chilling sense of déjà vu makes me close my eyes for a moment.

An attendant steps out of a little gatehouse and comes around to the driver's side of the car, carrying a clipboard. I press back the unbidden memory of a different hospital, a different time. I roll down my window.

"Morning. And who will you be visiting today?" His tone is friendly and courteous.

I force a smile in return. "I'm actually here to inquire about someone who was a resident here some years ago."

"You work for the state?"

"I don't."

"Anyone in the offices expecting you?"

"I . . . I didn't think to call first. Sorry. No."

"What's the name of the resident you're asking about?"

"Rosanne Maras."

"And your name?"

"Miss Calvert."

He writes both names down. "I'll call up and see if anyone in the offices is working today. Most everyone is taking a Christmas holiday."

The man steps back into his gatehouse and picks up a black telephone receiver. I watch through the window as he speaks Rosie's name into the mouthpiece. I see when his lips form my own name, watch as he listens. After what seems like a long stretch of seconds, he hangs up. Then he is unlocking the gate and opening it wide. He walks back to me.

"You're in luck. Dr. Townsend is in his office for a bit today and he said he'd see you."

"Dr. Townsend?"

"He runs the place."

I thank him as I put the car in gear. I slowly move past the opened gates and the two massive oaks. As I steer the Studebaker up the sloping driveway, I glance in the rearview mirror just as the man swings the heavy gates closed and locks them.

I park in a small visitor lot cut into the lawn on the right side of the multistory structure. As I step out of the car, I see now that the paned windows are barred on the inside on every floor except the first. I walk up the steps to the large double doors.

Inside the lobby are a waiting area and a large reception desk with a nurse sitting behind it. A miniature artificial Christmas tree sparkles on one corner of the desk.

"If you'll have a seat, someone will be with you shortly." The nurse nods to one of the sofas placed in the room.

Less than five minutes later, a door to the left of the reception area opens. On the other side of it is a young man in a pressed white shirt and dark tie.

"You the one who just called in from the gate?" he asks.

"Yes."

"If you'll follow me."

The man starts down a hallway with several doors on either side, some open to darkened offices, some not, and I follow. He stops at an open door at the end of the hall and then steps aside. The room is richly paneled and lined with bookshelves on three sides and framed academic degrees and awards. A man in a white doctor's coat sits behind a large cherrywood desk. He looks to me to be about my own age, maybe a little younger. His dark hair is strewn with strands of gray.

"Open or closed?" the young man says as he lays a hand on the doorknob.

"You can leave it open. Thank you," the doctor replies.

"Thank you for seeing me," I say. "You are Dr. Townsend?"

"I am. And you must be Mrs. Calvert. I remember the name from Rosie's file. A pleasure to meet you."

"Oh, I'm sorry. Mrs. Calvert is my sister-in-law. I am Miss Helen Calvert."

"Ah. I see. Please have a seat."

I sit down in one of two armchairs positioned in front of the large desk.

"And how is Rosie these days?" he asks casually.

"I . . . was hoping you might be able to tell me."

The doctor stares at me a moment, one brow slightly raised. "Why should I be able to tell you that? Rosie was discharged from this facility years ago. Did you not know?"

"I have been out of the country for a long while, you see. I was in Europe during the war, so I didn't know about Rosie's situation."

The doctor blinks at me, and I can tell my explanation is no explanation at all.

"Well," he says matter-of-factly. "I'm afraid you've troubled yourself to come here for no reason. Rosanne Maras was discharged from this institution in the fall of 1940." The doctor regards me for a moment before continuing. "And I'm sure you must be aware that your brother and sister-in-law ended their guardianship over Rosie before she was brought here."

"Yes, Celine told me that. I was hoping you could tell me where Rosie was discharged to. Actually, I am most interested in what became of the child she bore."

"And why is that, Miss Calvert?"

"Because, as much as it pains me to say it, my late brother, Truman Calvert, is the father. The child is my niece or nephew."

"So your brother told you he is the father? I ask because Rosie would not or could not tell us who the father of the child was. Your brother's name is not recorded on the birth certificate that we issued here."

I open my mouth to tell him Rosanne was paid for her silence, but shut it. That is not this man's business. When I open it again, different words are on my tongue.

"It's really not my place to discuss private matters about this unfortunate family situation, Doctor. I came here primarily to ask about the child. My niece or nephew. And I would also like to know where Rosie is."

"I don't know where Rosie is."

"Can you please tell me where she went when she was discharged? Can you tell me where her child was sent?"

"I'm afraid I can't. You aren't Rosie's next of kin. And as far as I know, you're not kin of the baby, either. So no. I can't tell you anything."

I feel my frustration rising even though I know I must remain polite and genial if I am going to get any information at all from this man.

"Is there anything you *can* tell me?" I ask as nicely as I can.

"Such as?"

"Such as why Rosie was brought to a place like this? I don't understand. It seems to me she should have been taken to a home for unwed mothers."

"That is your opinion and you are entitled to it, but unless you are a doctor—are you?"

"No."

"Well, unless you are a doctor, you can't possibly know what would've been best for her, could you? Rosie was a minor child who'd been placed in the care of the state, and this is a state institution dedicated to caring for people like her."

"Like her?"

"Yes."

"Are you saying she was crazy or mentally encumbered or psychopathically delinquent or any of the other things on your sign outside?"

"Nowhere on our sign outside do we call anyone crazy, Miss Calvert."

I take a breath and hold it a moment to calm myself. I am getting more annoyed by the minute at the doctor's tone. "But it does say the other things."

Dr. Townsend stares at me a moment. "How well did you know Rosanne Maras?"

"She was born at my brother and sister-in-law's vineyard. She'd lived her whole life there."

"But I asked how well you knew her."

I know my answer will only serve to prove his point, not mine. "That's not what really matters at the moment—"

"Well, of course it matters. It always matters how well we know a person if we are going to make decisions regarding his or her well-being."

I take another calming breath. The doctor waits for my reply, unruffled. Calm. Completely in control.

"Look," I say. "If this is about the colors and shapes Rosie said she could see—"

"So you know about that, do you? How much do you know?"

"Not much. My sister-in-law mentioned it."

"So you don't know, then, how much Rosie had to endure because of it?"

"So it was true? What she saw was real?"

"It was real to her. And since you didn't answer my question, I will tell you that I had many therapy sessions with Rosie regarding her condition, so I do know how much she had to endure because of it."

"What do you mean by her condition?"

"Her condition. She suffers from synesthesia."

I try to wrap my tongue around the strange word and find that I cannot. "What did you call it?" I ask.

"Synesthesia. Rosie's auditory and visual sensors are tangled. That's why she sees colors and shapes when she hears sounds. For people with synesthesia, stimulation of one sensory modality triggers an automatic response in another modality. For her, sound produced colors. For others like her, sound can produce taste. For others, it is some other kind of overlap and misfiring of two senses. The condition made Rosie's life very difficult."

"So you helped her with it?" I ask.

The doctor stares at me as though I've asked the wrong question. "Despite our best efforts, we were unable to rectify this sensory deviation during the time Rosie was here," he answers a moment later. "She left soon after her nineteenth birthday to live in a group home. She was discharged out of the state's oversight with the equivalent of a high school diploma and upon reaching her majority. And after proving she was able to live a responsible and independent life, which she learned to do here—even with her condition. It was important that Rosie learn to suppress it. She learned to not let her condition master her. So yes, we helped her."

"And the baby?" I ask.

"What about it?"

"What happened to the baby?"

"The child was placed into the state's care and taken to a receiving home where adoption by a suitable family was the objective."

When he says this, I sense that I knew all along this is what happened to my niece or nephew. Rosie wouldn't have had the means to raise the child unless someone stepped in to support her. God, how I wish I had known. I would have found a way to help her, even from Vienna. I could've wired her money. If Rosie had wanted to keep her child, I could have had George and Lila come get her and the baby and care for them until I had made other arrangements for them.

I know it is not likely Dr. Townsend will tell me where this receiving home is, but I decide to ask anyway. I need the assurance that my brother's child is all right. I want someone to be able to tell me that he or she was adopted by a family where there is love and affection and affirmation.

"I don't suppose you will tell me where this receiving home is?" I ask.

"If you can prove your brother is the father and can get a court order for me, I would be happy to oblige."

"My brother died in a training exercise in 1942. Preparing to go to war."

"I'm truly sad to hear that, but it doesn't change the fact that I cannot divulge information about a resident without proof of relation. Provide proof your brother is the father or get a court order, and I will open the file."

I sit for a moment, digesting the new information and feeling a sense of immense disappointment. George said he would help in any way he could, but even he cannot prove to a judge that Truman is the baby's father. Celine certainly wouldn't be willing to provide any proof. And what proof is there to be had, anyway? Truman is dead. Still, I will go back to San Francisco, share all this news with George, and ask him what I can do about what I cannot prove.

"If that is all, Miss Calvert?" the doctor says.

I look up at him. I wish it wasn't all. But I can tell we are done here. He will tell me nothing else. "Do you know how Rosanne came by this condition?" I ask as I start to reach for my purse by my feet.

"We are learning more about synesthesia every day, including what causes it. More studies need to take place, but I can tell you that it is often hereditary."

The word falls into my chest like a rock. "Hereditary? You mean it's genetic."

"Yes. It's likely someone in Rosie's family also had the condition."

If this doctor saw Rosie's hereditary condition as debilitating and deviant, something that made a person's life a burden to the state, then . . .

"Tell me you didn't," I say.

The doctor stares at me. "Didn't what?"

"Tell me you didn't sterilize her."

Dr. Townsend cocks his head slightly. "That truly is none of your business, Miss Calvert. I believe we are finished here."

"God Almighty, you did, didn't you?" I say with a gasp. "I know you do that here."

"Again," the doctor says calmly, "that is none of your business."

"But why?" I am unable to keep the accusing tone out of my voice. "Why did you do that? Rosie was just a young girl!"

"She could've easily passed her synesthesia on to a child. And as I said earlier, this genetic condition made her life miserable. Do you understand? Her life was handicapped because of it."

"But how do you know her life was miserable because of it? And what gives you the right to decide who is worthy to be a mother or a father and who is not? What gives you the right to judge whose life has value and whose doesn't as if you were—"

"As if I were God?" he cuts in. "I've heard that before from people like you who haven't seen what I've seen."

"I was going to say, 'as if you are better than everyone else.' God doesn't devalue people the way you do," I say evenly.

"Is that so? And yet he permits some to be born with the worst birth defects imaginable."

"But he doesn't love or value them less because of it! Do you honestly think because of her condition that God in heaven loves Rosanne Maras less than you or me? Do you honestly believe that he loves anyone who is blind, or crippled, or can't think straight, less than anyone else?"

"If I was of a mind to convince you," the doctor says coolly, "I might take you upstairs and show you the many men and women we have here with perfectly operating sexual organs but with the intelligence of four-year-olds. Do you think someone with the mind of a four-year-old would make a suitable parent or would produce a healthy child? I can show you women whose promiscuity has riddled them with diseases and who are of such low moral standards that they would fill the earth with miserable souls just like themselves, who would then grow up into a life of crime and depravity. Just because a person has the anatomical features to produce a child doesn't mean they should, Miss Calvert. Deviance is woven into the fabric of a person's genes, as is intelligence and moral fortitude. I would ask you how you could so cavalierly subject society to the immense financial and civic burden of caring for people like this and then their multiple offspring. But since you are not likely to be convinced, and you are no threat to our work here, I will kindly say, instead, good day, Miss Calvert."

Martine's words to Johannes that long-ago night are echoing in my head and heart. *Who are we to say their lives are meaningless, Johannes!*

Who are we indeed?

I rise from my chair, shaking with anger and regret for all that I did and cannot undo. "You think you know everything, have seen everything," I say. "But I'm the one who has seen where this takes us all in the end, how the way you're thinking right now can degrade and make you—yes, you, Doctor—just like Hitler and all his murdering Nazis. You want only perfect people living in the world, and for *you* and only you to decide what is perfect and what is not. Wake up! That's what they wanted! Can't you see? That's exactly what they wanted. And look what they did to get it. Look what they did!"

The man startles but quickly recovers his composure. "We are finished, Miss Calvert." Then he reaches for papers on his desk, as if I have already left the room.

I stand a moment longer and then turn from him and leave his office, two hot tears sliding down my face. I lost my temper. I said things I cannot take back, that can't be unheard, just like before when Fraulein Platz came to the Maiers' door.

I sweep the tears away with one hand as I walk quickly down the long hallway, wanting to believe, needing to believe, that George will somehow be the next one of us to walk down this hallway, and with a court order in his hand. Somehow I have to get one.

In the lobby, I stride past the nurse at the reception desk, who looks up at me but says nothing.

I swing the front door open wide, step out, and yank the door closed behind me. I pause on the top step, wishing I could go back in time and fix everything. I would tell Truman to be careful, to recognize he was unhappy in his marriage and deal with it so that he didn't make a mistake that would ruin three lives. I would tell Celine to put Rosie in school and to stop treating everyone like objects to be controlled. If I could go back in time, there is so much I would do differently. So much.

If only I could. Two more tears are spilling down my cheeks as I walk toward the Studebaker. When I am halfway to the vehicle, the door to the institution opens and the young man who showed me to Dr. Townsend's office steps out. He holds up a hand to indicate he wants me to stop and wait for him.

He hurries over to me. In his hand he holds a folded piece of paper.

"I heard you talking in there. I was just in the next office over. Here." He offers me the piece of paper. "It's the address of the hotel in Petaluma where Rosie Maras was given a job after she left here. I looked it up while you were talking."

I take the piece of paper, too stunned to thank him.

"I'd appreciate it if you kept this just between us," the man says. "My father would be livid if he knew I had given the address to you."

"Your father?" I ask, finally finding my voice.

"Dr. Townsend. I work for him when I'm on summer or holiday breaks from medical school. My name's Stuart."

I again look at the address in my hand: Hotel Pacifica, 104 Washington Street. Petaluma, California. Then I raise my gaze to the young man in front of me. "I don't know how to thank you."

"I'm the one who is grateful for the chance to help you. I remember Rosie Maras. She was kind to me. Quite kind. And I . . ." His voice falls away.

"You knew her?"

"My family has a house on the premises, so I pretty much grew up inside the hospital. My father was always giving me little jobs to do. I knew a lot of the residents. I liked Rosie, and I wish . . . I wish things had turned out differently for her."

"So do I."

We are quiet for a moment.

"I'd better get back inside." Stuart casts a glance toward the building behind him and then turns back to me. "If you happen to find Rosie, would you tell her something? Please? From me?"

"Of course."

"Tell her I'm sorry."

"It's not your fault what happened to her here," I say gently. "You couldn't have been more than a kid."

Stuart Townsend smiles, but it is not a happy smile; it is one full of old regret. "But you'll tell her anyway? I don't want her to forget that I was always very sorry about what happened here. And my part in it. So, you'll tell her?"

I tell him I'll pass on the message if I'm ever able to.

He starts to turn and so do I, but then another thought occurs to me. "Do you think you could do one more thing for me? Could you find out where the baby was sent? Please? It would mean a great deal to me if I could know what became of my niece or nephew."

Stuart thinks for a moment. "I don't know. Those records are in a different place. Maybe. If I can get to them without my father knowing about it."

"I would be forever in your debt."

"I could try. Is there a telephone number where I can reach you?"

I feel inside my handbag for a pen and scrap of paper, and I pull out the bill from the hotel in Santa Rosa where I spent Christmas Eve night. I write Lila and George's number on one corner, tear it off, and give it to him.

"Do you remember what it was?" I ask. "I mean, was the baby a boy or a girl?"

Stuart pockets the scrap of paper. "I do remember. She had a little girl."

I feel my heart lighten with the joy of knowing this. "Thank you for telling me."

"I'd better go," he says.

As he turns to head back inside, one last question springs from my lips. "Do you happen to remember if a name was given to the child?"

Stuart smiles as he swivels to face me again. "I do remember. Rosie asked that I make sure the home that was receiving her baby knew a name had been chosen. I can't remember the name of that receiving home, but I remember the name Rosie had given the baby. She was adamant about it. And it was a rather unique name."

"Please tell me."

"Amaryllis."

27

Before . . .
MAY 1940

A week had passed since Fraulein Platz had been to the house, and I settled into a contented confidence that I had come through for the Maier family. The turmoil all around Austria was alarming, and the family still prayed nightly at dinner for Captain Maier's safety, but inside the Maier home, when the door was shut on the worries of the world, I sensed ours was a peaceful haven. The town house on Rainergasse was the one place where I and the family I loved had relative shelter from the storms of war.

I took Brigitta to school on a warmer but still chilly May morning and came back to the house to straighten up the children's rooms. But first I wanted a cup of tea and a Berliner. I was just setting the kettle to boil when Martine rushed into the house from having been to the post office. She dashed inside as if she'd forgotten something important and had returned for it. She nodded to me standing at the kitchen counter and then tugged off her sweater and hat and tossed them on the kitchen table rather than on the hook in the entry behind her.

"You need to pack a suitcase," Martine said. "I'll pack one for

Brigitta. I'm sending the two of you to my parents' in Innsbruck, and I want you both on the first afternoon train."

I had been to Martine's parents' home in Innsbruck several times. It was a charming place, and the children loved going there for summer term breaks and skiing trips over the holidays. But it was only mid-May. There were several weeks of school left. Everything about Martine's demeanor told me that something was wrong.

"What has happened?" I asked.

But Martine was already turning for the escritoire around the corner in the parlor. I left my tea making and followed her. Martine began rummaging through the pigeonholes, yanking out identification papers and passports, no doubt looking for Brigitta's.

"Martine! Please tell me," I said. "You're scaring me."

"I don't want you to be scared." Martine didn't look up but kept rummaging through the nooks, pulling out Reichsmarks now. "I just want you to do as I say. Please go up and pack a bag. I'll be up in a moment to pack Brigitta's." Then she turned to me. "You might have to stay there for a long time. And you might . . . you might have to take Brigitta somewhere else after you get to Innsbruck. I'm not sure yet. I've wired my father and he's . . . he's working on it."

"Working on what?" I said, a shapeless dread spreading across me.

"I might need you to hide Brigitta for me." Martine's voice cracked on the word *hide* and tears sprang to her eyes.

I could barely breathe. "Why?"

"Because I was at the post office just now and I ran into Klaus's mother, Sigrid. Klaus is that little boy at Brigitta's school, the one who is in a wheelchair."

"I know who Klaus is."

"Sigrid told me she and Klaus are leaving within the hour for her sister's in Saint Pölten. There is a government woman going around to all the homes of the students at Brigitta's school asking questions about them and filling out forms and official documents about their disabilities and how much care they need. Sigrid said four children from another school like ours in the Meidling district were taken yesterday and transported to some hospital west of the city. Their parents were told after the fact that that's where their children would be residing now. Shut away in some hospital where no one could see them. They institutionalized them, Helen! We've got to get Brigitta somewhere safe."

Regret enveloped me. I'd been wrong to keep from Martine the news that the woman had already been by and that I had taken care of it. I placed my hand on Martine's shoulder. She stopped riffling through the escritoire, looked at my hand on her shoulder and then up at me.

"You don't need to worry about this," I said. "That woman, Fraulein Platz, has already been by, but I took care of it. You don't have to worry. I didn't mention the visit to you before because you'd been so anxious about rumors of disabled children being sent to live in institutions. I convinced Fraulein Platz everything here regarding Brigitta's care is fine. Exceptionally fine. She left here quite satisfied."

Color drained from Martine's face. "What do you mean she has already been by? What do you mean you've taken care of it?" Her voice was laced with fear and doubt.

"She came by a week ago, but I didn't say anything because she was happy with her assessment of Brigitta. I knew you were worried about so many other things. I didn't want you to worry about this, too."

Martine's expression and tone were now signs of building anger. "How could you think you were doing the right thing by not telling me?"

"Because you had been so upset by the things Captain Maier

was telling us. And I assure you, I did take care of it. We don't have to worry about Brigitta." I had never had an employer look at me the way Martine was looking at me in that moment. I'd never angered one of them like I had just now.

"How do you know you took care of it?" Martine said, her voice rising in pitch and volume.

"Because Fraulein Platz was only here for a few minutes and she was happy with her assessment. She was happy with what I told her."

"What did you tell her?" Martine said urgently. "What did you say?"

"I told her what you and I and the captain had talked about before. That Brigitta is loved here in this family and very well cared for. She is no burden on society and she never will be."

Martine stared at me, unconvinced.

"I assured her that Brigitta has me as her primary caregiver and that I'm very fond of her, and that I had a chance to go back to the States when Captain Maier suggested I go, but I didn't go. I stayed. I stayed to take care of her. I will stay as long as Brigitta needs me, even if it's always. You know that."

Martine's eyes had widened in astonishment as I spoke. Now she lunged forward and grabbed my shoulders. "How could you do such a thing!" Martine screamed. "How could you say that?"

My mouth dropped open in surprise. "Say what? What did I say?" I gasped.

She dropped her hands and spun away, clenching her fists. "How could you say that you are the one who cares for Brigitta, that you are the one who will always take care of her? You could be sent back home to the United States tomorrow! The Reich owns your work visa now. They could deport you with one stroke of a pen." Martine threw her head back and let out a muffled cry of rage. Then she turned back to me. "I can't believe you did something so stupid."

"I said I'd always be here for her!"

"That is a promise you can't keep! What you told them is that Brigitta will always need someone to take care of her. *That's* what you told them."

Full awareness swept over me like a rogue wave. Dear God, I'd made a horrible mistake. "I am so sorry, Martine. I promise I only wanted to keep Brigitta safe! You have to believe me."

Martine whirled away from me and into the kitchen. She grabbed the car keys from their hook on the wall and threw open the back door. I knew where she was going to go. Martine was going to dash to Sonnenschein and fetch Brigitta. The kettle on the stove began to scream.

"I'll come with you!" I shouted, dashing into the entry hall to grab my sweater and then racing back into the kitchen to turn off the flame under the boiling water. But when I opened the back door, the car was speeding down the alley. Martine had left without me.

I sprinted for the front door, grabbed my purse to lock the house, and then began to run the six blocks to Brigitta's school.

I had been a fool, and so full of self-importance that I put the child I loved in danger. I couldn't think about what I'd do if Martine told me she didn't want me anywhere near Brigitta anymore. The only thing that mattered was getting Brigitta and bringing her home. My lungs began to burn after the first three blocks, and I had to stop a moment at a lamppost and catch my breath before taking off again.

Perhaps Martine would be so desperate to get Brigitta to her parents that she would have no choice but to entrust her to me again, and this time I would make good on my promise. I would protect that little girl with my life. And I would keep my mouth shut.

By the time I reached the school, breathless and gasping, Martine had been inside for several minutes. The second I threw open the door, I heard a high keening sound, the wail of a woman in agony. Beyond the reception area was Martine, crumpled onto her knees in front of the administrator's office. The administrator, a silver-haired woman in her early sixties named Emilie Pichler, was bending over Martine, speaking softly to her. The reception-ist was standing at her desk, a handkerchief to her eyes. Several students had come out from their classrooms and were peeking from around a corner even as their teachers were trying to herd them back.

As I approached, Martine turned to me.

"She's gone!" Martine yelled. "They took Brigitta. They already took her!"

I felt my legs go weak, and I wobbled backward against the wall behind me. For a moment I thought I might faint.

"That's impossible," I said, my words little more than whis-pers. I turned to Frau Pichler. "You would have called the house."

"We were instructed not to," Emilie said, her voice hoarse with restrained emotion. "They said they would be contacting the families. Not us."

Martine gazed up at me. "You stupid, stupid woman!" she shouted, and then took up her weeping again.

I wanted to put my hands over my ears to block out the sound of those agonizing cries and the words that I knew now were true. I had been stupid. But I would be stupid no longer. We would get Brigitta back. I would not rest until we had.

"Who came for her, Frau Pichler? I need to know who came for her. Tell me who it was. Where's the paperwork? Who signed her out?"

Emilie Pichler stared at me a moment. "No one here signed her out," she said, indignant. "They had official papers for seven of the students. Seven! They took them because they could,

Fraulein Calvert. They came with armed police and we could do nothing."

"Where did they take her? Where did they go?" I said, undeterred.

The administrator exhaled heavily. "Am Steinhof."

"What is that? I don't know what that is."

"It's a . . . a special hospital in Penzing," Emilie said, as if choosing her words carefully while looking down at Martine.

I bent down. "Let's go," I said to Martine. "Let's go and get her."

"I don't think it's going to be that easy," Emilie said.

I snapped my head up to look at the woman. "I don't care how hard it is!" I turned and said the same thing to Martine. But Martine was now slumped against the receptionist's desk, her tearstained face blank. It was as if she had entered another room and shut the door behind her.

"Martine?"

She did not respond.

I stood. "Let me call one of her friends to come get her, and then I'll go get Brigitta myself."

"Fraulein Calvert," Emilie said wearily. "I know how fond you are of this family and especially of Brigitta, but I think perhaps this is a matter that Captain and Frau Maier will need to address."

"Captain Maier is in Poland until next week. Do you really think he would want us to do nothing while we wait for him to come home?" I said as politely as I could. I liked Emilie Pichler, but waiting was the worst possible next course of action.

Emilie sighed and then nodded. The receptionist turned the telephone on her desk toward me.

Minutes later, after having arranged for one of Martine's friends to come for her, I was taking the car keys out of Martine's skirt pocket and rushing out the door.

Vienna was a sprawling, beautiful city laid out in twenty-three numbered districts; Penzing was the fourteenth, and nine kilometers away from the Maiers' home in the Wieden district. In the eight years Vienna had been my home, I'd had little occasion to travel to the outer districts. As I made my way northwest, I couldn't remember the last time I'd been in this direction. The Maiers liked the city—and spent most of their leisure time in the *innere Stadt*—the city center.

As I maneuvered my way out of the busier part of the city, I practiced in my mind what I was going to say when I arrived at Am Steinhof. I would calmly but authoritatively ask to see who'd been in charge of transporting the schoolchildren from Wieden that morning, as there had been a mistake. Brigitta Maier was the daughter of a captain in the führer's Wehrmacht, a brave soldier who was at that very moment serving his country. That was the mistake.

I knew those who had taken Brigitta surely knew who her father was, but it was obvious they hadn't considered the ramifications of taking the child of an army officer. I would loudly announce who Brigitta was. If it was a large hospital, then there had to be a great many people inside it. All within earshot would hear me state why I was there. I would make sure they heard it.

The metropolitan landscape of the city fell away, and in its place were large expanses of verdant pastures and woods, broken here and there with residences and roads leading to smaller towns. Soon I was slowing to study the map Frau Pichler had quickly sketched and glancing at addresses. I stopped in front of a large multistory building, painted white and fenced in and surrounded by trees and hills and lush lawns. Behind it were additional buildings, smaller, also painted white, also edged with grass and trees and flowering shrubs. It looked like a peaceful college campus.

But as I came to a stop in front of its gate, I saw that this was no college. It was not even a typical infirmary. The sign read AM STEINHOF PSYCHIATRIC HOSPITAL. A burst of alarm pulsed through me.

I stepped out of the Maiers' car, my eyes taking in the grandeur of the facility and the absolute quietness. There was no sound coming from the buildings. All I heard was birdsong and the rush of another vehicle passing by me on the road.

I walked up the path to the main building—its front entrance was on the street side of the fence—and opened the heavy door leading to the visitors' lobby. Inside were shining linoleum floors, comfortable chairs in which to sit and wait, pastoral artwork on the walls. There was no one else in the room except a woman behind a reception desk. She looked up when I approached.

"Can I help you?" she said in German.

I cleared my throat, steeled my resolve, and spoke my best German as well. "Yes. A child was brought in here today from her school in Wieden. But she should not have been. It was a mistake. Brigitta Maier is the daughter of a decorated officer in the Wehrmacht. I've come to collect her."

The woman stared at me as if I had just asked for a table for two.

"And who are you?" she said.

"My name is Fraulein Calvert."

She cocked her head and frowned. "You are not from the T4 offices. You are American."

I was disappointed my accent was so obvious but said, "What of it?" I didn't know what T4 meant, and I could hear the insecurity in my own voice.

"You are not the child's mother," the woman went on.

"I am Brigitta Maier's nanny. I am employed by Captain Maier to care for her."

"The hospital only speaks to next of kin and legal guardians regarding patients here," she said calmly.

"But Captain Maier is deployed to Poland and Frau Maier is . . . ill. So I am here. Because as I said already, a mistake was made. Brigitta Maier is not to be a patient here. I've come to fetch her home. And I'd like to speak with someone in charge, please."

The woman sighed and picked up the handset of the telephone on her desk. She pressed a button. "There's another one out front here. Not a parent this time. She believes a mistake has been made . . . No . . . The child's surname is Maier . . ."

The woman listened and I waited.

"All right. Thank you." The woman hung up the phone and looked up at me. "No mistake has been made, Fraulein."

"I assure you one *has* been made," I said, fighting back tears of frustration. "I would like to see Brigitta."

"Only family is allowed to visit, and only when visitation is allowed."

"But I must insist that—"

"Unless you wish me to summon guards to escort you out, you should go, Fraulein." The woman's demeanor and voice were so calm, almost bored. I wanted to shake her.

"How do you sleep at night?" I said instead. "Taking these children from their parents and hiding them away here to live like lepers, away from the people who love them. How can you live with yourself?"

The woman serenely picked up the phone, surely to call for guards to toss me out.

I turned on my heel and stormed out of the building, vowing aloud to come back with Captain Maier when he returned next week.

Brigitta did not belong in that place, as pretty as it was on the outside. She belonged home with her family.

Johannes would be able to use his influence, I was sure of it. Maybe he could not rescue all seven of the children who had been taken from the school that morning, but he could get Brigitta.

He must.

And when he did, I would be on the next train with her to somewhere safe. Somewhere far away. Farther away than Innsbruck. I would take her to America. To the vineyard. I would find that safe place. I would.

28

I sit for a moment in the Studebaker staring at the address Stuart Townsend gave me, not seeing the words as much as hearing a name.

Brigitta. Brigitta. Brigitta.

I lean forward and rest my hands and forehead against the cool steering wheel, the paper crinkling in my hand, while I wait for the reverberations to still. My words to the doctor had fallen on deaf ears, but they'd set in motion an old bell in my head that had never really stopped ringing.

The past cannot be undone. I know this. I know I only have now. Today.

And today I am holding a piece of paper with an address I didn't think would be given to me.

I pull back from the steering wheel to study it. Rosie named her daughter Amaryllis. It can't have been a coincidence. She hadn't even known what an amaryllis was before I sent one to her. She'd told me as much in her thank-you note. She'd also written that it was the most beautiful flower she'd ever seen. I suddenly feel connected to Rosie by a thin but luminous thread: the amaryllis. The bond is new and loose but real. As real as the link we already share as mother and aunt to the same child.

Perhaps with this address I can find Rosie, and together we can look for Amaryllis.

I know the town of Petaluma, know it is less than twenty miles away, and I am glad it's still early in the day. The revelations of the morning have wearied my heart but not weakened my resolve. I start the car, and when I get to the bottom of the little rise, the attendant smiles and waves like we are old friends as he opens the gate wide.

Forty minutes later, I am in Petaluma and looking for Washington Street, which I follow to the 100 block. The hotel, constructed of creamy golden brick, is five stories high and situated on a busy corner. I park, check my appearance in the rearview mirror, and go inside.

The lobby is nicely appointed, with tall ceilings, stylish rugs, and smartly upholstered furniture. Holly garlands and Christmas wreaths decorate the walls, and a large lighted fir tree sits in one corner of the lobby. The hotel desk clerk, a young woman in a red wool blazer, smiles and wishes me a good afternoon.

I'd thought about what I would say as I drove. The little fib is going to be easy. Rosie is almost like family. Amaryllis makes it nearly so.

"Good afternoon," I greet the hotel clerk in return. "I'm looking for a relative who worked here and with whom I lost contact during the war. I was stuck in Europe, you see, and unable to stay in touch with her. Now that I'm home, I would very much like to find her."

I am counting on the deprivations of the war to win me some sympathy, and I can tell that they do.

"I'd be happy to help if I can," the woman says kindly. "What is the name?"

"Her name is Rosanne Maras. It would have been the fall of

1940 when she started her job here. I don't suppose she is still employed at the hotel?"

"I'm afraid there is no one by that name currently working at the hotel, but I can ask the manager. He's been here longer than me. If you want to take a seat, I'll inquire for you."

I thank her and sit down in the lobby. Five minutes later an older, gray-haired man comes out from an office located behind the reception desk. I start to rise, and he motions me with a smile to keep my seat. He chooses an armchair across from me.

"I'm Douglas Brohm," he says, his smile widening, "manager of the Pacifica."

"Helen Calvert."

"So you're asking about a former employee, Rosanne Maras? She's a relation of yours?"

"Yes. I've been overseas. The war made it difficult to stay in touch."

"It was quite a while ago when she worked at the Pacifica. Might I ask if you are aware of how she came to be here?" Mr. Brohm says this cautiously, as though a relative of Rosanne Maras will surely know that.

"Yes. She came to you from the Sonoma State Home for the Infirm."

He nods, satisfied, it seems, that I know the finer details of Rosie's history. "Yes, we were happy to participate in that release program for a number of years."

"So, did she stay here for a while after being fully released from the state?"

"For a time. She resigned in 1943. I checked her personnel file before coming out to see you."

"And do you know if she quit to take another job elsewhere, perhaps?" I hear the longing in my voice. I see in Mr. Brohm's expression that he hears it, too.

"She did not say where she was going. She was quite cordial

when she quit, though. Thanked me and the staff for giving her the chance to make something of herself."

"Did she stay in contact with any of the other staff that were here at the time?"

"As I recall, she did not. I can ask the head of housekeeping if she is aware of anyone having been in contact with Rosanne over the years, but my guess is no one has. I have not heard her name mentioned since the day she left, until today. Rosanne was a good worker, but she kept to herself. Again, I'm very sorry."

"I am, too." I sigh. "Do you know where in Petaluma she was living when she worked here? Might she have had roommates or a landlord who she stayed in touch with?"

He hesitates before answering. "Sorry, but I don't think I'm at liberty to divulge an employee's personal information to someone I've just met. I take it none of your other family members have stayed in touch with her?"

"No. It's . . . it's complicated with my family."

"I see." He stands, signaling he has nothing else to offer me.

"May I leave you my phone number in case your head of housekeeping might know where Rosanne went when she left here?" I ask. "And would you be willing to contact the landlord of the last residence you have on record and inquire about Rosie? I know it's a lot to ask. I wouldn't trouble you if it wasn't important. That person can just call me, then, if they have been in contact with her."

"I can have one of the clerks look into this for you." He reaches into the breast pocket of his suit coat and removes a hotel business card from a little brass case. He hands it to me. "Jot your name and telephone number on the back of the card there. If we hear that anyone might have information for you, I will call you."

I write down George and Lila's phone number and hand the card back to him. My frustration seems to keep me pressed to the chair, and I rise as if burdened by the weight of it.

"I can see you had hoped for better information about your relative, and I'm sorry I can't provide it, but I can tell you when she left here she seemed happy," Mr. Brohm says.

The heaviness in my chest lessens a bit. "She did?"

"Yes. Happy enough for me to remember it, Miss Calvert. I hope you can take some comfort in that."

"Thank you for telling me. It actually means a great deal." I shake his hand, leave the hotel, and return to the Studebaker to head back to San Francisco.

I spend the next two days alternating between feeling like I'll never know what has become of Rosie Maras and nursing the hope that I will.

I check the local and regional phone books in the downtown library, looking for a Rosanne Maras to no avail. I place calls to directory assistance in Los Angeles and San Diego and Sacramento. No Rosanne Maras is listed.

I call the Sonoma County social services office and ask for Eunice Grissom, the name on the letter I found in Celine's file cabinet, not knowing if she's still a social worker employed there. She is, but she offers me no more than what I already know: Rosie was released from county oversight on her twenty-first birthday.

"I've not heard from her," the woman tells me. "And it's not likely that I would have. She wasn't under any obligation to keep me informed of her whereabouts."

"Do you know where her baby was placed? Or perhaps what kind of family adopted her?" I ask next.

"Even if I did, I couldn't tell you," Mrs. Grissom says.

I'd figured as much.

"Can you tell me if Rosie was agreeable to her daughter being adopted? Can you tell me that?" I ask.

"I'm not telling you that, either."

"She wasn't, was she? That's why she named her. Rosie wanted to keep Amaryllis."

"Rosanne Maras was seventeen, homeless, and with no means to support herself. It doesn't matter if she did or didn't."

"It matters because Amaryllis will be the only child Rosie will ever have."

Mrs. Grissom is quiet for a moment. "So you know about the procedure she had done at the institution."

"I do. Dr. Townsend told me all about it." I suddenly don't care if I burn a bridge here. This woman will be of no help to me. "And she didn't have it done. It was done to her."

Mrs. Grissom's tone changes when next she speaks. "I didn't make that decision. I wasn't consulted."

"But you knew they did that sort of thing when you took her there, didn't you? My sister-in-law knew. And how could Celine have known unless you told her?"

"Look, I do the best I can with what I am actually able to do. Try doing my job and see how well you can make the laws work perfectly for the people under your care. I have to go. I've got far more to do today than time to do it."

"Wait, please. Just answer that one question," I say. "Please?"

She huffs. "Which one?"

"Did Rosie want to give my niece up for adoption?"

The woman pauses a moment before answering. "She didn't. She wanted to keep her baby. But that was impossible. You know that, don't you?"

"I would have taken her."

"But you weren't here. I need to go."

Before I can say anything else, the line falls dead.

For hours after we hang up, I console myself with the knowledge that at least when Rosie left Petaluma, she seemed happy. Somehow, despite what happened to her, she found contentment.

When I strike out with the county, George offers to consult a partner in his firm who practices family law about getting the court order.

"But it might take time and effort to convince a judge you're Amaryllis's aunt with no proof of paternity," he tells me. "And even if we get the order and are able to learn which receiving home the baby was sent to, the adoption records are most likely sealed. Your being Amaryllis's biological aunt won't matter then. The child will be her adoptive family's legal daughter."

"I know," I tell him. And I do know. Yet I yearn for assurance that Amaryllis is safe and loved and cared for. It's likely that some family in Northern California or south of San Jose or somewhere in the vastness of San Francisco is happily raising Amaryllis. But I want to *know* it for fact, not just hope it.

As George and Lila are in no hurry for me to start looking for my own place, I unpack most of my belongings into one of the bedrooms on the third floor and begin using the other room as a little sitting area so that I can have time to myself at the end of the day, and also give my friends some time alone as well. They tell me not to rush to look for a job, and to use this time during the holiday season to conduct my search.

I find that I get along quite well with George and Lila. If I'd stayed in the Bay Area instead of moving to Europe, I might've found the man of my dreams here and married him, and my husband and I and George and Lila would have been couples who took their children to the circus together and had dinner parties and celebrated the holidays together just as I was celebrating with them now. I don't regret the life I've led, but I'm acutely aware that if I'd made different choices, my life would have had a far different trajectory, and not only my life but other lives, too. So much would be different at this moment if I had stayed.

On the last day of the year, I summon the courage to give Celine a call to wish her a happy New Year and to apologize for how we ended things on Christmas Eve.

"Why are you really calling?" she says calmly after I've done both, rightly guessing I've an ulterior motive in phoning her. "Do you honestly think we have more to say to each other?"

"It's New Year's Eve and the perfect time to bury the hatchet, don't you think? I am really sorry that I upset you and then left without saying good-bye."

"What do you want, Helen?"

I pause before answering, even though there is no point now in beating around the bush.

"I just want you to sign an affidavit that Truman was the father of Rosie's child. I'll never mention this again to you, Celine. Or anyone else. Ever. I promise."

She laughs lightly. "You must be mad. Why on earth would I do that?"

"Because it will allow me to find out what receiving home my niece was sent to."

"Your niece."

"Rosie had a little girl."

She pauses, but only for a moment. "I'm not signing any such paper, and I'll swear to anyone who asks that I have no idea who fathered that tramp's child."

"Please, Celine? I'm begging you."

"I don't care if you crawl back here on your hands and knees to get it, Helen. No."

"All I want is to know my niece is all right, that's she's living a happy life."

Again Celine laughs. A mirthless guffaw. "I don't give a damn what you want. Do you actually think I'd drag my family's reputation through the mud for what *you* want?"

"No one has to know. It's just for one judge in one courtroom."

"Don't call me anymore, Helen."

"Celine—"

But the line clicks off. She is gone.

I set the handset down hard, despite knowing it had been a long shot thinking Celine would want to help me.

I can only hope that George and his partner will be able to craft a compelling argument without her help.

That evening, George and Lila invite several friends over, and I find myself enjoying the festivities more than I thought I would. We play charades and Parcheesi and eat oysters on the half shell. There is dancing and singing and card games. It is the most joyous I have felt since my happiest days in Vienna.

The following day, the three of us get up late. We are enjoying coffee and leftover Parker House rolls from dinner the night before when the telephone rings. George comes back to the breakfast nook after answering and tells me the call is for me.

"It's a Mr. Stuart Townsend," George says with a smile. I spring from my chair to pick up the receiver on the telephone table between the kitchen and dining room.

"Hello, Stuart," I say. "Please tell me you have news for me."

"I do," he replies. "I figured I could sneak into the offices unnoticed this morning with it being New Year's Day. There's no one on the first floor except me right now. I found the name of the receiving home where Amaryllis was taken. It's called Fairbrook Children's Home and it's in Oakland. Do you want the address?"

"Yes, yes!" I fumble for a pencil and a piece of notepaper. He speaks the address and I scribble it down. "Thank you so much for this, Stuart." My voice starts to break. "I really am so very grateful."

"You're . . . you're welcome."

I hear emotion in his voice, too.

"Did you happen to find out if Rosie is still working at that hotel?" he asks.

"She left that place some years ago."

I tell Stuart about my visit to the Pacifica and my conversation with Mr. Brohm.

"I'm beginning to think I'll never find out what became of her, but the manager said she seemed happy when she left, Stuart. There is that."

"All right," he says, but I can tell it isn't all right.

"What is it?" I ask him. "Why is it so important to you that I find her? What is it that you are sorry for?"

He is quiet for a moment. "Rosie and another resident had a chance to escape when I was on security detail," he finally says. "I ruined it for them. I blew my whistle."

"Weren't you just a boy?"

"I had just turned fourteen. The other resident got away, but Rosie had just given birth and she couldn't run. I don't know if Rosie would've been able to make good her escape, but she might have had a chance if I hadn't blown the whistle. I wish I hadn't. She was a nice person. And smart. I didn't think she belonged here, and I've always wished I had done things differently."

"All of us, at some point in our lives, wish for a way to go back in time and make different decisions. I wish for it, too. You have no idea how much."

We are both quiet for a moment.

"Do you want me to let you know what I find out about Amaryllis?" I ask him.

"I would. Please write to me at the university, though. Don't try to call me here."

He gives me his address.

"I'll stay in touch," I say. "Thank you, Stuart. So very much. And happy New Year."

"Same to you."

When I hang up, I consider, only for a moment, calling the Fairbrook Children's Home right then. But I want to see the place, want the people who run it to see me. I want to see for myself what kind of environment my infant niece was placed in, and I want its managers to see for themselves what kind of person I am. I want them to meet me, not just hear my voice. I want them to want to help me.

I know I'm not going to be given the name of the family who adopted Amaryllis or the address where they live. But I am hoping compassion will win out and I'll be told in general terms about the couple who chose her. Took her home. Gave her their last name.

And yes, I want the people who run this children's home to decide it might be wise to contact this family and let them know their adopted daughter has an aunt who just learned of her existence. What if Amaryllis is wondering where she came from? What if she is troubled, as any eight-year-old might be, by not knowing? Maybe Amaryllis desperately needs to know the mother who bore her wanted very much to keep her but couldn't. I can give Amaryllis that assurance. I can tell her a lot about her mother if given the chance.

I'm fully aware that the adoptive family may not want anything to do with me. It's possible they haven't even told Amaryllis she is adopted. But what if the opposite is true? What if they have?

I walk back into the kitchen. "May I borrow the Studebaker tomorrow, George?" I ask. "I need to go to Oakland."

29

When I returned to the Maier house from my unsuccessful trip to Am Steinhof, the older children were not yet home from school, and Martine, who'd been given a sedative, was asleep in her bed. The friend whom I'd phoned to come for Martine, a fellow officer's wife named Therese, had called for the family doctor, and he had just left after supplying additional calming pills for Martine, should they be needed. Therese had also learned that Johannes had been contacted by the Viennese field office overseeing the transfer of disabled children to Am Steinhof and was now arranging to be granted several days' leave. Therese had spoken to him on the telephone.

"What did he say? Can he get her back? Is that why he's coming home early?" I asked Therese. We were standing in the Maier kitchen as Therese made us both a cup of tea.

"I don't know that he can get her back," Therese said doubtfully.

For several seconds, I couldn't make sense of her answer. Of course he could get her back. Of course he could.

Couldn't he?

"Did he actually say that?" I said, when I was able. "Did he say he can't?"

Therese poured the hot water atop the tea leaves in their strainers. "He didn't say that's why he's coming back early. I think he's coming back because of Martine."

"But surely he's going to try," I said, incredulous. "He has to try to get Brigitta back."

"I would. You would. So I guess he probably will, too. We didn't talk long, Helen. I could hear other people in the room with him. He wasn't alone."

"I can't believe this is happening." I folded myself onto a chair at the kitchen table. "I didn't mean for it to."

"I know you didn't," Therese said. "And deep down Martine knows, too."

"I'm afraid this is it for me. Even if we get Brigitta back—and I will not rest until we do—I don't know if Martine will ever forgive me for not telling her that woman had been here."

Therese removed the strainers and brought the two teacups to the table. She handed one to me and took the chair opposite me.

"I think in time she might," Therese said. "Just don't expect too much from her too soon. She needs someone to blame, and right now it's you."

"But I *am* to blame."

Therese shrugged. "I don't know that there's any way to have avoided this. I think it was always the Nazis' plan to do what they did today, to do what they're doing everywhere else, every day."

"Surely you are not in agreement?" I was astonished at Therese's casual tone. "The way they treat the old, the sick, the disabled, the Jews, the Roma, men who love other men? It is as if they want no one around them but their idea of perfect people. Surely you don't agree with this?"

Therese took a sip of her tea and then set the cup back on its saucer. "It doesn't really matter what I think, does it? I don't have the power to change what is happening, and neither do you. The Nazis are the ones in control, and they have decided this is the way it will be. And so it is."

"But we can't sit here and drink tea and do nothing! Isn't that the same thing as being in agreement?"

"I don't think it is. And you need to be careful what you do and say, Helen. Austria is not a safe place for dissenters, especially if they are foreigners. You shouldn't be saying what you are saying right now to other people. You really shouldn't be saying it even to me. I'm telling you this for your own good."

I was quiet for a moment, letting that warning settle over me. Perhaps Therese was right that I had no power to change the current situation. But that didn't mean I had no power at all. "I have to try to get Brigitta back. I have to."

"It's not completely your fault they took her. I think she was on their list. Even before you talked to that woman."

"But I should have told Martine that Fraulein Platz had been here."

"Maybe so, but would Martine have known to flee with Brigitta that very day? To send the two of you to Innsbruck? She wouldn't have known they were taking children from other schools. It hadn't happened yet."

"She might have."

"Well, we'll never know, will we?"

We both sipped from our cups.

"Martine wanted to let you go," Therese said a moment later, "but I convinced her that she needs you now more than ever. And I tried to convince her that they were probably always going to come for Brigitta, no matter what you said or didn't say. They would have come for her in Innsbruck, too. Innsbruck is Austria and Austria is Germany. They would have found her there."

"There has to be somewhere safe to take Brigitta," I said. "If I could just get her to England, I have friends there. And from there maybe I could take her to America."

Therese laughed ruefully. "You have forgotten we are at war with England. Listen to me, Helen. The best thing you can do right now is care for Martine and her other children. Her heart is broken. She may be angry at you right now, but she is hurting. Let her be angry with you. She has to be angry at someone. And the other children will not understand this. They will need you, too."

Therese finished the last swallow of her tea, stood, and took her cup to the sink. "I need to go. My own children will be coming home soon."

I walked with her to the front door. Therese reached for her lacy shawl hanging on a hook on the hall tree.

"You'll remember what I said, won't you?" Therese said as she wrapped the shawl around her shoulders. "I mean about speaking out against what is happening. You could get yourself deported. Or worse."

I nodded. "I'll try to be careful."

Therese looked past me to the rest of the house. "This home already seems different without Brigitta."

I couldn't summon words in response. Therese turned and left.

The next two days as the family waited for Johannes were tension-filled. Werner and Kurt quietly sorted out the sudden absence of their youngest sister, saying little to anyone. The girls, especially Hanna, dealt with it by asking questions no one could answer.

Martine managed to leave her bed for short periods, but she couldn't bear to see the reminders of Brigitta around the house— her photograph on the mantel, her slippers by the bathroom, her artwork tacked to the pantry door. She often retreated to her room after only minutes with her other children, overcome by the visible evidence that her youngest daughter, who should have been at home with her, was not.

Werner had noticed his mother distraught at the sight of Brigitta's hair ribbons on the banister and offered to put them away. Martine had yelled at him to leave them alone and then had broken down and wept for having spoken to him that way.

The hours when the children were at school were the hardest, because then I was alone in the house with Martine. The first time she had ventured downstairs, Martine told me she did not want to discuss what happened.

"I know you're sorry," Martine said tonelessly, "but I don't want to hear you apologize. I don't want to hear it."

"What do you want to hear?" I'd asked. "What can I do for you? I'll do anything."

"There is nothing you can do."

And so I had kept my distance, busying myself with the children's needs and taking care of all the meals. Twice that first day after Brigitta was taken and three times the second, friends came by to call on Martine. One brought a bouquet of freesias, another a plate of crullers. Martine refused to see them. I had to send them away, suggesting perhaps they try again the following week.

"How is she?" each one had said, and to each I had replied, "She is devastated."

Finally, just before dark on the third day, Johannes arrived home by taxi. The children and I were at the dining room table eating cassoulet that I had made. He came in through the front door, stepped into the narrow entry with his duffel and travel bag, and the three girls rose as one from their seats to run to him, each one talking at once about the horrible thing that had befallen the family while he'd been gone. "Brigitta is gone!" "Brigitta has been taken." "When are you going to get her back?" The two boys stayed in their chairs, watching with pensive interest as their father embraced their sisters and struggled to answer them.

The man looked haggard and ill-equipped, despite the commanding appearance of his military uniform, to handle his daughters' many questions. He turned to me, and his gaze said, *Help me.* I rose from my chair.

"Come, girls." I gently nudged the girls back to their places. "Let's allow your father to sit down and have his dinner, too, and then he can answer your questions."

Johannes looked both grateful and terrified as the girls led him to his seat. He noticed right away that at the other end of the table, Martine's chair was empty. I dished him up a plate of cassoulet and brought it to him. As I was retaking my seat, Martine appeared in the doorway to the dining room. She had apparently heard the commotion of her husband's arrival.

Johannes sprang from his seat and rushed to his wife, pulling her to his chest. Martine was like a rag doll in his arms. She closed her eyes against the strength of his embrace, as if needing to steel herself against feeling the intensity of it.

"I'm so sorry about all of this, *Liebling,*" he said softly. "I'm so very sorry."

"Can you get her back?" Martine asked flatly. I noticed with alarm that she hadn't asked when he'd get her back, but whether he could.

Johannes took a step back to look at his wife, his hands resting on her shoulders. "I came home as soon as I could, Martine."

"But can you get her back?" Martine said again, the same way.

"Please, can we talk about this later?" Johannes dropped his hands and motioned with his head to all the children seated behind them.

"This? What is the *this* to talk about later? There is only the question. Can you get her back? Yes or no?"

It seemed to take a long time for Johannes to answer.

"I don't know."

Martine stared at her husband for a long moment before she spoke again. "You knew they were coming for Brigitta and you said nothing."

"I didn't know," Johannes said quickly.

"You've known about the other terrible things the Nazis are doing. How could you not know about this?"

"This is not a military matter, Martine. It has nothing to do with the fighting, or the men I fight with. I did not know."

Martine held his gaze for a second and then turned from him and left the room.

Johannes watched her go and then slowly made his way back to his chair. He slumped into it but did not pick up his fork.

"Why did they take Brigitta, Papa?" Werner asked.

Johannes took a long breath and exhaled before answering. "The new government thinks children like Brigitta will have a better life if they live in a place that is specially designed for people with . . . difficulties."

"Why do they think that?" Liliana asked.

"I guess . . . I guess because people like our Brigitta will have a hard time getting a job when they are older and making a living."

"Brigitta can live with me when I'm a grown-up," Liliana said. "I don't care if she can't work."

"She can live with me," chimed in Amelia.

"No, with me!" Hanna said.

Johannes lifted a hand to rub his forehead, as if trying to wipe away a dirty smudge.

"Why can't you get her back?" Kurt asked.

Johannes kept massaging his forehead. "Because I don't make the rules, son. There are new rules now. And I didn't make them."

"Does she have to live at that place forever?" Amelia's voice broke as she asked.

Johannes did not immediately answer her. I felt tears burning in my eyes and a searing pain in my gut.

"I hope not," he finally said.

No one said anything for a stretch of seconds.

"Can we go see her?" Hanna finally asked. "I want to see her. I drew her a picture."

Again, Johannes did not answer.

"I'm sure you can," I said, swallowing my emotion. "I went there to try to get her. They said families can visit. On visiting days."

Johannes lowered his hand. "You went there?"

"I did. I wanted to bring her home, Captain. I tried."

He looked at me and said nothing. A moment later, Johannes picked up his fork, and the rest of the family followed suit. The Maiers ate their dinner in silence.

The following morning, I woke early. The third floor I'd always shared with Brigitta was painfully quiet. I went downstairs to make the coffee but found Johannes in the kitchen with the French press already out. We had not talked again after dinner the previous night. After the kitchen was cleaned up and the children were in bed, Johannes hadn't emerged again from the master bedroom. He made the coffee now and spoke to me as if no time had passed since our last words at the dinner table the night before.

"It served no purpose going to Am Steinhof yourself," he said as he scooped the ground coffee beans into a measuring cup.

"It was the only thing I could think of to do. So I did it."

"But that hospital didn't take her from us. It was an administrative office here in Vienna that ordered it. I will go there tomorrow."

"I'll come with you."

"I need you to stay here and do your job."

He sounded angry with me. Like maybe he believed it was my fault, too, that Brigitta was gone.

"If I had known this would happen, I never would have let that woman in the house," I said.

Johannes set down the tin of coffee and stood silent and still at the counter for a moment. "I am not saying this is your fault," he finally said.

"But I told Fraulein Platz I would be here for Brigitta for years to come. Years. I made it seem like she would *need* someone for years to come."

"These people don't need a nanny to tell them what kind of care someone like Brigitta needs and for how long. This isn't about whether or not you will be able to keep renewing your visa for years on end. It's not about you at all. This is all about Brigitta. All they had to do is look at her medical file. The visit here just confirmed what they already supposed."

"Then I should have told Martine that woman had been here."

Johannes sighed, picked up the tin again. "Maybe. I'm not sure. I'm not sure of anything anymore."

The kettle of water began to boil, filling the kitchen with its trembling wail.

Over the next three days, Johannes was in and out of the house, tending to his wife when he was home and making the case for his daughter at the local administrative office for the Reich when he was not. I went to Brigitta's school to ask Emilie Pichler if any more children had been taken. None had, but I learned the parents of the other six students snatched the same day as Brigitta were also visiting the local administrative office and writing letters to higher-ups. I learned parents of children too young yet for school had been forced to hand over their disabled babies and toddlers, and they were doing the same. Some of these parents, Emilie said, were in the beginning stages of planning a joint trip to Berlin to advocate for the return of their children.

Johannes also made daily calls to Am Steinhof to ask about visiting Brigitta. Each time, he was told there had been such a large influx of new residents that visiting hours were still temporarily suspended.

"When will they be reinstated?" he'd asked.

"Soon," was the answer.

By the afternoon of the third day, however, Johannes's leave was nearly up. He was to depart in the morning to return to his division, which was still deployed for control measures in Poland. As he placed one of his bags at the door for the next day's early departure, Martine implored him to ask for an extension.

"I won't be granted one, Martine," he said. The children were still at school and only I was in the house with them. "I was lucky to get the time off that I did."

"But you haven't even asked for it. You can at least ask!"

"It won't do any good."

"Give me your commander's telephone number and I will ask him myself!" Martine shouted, and Johannes finally said he would make the call. But he insisted he needed to finish packing first. Martine, furious with him, climbed the stairs to their room and slammed the door shut.

I wanted to be anywhere but in the same room while they fought, but I'd been right there at the kitchen table, just a few yards from them, mending one of Liliana's blouses.

Seconds later, Johannes stepped over to the telephone on its little table by the entrance to the kitchen. Apparently he was not going to pack his second bag before making the call. Now he was only a few feet away from me on the other side of the wall. In another short stretch of seconds, he was talking to one of his superiors. I heard him ask if he might be granted an extension of his leave, as his wife was not well. The person on the other end of the line began to yell, his voice clearly projecting out of the handset and into the airspace where I sat.

"We are at war!" the man yelled.

And then the man said something so vile I stabbed my finger with the needle.

"Stop obsessing over your monkey child, Captain Maier, and get back to your duties."

When I heard Johannes answer, "Yes, Obersturmbannführer," I dropped the mending and bolted for the back door to the alley to get away from the phone call, the house, the madness. I came back inside only after I was sure Johannes was no longer downstairs.

Early the following morning, Johannes kissed his children good-bye and called for a taxi. When it arrived, he instructed me to keep calling Am Steinhof to inquire about visiting hours. He would continue to write letters from his posting. He would appeal to ranking officers who had known him for years, knew Brigitta, knew what a sweet and happy child she was, and ask them to intercede on the Maiers' behalf.

And then he left.

Each day after Johannes's departure seemed endless. I waited to hear good news either from Johannes by telephone or directly from Martine. No news came. Every day was the same.

The first week of June, fourteen days after Brigitta had been taken, Martine was at last told by a staff nurse on the children's ward at Am Steinhof that she could see her daughter the following afternoon. But as she readied to leave the next morning, there was a phone call. Brigitta had come down with pneumonia and could not have visitors.

For a week, Martine called and begged to be allowed to see her sick child. She called Johannes's unit incessantly to plead with him to intervene until he told her she had to stop. He was going to be officially reprimanded if she did not. That would not help Brigitta.

Twice Martine drove to Am Steinhof to beg to see Brigitta. Twice she was turned away. Because, she was told, her little girl was too sick for a visit.

I could only watch over the older children and pray. Martine did not want my help and would barely look at me.

Martine's parents came from Innsbruck to cry with their daughter and comfort their other grandchildren. They offered to take them all back to Innsbruck when their visit was over, but Martine would not be parted from any more of her children. After four days, Martine's parents left, sad and worried for their daughter but unable to get her to change her mind.

I took long walks to find a measure of solace and to have time away from Martine. I'd often find myself in front of Brigitta's school—the last place I'd been with her. I had braided her hair that day, had walked her to school while we counted squirrels and pigeons, had told her to have a good day, had waved good-bye.

On the eighth day since we'd been told Brigitta had taken ill, Frau Pichler saw me from the window of the school and gave a slight wave. It seemed to be a wave of farewell, though, and not hello. I couldn't shake the feeling that Brigitta would never be coming back to Sonnenschein Grundschule, that I would never step inside it again to collect my sweet girl for home.

She was never going to leave that place she'd been taken to. They were going to keep her there forever, hidden away from the rest of the world.

Only a few days later, on a humid day in late June, and the last day of school before the term break for the remaining Maier children, Johannes arrived unexpectedly in the early afternoon. His face was wan and his countenance that of a grieving man.

"Where is Martine?" he said to me in a voice empty of strength.

The spinning world seemed to teeter to a stop. "What has happened?" I said. But I could tell by the look on his face and by the sudden splintering of my heart within me. I already knew why he was home from the war in the middle of the day. I knew before he answered me.

"The pneumonia was too much for our little girl," Johannes said, his eyes suddenly rimmed with silver. "She is with God, Helen. He will watch over her now."

I knew in my soul it was true. Brigitta was dead. But still I whispered the word: "No."

Then I said it louder. Then I yelled it.

Johannes turned from me to find his wife.

I dropped to my knees on the rug on which Brigitta and I had worked on puzzles, played games, read stories, sipped hot chocolate.

I covered my face with my hands and wept.

30

The last time I traveled to Oakland was long before the Bay Bridge had been erected, and the drive combined with a ferry ride had taken more than an hour. But now as I cross over the glittering water, Oakland lies ahead as if it is San Francisco's cozy next-door neighbor.

I find Fairbrook Children's Home easily enough after turning south from the bridge and making my way to a part of the city where fruit trees had once been as plentiful as the houses and buildings and streets are now. The home is located on one of these streets, flanked on either side by houses that had clearly been built after it. The three-story building is of wood and stucco and trimmed in creamy brown. A two-story residence is connected via a breezeway. From the curb where I've parked, I can see a fenced backyard and a small playground of sorts, empty at the moment of any children.

I step out of the car, walk up to the entrance, and ring the bell. A woman about my own age answers.

"How do you do?" I say cheerfully. "My name is Miss Calvert

and I'd like to speak to someone in management, if I may." I hope I sound professional and confident, and I must be successful, for the woman doesn't so much as raise an eyebrow.

"If you're from the county and have a child to bring, I'm afraid we're full," she says. "I don't expect we'll have an opening for several weeks, if that."

"No, I'm not from the county."

The woman looks at me as if to assess me, glancing at my face and noting my graying hair. "I don't suppose you've come about adopting one?" she says skeptically.

"No. I'm here on a personal matter," I say, maintaining my smile and courteous tone, "and I'd be grateful if I could speak to someone in charge."

"All right." The woman shrugs as she opens the door wide.

I step into a small foyer. Three wooden chairs are set along a wall and are the only pieces of furniture in the room. Above the chairs is a painting of apple-cheeked toddlers crowding happily around a basket of kittens. Ahead is a wide staircase leading to the upper floors. On my left is a hallway revealing closed doors on either side, and on my right, a sitting room with plentiful windows along its back wall. I hear an outburst of laughter somewhere in the home, and the sound makes me glad.

"Have a seat in the sunroom there and I'll see if Mr. or Mrs. Sommers has a moment to spare," the woman says.

"Thank you." I walk into the well-lit space where all the windows are and take a chair.

Within five minutes, a woman, rail thin but looking very much in charge, comes into the room. Her hair is a soft gray at the temples, and she wears a golden chain around her neck sporting a key, a tubelike brass whistle, and a folded pair of reading glasses.

I rise to my feet.

"I am Mrs. Sommers," the woman says. "My husband and I

are the directors here." Her tone makes it clear she hopes this unscheduled visit will be quick. "Please have a seat."

I retake my chair and the woman sits in one opposite me.

"How can I help you?" Mrs. Sommers asks briskly.

"Thank you for seeing me," I begin. "My name is Helen Calvert, and I've come with a plea for help, actually. I'm inquiring about my niece, and I only know that she was placed here as an infant some years ago."

The woman blinks, waiting for more.

"I was stuck in Europe during the war, so I was not able to stay in touch regarding everything happening back here at home. With regard to my niece's coming here, I mean."

Mrs. Sommers seems to soften the tiniest bit. "I see. Well, I suppose I might be able to help you in some respect, but if your niece came here as an infant during the war years, she's likely been adopted, and the information pertaining to that is something I cannot share with you."

"No, I'm sure you can't. But perhaps you could just let me know that she is being well cared for and in a good home?"

"I can assure you that all of our adopted children are placed in good homes, Miss Calvert."

"I'm sorry. I didn't mean to suggest that they weren't, I'm just . . . The situation was difficult for my family, you see. And I feel very bad for what happened to the child's mother. Peace of mind would be a balm to me."

Mrs. Sommers regards me for a moment and then withdraws a little notepad and pencil from her skirt pocket. "When was this?" she asks in a tone that gives no indication of how much information she is going to provide.

"It would have been late summer of 1939."

"And how did your niece come to be in our care?"

"She came to you from the Sonoma State Home for the Infirm," I say. "That's where she was born."

The woman looks up from her notepad, eyes wide. "And you said this was the summer of 1939? Are you here inquiring about Amaryllis?"

I nearly fall forward in my chair. "Yes! Yes, I am."

The woman continues to stare at me as if still trying to fit puzzle pieces together. "And you are the birth mother's aunt?"

"No. Um, no. My brother was the father of the baby. That's why it was so difficult. He was married to someone else. Amaryllis's mother was a maid in his household, and someone who didn't have any family to care for her when she became pregnant."

"Good Lord," Mrs. Sommers says, clearly taken aback.

"So you can see how difficult it was for my family and for Amaryllis's mother," I continue, surprised by the woman's astonishment.

And still Mrs. Sommers stares.

"I know it's not customary for you to divulge details about an adoption, but perhaps you could just tell me about Amaryllis's new family without giving me their names. Even that much would mean a great deal to me. Or maybe you could contact them and let them know that Amaryllis has an aunt who would love to meet her."

Mrs. Sommers sets the notepad and pencil down on a little table between us. "Amaryllis wasn't adopted."

"Beg your pardon?"

"Your niece wasn't adopted. She is here."

31

Over the next few days, I was one moment numb with disbelief that Brigitta was dead, and the next either consumed with sorrow or seething with anger that we'd all been kept from her as she lay dying. Martine, at least, should have been allowed to see her sick child. What if Brigitta succumbed to her illness because of loneliness and fear, begging for her *Mutti* with gasping breaths as she grew weaker? What if Brigitta could have rallied if only she'd been able to have her mother hold her and soothe her fevered brow and sing to her? Visions of such scenes tormented me day and night.

Martine refused to believe that her child was gone, insisting it was a trick of the government to keep them parted. It made no difference when Johannes told her that those in power had no reason to tell them their daughter was dead if she wasn't.

"It was just Brigitta's time," he'd said to his wife that first terrible day. "Pneumonia can be a difficult disease, Martine. You know this. Your own grandmother—"

"My grandmother was seventy-two years old when she died!"

Martine had shouted. "And my baby girl is only seven. She's seven, Johannes. She needs a step stool for the bathroom sink. She still has baby teeth!"

As their parents argued nearly hourly about this, the remaining Maier children wandered aimlessly around the house. The boys seemed in a brooding daze and the girls acted out in agitated confusion. I knew I had to be strong for them, and as I summoned the resolve to do so, I discovered that attending to Brigitta's siblings kept me from caving into despondency myself. The children needed to be listened to and cared for. And they needed answers.

"Did it hurt when she died?" Liliana asked me on the second day.

"I don't think so," I answered. "I think Brigitta probably just went to sleep one night and, because her tired lungs could not give her all the air she needed, she just slipped away without waking up."

"Is she in heaven?" Hanna asked.

"Absolutely."

"Does she have all her fingers now?" Amelia asked. "And straight legs?"

I thought for a moment. "Maybe. I don't know. We loved her just the way she was, didn't we? So maybe it's quite all right to think of her there just the way we loved her."

They nodded, relieved, it seemed.

The boys had different questions. How come the hospital didn't let anyone see their sister before she died? I didn't have an answer for that. How did Brigitta get pneumonia? It was June. Warm and sunny. I didn't have an answer for that, either. But I thought they were good questions.

On the third day, Martine's parents arrived from Innsbruck, and the children naturally turned to them for comfort. I couldn't help feeling cast aside. I tried to busy myself with answering the doorbell and receiving the covered dishes, baked goods, and flowers brought by neighbors and friends, but Martine's mother stepped into that responsibility, too. When callers came to offer their sympathy, they wanted to talk to the family, not the nanny. I spent much of the fourth day trying to stay out of the way.

It took five days for Brigitta's remains to be released. Johannes had offered to hire a driver from a funeral home to go to Am Steinhof and collect his daughter's body but was informed her remains would be sent to the house by an official transport. Martine was expecting a casket and one last look at her little girl. I assumed this, too. But Brigitta's remains arrived in a wooden box the size of a breadbasket. She'd been cremated.

Again Martine raged that Brigitta was still alive and being kept from her, and again Johannes struggled to convince her that the Reich had no purpose for doing such a thing. The Reich was all about its purposes. He showed her the death certificate and she screamed that it was just a piece of paper. When her mother tried to calm her down, Martine stormed from the house. After an hour had gone by and she'd not returned, Johannes got into the Opel to look for her. On instinct, he drove the nine kilometers to Am Steinhof and learned Martine had just been arrested for refusing to leave the property. She had taken a taxi there. He'd been able to convince the local magistrate that his poor wife was overcome with grief. Martine was released, the charges were dropped, and the couple arrived home well after dark.

On the sixth day, the family brought the little box of ashes to St. Elisabeth's so that the priest would bless Brigitta's remains and conduct a funeral mass, which was to be followed by an interment in the mausoleum at the central cemetery in Simmering, where Johannes's parents had been laid to rest years before. Martine had at first refused to go to either place. Johannes, who never raised his voice to his wife, did so then, telling her she would go and pay her respects, and he would not stand for her not to.

The family dressed in black and sat in the front pews of the church, with me just behind them. There were music and prayers and words of reassurance from the priest, but the longer I sat there listening, the angrier I became. What had been a comfort a few days earlier—picturing Brigitta in heaven—was now a jagged thorn. Brigitta was no doubt flooding the halls of paradise with her laughter and smiles, but she belonged here on earth with us, not up in the clouds.

And for the love of God, why had she been sent home in ashes? What kind of thoughtless, heartless regime does that? Unless those were not Brigitta's ashes in that little box. I couldn't help but share Martine's doubts. What if the Reich had some dark purpose for children like Brigitta, concealing them away, intent on everyone forgetting about them? As I sat in the hard wooden pew, I couldn't shake the nauseating feeling that something dark and malevolent was now hovering over that pretty hospital campus called Am Steinhof.

I impulsively stood up and turned to flee the sanctuary, my shoes tapping out a noisy retreat. People turned to look at me as I passed them, including Emilie Pichler, whose gaze lingered on me in a curious, telling way. It was almost as if Emilie had discerned why I couldn't sit there any longer listening to empty consolations, almost as if she shared my contempt and suspicions but was better able to conceal it.

Two hours later, back at the town house, as friends served coffee and little sandwiches and Martine sat glassy-eyed in the parlor, I caught Emilie Pichler looking at me again, in the same penetrating way. Our eyes met for a few seconds, held each other's gaze, and then Emilie made her way to me.

"Fraulein Calvert." The woman's voice was quiet, as though she was intent on not being overheard. "Perhaps you could come by the school the day after tomorrow? I have some artwork of Brigitta's that she told me she'd created especially for you. Shall we say ten o'clock?" Before I could say I would be there, Emilie Pichler bowed slightly in farewell and left.

The following day, I overheard Johannes tell the children seated at breakfast to pack their suitcases when they were finished with their muesli, because they were leaving with their grandparents that morning for Innsbruck. Their mother was going, too. When I started upstairs from the kitchen to pack my own bags—I always accompanied Martine and the children when they went to Innsbruck—Johannes called me into the parlor.

He asked me to have a seat on the sofa, and he took an armchair opposite me.

"The children and Martine are going to be staying with her parents for the foreseeable future, not just the summer," Johannes said. "My deployments are only going to get longer as the war gets more complex, and Martine cannot stay in this house. Not now. Not after what has happened."

"I understand," I said. "I'm happy to relocate to Innsbruck with Martine and the children."

"Martine does not want you to come. I'm sorry."

I swallowed an immediate knob of sorrow and waited for Johannes to tell me that in a month or two, when Martine's grief had eased, I would be following along.

He said something else instead. "She knows how much you love our children. In fact, it is probably because you loved Brigitta so much that she doesn't want you to come. You were like a second mother to Brigitta. But you made decisions that I'm afraid Martine cannot forget. She would like to, but she can't."

Tears sprang to my eyes, hot and accusing. "If I could get that day back . . ."

Johannes shook his head as though to gently sweep away my regret. "It's not just that, Helen. The larger truth is, as long as my family is with Martine's parents, we don't actually require your services. The boys certainly don't need a nanny. The twins are moving past the time that they need one, and Hanna will have her grandmother there. The children might be in Innsbruck with their grandparents for a long time. We've . . . we've outgrown our need for you."

As soon as the words were out of his mouth, I knew Johannes was right. This family, without Brigitta, didn't require a nanny anymore. The children were growing up, as children do. This had happened to me before. Several times before. I'd be with a family for a stretch of happy years, and then a day would come when the little ones weren't little any longer. And I had moved on. There had been sad good-byes, but they'd been expected. I had failed to consider that even if Martine felt differently about me, without Brigitta, this family did not truly need me.

"I will write you a letter of recommendation that you can take anywhere," Johannes continued when I said nothing. "You've served us well. I will make sure to include in the letter how resourceful and devoted you are to the families you work for."

"Thank you," I finally managed. "I understand."

He seemed to relax a bit. The hardest part of this conversation for him was over. "I am so glad to hear that. I . . . I wonder if I could ask a favor of you? For the children?"

"Anything," I said. "You know I will do anything for this family."

"Your departure will come as a surprise to them. They are fond of you and they have already had to bear such a tremendous loss. I wonder if, when you say good-bye, if you could not let on how sad you must be right now to be leaving them. Perhaps you can say that it's wonderful that they will be with their grandparents and that you are wanted by another family who needs you like ours once did."

"You want me to suggest that leaving them was my idea."

Johannes looked at me thoughtfully. "More like, you sense the time has come to move on. Because you surely know that it has. I think it would ease any discomfort regarding your departure, especially for the girls. I would greatly appreciate it."

I pondered his request for a moment. I didn't want to add to the children's sadness right now. But I would not do this for Johannes, not for this man who, when his superior called his child a monkey, said nothing. I would do it for his children, though, whom I loved. I nodded.

"I have to go back to my division tomorrow, and I'm shutting up the house. Today," Johannes went on. "I am giving you your next month's pay, and I've reserved a room for you, starting tonight, at the Hotel Edelweiss. You can stay there as long as you need to while you make other arrangements. I strongly suggest you return to the States while you still can. The world is an uncertain place right now. If I were you, I'd go home."

"I'll think on it. And thank you for providing me with accommodations." I stood up and so did he. I turned to leave the room but pivoted to face him again. "But I wonder if you could do one more thing for me, Herr Maier."

"Of course."

"Tell me truthfully. Is Brigitta dead?"

He hesitated only a moment. "Yes, she's dead."

"You swear to me? You'd swear on your mother's Bible?"

"I would. I promise you, if you went to Am Steinhof, you would not find Brigitta there."

"Or anywhere else?"

"Or anywhere else. I know this for a fact."

I stared at him for a second. "Did she die of pneumonia?"

Johannes held my gaze. Took a breath. Let it out. "She died. Isn't that horrific enough?"

His anemic, resigned tone angered me. "No, it's not," I said sharply. Disrespectfully. "Not if that's not how she died."

Johannes's face registered neither shock nor outrage that I'd spoken to him that way. "I'll have the letter ready for you this afternoon. Before the children and Martine leave for Innsbruck, I will gather them here so that you can say good-bye." Then he turned and left the room.

For several seconds, I could only remain where I stood as fresh tears pooled in my eyes. There seemed to be no end to fresh tears. Everything was changing so fast and so hard. I wanted the world to stop spinning for just a tiny stretch of time so I could get my bearings. So I could grasp a new handhold, figure out what to do next. I didn't want to go home to the States. Not like this. Not in defeat and failure.

There had to be another family in Vienna that needed me, didn't there? I only had to find them. But would the new governing officials in Vienna renew my work visa, due to expire in just a matter of months, if I had not yet found a new posting? America had not joined the coalition of nations united against Germany, but tensions were high. What if my work permit wasn't renewed? I might be headed home to California regardless of what I really wanted to do.

And meanwhile I'd have to find a way to live with Johannes's cryptic words. He hadn't answered my question. It would have been simple enough to reply that of course Brigitta had died of pneumonia, as easy to say as "Yes, she's dead," which he'd had no trouble confirming just seconds before. The thought that something worse, something sinister, had happened was too appalling to ponder.

I started for the staircase to my room to pack my things, my heart heavy.

As I climbed the stairs, I was reminded of what a seasoned nanny told me decades ago in London's Hyde Park as we both pushed prams with babies tucked inside them.

"Don't make the mistake of thinking the children you nanny—

or their parents—are your family. They're not. And you're not theirs."

I had forgotten, grown careless, when it came to Brigitta. I'd given in fully to love.

If I could see that other nanny now, I'd tell her that though my soul felt fractured in this moment, I had no regrets over having loved her.

None.

I didn't sleep well that first night, although the Hotel Edelweiss was located on a quiet, tree-lined street near the prettiest part of the *innere Stadt*. The gaping unknown and my unease about what might have really happened to Brigitta peppered the long wee hours with fits of wakefulness.

In the morning, I set about looking into nanny service organizations willing to take me—an American on a work visa—into their employ. I had never used a service before; I had been hired in London, Paris, and Vienna by word of mouth. I hadn't known to that point how unnerving it was to stand in front of strangers, offer them the letter of recommendation from my last employer, and watch them read it word by word with no indication of any interest.

The service I visited in the morning did not want to hire an American whose work visa was due to expire. The service I went to in the afternoon wouldn't speak with me at all other than to intimate that I was a fool for wanting to remain in Vienna. Though the American government hadn't denounced the absorption of Austria into Germany, the American press had firmly done so. Not only that, but the Americans had only a consulate in Vienna now, not an embassy.

I returned to the hotel in the late afternoon, my thoughts

somersaulting. I didn't want to go back to the States after nearly forty years in Europe—most of them wonderful—and especially not after having been let go. When I did return to America for good, I reasoned, it would be to retire. I would not go back before that, and certainly not when I was feeling like a failure. Maybe I needed to get outside of Vienna to look for a new posting. Salzburg, perhaps. Home to America, if it could be called that, was my last resort.

The second night at the hotel, I slept as fitfully as the first, and my dreams were filled with wraithlike creatures chasing me through a sprawling house with too many rooms and too many hallways, across floors that were crooked and splintering, and past walls mottled with mold. And all the while I was calling for Brigitta and unable to find her. I realized upon waking that I could not leave Vienna without some kind of answer. I had to know the truth of what had happened to Brigitta. I could only hope that Emilie Pichler wanted me to come that morning because she needed answers, too, and wanted me to help her uncover them.

After breakfast in the hotel, I took a tram back to Wieden.

The school's front door was open, but the receptionist was not behind her desk and there were no sounds at all coming from the hallways or the classrooms beyond. The inside of the small one-story school was deathly quiet, even for summer break. Several boxes stacked one on top of another lined the hallway that led to the classrooms. Emilie Pichler appeared from her office directly behind the receptionist's desk.

"Fraulein Calvert. I'm so pleased you came." Emilie Pichler looked tired. "Please come in." She motioned for me to join her in her office.

The little room was filled with bookcases and cabinets in various states of fullness and emptiness. Like in the hallway, boxes were stacked here, too.

"You are packing?" I asked as I took an offered chair.

Emilie sat down behind her desk and smiled weakly. "I am closing the school."

"Closing it? Is the new government forcing you to?"

"No. This was my decision. My mother is in failing health. I am moving to Theresienfeld to care for her."

"I see. I'm . . . I'm sorry to hear that." I sensed there were other reasons but didn't ask what they were. "This was a wonderful school," I said instead. "You did amazing things here, Frau Pichler."

Emilie's weak smile intensified slightly. "Yes. For many years we did. And please call me Emilie. May I call you Helen?"

"Of course."

A stretch of silence followed. I noticed there was no artwork on the woman's desk, nor was she reaching for it in a drawer or a cabinet. Emilie was staring at me almost as if she wanted me to speak first.

"There is no artwork of Brigitta's for me, is there?" I asked.

"I'm sorry I lied to you about that. I wanted to talk with you. Privately."

"I wanted to talk to you, too."

Emilie tipped her head in slight curiosity but didn't respond. She was being careful.

"I don't think Brigitta died from pneumonia," I said boldly.

She didn't raise an eyebrow. "I don't think she did, either."

"Do you know what happened to her?"

Emilie shook her head. Her voice when she spoke again was wrapped in restrained emotion. "I only know that seven of my students were taken to that place, and three of them have died recently from sudden illness, or such has been communicated to their families. The same thing has happened to children from another school like this one in another district."

My blood chilled beneath my skin. "Good God," I said as

anger and fear and dread bubbled up inside me. "What is going on?"

Emilie cleared her throat and shook her head to toss away gathering tears. "I have a family member who knows someone at the Reich Chancellery in Berlin. The führer has come up with a scheme to, as his friend would say, ease the burden of those whose quality of life has been impacted by age, illness, or disability."

"Is this scheme called T4?" I asked.

Emilie's eyes widened. "Yes. Aktion T4. Where did you hear of it?"

"When I went to the hospital to try to get Brigitta back, the front desk nurse asked me if I was attached to that program. What is it?"

Emilie leaned forward in her chair, as if to keep the walls from hearing her. "I only know because this family member told me, and he only did so because he cares for me and he knows what kind of school I run. I'm asking you not to disclose to anyone where you learned what I am about to tell you. My instincts tell me that I can trust you. I want you to know that it's real, and it's happening."

"You have my word," I said quickly. "What is the T4 program?"

"It's for one purpose only." Emilie swallowed before continuing, as though to fortify herself for speaking the rest of the answer. "*Krankenmorde*."

The word fell on my ears like a hammer. *Krankenmorde*. Mercy killing.

"What are you saying, Emilie?"

"They are killing disabled people in the name of mercy."

"Brigitta?" I said, stricken. "They killed her?"

Emilie nodded and brought a handkerchief to her eyes to dab at sudden tears threatening to spill. "She is not the only one, Helen.

There have been others. Some they've murdered with gas, others with injections."

"How many?" I whispered, tears gathering at my own eyes. "How many have they killed?"

"I don't know. No one does. I just know it's dozens upon dozens. And they're still doing it. They are gathering up disabled people of all ages: babies, children too little for school, boys and girls like Brigitta, adults young and old. In Germany and Austria. Perhaps in Poland and Czechoslovakia, too. They're being taken to places like Am Steinhof, and their families are being told they're being institutionalized for their own well-being. But they are not caring for these people at these places. They are killing them."

I sat back in my chair. The tears I'd been holding back slid down my cheeks. For several moments, neither of us said anything.

"We must do something!" I finally said. "We must stop it."

"You know as well as I that we can't. No two people can."

"Why did you tell me this if it's impossible to stop!"

"Listen to me," Emilie said urgently. "We cannot save them all. But I think you and I can save one."

"What are you talking about?"

"I have been watching you from the moment Brigitta was taken. You refused to give up on her. You refused to do nothing. You can help me save one."

"How?" I said, instantly hungry to know more.

"I know all the children who would've been starting school here in September. I have completed their assessments and I know which ones will likely be added to the terrible list of those bound for Am Steinhof. And . . . I have spoken to their parents. Most of the parents won't consider being parted from their children. They didn't believe me when I said their children are in danger. But there is one family who wants us to take their little boy and get him out of Austria."

Though invigorated by the thought of rescuing a child destined for Am Steinhof, I shook my head. "I don't see how I can help. Captain Maier let me go. I don't have a posting anymore and my work visa is going to expire in a few months."

"I know Herr Maier let you go," Emilie said. "He told me at the funeral that was his plan. I know you need a new job, so I telephoned my sister-in-law. She's a Cistercian nun at a Catholic school in Switzerland. Switzerland, Helen. It is the last safe place left in Europe. Martine told me once that you studied at university to be a teacher. My sister-in-law—she goes by the name Sister Gertrude—told me the school needs another live-in teacher, especially one who can teach the English language. You could have a place there, if you want it and if you can persuade the Swiss to give you a work permit. You could be on a train tomorrow or the next day or the next—whenever we can get you your travel visa—taking your new charge, Wilhelm, to see his auntie, couldn't you?" Emilie said hopefully. "You could give that story to anyone who asks, yes? That you are a nanny taking a young boy to visit his elderly aunt in Lucerne."

"His aunt."

"At the border, you won't say why you're really traveling with him. Just in case."

"Why should the Nazis care if one disabled child is taken out from under them? Wouldn't they think I'm doing them a favor?"

Emilie Pichler sighed. "I have given up trying to understand how they think. Every day they surprise me with what they do. They won't suspect he's disabled, anyway. Wilhelm looks fine; it's when he tries to speak that his deafness becomes apparent. And it's not the German border I am most worried about. The Swiss are being careful with who they let in, even on a tourist visa. You need a good story for why you're bringing Wilhelm, a child with a German passport, into the country. It needs to seem like it's just for a visit. And the rescue must happen as soon as we can arrange it. That woman, Fraulein Platz, has just been to Wilhelm's house. They know about him. Sister Gertrude has arranged with a Lucerne family to take Wilhelm in for as long as his life is in danger. There is a Catholic relief agency there, Caritas, who will vouch for this plan and for you after you get there. Will you consider it, Helen?"

For the first time since Brigitta was taken, I sensed something other than the vise of powerlessness. Out of my deep sadness, I felt a bolt of energy, crackling past all that I couldn't do to protect Brigitta and igniting a new flame within me. I couldn't save my sweet girl; I didn't know about the Nazis' diabolical and secret scheme and how they'd used me to execute it. But now I would have a secret plan of my own.

"Absolutely," I said.

"I must tell you that there is some risk. I don't know what will happen if a German guard on the train or an agent at the Swiss border figures out Wilhelm does not have an aunt in Lucerne. But if you are successful, Sister Gertrude and I might try to rescue more, if we can. We might need you to help again, you and my sister-in-law from Lucerne and me from Theresienfeld. I am actually asking your help for more than just this one time."

"I'll do it," I said.

32

"Amaryllis is here?" Surprise and delight course through me, but so do shock and dismay. This means no one chose her. All these years and no one wanted her. "She's been here this whole time?"

"It happens sometimes," Mrs. Sommers says. "Most infants are quickly adopted, but occasionally they aren't. Prospective parents are informed of a child's family background if we know it. We do not hide from them how the children come to us. It was in Amaryllis's records that her mother was an inpatient at a state hospital. To many people wanting to adopt, that translates into risk."

I think back for a second to what Dr. Townsend said about Rosie's odd ability being hereditary.

"Has Amaryllis ever displayed any . . . um . . ." I struggle to find the right words to frame my question, but Mrs. Sommers senses what I want to know.

"Amaryllis has displayed no tendency toward the same delusions her birth mother had," she says.

"There's a medical term for her mother's condition," I say in quick defense. "Rosanne Maras wasn't delusional."

"Call it whatever you want, but prospective parents are often afraid to take a child whose biological mother was institutionalized, for whatever reason. You can't blame them, really."

"So Amaryllis is available for someone to adopt?"

"Yes."

"I can take her," I say without so much as a second's thought. "I can adopt her."

Mrs. Sommers hesitates before answering, and when she does, it seems she is choosing her words carefully. "You appear to be quite a bit older than most adoptive parents. And you are unmarried?"

"But if I can provide her a good home where she will be loved and wanted, isn't that more important than how old I am or the fact that I'm not married? And besides. She is my niece."

"Perhaps if you could get a good lawyer to help you with stating your case before a judge?"

"I know a good lawyer," I say, inwardly thanking heaven for George Petrakis.

"I can see where a court would be disposed to let you have Amaryllis, provided you can prove that you can give her a good home. It is always harder to place the older children," Mrs. Sommers says, tipping her head as she studies me. "I will help you with the application. It has always bothered me that we could not find a home for her. We came close once. Amaryllis is a sweet child. She deserves a real home."

"I would appreciate any help you could give me."

"Maybe before we continue this conversation, you should meet the child."

"I would like that very much, even though I know I won't change my mind."

"I'll go fetch her. I'll tell her a visitor is downstairs and wants to meet her. You can decide how much about yourself you want to tell her. If anything."

"All right."

"Wait here a moment."

She returns minutes later with a brown-haired girl in tow behind her. Amaryllis's heart-shaped face and dark hair are her own, but her eyes—locked on me—are Truman's eyes, large and luminous.

Mrs. Sommers walks back into the room briskly, but Amaryllis hovers at the doorway, peering at me. She is wearing a plain blue dress that looks like a school uniform and scuffed patent leather Mary Janes.

"Come inside, Amaryllis," Mrs. Sommers says, beckoning the child forward.

Amaryllis doesn't budge.

Mrs. Sommers repeats her words in a louder, slightly more authoritative tone. "Come inside, Amaryllis."

When the child again makes no move, Mrs. Sommers opens her mouth to no doubt repeat the request and maybe add a warning, but I speak before she does.

"Hello, Amaryllis. My name is Helen. I'd like to talk with you if that's okay."

"I don't know you," the child says in a voice void of emotion. She is making an observation and nothing else.

"I know. I would like for you to know me, though."

"Why?" The child narrows her eyes slightly, as though she'd been studied by prospective parents in the past and then ultimately not been chosen. The look in those Truman-like eyes speaks of far more heartache than eight years on the planet should. It is as if Amaryllis is already done with pretense and half-truths. The answer I give must be as truthful a one as I can give.

"Because," I say, and I can only hope my next words are the right ones, "we are family, you and me. You are my niece."

Amaryllis stares at me for a long moment before saying, "I don't have a family."

"It may not be a big family, that's true. But I am your aunt, and that makes us family."

"How are you my aunt?" the child says, her brows slightly furrowed.

"Well, my brother was your father."

Amaryllis stares at me in obvious disbelief. "I don't have a father."

"Everybody who is born has a father," I say. "I know you never knew yours, and I wish my brother were still alive so that you could meet him. He died during the war. I'm sorry to have to tell you that."

Amaryllis does not react to this news, either, at least not that I can see.

"Was he nice?" she asks seconds later.

"He was a good brother to me." I hope that is answer enough. "I'm a little older than he was. We lost our mother when we were young, and so we sort of looked out for each other when we were children."

"What was his name?"

"Truman."

Still Amaryllis does not move.

"I knew your mother, too," I say.

At this, Amaryllis's face seems to crumple the tiniest bit. "Is she dead, too?"

The child's words pierce me, but I keep my voice light. "I don't think so. I've been looking for her, and I haven't found her yet. But I did talk to someone who said she was well when he last saw her."

Still Amaryllis does not move.

"And there's something else. I think I know why your mother gave you your name."

Amaryllis holds my gaze as her cocoa brown eyes suddenly begin to shimmer.

"Won't you come sit with me so we can talk?" I ask.

She hesitates only a moment more before joining me and Mrs. Sommers at the little sitting area.

I watch as Amaryllis wipes her eyes of their unfallen tears and turns to stare at me as we sit next to each other on the sofa.

"Why don't I know about you?" she asks.

"It's because I didn't know about you. I didn't know you had been born. I wish I had. I only just found out on Christmas Eve."

"Who told you?"

I know I can't explain the intricacies of how Amaryllis came to be in my life, nor would telling her about Celine be easy or helpful. "It seems like it might be important to know who told me, but it doesn't really matter. What matters is, as soon as I knew about you, I wanted to come find you. I wanted to find you and your mother. I haven't found her yet, but I did find you."

"My mama didn't keep me."

The five words are razor-sharp and yet somehow also delicate. Fragile.

"I think she wanted to," I say. "But she wasn't allowed."

"Why?"

"We've gone over this, Amaryllis," Mrs. Sommers interjects, and then she turns to me. "Amaryllis knows her birth mother was very young, she wasn't married, and she didn't have a home or a job and was living at a state institution, so she couldn't take care of a baby."

I let my gaze fall back on my niece. "I bet it was hard for your mother to let you go. I bet she did it because she loved you."

"One of the older girls here says my mama was crazy. That I was born at the loony bin."

"Amaryllis!" Mrs. Sommers exclaims. "I—"

"It's all right," I interrupt. "Please, Mrs. Sommers."

The woman shuts her mouth on the words she'd been poised to say.

I turn again to Amaryllis. "I know for a fact your mother wasn't crazy. And I've been to the place where you were born. It is not a loony bin. It's a pretty building made of bricks on a grassy green hill, and there are two big oak trees in front that look as if they are as tall as the clouds. It's . . . it's a place that tries to help people."

Several seconds of silence hang between us as Amaryllis appears to be picturing this image in her head and fitting it all in with what she knew before and what I am telling her. Then she speaks again.

"Do you think my mama remembers me?" she says.

"I am sure she does."

"Why did she name me Amaryllis? You said you knew."

I smile at her. "I lived far across the ocean for a long time, and I didn't get home to America very often. But I met your mother when she was a little girl, and we were friends. She grew up on a vineyard my brother and his wife owned. The Christmas before you were born, I sent an amaryllis plant to your mother at my brother's house, and I know for a fact she loved having it. Her name is Rosanne, but we all called her Rosie. Rosie worked as a maid at my brother's house, and she liked keeping the letters I wrote to my brother's family because of the pretty stamps. And that Christmas was her first without her parents and little brother, because they had died in a tragic accident. I hadn't seen her for a few years, but I thought the amaryllis would cheer her. An amaryllis flower is very beautiful."

I pause a moment to gauge how all of this new information is falling on the little girl. But her expression reveals only quietly intense interest. I continue.

"I told your mother you can always see an amaryllis bloom again. I wrote a letter with the instructions. All your mother had to do was put the amaryllis bulb in a quiet, dark place and then plant it the following autumn. I told her it would bloom every year if she did that, if she just took care of the amaryllis in a special way. I think maybe that's why she gave you the name. She was taking care of you in a very special way, and she knew with every birthday that you'd celebrate apart from her, you'd be blooming, just like you are right now. And she'd be able to picture it."

The child's eyes are suddenly shimmering again, and this time two tears slide slowly down her cheeks. "I wish I could see her." Her voice is full of longing.

"I wish you could, too."

"I talk to her at night in my bed. I pretend she hears me."

"I like that. I think I'll believe she hears you, too."

Amaryllis palms the tears away. "I talk to her because I'm still here. Lots of kids get new moms and dads, but not me." The tenderness in her voice is gone and the observational tone back. "One mom and dad almost chose me, but they changed their minds."

Amaryllis's words are piercing, and again I keep my voice soft and gentle, as though I didn't feel the prick. "That must have been sad for you."

The child shrugs. "Mr. Allred was nice, I guess, but I liked Mrs. Allred a lot. I was starting to love her. She bought me these shoes. They were black and shiny when she gave them to me. I thought she was starting to love me, too. But she wasn't."

I can stand it no longer. I scoot over to Amaryllis and put an arm around her, bringing her into my bosom. When she doesn't resist, I put my other arm around her and hold her close. As Amaryllis eases into my embrace, I feel her shudder with the weight of owning far too much sadness.

"I want you to listen to me carefully," I say into the child's soft brown hair. "You are worthy of love, Amaryllis. And I swear to you, I will spend the rest of my life making sure you know it."

"I don't want to live here," Amaryllis whispers after several long minutes.

"I don't want you to, either." I pull away slightly so that I can look at her and hold her gaze. "What I really want is for you to come live with me. I know it might be hard for you to trust grown-ups, but if you would have me, I would like very much for you to come live with me. You're my family, Amaryllis. Your blood and my blood are the same. I know I'm older than most mothers, and I don't have a husband to be a father to you. It would be just you and me. But I promise you I will do my very best to give you a good and happy home, and I will love you from this day forward as if you were my own daughter."

All those decades of caring for other people's children, and even the desolation of losing my beloved Brigitta and then the years at the convent school in Lucerne, have prepared me in both wonderful and terrible ways for this moment. I will not rest until Amaryllis is mine in law as she is mine in my blood and now in my heart.

Tears are now sliding down my own face. Amaryllis reaches up and touches my wet cheek, as if needing assurance I am real, and my tears are real.

"Can I go with you today?" she asks.

"Oh, how I wish you could. But I have to convince some people that you and I belong together, so I need you to be brave just a little while longer. I have a good friend who's going to help me, and I promise we will work very hard to make it happen as fast as we can. I will not stop until you are with me. And I will come visit you, every day if I can. In the meantime, though, I need you to be brave. Can you do that, Amaryllis?"

My niece regards me with an unreadable expression; it might be resignation or doubt or defeat or perhaps the beginnings of hope, but she nods.

I draw Amaryllis back into my arms. "I will come back for you, I promise you."

33

I stood on the platform at the train station in Favoriten, my hard-won travel documents clutched in one hand and the hand of the little boy who stood next to me in the other.

At my feet was a travel case, all that I was bringing with me from Vienna, all that a person who was supposed to be in Switzerland only a week would need. Wilhelm's—an even smaller one—rested atop it.

No one had come with us to the station to wave good-bye or to help us board the train. It had been collectively decided that any tearful family farewells had to be said in the privacy of the Leitners' house. Wilhelm Leitner and I had said a final good-bye to his parents and older sisters, all of whom struggled to rein in their tears, from inside a taxicab. Emilie had stayed behind to comfort them after we were no longer in view.

I squeezed Wilhelm's hand now and smiled at him.

"You are very good at this game," I murmured to him, moving my lips carefully so that the six-year-old could read them. He smiled back at me.

The object of the game was not to make a sound, not a peep, until we got to Lucerne. A box of chocolate-covered cherries was waiting for him in my travel case if he won. I had spent the last three days at Wilhelm's house to get to know him and his parents and siblings so that he would willingly board a train with me with no family present. I had also learned the few signs he used to communicate everyday things like hunger, thirst, weariness, and the names of his family, as well as simple finger spelling.

"Wilhelm doesn't know it's uncertain when he can come home," Emilie had told me the last time we'd taken the tram together to the Leitner house. "He thinks he's going just for a visit to see the Swiss cows with their colorful collars and tinkling bells."

"Even though he can't hear the bells?"

"Even though he can't hear them," she'd said. "I'm afraid you will have to be the one to tell him the truth when he is finally safe. Or maybe my sister-in-law can tell him if you'd rather."

The little boy had already become precious to me. "I'll tell him," I'd said.

I finally caught the eye of a porter, who brought our luggage aboard and hoisted it up onto the rack above our seats.

Wilhelm and I settled down, he at the window and me next to him. The train car was quickly filling with fellow travelers, civilians like us but also Nazi officials, and the occasional SS officer. We were no one to them; just a grandmother perhaps out with her young grandson, a quiet boy who wasn't running around and shouting and being intolerable.

A woman walked by us in the aisle and said to Wilhelm, "What a cute little fellow you are."

Wilhelm, with his concentrated gaze on the window and all that was soon to happen on the tracks below, didn't look at her.

"He loves the train," I said enthusiastically, and she smiled and moved on.

This was going to be the easiest part of the trip; I knew that. The farther we got from Vienna, though, the more I knew I'd worry about being noticed, remembered, or questioned. We had a very long day ahead of us and several transfers to make. Wilhelm had been warned by his parents that it would take a while to get to where the Swiss cows lived, that he'd be playing the game with Fraulein Helen for a very long time. But he also knew there was going to be a fabulous tunnel over the Tyrol and deep within the Alps where dwarves lived. And he knew that if a policeman came to us and asked to see any papers, he was to do nothing except play the game. If he got agitated or cranky, I had a small dose of sleeping powders to put in his can of juice. By the time we reached the German-Swiss border near Höchst, twilight would be falling.

The train began to puff and wheeze and Wilhelm turned to me and smiled. Then he put his hand on the windowsill to feel the vibrations from the rails below. The train lurched forward, and a whistle blew that the boy did not hear. The platform began to fall away, and with it, Vienna. I didn't know if I would ever be back. The future looked so dark and unclear.

As I watched the city drift past, I practiced in my mind what Emilie and I had decided I would say to the Swiss canton officials when I at last arrived in Lucerne.

I had procured my Swiss travel visa by stating that I, as Wilhelm's nanny, was bringing him to Lucerne to see an elderly aunt and also visit the school that his parents wanted him to attend when he was older, Sister Gertrude's school. We were to be in Lucerne only seven days. That was what I was going to tell both the German and the Swiss border officials.

But that was not what I was going to be telling the canton officials in Lucerne.

I was instead going to be begging for temporary residency for Wilhelm. I knew I'd have the backing of Sister Gertrude's convent and school, and also the local Catholic relief agency and the family who had agreed to care for Wilhelm until he could go home safely to Austria and not be in danger. But still.

"When I tell them that, the canton officials will know that I lied when I got the visa," I'd said to Emilie as we were making these plans.

"No, they won't," she'd said. "I'll send you a telegram two days after you arrive telling you that Wilhelm's life is in danger and he shouldn't return home. And that's when you will go to the canton. That's when you will ask if you can stay also. It's widely accepted that it's not wise for Americans to reside in Nazi-occupied territories right now, Helen. You can remind them of that, and you can say that your Austrian work visa is about to expire. You tell them you will require nothing from the canton except permission to stay. Sister Gertrude will tell them she will provide you room and board in exchange for teaching English, so that you will not be taking any wages from a Swiss worker. Oh, and offer your services to the canton as an interpreter. You speak English, French, and German. You can be an asset to them during this uncertain time."

"And if they say I can't stay?"

"If they say no, you will be no worse off than you are now. But you'll probably have to attempt to find a way home to America. It's not that easy right now to travel to the U.S. Ocean liners from Europe aren't crossing the Atlantic anymore. It's full of German submarines and the Swiss know it. So you can just make a show of trying to get home. Perhaps you will actually find a safe way to do it, Helen. But until then, we can try to get more disabled children out of Austria."

"But how will we do it?" I ask. "I can't go back into Austria and do it this way again."

"No, you absolutely cannot. We will have to find another way. I don't know yet how, but we will. We have to."

The hours on the train passed slowly, and I couldn't help but flinch every time someone walked by our seats. Wilhelm gazed out the window, looked at books his mother had packed in his rucksack, and played with little farm animals also tucked in his pack. We ate sandwiches his mother had made and dozed. Finally, in the late afternoon, we entered the Arlberg Tunnel—fifteen thousand meters of railway inside the heart of the Alps. Wilhelm loved it.

By the time we had changed trains again and arrived at the last station before the border, it was after eight in the evening, but the long July days meant dusk was only just beginning to fall.

Sister Gertrude had instructed me to use the Rhine River border crossing at Höchst, two hours north of Lucerne. She had friends in St. Margrethen on the Swiss side who would be waiting for Wilhelm and me and would give us lodgings for the night and get us to the train station the following morning.

Again I needed a porter to help us get our travel cases to a waiting taxi, which then took us to the border crossing on the St. Margrethen Bridge. Wilhelm and I joined a dozen other people who had queued to walk across the Rhine to Switzerland on foot. I used hand signals to tell Wilhelm to hold on to my skirt with one hand and his rucksack with the other as I carried both our travel cases and my handbag over my shoulder. I could tell Wilhelm was tired of traveling, and the thrill of seeing Swiss cows had waned. He looked at me, signed the word for his mother, and mouthed the word *Mutti*.

"I know. Soon," I said, enunciating all three words carefully so that he could read my lips.

Finally it was our turn.

I handed our documents to the German official who asked for

them. He looked at mine, looked at Wilhelm's, and then at mine again.

"Why did you come this way?" he said curiously.

"Sir?"

"Feldkirch would have been quicker for you. Why this crossing?"

I mentally tamped down a little knob of alarm. "I have friends in St. Margrethen I wish to see before we go to Lucerne. Just for overnight."

Then he looked down at Wilhelm. "And how old are you, little one?"

"Wilhelm is shy around strangers," I said. "And you can see on his documents that he is six."

The official stared at me. My heart began a staccato beat in my chest.

But then he stamped our documents and we walked the few meters to the Swiss side of the bridge, where we would have to do this all over again.

There was the same scrutiny, the same careful study of our documents.

"And why are you coming to Switzerland for these seven days?" the Swiss official asked disinterestedly.

I gave him the answer I'd practiced. "To see Wilhelm's aunt and visit the Catholic school that his parents wish him to attend when he is a bit older."

"This Austrian boy has a Swiss aunt?" the official asked.

"He does." I didn't offer an explanation. Emilie had said to seem nonchalant if I was asked additional questions, rather than too anxious to comply.

"Aren't there plenty of Catholic schools in Austria?" His tone now sounded like that of a disgruntled man, a father of young children perhaps, as though he might've been wondering why

Wilhelm's parents would do such a thing to their young child, sending him so far away for school.

"It's a very good school," I said simply.

He appeared to be about to stamp our documents when Wilhelm's weariness got the better of him and he let out a sound of exasperation. It was a strange, otherworldly sound. The official looked down at Wilhelm and then back at me.

"What's wrong with him?"

"We've been traveling all day. He's tired."

Wilhelm pulled on my skirt and another odd, guttural sound escaped him. My pulse was racing as I raised a finger to my lips and said, as though Wilhelm could hear me, "Shh, darling. Be a good boy now. Almost done."

The official was staring at me. So, too, was a second official now, who was standing behind the first in the doorway of a small building; it seemed to be an office of some kind just over the Swiss side of the bridge.

"What kind of school is this that you're taking him to?" the first official asked, his brows puckered.

"Like I said, it's a good one."

"And you're American," he said, as if suddenly realizing I was in an odd place at an odd time for a U.S. citizen.

"I am." I tried to sound confident, but I heard the nervous lilt in my words.

The second official took several steps forward and spoke to the first one.

"I want to see them in my office."

"But why?" I said to this second man, my voice still slightly trembling. Had they picked up on it? "Our documents are in order."

"If you would come this way and step inside, Fraulein," the second official said. I could tell then that this other man was in charge and I was in trouble.

The first official took a side step so that I could do nothing other than move in the direction of the little office. I looked down at Wilhelm.

"It's all right, sweetheart," I said, knowing full well the boy couldn't hear what I was saying. I took his hand. "I'm sure this will only take a moment."

We left our travel cases and followed the second official inside and to a smaller room behind an administrative area consisting of two desks and an electric kettle on a small wooden table flanked by an assortment of teacups. No one was sitting at the desks. When we were inside the smaller office, the official closed the door. He took a chair behind his desk. Stacks of papers, ledgers, and half a sandwich on waxed paper lay atop it.

"Please. Sit." He pointed to one of two chairs situated in front of him. Inside his well-lit office, I could see now that he was perhaps only in his mid-thirties. Young, I thought, to be in charge of this border crossing. He'd either proven himself or had family connections, I imagined.

I obeyed, pulling Wilhelm close to me. He crawled up onto my lap and laid his head on my shoulder, his eyes opening and closing drowsily.

The official held out his hand for my documents and I gave them to him. He studied each one carefully.

"What is wrong with the boy?" he said, but gently. Kindly.

"There's nothing wrong with him."

"Tell me truthfully, Fraulein. Does this child have an aunt in Lucerne? I want the truth, and unless you want to spend the night in jail, you better give it to me."

Despite his polite tone, I felt all the carefully made plans to rescue Wilhelm falling to dust. "Aren't I going to spend a night in jail now no matter what I say?" I replied.

"No." His voice was still gentle. There was something in the way he was speaking to me that made me feel like I should trust him. I sensed compassion.

"He does not have an aunt in Lucerne," I said.

"Why are you here with him?"

"His life is in danger, sir. Wilhelm is deaf, and Adolf Hitler is killing disabled children like Wilhelm. I know how unbelievable that sounds, but it is true. The Nazis killed a little girl who I loved because her arms were deformed and she walked with a limp. They are killing all kinds of people they don't like. Wilhelm is on a list of children to be taken from their homes and sent to a place where, I assure you, he will be killed."

The official hesitated a moment. "Who are you with?" His voice was soft now, just above a whisper.

"I beg your pardon?"

"What group are you with? You need to trust me now."

"I'm not with any group."

"Who is working with you?"

"It's just me, a teacher in Vienna, and a nun in Lucerne. That's all."

The official leaned forward in his chair. "Listen. I will help you now, but you can't do this again. You're going to get yourself arrested and deported, maybe even jailed for smuggling. Don't do this again."

"I can't make that promise," I said.

"What do you mean, you can't make that promise? Did you not hear what I said?"

"There might be others we will want to save."

"But you don't know what you're doing."

"Well, I'm new at this. I need to learn. And all I required tonight was help, which you say you will give me." And then, feeling braver, I added, "And could give me again, couldn't you?"

The man said nothing.

"Hitler is killing children," I said again. "You have to believe me."

"I never said I did not. How are you planning to take care of Wilhelm in Lucerne? You cannot expect to hide him for months, maybe years on end."

"We're not going to try and hide him." I quickly told the officer about Sister Gertrude's convent and school in Lucerne and the telegram Emilie was going to send me in two days' time.

"I hope for the child's sake you are successful. But if you truly intend to rescue other children, you can't expect that to work the next time," he said.

"Yes," I said. "I know. We need someone on the inside to help us. Look, I can come back here to this crossing as often as I must to fetch more children. Somehow my friend Emilie will get them here to the Austrian side. She will find a way. I know it. And if you can just get them across the river, I will take them. That's all you would have to do."

"No. That is not a solution, Fraulein. You would be back at the local canton office each time begging for asylum for another disabled child from Austria. Switzerland is not officially nor broadly extending refuge to beleaguered citizens of the Nazi regime, and that is who these children are."

"And why isn't it?"

"You and I may not like the reasons, but surely you can see that Europe is a sinking ship and Switzerland is just one little lifeboat. Everyone cannot climb aboard. There would be too many. The lifeboat, too, would sink."

An idea suddenly came to me. "Switzerland *does* shelter its own children."

I paused, thinking. Imagining. It might work. It just might . . .

"Continue," the official said.

"A child dropped off anonymously on the doorstep of Sister Gertrude's convent," I said slowly, "would not draw suspicion if pinned to the child's clothing was a tearstained note asking the sisters to please take care of the presumably Swiss child . . ."

He tipped his head, waiting for me to finish the thought.

"Churches have always been safe places for desperate parents to leave children they cannot care for, haven't they?" I went on. "And if it seemed word had gotten out that Sister Gertrude's convent was taking in abandoned children in these troubling times, it would not be unreasonable then if it happened again. And then again. But the sisters and I would be expecting the children each time. We would know who they were because you and I would've been in contact. The sisters could find homes for the children within the parish, homes where their true identities could be kept safe so if this madness ever ends, we can return these children to their rightful families. But everyone would naturally assume they were Swiss. Wouldn't that work?"

"Maybe. But perhaps it would be better if you tried the normal channels first. There are many relief organizations in Switzerland working to do legally what you are trying to accomplish under this ruse. There are groups in Geneva—"

"But that would take too long, sir! Children just like Wilhelm are being murdered every day. We can't wait. This other way will work if you help us. Once the children are safely in the country and housed with church families, then Sister Gertrude and I can ask for legal asylum—if we must."

He exhaled heavily, as if to expel the notion of there being any other viable option. "If the children are young, yes, this way might work. They must be young, Fraulein, or unable to answer questions. You can't expect a child to lie."

He was right. I knew it. But it pierced me to think that a fully conversant disabled child like Brigitta would not be a candidate for this kind of rescue. A child like Wilhelm, yes, but not someone like Brigitta. We would have to find another way for older children, if another way could indeed be found.

"I understand," I said. "So I would come and get the children and secretly make my way back to the church and then—"

"No. You should not come back here at all. Any child would need to be brought by courier under cover of darkness. It could take several days from the time your friend Emilie gets them to the border until they show up on the church doorstep in Lucerne. How many are you planning to save?"

"I don't know. As many as we can. For as long as we can."

He paused a moment and then reached into his pocket and pulled out a business card. He wrote something on the back of it and then extended it across the desk.

"This is my home number. Only call me at ten p.m. so I'll know it's you. If I don't answer, it means I am not at home or I can't."

Relief and gratitude flooded me. "Thank you," I whispered.

"Put my card away, please."

I slipped the card into my handbag, but not before noticing his name, Franz Kohler.

"Thank you, Herr Kohler," I whispered again.

"Call me Franz. Do not call me for at least two weeks. I need to talk to some people. Hopefully you will have made your case before the canton officials by then and been granted at least a temporary visa to stay in Lucerne." He stamped my documents and handed them back to me. "You should go now."

For half a moment, I wanted to ask Franz Kohler why he would do this. Why would he risk his job and maybe imprisonment to help me? But in the second half of that moment, I realized he was not doing it to help me; he was doing it to save these children, and for the same reason I was. Because it was the right thing to do. He had also clearly done something along these lines already, perhaps many times, and was connected with other people who also couldn't stand by and do nothing. The world was full of evil people, to be sure, but there were also good people in it.

"God bless you, Franz," I said instead.

I rose to leave, stirring Wilhelm awake. He frowned as I set him on his feet so I could take our suitcases outside the office. The child looked up at me with tired eyes.

"It's best if the agents out front do not remember me assisting you or calling for one of them to assist you with your luggage," he said.

"No, I understand. We will manage. Thank you. For everything."

We exited the building and then I wrangled our travel cases with some effort. Night had crept in while we'd been in Franz's office. I showed the official who had first stopped us our stamped documents, and I motioned for sweet Wilhelm to again hold on to my skirt as we walked through the last barrier to safety.

I was as exhausted as he was, and all I wanted to do was find Sister Gertrude's friends on the other side of the gate, give Wilhelm the chocolate-covered cherries he deserved, and collapse in relief and joy. Tomorrow before I boarded the train for Lucerne, I would post a quick letter to Emilie so she would know we'd made it across the border to Switzerland.

We had saved Wilhelm, I'd tell her. I was already confident that we had.

And I would tell her as soon as I safely could that we had someone on the inside now who would help us save another child like him. And another. And another. And another.

34

A flurry of activity begins when I return home from Oakland, including the filing of court documents and investigations into my private life to make sure I'm a suitable parent. George Petrakis is happy to help with the legal aspects and, thankfully, so is Mrs. Sommers. Both are intent on accelerating the petition within the court system so that Amaryllis can be adopted that much quicker.

When I told George and Lila my plans to adopt and that it was now imperative that I find my own place and secure a job, they told me a few hours later that they had a plan of their own. Over dinner, Lila reminded me that she and George already knew my only assets are my father's property in Oregon—which he'd bequeathed to Truman, and then Truman to me—and a bit of savings I brought from Austria and converted into dollars.

"We want you and Amaryllis to live here with us," Lila said. "The third floor is perfect for you. You would both have your own room and bathroom and some privacy. We know you're worried about finding a suitable place to rent, and it's expensive here in the city. You could live with us rent-free so any job income could be used to support you and Amaryllis. And then you could save your father's property for Amaryllis's future."

"I could never ask you to do such a generous thing," I responded in what was surely wide-eyed shock.

"But you're not asking," George said. "It's what Lila and I want to do, and it would solve a huge problem for you."

"And I love the idea of having a child in the house again," Lila continued. "Especially a little girl. I'd always hoped for a daughter, and we never had one. I love our three granddaughters, of course, but they don't live here in the house. I don't get to see them every day or hear their prayers at night. I think it would be wonderful to be a part of helping you raise this child. And George could be somewhat of a father figure to her. That's important, you know."

I'd begun to cry at the kindness of such good friends. "I don't know how to thank you."

George smiled. "You can thank us by letting us help you."

Lila and I have since been working on the second third-floor bedroom to make it a haven for an eight-year-old. I find a girl's bedroom set at a secondhand store that merely needs a fresh coat of paint, which George sees to. Lila buys new curtains, I use her Singer to create a pretty coverlet for the bed, and a church friend of Lila's brings over a box of clothes her granddaughter has outgrown, all Amaryllis's size.

The following week I find a job at a stationer's store near the university—so very like one I loved in Lucerne—that sells fancy writing papers, journals, and pens. The owner allows me to arrange my hours so that I will be home with Amaryllis in the mornings until she leaves for school and then to meet her at the front door when classes are let out.

Two weeks after that, the Petrakis home is inspected by a county social worker who introduces herself as Mrs. Whitman. When she is finished with her assessment of the house, George,

Lila, and I sit down with her to discuss my continued welcome in
the house, and George and Lila's willingness to partner with me
in this venture. We seem able to assure her that Amaryllis and I
will always have a home with George and Lila, but she is concerned about our ages.

"You are all in your early sixties," Mrs. Whitman says. "When
Amaryllis reaches adulthood on her twenty-first birthday, you
will all be in your mid-seventies. Perhaps I don't need to tell you
that's several years older than the average life expectancy in this
country."

"But I am healthy," I counter, my slightly wobbly voice betray-
ing my anxiousness. "I have a clean bill of health from a doctor
right here in San Francisco. I just went for a physical last week. I
can show you his report. And George and Lila are healthy, too.
Seventy is just an average."

"Yes, but it's an average because many people don't live any
longer than that, Miss Calvert," the woman says. "It's going to
be in my report that this is something the judge will have to
weigh. I can't leave it out."

George, who seems to be deep in thought, suddenly speaks up.
"Mrs. Whitman, would you consider coming back tomorrow
around noon? I know it's a Saturday, but there's something I'd
like to show you."

I can't think what it might be that George has thought of, but
the county worker is intrigued and agrees. When she leaves,
George tells me and Lila his plan, and I'm again overcome with
gratitude for these friends.

When Mrs. Whitman returns the next day, the living room is
filled with George and Lila's sons, daughters-in-law, and grandchildren. They'd all arrived that morning, and I'd told them
everything—about Amaryllis, about Rosie, and even about Brigitta.

"All of these young people will be Amaryllis's family," George tells Mrs. Whitman now. "Our sons will be like her uncles, our daughters-in-law her aunts, and our grandchildren, her cousins. If anything should happen to Helen, Lila, and me, Amaryllis will not be left without family. I guarantee it."

And then the Petrakis sons and their wives, down to a one, tell Mrs. Whitman that Amaryllis can have her pick of where she would want to live if the unthinkable happened, because she'd have a home with any of them.

Mrs. Whitman offers us a smile. "I'll put that in my report, too."

As the days progress, I make the trip into Oakland as often as I can to visit with Amaryllis and to keep her focused on the future. The visits are as much for me as they are for her. Several times, I bring George and Lila with me.

Finally, on the fourth of March, I am standing before a judge in an Alameda County courthouse, and George and Lila and all their family are there with me. The judge has studied the case file; he has heard from the county and Mrs. Sommers. And he has heard from Amaryllis.

He renders his decision, and I can't help crying as I'm officially made the sole parent of Amaryllis Smith—Smith being the last name given to every orphan who arrives at Fairbrook without one. The first thing I do before leaving the courthouse, and at Amaryllis's request, is submit a petition to have her last name changed to Calvert.

And then it's over to the orphanage to get her things and bring her home.

I know that our new life as aunt and niece—almost mother and child—will not be without its difficult moments. I have seen enough as a nanny and teacher to know that children, as they grow, learn about the world and their place in it by testing what they know and experimenting with what they don't. I'm aware there might be days, maybe many of them, when Amaryllis and I will clash. When Amaryllis will be angry with me. When I will have to correct her.

But I also know that love is a powerful force. Far more powerful than the strength I saw on display in Nazi-occupied Austria. Love, to overcome that kind of power, just needs to be unleashed from fear.

"Am I to call you Mother?" Amaryllis asks an hour later as we cross the bridge into San Francisco.

I hear in her voice twinges of conflict and unease.

"You don't have to, Amaryllis," I tell her. "You can keep calling me Aunt Helen if you want. Legally I am responsible for you as a parent, and I already love you as a mother would, but I know you still love the mother you never knew. And I understand that."

"So I can keep her?"

I smile at the simple request worded in a way that wouldn't make sense to anyone else. But I know what Amaryllis wants. She wants to keep the mother of her dreams, the one in her heart whom she has been whispering to, perhaps for as long as she can remember.

"Absolutely," I tell her.

In the beginning, Amaryllis is guarded in her trust, reluctant to speak her own mind, afraid to give in to laughter, careful with her affection. But also, with each new day, I see those protective behaviors diminishing, little by little, especially as Amaryllis settles into school, meets new playmates, and finds a good friend and confidant in George Petrakis.

I often find Amaryllis in George's study playing checkers with him or out on the patio with him talking about something she heard on the playground or from friends. It is George to whom Amaryllis most often goes for help with her schoolwork, and

George whom she wants to sit with on train trips. And when all the Petrakis children and grandchildren come to the house for weekend celebrations, it is George whom Amaryllis stays close to, until the weeks and months make her completely comfortable around the extended family. Lila had been right about Amaryllis needing a father figure in her life.

She asks me about Truman from time to time, wanting to know more about what he was like, what he loved, what he didn't. I show her photographs of Truman and me as children and answer every question the best I can. She asks if she can keep the photographs in her room, and I give them to her. When the time seems right, I ask Amaryllis if she would like to see the place where he is buried, and she says yes.

Amaryllis has been with me nearly eight months when we pick a Saturday to go to the national cemetery in San Bruno, seventeen miles away. As we set out on the forty-minute drive, she asks me, in a puzzled voice—as if she'd been pondering this for a while—how her mother and my brother had a baby. I know this is ground we're going to need to cover, but Amaryllis is only nine. That longer conversation is a few years away, in my estimation. I fumble for an answer for right now, and in so doing, I hesitate too long.

"You said my mama was a maid at your brother's house," she says next. "So that means . . . that means she wasn't the bride?"

"No, she wasn't."

"Why was she a maid and not the bride? Didn't she want to be the bride?"

"I don't know if she did, honey. It's . . . it's complicated, Amaryllis. There's so much I will tell you when you're older about your mother and father. You're going to have to trust me that now's not the right time. For now, just know that I'm so glad you're you. And so glad you're here."

She seems satisfied enough with this. When we arrive at the cemetery and find Truman's grave, she sits in front of it for a long while, looking at his last name, which she now shares.

After we return home, it's almost as if Amaryllis has fixed something that was crooked in her mind, at least for now. Her questions about Truman began to taper off.

Rosie, though, is another matter. Amaryllis peppers me with questions about her mother, wanting to hear everything I know about her on a continuous loop. I tell her nearly weekly about the month I spent at the vineyard when Rosie was just a toddler who followed me around and begged to be held and sung to and played with, and Amaryllis will want to hear it again. And then again. Then she'll want to hear about the three weeks I spent at the vineyard when Rosie was nine, just her age, over and over. I tell her about the stamps and letters Rosie liked, and then I am asked to repeat it a week or two later. I tell her about the amaryllis at Christmastime, her favorite story. I tell her about the accident that took Rosie's family, not because I want to but because Amaryllis insists on hearing it multiple times.

I continue to dig for Rosie's whereabouts despite never seeming to gain any headway there. George even asks a friend at the police department to run a check of the name Rosanne Maras and finds nothing, either, not even a driver's license. As time passes and we continue to come up with nothing, it is Lila who suggests to me that perhaps with everything that happened to her, Rosie doesn't want to be found. Perhaps she has forged a new life and left the sorrow of her past far, far behind her.

Lila may be right.

I decide it's probably time for Amaryllis and me to begin to come to terms with that.

A few nights later, as I'm putting Amaryllis to bed, I tell her that I've sadly had no luck finding Rosie.

"I'm guessing your mother moved from California, perhaps

far away," I tell her. "She surely believes you were adopted, Amaryllis, just like I did. So maybe she was thinking there was no reason to stay here. And so she moved far away."

Amaryllis exhales, puckers a brow. "Can't you find her in the faraway place?" she asks after a moment's pause.

"Maybe. But I'm thinking until I do that, you just keep your mother where you have always kept her."

She stares at me, not understanding.

I press my hand to her pajama top. "In your heart. Just like you are probably inside hers. She's there, isn't she? You feel her there, yes? It's why you whisper to her at night in your bed. Because she's right there inside you."

Amaryllis blinks slowly as she considers this, and then she nods.

I can see in her eyes that this is not the same as seeing Rosie's face, hearing her voice, holding her hand.

But I know too well this is the way, the only way, to keep close to you someone who is gone from your life. It is better than the alternative—isn't it?—which is never having had them at all.

35

Before . . .
LUCERNE, SWITZERLAND
NOVEMBER 1947

I stepped out of the post office on Zürichstrasse, clutching an envelope tight as an autumn breeze tried to tease it out of my hand. It'd been a while since I'd opened my mailbox to find anything inside, though the postwar mail service had resumed long ago. I'd expected only to receive word that my Swiss work visa had finally been renewed, but then I saw the nonbusiness-type envelope and my hopes rose. The envelope looked like personal stationery that had traveled a bit of a distance.

And indeed it was. But it was my own personal stationery: the most recent letter I wrote to Hanna Maier in Innsbruck returned to me, undeliverable, like the others before it.

I went every Saturday to the post office, stubbornly hoping for news of the Maiers each time, even though no word from them was ever waiting for me. I liked the two-kilometer route to get there. I liked walking past the bakery and the little music studio where young violinists learned from the elderly maestro who lived inside it. I liked strolling past the house where the two gray cats sunned themselves on the front windowsill and stopping in at the stationer's store to look at his beautiful Italian writing papers. I liked meandering down to the tip of the lake to marvel at the water's glacial blue majesty.

I had learned to rely on Lucerne's loveliness for uncomplicated joys like these, especially during those thirteen intense months— until the borders closed for good and Franz was transferred to Bern—when Emilie and I rescued nearly a dozen disabled children out of Austria. Franz had been right. It was only with great reluctance that the canton officials in Lucerne allowed Wilhelm to stay as a temporary but long-term guest of a generous parish family. Finding homes for the sudden influx of "Swiss" youngsters left on the steps of the convent had been easy by comparison, but I'd daily worried our deception would be exposed and I'd be arrested.

About the same time Franz was transferred, Emilie got word that the T4 program in its official capacity was ending, but we both knew the killing of the innocents would likely not stop. Indeed, in that August of 1941, it was only beginning.

But we rescued no more children after that.

Lucerne had survived the war intact, as had most of Switzerland. The undisturbed respite I'd enjoyed here had come at an emotional price, though. Every time I heard a report that Innsbruck had been bombed by the Allies, I could only hope and pray that Martine and the children were all right, and all while I sat in relative ease. Those were the worst months. Feeling safely tucked away in Lucerne and knowing that Martine and the children were not safe at all.

The last word from the Maiers was a letter from Hanna in June 1945. Then fifteen, she had thanked me for my letters the past few years—they'd finally received most of them—and told me they had all survived the war, including the boys, who'd been conscripted at eighteen and sixteen for the invasion of Slovakia.

Johannes had survived, too, though he was in a prisoner-of-war camp in Britain and Hanna didn't know when he would be returned home. Hanna had also said that her grandparents were selling the house in Innsbruck and they were all moving, but the final plans were still undecided. I had written back straightaway but had heard nothing since.

For two and half years, there had been nothing.

After swinging by the lake, I opened the back-door entrance to the little Cistercian convent and primary school that had been my home and refuge for the last seven years. I stepped through the school's kitchen and cafeteria and down the darkened hall to pass by Sister Gertrude's office. I was surprised to see the nun sitting behind her desk on a Saturday. She looked up at me and smiled.

In the years that I'd been Sister Gertrude's friend and a teacher at the little school she and the other nuns ran, I'd grown to think of her as a true sister, the one I had never had and had always wanted. It had been a long time since I had enjoyed a sibling bond that felt intimate, and I knew this had been my fault. I had moved away from Truman and stayed away. For decades. We had exchanged letters, and I had taken those two trips home to see him and his family, but I regretted not having invested more time and effort into our relationship. And, of course, it was too late now.

I stopped at the open door to Sister Gertrude's office. "I wasn't expecting to see you in your office on the weekend."

"Just finishing up some correspondence. Any word on the extension of your visa?"

I shook my head. "Not yet."

"What's that, then? Did you finally hear from the Maiers?" She nodded to the envelope in my hand.

"Return to sender. I suppose it was silly to think the Austrian postal service might still forward something after two years. I don't know why I tried again. I was just feeling . . . optimistic."

"Nothing wrong with that. Nothing ever wrong with that."

I smiled. Sister Gertrude never failed to see the possible and pleasant, no matter how hopeless a situation seemed.

"You know, it's quite possible the Maiers returned to Vienna after all," the nun continued.

"I don't think so. In Hanna's last letter she said Martine vowed she was never taking them back there. I'm not surprised, really. But I am perplexed Martine chose to leave no forwarding address and that neither Hanna nor the twins have written to me."

"And tell me again how old the youngest would be now?" Sister Gertrude motioned for me to take the chair in front of her desk.

I stepped fully inside and sat down. "Hanna would be seventeen now. I know what you're thinking. It's been a very long time since those children needed a nanny and I should just let them go. Perhaps that's what they've done with me."

"Actually, I was thinking you might want to see for yourself if perhaps the Maier family has returned to Vienna. Maybe they did. Maybe enough time has passed and Frau Maier changed her mind."

"Do you think I should write to them at the address in Vienna?"

Sister Gertrude stroked her chin. "Perhaps you should just go. Go back to Vienna. I have felt for a long time that you need to return, and not just to seek out those children but to set your soul at peace. It bothers you that you do not know what has become of this little family, doesn't it? Especially after all that happened to them, and to you when you were with them."

"It does bother me." I sat back in the chair. I had spent many an evening with Sister Gertrude like this, after the day was done and especially after the last child was rescued, as we sipped schnapps and spoke about what mattered most to us. "But I can't just hop on the next train for Vienna. I have classes to teach."

"Sister Agathe is quite capable of taking your classes. As you well know."

"I suppose. But it's still such a complicated trip, isn't it? All those occupied zones to go through."

The end of the war and the ousting of the Nazis from Austria didn't mean it was again its own sovereign nation. Four occupying powers controlled the country.

"A bit complicated, perhaps. But not impossible," she said. "I took that trip to see Emilie in Theresienfeld without too much trouble."

We were silent for a moment.

"I think you should at least try to take care of this, Helen. As your friend, I am asking you to. And as headmistress of this school, I am telling you. You are a good teacher, the children are fond of you, but I have long sensed that you have unfinished business in Vienna."

I felt a pang in my chest, and the opening of a box I'd thought was nailed tightly shut. "You've never said anything about this before."

"I know. I should have."

"Have I not done a good job here?"

"On the contrary, you've performed remarkably well considering your heart seems to be so unsettled. I thought perhaps it was just the loss of your brother, but that was five years ago. I should've figured it out before. It's this family and what happened to that little girl that still troubles you. I think you owe it to yourself to find the peace you lack."

I was quiet as I sat in the chair, thinking. It wasn't as if the sister was suggesting something I hadn't thought of myself, but every time I'd considered returning to Vienna, for even just a short visit, I'd tossed the notion away. What was the purpose of going if the Maiers weren't there? I wanted Martine to absolve me. To forgive me. I had worked through some of my remorse by helping to rescue other children, but Brigitta was the one I had loved. She was the one I had failed.

"Don't you think it's time you went back?" Sister Gertrude asked.

"And if the Maiers aren't there? If someone else is living in that house now, what then?"

"Well, maybe you ask around. Call on their friends or visit the church they attended. If you still come up with nothing, stop in Innsbruck on your return to Lucerne. Go to the address you last had for Frau Maier and her children and inquire. You might not be able to find this family there, true. But you haven't even tried. And yet you keep writing letters, hoping against hope they will be delivered. I know you pretty well now, and I think you have convinced yourself that you're happy here. But I'm not sure that you are."

"I love Lucerne."

"But I don't think you love *you* in Lucerne. You're troubled here."

"I feel like you're sending me away." A strange sadness filled me, though I knew Sister Gertrude was right. I did have unfinished business in Vienna.

"I'm telling you to listen to your heart, Helen. It is restless within you."

When the war had finally ended and the families of our rescued children began to come for them, I'd worried that Austria would receive the same treatment as vanquished Germany. I had felt tremendous relief that the country had been viewed not as the Reich's accomplice but rather as the first victim of Nazi aggression. But like Germany, postwar Austria had been parceled into occupied zones, with the French governing the west, the Americans controlling the middle north, the British the middle south, and the Soviets—who'd marched into Austria a month before the Western Allies had—taking everything east, from Linz to Fürstenfeld. Vienna, like Berlin, was to be controlled by all four victorious powers, but also like Berlin, it was surrounded on all sides by Communist forces intent on making Austria a Soviet state.

My journey to Vienna would begin with the first morning train headed east from Zurich and across the Austrian border into the French zone. Then a platform and passenger check in the American zone near Kitzbühel, and finally—the stop I was most unsure about—the transition to the Soviet-controlled zone at Linz.

The stops made for a long travel day—and sixteen hours instead of the prewar thirteen—but unexpectedly, it was not a troublesome one. As I progressed through the zones, I wasn't questioned at length by anyone—not even the Soviets—regarding my reasons for traveling to Vienna. It had been enough to tell the official at each stop that I was merely reconnecting with the family for whom I used to nanny. My American passport apparently made me automatically one of the trusted Allies.

Vienna, being the capital, had been apportioned to the occupiers by districts; only the city center was jointly controlled. Wieden, where the Maiers had lived, was under the authority of the Soviets, as was the nearby main train station in Favoriten.

I arrived at the Hauptbahnhof at a little after ten at night and found a room at a pension one block away. I told the proprietor I might need the room for several nights. He was happy to have guests at all and told me the room was mine for as long as I wanted it.

In the morning light, I was able to finally see the evidence of what I'd seen in the Zurich newspaper following the end of the war. Vienna had been bombed more than fifty times, and tens of thousands of houses and buildings had been flattened. But I knew this was nothing compared to the destruction in Berlin and Dresden and Cologne. As I emerged from the pension and began the short, one-and-a-half-kilometer walk to Rainergasse, there was a pervasive sense of not-quite-all-thereness all about me. I passed scaffolding and barricades, and then a bomb crater in the street. All seemed misplaced, like parts of a movie set that needed to be trucked away so that life in Vienna could get back to normal. I couldn't see the skyline of the *innere Stadt* three kilometers away; the surrounding buildings were too tall. I didn't know if I'd take the tram—if there was a tram to take, as I'd read four thousand of them had been destroyed—to see for myself the city center I loved. I'd heard the massive and elegant St. Stephen's Cathedral was still without a roof.

No, perhaps I would not go.

As I walked, I saw that much debris had indeed been cleared away and some of what had fallen was beginning to be replaced. But Vienna was not the city it had been before. It was as if the city were a man who'd always worn a beard, but he'd been suddenly and inexpertly shaved. He was not recognizable as the same man.

I found Rainergasse and turned down it.

As I neared the Maiers' town house, I was relieved to see it and every other home on the street still standing, and yet as I came to stand on its front step, a feeling came over me that the house was a ruin nonetheless. I could tell in an instant, just by looking at the weed-filled planter boxes at the dirty windows, that Martine and the children had not returned. A light was on in one front window, and on the postbox the name still read MAIER, but this was not a house where the Maier family still lived. I rang the bell and waited.

The door opened, and before me stood Johannes. It had only been seven years since I had seen him last, and at this very same place—framed in his doorway—but he appeared twenty years older. His hair had gone silver and worry lines crossed his face. An ill-fitting cardigan hung on him, and his wrinkled trousers looked like they belonged to someone taller and younger. A name tag pinned askew to his chest bore in small letters the company name EISCHEN HARDWARE. Johannes looked like an old man who had forgotten who he was.

"Hello, Johannes." I didn't realize I'd called him by his first name until after I'd said it.

"Fraulein Calvert," he replied in a voice stronger than his appearance suggested he could muster. "What a surprise. And what brings you back to Vienna?"

His demeanor and the casualness of his greeting first needled and then alarmed me. "Why do you think I came back here?"

He stared at me, apparently waiting for my answer.

"I came to see Martine and the children."

"I'm sorry to say you've come a long way for nothing." His tone was emotionless. "The children aren't here. They are not even children anymore, you know."

"That doesn't mean that I don't still care about them. And Martine, too."

"Martine is not here, either."

His tone was strange. Wrong. I was instantly afraid that something terrible had happened to Martine and the children and this shattered man in front of me was alone now. "Where is everyone, Johannes?"

He stared at me a moment. "Martine and the children moved with her parents to Salzburg after the war," he finally said, calmly.

"And why aren't you in Salzburg?"

"I am not wanted there."

Something dripped onto the threshold. I looked down at our feet and saw little spatters of blood on the floor between us. And then I noticed Johannes's hand on the doorknob was bleeding.

"Your hand," I said.

Johannes looked down at the doorknob. "Oh, that. I was careless with a knife just now, cutting some bread."

Again his tone didn't match the moment.

"Maybe you'd let me take care of it for you?"

"I suppose it won't do to go to work today and bleed on the customers, will it?" He glanced back up at me, and for a second I caught a glimmer of the determined man I used to know. But the look vanished as he let go of the doorknob and stepped back so that I could enter.

The house was the same on the inside and yet not. The furniture was where it had always been, and even Martine's little touches, like the art on the wall and the decorative pillows on the sofa and the vases on the tables, were the same, but there was no longer any life in the house.

I turned to Johannes. "How about if you take a seat at the kitchen table while I find what I need?"

He said nothing as he went into the kitchen. I made my way to the first-floor bathroom to rummage through cupboards for bandages, tape, and iodine. When I returned to the kitchen, I sat down next to him.

Johannes extended his hand onto the tabletop. On the flat of his palm was a clean slice into his skin at least an inch long.

"It's a little deep, Johannes. Maybe you should have a doctor stitch it?"

He shook his head. "Just tape it up. I'll be fine."

Johannes didn't wince as I cleaned the wound, nor as I began to wind the gauze around it.

"When were you released?" I asked.

He didn't seem surprised that I knew he'd been a prisoner of war. Or maybe he didn't care that I knew.

"Six months ago."

"You were in England?"

"At a camp near Liverpool. It wasn't so bad. But you couldn't get a decent cup of coffee to save your life."

I almost laughed. Almost. We were quiet as I cut the gauze and then reached for the adhesive tape.

"I didn't think I would see you again after you'd gone back to the States," he said. "Especially now. Vienna is a mess. Wieden's streets are crawling with Communists."

"I didn't go back to the States." I snipped a short length of tape. "I spent the years of the war in Lucerne teaching English at a Catholic primary school."

He looked up at me in wonder. "This whole time you've been in Switzerland? Why? Why didn't you go back home?"

"I didn't want to. I wanted to be where I was. And actually, after you let me go, there were things I wanted to do."

"Like taking in a few last visits to the opera?" He said it cynically, as if a couple of nights at the opera house in Vienna had been all I'd wanted after having lost so much. I knew he wasn't serious, but it irked me that he said it at all.

"No. Like helping disabled children escape to Switzerland so the Nazis wouldn't do to them what they did to Brigitta." I hadn't meant to say something so callous, but my words were true, and once they were out, I didn't regret them.

He flinched at my answer but recovered quickly. "You did that?"

"I did. I helped save eleven children. Six boys and five girls. One was just an infant."

Johannes stared at me, a mix of disbelief and awe on his face. "But how? Switzerland wasn't accepting refugees."

"We found a way. And these children were not refugees. They were just little ones who needed a safe place to live for a while. Loving Swiss families were found for all of them. These families fed the children we rescued, clothed them, saw to their schooling and medical needs. The children were a burden to no one, not that they ever had been, and all were returned to their families after the war. Unlike so many other disabled children. Right?" Again my boldness stunned me, but I was finally saying to Johannes Maier what I'd wanted to say for a very long time.

He stared and said nothing.

"I know about the T4 program, Johannes. I know all about it."

He looked down at his wounded hand, now fully bandaged, resting on the table. "Then you know it ended in 1941."

"Did it, though? Perhaps it did if all the disabled and ill and elderly had already been killed by then," I said coolly. "Or perhaps T4 was halted because the Nazis needed their many gas chambers for other horrific purposes."

Johannes shook his head but did not look at me. "I had nothing to do with that. I had nothing to do with those camps."

"You were an officer in Hitler's Wehrmacht."

"I was just following orders. None of this was my idea. None of it."

His words were calmly spoken, as if he felt no emotion at all in saying them. Rage boiled up from within me. "And you think that excuses you? That you were just following orders? My God, Johannes. You objected to nothing, you challenged nothing! Not even when your commander shouted over the phone that your own daughter was a monkey! Every Nazi order you obeyed furthered their cause. Don't you see it? Every time you said nothing, you were saying you agreed with them. Every time you did nothing to stop the madness, you were pushing it forward!"

He smiled weakly. "Says the American who sheltered in Switzerland while the rest of the world burned."

The barb landed swiftly in my chest as if it were a tangible thing. With its sting, I realized I'd always known I could have done more to stand against the evil that was the Third Reich. And so could my homeland. We could have done so much more. America could have provided safe haven to European Jews who had been desperate for asylum. We could have done that easily. I saved eleven children, yes, but when the Swiss borders closed and rescuing anyone from Nazi-occupied countries became exceedingly dangerous, what did I do? I retreated into the safety of fear. I'd heard the news that Jews were being apprehended on the shores of Lake Constance after rowing all night from Germany to Switzerland. I could've asked Franz before he left for Bern for the names of all the people who'd helped rescue the Austrian children. I could have told those people to be on the lookout for refugees crossing the lake at night. Could have coordinated with them to bring these people down to Lucerne to hide them. I wish I had. Perhaps I would have been quickly found out, arrested, and deported, but I wish I had. Oh, how I wish I had. Maybe I could have only saved one Jewish person before being discovered and the operation shut down. But if every one of us who could have saved just one had done so, how many could have been saved from the concentration camps? It was staggering to ponder.

But Johannes was looking at me now like we were the same in this respect. We were not the same.

Not when it came to Brigitta.

"You're right, Johannes," I said. "You're right that I could have done more when I left Vienna. But at least I did everything I could to save Brigitta. At least I did that."

He startled, but only slightly.

"You knew all along she didn't die of pneumonia, didn't you?" I went on. "You knew they had killed her, and you pretended it was just her time. You even told Martine pneumonia could be a difficult disease. I heard you say it."

He looked at me, held my gaze, and then nodded. "It's all right if you want to blame me for what happened to Brigitta. And yes, that is what I said. I thought at the time it was the most merciful thing to say to Martine."

"Don't talk to me about the Nazi brand of mercy," I hissed, leaning forward. But when he didn't recoil or lash out in return, I sat back. "And I don't blame you directly for happened to Brigitta, but I can't understand how you were able to live with it. You knew what they were doing! You went back to your panzer division as if losing Brigitta was nothing!"

"I went back to my division because I believed I had no other choice. As I have already said, you have every right to blame me for what happened to Brigitta. Martine does. The other children do."

"Why? Why should I blame only you?"

He closed his eyes and swallowed before answering, as though he expected the next words coming from his mouth to scrape his throat raw as he spoke them. "Because I'm the one who asked—begged and bribed—for Brigitta to be given the injection that killed her."

The air seemed to be swept from the room, and I sat unable to draw breath. What he was saying was impossible. No father would do that.

"I don't believe you," I said.

"It's true. I'm the one that had her moved from Am Steinhof to the killing center at Hartheim." He opened his eyes to look at me. "That's why Martine and the children blame me."

"No." I shook my head. "No!"

"Yes." Tears were now slipping down Johannes's face.

"How could you do such a thing?" I whispered.

For a moment, Johannes did not answer. It was as if he could not summon the words or convince his tongue to form them. When he finally spoke, his voice seemed to splinter in two. "Because I'd learned from someone inside Am Steinhof that they were doing experiments on her. They were doing dreadful medical experiments on all the children. I could not bear it, Helen. I could not! I paid someone to take her to the place where they killed them, so that it would stop."

Johannes leaned forward, dropped his head to the table atop his folded arms, and began to quietly sob.

I sat still in my chair, afraid I would shatter into a thousand pieces if I moved. For many long moments, I sat frozen as the man next to me cried. I wanted to hit Johannes; I wanted to hold him. I wanted to scream at him; I wanted to soothe him. I wanted to find every doctor who'd tortured the children at Am Steinhof and every nurse who'd stood by and helped and cut them down with a sword. I wanted to push them into hell myself.

I wanted to forget I had ever known this family; I wanted to remember them always.

I wanted to hold on to all the love I'd known there in Vienna—there had been so much—and yet still hang on to all the anger that had now seized me as if it had talons.

I realized what I really wanted was to go home. To California. Back to the place where my life had begun, back to the place where, forty years earlier, I'd left full of dreams. I was done with Vienna. Done with Lucerne. I was so tired and done with all of it.

"They would have killed her anyway, Johannes," I finally said as tears slipped down my own cheeks. "You didn't kill her alone. We all did."

"It was me, it was me."

"Yes, it was you. But it was Martine, too. And me. We all should have fought back the moment the Nazis first showed us what they wanted. What they hated. Every good person every-where should have."

"It wouldn't have made a difference."

"That's not true."

"Power like that can't be stopped."

"Of course it can. It *was* stopped. It was stopped when the rest of the world finally said, 'No more.' But we waited too long. We should have said 'no' at the very beginning. There shouldn't have been a 'more.' We waited too long."

Johannes, still weeping softly, said nothing.

How much time passed as we continued to sit there, I wasn't sure. When I rose to leave, he was no longer sobbing, but his head was still cradled in his arms.

I reached for his uninjured hand, laid my own across it, and held it there. He placed his bandaged one atop it, and for a moment, we remained that way. Then I withdrew my hand, turned from the despairing man, and walked out of his house.

Rain clouds had gathered while I'd been inside and were now rumbling overhead. As I walked back to the pension to collect my things, I couldn't help but think that Johannes Maier would spend the rest of his life having bad dreams of being chased by demons through that same decrepit house of my own nightmares, while calling out for a daughter who would not answer him. When I reached the pension, the sky opened and the rain began to fall.

36

I am sitting at the patio table in the backyard with the invitation to come to New York in front of me when Amaryllis arrives home from school. I hear her greet Lila in the kitchen, lower her books to the kitchen table, and open the fridge for a drink.

Seconds later she is on the patio saying hello to me, too.

She is so tall and pretty, with wavy brown hair—so like Rosie's—and Truman's radiant eyes. I remind her often how much she favors them both in appearance. She is introspective and insightful like Truman was, but also unafraid to go after what she wants. And unfailingly kind. Her fourteenth birthday is fast approaching, and I can hardly believe how fast five years with her have flown.

"What's that?" Amaryllis takes a chair next to me and nods at the letter. She has a glass of chocolate milk in her hand.

"I've been asked to speak in New York City. At a university."

"Auntie! That's terrific. You're going, aren't you?"

It is the first time I have been invited to speak somewhere that isn't on the West Coast, and I am surprised and humbled and, if I'm being honest, a bit terrified.

"I suppose I should," I say.

"Of course you should."

I smile at her bold confidence and remind myself this was what I'd wanted when I first began speaking out against forced sterilizations at California institutions; I'd wanted from the get-go for the message to go well beyond me and the California state line. But now that it seems like it is finally starting to happen, I feel unequal to the task.

But then again, I had started out feeling the same way.

George and Lila had been my best cheerleaders early on, telling me I was more than capable and qualified to speak to audiences on the inherent dangers of eugenic ideology. And even Amaryllis in her own uninformed way encouraged me, though it's just been in the last year that I think she suspects she's somehow a part of what I speak to audiences about. She heard me mention Rosie's name a while back when I was talking to an interviewer on the phone and I couldn't get out of earshot quick enough. She doesn't yet know all the complexities of how she was born, but I've promised myself to tell her this year on her birthday, now only a couple of weeks away. She's been patient about being told the full truth, and I've been grateful for that.

I waited until a year after Amaryllis came to live with me to begin looking for a way to change California's eugenics laws. Partly because I wanted to devote that first year to her and her alone, but also because I knew I'd be beginning a potentially long and difficult battle. Forty years of a legalized state-run practice wouldn't disappear overnight. I knew that without George even telling me. I'd asked him how an ordinary citizen can change a law, and after reading his books on California legislation and the long process of getting a bill signed and old regulations repealed, and after too many unanswered letters sent to Sacramento, I realized I wasn't beginning with the most convincing thing I could bring to the conversation. What I possessed to light a fire, even if it was to be a small one at first, was my experience in occupied Europe. There was tremendous interest in the personal stories of those who had witnessed the atrocities of the Nazi regime. The shocked American public wanted to bear some of the weight of millions having perished by hearing the stories and taking on the pain as appalled listeners.

I realized I had a story to share about the disabled children of Austria, and at the end of my tale was the perfect entree to telling people what was happening right here in California in institutions up and down the coast. I could show them how it was all connected. I had read in George's books that one person with a desire for change might struggle for years to get noticed by elected legislators, but a groundswell of public opinion probably would not.

I offered first to speak at church groups, which led to invitations to speak at civic clubs, and then college campuses and high school gymnasiums. I would always begin by saying, "I'd like to tell you a story about a little girl named Brigitta . . ." Audiences young and old hung on my words, and when I got to the part near the end where I told them the eugenic thinking that killed Brigitta and sought to kill Wilhelm was alive and well and all around us, every eye widened. And then I would tell them about another girl I cared about named Rose, a derivation of Rosie's real name. I always left out the more specific defining details, like Rosie's last name, so that I could protect her, wherever she was. And I left out the part that I was now raising Rosie's child; that was to protect Amaryllis. But the speech was always impactful nevertheless. I encouraged every listener to write his or her legislative representative and join me in the effort to halt forced sterilizations in state institutions.

Three years in, Stuart Townsend, then in his internship at a hospital in the Bay Area, wrote and told me that he was studying pediatric medicine now and was not going to be returning to his father's institution. He'd heard I was going to be at his alma mater to give my talk, and he was disappointed he would have to miss it. He told me I could count on his future support in any way I needed it.

In the past five years, I have given the talk a hundred times in California, and a few times in Oregon and Washington State.

And now here is an invitation to give it at an East Coast university to an auditorium that is expected to be filled to capacity.

It's starting to happen, the amplification of what I and a handful of others like me whom I have met along the way have been trying to shout for the last five years.

I look up at Amaryllis, my niece and the daughter of my heart, and on impulse I ask her if she wants to come to New York with me.

"Really?" she says, happily surprised.

"You'll still be on your summer break in late August. Yes, I think you should come."

And then I sense the urge to tell her what she's been waiting to hear since I first brought her home, what I thought I'd be telling her a few weeks from now.

The time is right. I can feel it. It is spontaneous and natural and organic to the moment.

But I want her to feel it's the right time, too.

"Amaryllis," I begin. "You know I've been waiting until you were older to tell you about your mother and Truman. And maybe you've noticed I haven't shared much with you about why I am speaking out against what is happening in state institutions . . ." I let my voice trail off and watch her.

"Yes," she says, not taking her eyes off me.

"I'm thinking I'll tell you now. About both. The time seems right for it, but I want you to feel like it's right, too."

She nods. "I want to know."

"What happened between your mother and Truman, I can't fully explain. I wasn't there. Truman died before I could ask him. But somehow my brother and your mother, they . . ."

"They made love," Amaryllis says plainly.

She and I had the talk about how a baby is made when she was twelve and began to menstruate. I kept it general, without specifics, to keep it as uncomplicated as possible. There was more I would tell her when she was older. I had called it intercourse. I suppose she has heard this other term at school. I wonder what else she has heard. I try to hide my surprise.

"Uh, yes. Yes, they did. And the problem was . . . well . . ."

"The problem was my father was already married to Celine."

Celine was a woman Amaryllis had never met, but she knew Celine was the mother of her half brother, Wilson, whom she had also never met. I told Amaryllis she had a half brother because I thought she had a right to know. She's long since stopped wondering when she would ever meet these estranged people.

"Yes, that was the problem," I say. "But there were other problems, too. Your mother was an orphan, and she was only seventeen, and she was living with Truman and Celine then, if you remember. She couldn't live with them after that happened, and so the county, who was responsible for her, sent her to the place where you were born. There's a reason why she went to that place rather than just a special home for young pregnant women who aren't married."

I have Amaryllis's full attention now; unlike the other details she had deduced, she hadn't been able to figure out why her mother had been sent to an institution.

"Rosie had an ability that most people don't have. When she heard sounds, she would see colors. Like . . . like a kaleidoscope, I guess. The sounds brought the colors to her mind, just like the noise brought the sound to her ears."

"She saw these colors all the time?" Amaryllis asked.

"I think so, yes. I was told once that other people sometimes have this ability, too. They are born with it. But the people at the institution thought her brain wasn't working properly; they thought it was abnormal for a person to see colors when they heard a sound. These people didn't like it when a person wasn't like everyone else. They thought only they knew what was right and good and normal."

Amaryllis frowns. Lines of concern are now etched across her face. "What did these people do?"

I tell her.

I tell her everything, as gently and succinctly as I can.

"The doctors there were afraid *I* would also see those colors, because Rosie was my mother?" Amaryllis says when I am finished.

"Yes. That's what they were afraid of."

"But I don't see them. I don't see colors when I hear sounds."

"I know."

"What are these colors like? Are they pretty?"

"I don't know exactly. Perhaps."

Amaryllis sighs, lets her gaze wander as she thinks for a moment. "I bet they were pretty. I wish I could see colors like that."

"There have been plenty of days when I've wished I could, too."

We are both quiet for a few moments.

"This is why I speak to people about what I experienced in the war," I say. "It's because I want to change what is happening here in California. What was done to your mother is still happening here, and not just in California but all over the United States. It's still taking place because there is a way of thinking that allows for it. This kind of thinking, that one person can say he or she is a better human than another, is not only cruel, it is dangerous. I saw with my own eyes what can happen when this way of thinking flourishes without restraint."

I have given Amaryllis so much to think about. I worry for a second that my spontaneous move to tell her so much about Rosie without warning was a mistake.

"I'm glad you told me," Amaryllis says, partially relieving my fear. "And I'm glad you asked me to come to New York with you. I really do want to come."

"I'm glad, too. I'm sorry if this is too much to take in."

She chews on her lip in thought and then stands. "No. I've wanted to know for a long time. I was ready for you to tell me. But . . . I'm going to go inside now."

"You okay?"

Amaryllis nods. "I just want some time alone to think."

"I understand."

She starts to walk away but then turns back. "Thanks for doing this. What you're doing. I'm . . . I'm proud of you. And I think my mother would be, too."

She is gone before I can react.

Two weeks later, I receive a second letter from New York, this time from a Manhattan publisher. They want to meet with me when I am in town to discuss my writing a book. They are prepared to make me an offer on my memoir of the war. One of their editors heard me speak at a college event in the Bay Area a couple of months ago and was moved by my story.

They wish for me begin work on the book right away.

I've never thought of myself as a writer, but I immediately feel that I can share on paper as easily as I can at a podium. At least I believe I can, and isn't that half the recipe of any successful endeavor? The belief that you can do it?

A book is always in many places at once. That is its singular wonder. A book takes one voice speaking and makes it many. A book can shine far brighter and longer than I ever could on my own.

As I press this second letter to my chest, I hear the echo of Johannes Maier saying, "Power like that can't be stopped," and my own voice saying back to him, "Of course it can."

It can.

It is stopped. All the time.

Not with a magic wand or hopeful thoughts or wishful thinking or mere words, but with courage and resolve and the refusal to allow those without voices to remain unheard.

This is what makes us sublimely human, isn't it? Not unsullied genetic perfection, but when we stubbornly love and honor one another.

Just the way we are.

EPILOGUE

The crowd at the Los Angeles bookstore is bigger than I thought it would be with the memoir having been out six months already. The manager, pleased with the turnout and the sales this evening, isn't surprised.

"There's no waning lack of interest in your book," he murmured to me just before I rose to speak, and when the last chair had filled. "If anything, it's gaining in popularity. I've sold dozens upon dozens of copies, and not just tonight. People are drawn to your book. They want to know how an ordinary person just like them was able to do something extraordinary. It's inspiring, Miss Calvert. That's why they are here."

I imagine he is right. They want the story of the rescue. What draws people when I speak about this book is not the tagged-on plea I give to consider what is happening all over America in state institutions. They come to hear the tale of smuggling disabled children—the few that I could—out of Nazi-occupied Austria. They come to hear about Wilhelm, who survived, and Brigitta, who did not. I still have much work to do to bring audiences past the point of saying, "Isn't it awful what happened over there?" to "Something awful is happening right here."

I'm proud of the book, and glad it is not a work of science or politics or sociology. I am an expert on none of those things. The publisher didn't want a book exposing the evils that lie in wait on the eugenics road, anyway; they wanted a story about what I did—with help—to save a handful of victims of intended Nazi cruelty. I gave them that, but I was also allowed to share, in the last chapter, how my wartime experience changed me, how the focus of my life was transformed when I returned home to America and learned what had become of another girl I cared about, a girl who had the ability to see beyond the confines of this world every time a sound fell on her ears, a girl who was also a victim of the quest for perfection, albeit to a lesser degree.

The audience claps heartily when I am done speaking about my experiences and the writing of the book. I am grateful for the enthusiastic response, as always, but I'm ready to sign books and return to the hotel where Amaryllis is waiting for me. I've promised her a trip to Sunset Boulevard tomorrow and a matinee at Grauman's Chinese Theatre.

The patrons who have bought books crowd around the signing table. Some want to chat with me a few minutes; many want to know why, as I said in my talk, none of the designers and doctors of the T4 program have been brought to court on war crimes, like those in the Nuremberg Trials. I tell them I wish I knew. I don't have an answer. I wish I did.

The line begins to dwindle, and I see a man and woman at the end of it, hanging back as if they wish to be last. Perhaps they want to have a longer conversation with me. I'm tired and feeling every one of my seventy-one years. But if they want to talk about what I shared, I will. How we treat one another is what we are still able to do something about.

I redirect my attention to the person in front of me, a teacher who says she will be using my book in her high school sociology class next fall. I thank her.

Finally the last person in line is finished with me, and I can see in fuller detail the couple who's been hanging at the back. They move forward. The woman has my book in her hands. They walk toward me with uncertain steps—she especially.

When she is only a few feet from the table, I do a double take. I know that face, those cheekbones, that nose. They are Amaryllis's. Suddenly it's as if two worlds are colliding: the one I've been living in for most of my life and the one I had hoped to occupy again someday—the one Rosanne Maras inhabits.

"Rosie?" I say.

She smiles. "Hello, Helen."

For a second, I am frozen in my chair, and then I am up out of it, on the other side of the book table, and she is in my arms. Tears of joy, relief, and utter surprise are cascading down my cheeks. She is crying, too.

When we part, I step back to look at her. I see traces of the girl I knew among the grapevines all those years ago, but I see Amaryllis, too, in every feature on Rosie's face, except for her eyes. Amaryllis has her father's eyes.

"I tried to find you!" I say to her, wiping the wetness from my face. "I could find no record of Rosanne Maras anywhere."

Her smile deepens. "I haven't been Rosanne Maras for a long time. I go by Anne now. And my last name is Drummond." She turns and extends her hand to the man standing behind us, and he steps forward. He is of average build, has a kind face and dark brown hair with the first scatters of gray at the temples.

"This is my husband, Dr. Robert Drummond," Rosie says.

"What a pleasure it is to meet you, Miss Calvert." He stretches out his hand to me.

"The pleasure is all mine," I say.

"Robert is a professor in neuroscience at UCLA," she continues, smiling at him. I can see that she loves this man very much. And that he loves her. I am so, so glad.

"And you've been here in Los Angeles all this time?" I ask.

"For the last fifteen years, anyway. I moved here in 1943. Robert and I were married two years later. He and I met at the hotel in Petaluma where I was working after . . . after . . ." Her voice trails off.

"I know what happened before that, Rosie," I say, grasping her hand.

She nods, swallows down a bit of emotion, blinks back a few fresh tears. "Of course you do. Robert was in Petaluma speaking to a group of scientists about the very condition I have that sent me to that awful place."

"Synesthesia," I say. "I went to the Sonoma County institution looking for you when I first returned to the States. It was Dr. Townsend who told me about it."

"Ah. I should have guessed that's where you learned of it. I read in your book you knew why they cut into me."

"You've already read it?"

"Robert and I both have. I recognized your name right away when I saw it the first month it came out. And I knew you were talking about me in the last chapter. I almost reached out to you then."

"I'm so sorry if I shouldn't have used that variation of your first name. I was thinking if I called you Rose, you'd still have a measure of anonymity. I just wanted people to know you were real, and that what happened to you was real."

"I don't mind. I've had some time to get used to the idea. I think it's important what you've written about and what you're doing now by talking about it. I'm grateful. We both are." She nods toward Robert.

It hits me like a sledgehammer then that Rosie doesn't know I have her daughter. I didn't mention Amaryllis in my talk or in the book. But how to say this? I can't tell if her husband knows she bore my brother's child before she married him.

"Might I have a quick word in private?" I say to her. "There's something I need to ask you." I turn to her husband. "Robert, I hope you don't mind."

He smiles. "Of course not."

Robert moves away and begins helping the bookstore owner collapse the folding chairs. I like this man Rosie has married.

I step back toward the wall of bookshelves behind me, and Rosie comes close with a puzzled look on her face.

"Does Robert know everything?" I ask in a near whisper. "Does he know about Truman? About what happened?"

"He knows everything, Helen. And I've always wanted to tell you how sorry I am about that night with your brother. I was so young then, and missing my family. He and I had both been drinking to soothe our hurts, and we were drunk and I didn't know how to stop him. I wanted to, I asked him to, but—"

I cut her off. "That's not why I asked to speak with you alone. You don't owe me an apology or an explanation. I have always considered what happened my brother's fault. He was your guardian. He was . . . But we can talk about that at another time. What I want to tell you now is that I was able to find Amaryllis. I didn't even know she existed until I returned to America in 1947. But I found her. She was still at the children's home that she'd been sent to as an infant, and still waiting to be adopted. I adopted her, Rosie. And she's here with me in Los Angeles."

Color drains from Rosie's face. "What?"

"Amaryllis is here. At my hotel."

"Amaryllis."

Rosie whispers the name as if it is a long and reverent prayer that is somehow only the length of four short syllables. The moment seems sacred, and Rosie appears to be on the verge of fainting at the sheer holiness of it. I reach out to her. Robert notices the movement and looks up in concern. Then he is instantly at his wife's side.

"Anne, what is it? Are you all right?"

Rosie swings her head slowly to face him. "Amaryllis."

"What about her? What's wrong?"

"She's here."

Robert turns to look at me, his mouth open slightly, his eyes wide in surprise. I tell him what I just told Rosie.

"How is she? Is she all right? Is she okay?" Rosie asks me, her cheeks shining now with new tears.

"She is fine. She is . . . wonderful."

"Does . . . does she have . . . does she have what I have?" Rosie's voice splinters as she asks this.

"She doesn't. But she's often told me she wishes she did."

Rosie smiles and a laughing sob escapes her. It is one of relief but also pure pleasure. "She knows about me?"

"Of course. I've told her everything I know about you. She loves you very much, Rosie, even though she can't remember ever meeting you. I adopted her, but she calls me Auntie. You are still her mother. You've always been her mother."

Rosie leans onto Robert's chest. He embraces her as she cries quietly against him. The bookstore owner has put away all the chairs and has locked the front doors so new customers can't come in, and he is staring at us in curious fascination.

Rosie lifts her head and turns to face me again. "Can I see her?"

"Of course. We will go right now if you want."

She nods. "Yes, yes."

"I'll get the car," Robert says.

Minutes later, I am sitting in the back seat of the Drummonds' vehicle. Rosie is in mute wonder in the front. Robert fills the silence on the short drive to my hotel. He tells me he was a widower when he and Rosie met, and that she moved to Los Angeles to be part of a study he was doing at UCLA on synesthesia. They fell in love, and two years later they were married. Robert's sons were seven and nine at the time and very much needing a mother in their lives again. One is married now with a new baby, and the other is in college studying microbiology.

When we get to my hotel, I leave Rosie and her husband in the expansive lobby. I reassure Rosie that it won't be too much for Amaryllis to suddenly be told her mother is waiting downstairs to see her.

"She has been wanting this from the moment I met her," I say, and then I head for the elevator.

My heart is pounding with both anticipation and amazement as I ride up to the twentieth floor. When I walk into the room, Amaryllis is out on the tiny balcony reading, and still wearing her pleated skirt and coral-hued blouse from our flight to Los Angeles hours earlier. She'd asked if I wanted her to come with me to-night, but because she's already heard me give this talk dozens of times, I told her to enjoy the view of the city lights from twenty stories up. Now she comes into the room, smiling and asking if it was a good evening.

"It was definitely a good evening," I answer. "The best."

"Oh yes?" she says, smiling wider. "How come?"

I pat one of the two beds. "There's something you need to know."

When I tell her that her mother came to see me at the book-store, she doesn't seem incredulous or even overly surprised. It's as if she's been expecting news like this all her life, and now it has finally come. Amaryllis merely closes her eyes for a moment, as if needing to make sure the moment is indeed real, and then opens them to ask where Rosie is.

"She's here. In the lobby. Waiting for you."

We head to the elevator.

As Amaryllis expectantly paces in place waiting for the car to arrive, I am suddenly aware that everything is about to change. The minute Rosie and Amaryllis are reunited, I will be giving my girl back to her real mother, this precious child whom I love as my own daughter.

With giving, there is cost, isn't there? There is always cost. Sometimes it is an easy sum to hand over.

And sometimes it exacts from you the whole measure of your heart.

I will pay it, though. It is the right thing to do. And in a way, I will be righting a wrong the only way I can. I am at last returning to a mother the child that was taken from her.

Beside me, Amaryllis takes a long breath, her eyes on the half circle of numbers displaying the elevator's ascent. I want to tell her so many things in these seconds before the double doors open and the time for saying them is gone. I want to tell Amaryllis how proud I am of the young woman she has become, especially in light of the heartaches she had to endure far too young in her life. I want to tell her that she will always have a home with me, and that no matter what happens after tonight, I will forever be no farther away than a phone call at any moment of the night or day. I want to tell Amaryllis that no single thing I have ever done in my life has brought me as much joy and delight as taking her home to the house in Laurel Heights and now bringing her to this moment in time. I want to tell her that I love her. But the elevator car is suddenly here, and Amaryllis is dashing inside the second the doors open. And which of these things does Amaryllis not already know?

Amaryllis takes in another deep breath as the car begins descending.

"You all right?" I ask.

"I am. I just want this part to be done."

I think I know what she means. It is absurd for a mother and her child to be virtual strangers to each other. She wants the absurdity of that to be gone.

Seconds later, we are in the lobby and walking toward Rosie. She sees us, stands, and takes a step in our direction. The next instant, Amaryllis is running to her, and I know, as I have always known, that the two of them have never been truly and completely apart.

Robert and I watch in awe as Rosie and Amaryllis embrace, all the years and distance seeming to fall away like fractured shackles.

Rosie and I will likely not talk today about all that has transpired in the last sixteen years. Perhaps not tomorrow, either, or the next day. In time, though, I will tell her, if she does not already know, of Truman's passing. I will tell her about learning from Stuart of her attempt to escape, and his regret, and that he was the one to tell me where Amaryllis had been sent. I will tell her of every milestone of Amaryllis's that I got to witness.

Mother and child part to look at each other, happy tears streaming down their faces. Rosie looks past Amaryllis to where I stand a few feet away and mouths the words "Thank you." Then she turns her attention back to her daughter, stroking her hair and touching her face.

"Oh, Mama. I've missed you so much," Amaryllis says.

At these words—the first she has ever heard her daughter say—Rosie tips her head back in wonderment, her eyes glittering with delight.

I can very nearly see what Rosie is surely seeing at the sound, finally, of her daughter's voice—the bursts of color, the whorls of perhaps magenta, cerulean, and goldenrod, tumbling about like jewels from heaven.

I can almost see them.

And they are beautiful.

Acknowledgments and Author's Note

Every author friend I have has a book they wrote with great effort during the creativity-hindering, strength-sapping months of the COVID-19 pandemic; this one is mine. I absolutely could not have written *Only the Beautiful* without heaps of help, encouragement, and support during this uniquely complicated stretch of time.

I am exceedingly grateful to my editor at Berkley, Claire Zion, who somehow saw the story I was trying to tell in those early, unsuccessful drafts and who kept sending me back to the beginning to try again. I am in awe of her talent to see what could be there and wasn't yet. I am also indebted to my agent, Elisabeth Weed, whose instincts about plot details at every juncture—and in every draft—were spot-on. There wouldn't be a book without the insights of these amazing women.

I am immensely thankful to the Synesthesia Facebook group, including Jennifer Merrill, Kathryn Schneck, Emily Holt, Rachel Harding, Brigit Bishop, Melissa Davis, Chris Bermudez, Chris Salarda, Laura Middleton-Addison, Sarah Grace Kraning, April Strickland, Jona Markgraf, and especially Galit Sorokin for sharing their personal experiences with synesthesia. Any inaccuracies in the pages regarding this condition are mine alone.

Special thanks to Alexandra Minna Stern, Ph.D., founder and codirector of the Sterilization and Social Justice Lab, and research fellow Heather Dron for answering my many questions regarding the eugenics movement in California.

San Diego author friends Michelle Gable, Shilpi Gowda, and Tatjana Soli, as well as Kristina McMorris and Ariel Lawhon from afar, were unflagging in their encouragement when the writing was at its most difficult. I am also immensely grateful to Linda Hamilton and the rest of the Wednesday morning study group at New Life Presbyterian Church in Escondido for the prayers and reassurance.

A fond thank-you to my mother, Judy Horning, who proofread two full and very different manuscripts.

When I first learned of the young woman named Carrie Buck, whom Helen, George, and Lila discuss in that scene on Christmas evening, I knew I needed to know more of her story, and the role eugenics played in what happened to her. When I began the research to write *Only the Beautiful* at the start of the pandemic, I confess I didn't know what the eugenics movement was. Many people I mention the term to now don't, either. It's a movement that has thankfully gone by the wayside, but sadly the ideology, I believe, is still with us, and that's why I think the movement itself should not be forgotten. If we forget our history, we are more apt to repeat it, aren't we? Hence this book.

The 1927 Supreme Court ruling that allowed Carrie Buck to be forcibly sterilized gave every state the green light to continue or begin sterilizing those deemed unfit to produce children, all in the name of "race betterment." Over the next five decades more than sixty thousand men and women in thirty states were forcibly sterilized. And while these sterilizations diminished somewhat after eugenic ideology at its worst was exposed in the liberated concentration camps of Nazi Germany, the practice continued in some states for decades afterward. Many states had eugenics laws in place until the 1970s.

The Sonoma State Home for the Infirm is a fictional place that I created, but I patterned it after a real facility, the Sonoma State Home, which sterilized more people than any other institution in California. Dr. Townsend is also fictional, but I styled him after early eugenic leaders like Sir Francis Galton, Charles Benedict Davenport, Harry Laughlin, and Margaret Sanger. Galton, the premier pioneer of eugenic thinking and Charles Darwin's cousin, has long been credited as giving eugenics its name. He was also very interested in synesthesia for reasons that were not advantageous to synesthetes, as you might imagine.

More than twenty thousand people were sterilized in the state of California from 1909 to 1964, the highest number of forced sterilizations in the United States and one-third of all sterilizations nationwide. In March 2003, then governor Gray Davis issued a formal apology, saying in part, "To the victims and their families of this past injustice, the people of California are deeply sorry for the suffering you endured over the years."

In 2021, and while I was still wrangling with the writing of this book, the California legislature announced it was setting aside $7.5 million for reparation payments to victims of the long-passed eugenics movement. Of the twenty thousand people affected before the California eugenics laws were repealed in 1979, only a few hundred are still alive, and finding them might be difficult. Advocates of the legislation estimate only one-quarter of those still living will ultimately apply for this compensation.

For further reading, I highly recommend Dr. Stern's excellent book *Eugenic Nation: Faults and Frontiers of Better Breeding in Modern America*, 2nd edition. If you would like to learn more about the *Buck v. Bell* case, *Imbeciles: The Supreme Court, Ameri-*

can Eugenics, and the Sterilization of Carrie Buck, by Adam Cohen, is excellent.

As always, I would love to hear your thoughts on this book and I welcome invitations to visit virtually with book clubs as you discuss it. All the details on arranging for that are on my website.